CRUSHED

CRUSHED

CITY OF ELDRICH — BOOK TWO

LAURA KIRWAN

BURNT BARN PRESS

ISBN: 0-9913023-3-8
ISBN-13: 9780991302338

CHAPTER ONE

D ARK TREES LOOMED over the clearing where the small fire burned.

The rainy gray daylight barely penetrated the thick canopy of forest. It was afternoon in the rest of the world, but in the trees a murky twilight filled the air.

Two figures hunched near the fire and peered into the small iron dutch oven that hung above the flames.

"You're doing it wrong," said the first, a pudgy blonde girl wearing jeans and a green polo shirt.

"I am not. I'm doing it exactly like the book says," the second said, tossing her tangled dark hair over her shoulder. She sat on a boulder next to the fire, a black leather jacket over her blood-red velvet dress. A heavy silver pendant—a five-cornered star enclosed in a circle—hung from her neck. It brushed against the large dusty book balanced on her knees.

"Then why does it look like cat barf?" The pudgy girl stuck

an iron spoon in the dutch oven and scooped up a sample. "See?"

"Well, maybe if you took this more seriously . . ."

"What's that supposed to mean?"

"Maybe if you tried to dress for the part a little? At least I'm trying to look like a witch."

The pudgy girl snorted. "It doesn't matter how you look."

The other girl twirled a strand of hair around a black-lacquered fingernail and squinted at the book. "Maybe if you're not doing *real* magic."

The pudgy girl sighed. "Heather, you don't—"

"Circe," the dark-haired girl said impatiently. "Don't call me Heather. Real witches aren't named Heather." She looked up and glared at her companion. "Or Dana."

Dana rolled her eyes. "What about Kady? Or Natalie? You're telling me Natalie doesn't do real magic? I've seen Natalie do big scary magic in sweaty running clothes. Using Gatorade in place of ram's blood." Dana grimaced at the dutch oven. "I bet Natalie's version wouldn't look like cat barf."

Heather ignored this comment. "We have to make it work. I know I'm the one for him if I can only make him see it."

Dana rolled her eyes again. "He's like thirty years old. And he's gay. That was his *boyfriend* who died when his world blew up."

"I don't think he's all that gay," Heather said. "I've seen him looking at me."

"Yeah," Dana said. "Along with everybody else and the wall and the floor and—"

Heather slammed the book shut and glared at Dana. "Why do you always have to be so negative about everything?"

"Accepting reality isn't negative. It's grown-up. Like having a job." Dana pulled a cell phone from her back pocket. "Like the job I'm gonna get fired from if I don't leave now." She looked up at Heather. "Can you clean this up without me?"

Heather refused to meet her eye. "Whatever. I'll clean it up. Go to your stupid job. If you really cared about the craft you wouldn't bother with a job."

"We're not in high school anymore. Witches need to eat and pay rent like everybody else." Dana paused a beat. "At least everybody not still living with their parents."

Heather gave her a sour look, but said nothing.

"Thank you," Dana said in a syrupy voice. She ran to her small, beat-up car, and drove away without a backward glance.

"She's just jealous," Heather muttered.

"Of course she is," a feminine voice purred. "All women are jealous. Particularly witches."

Heather squealed, dropped the book, and nearly fell off her boulder. She looked up and saw a woman, dressed in black, standing on the other side of the fire.

The woman had thick, flowing blonde hair. She wore a tight-fitting black leather jacket that plunged into a low V-neck. Underneath, black lace peeked through, accented by the emerald green satin scarf wrapped around her pale throat. Her black skirt was velvet like Heather's dress, but tighter, falling to mid-calf. A slit in the front revealed a pair of black leather laced-up boots with a high spiky heel.

Around her neck, the woman wore a silver pentacle

necklace identical to the one Heather wore. She glanced at Heather's pentacle, and she smiled, small white teeth glistening behind dark red lips.

"You scared me," Heather squeaked.

"I've been looking for you," the woman said in a low musical voice.

"Me?"

The woman nodded. "Yes. *You.* I can feel your power from where I stand. I could feel it before I arrived. Your power, your potential, led me here."

Heather's mouth dropped open. "How do you . . . who are you?"

"Someone who understands that real magic requires real witches. Someone who honors the traditions of the craft. Someone not afraid to show the world what she is."

"You're a witch," Heather said, breathlessly. "A *real* witch. You . . . you *get* it."

The woman nodded. "I do get it. Much better than those work-a-day drabs who infest this town, with their sloppy demeanor and slipshod spell casting. Natalie Segretti, for instance. She is powerful, I'll give her that, but she sorely lacks style. It denigrates the craft."

Heather nodded. "Style matters. That's what I keep telling everybody and they laugh and treat me like a dumb kid."

"Even your friend," the woman said in gentle voice. "The one who ruined your spell and left you behind to clean up her mess." She shook her head. "Shameful, the way standards have slipped in this town."

"Will you teach me?" Heather asked in a rush. "Please? I'm apprenticed to this stupid rich woman who wears pastels and plays golf. She's awful."

The woman smiled. "Perhaps, but first you must prove yourself. Raw talent is not enough. You must show me that you have the necessary cunning and strength, that you understand the sacrifices that must be made to achieve true power." She paused a moment. "And true love."

Heather flushed. "He's . . ." She stared down at her lap. "I see how the other witches look at him. They tell each other he's gay, but I know they think they can make him forget all that."

"While they squabble, do you have the will to take him? To fight for him?"

"Dana says it's a crush, not love, but she's wrong. I know he'll fall for me if I can only get him to forget that man, and if I can keep the other witches away. If I could only get the spell to work."

"Here, little one," the woman said. "Let me help you."

CHAPTER TWO

ON JAMIE SMITH'S third day back at work, office supplies began turning up in odd places.

Like the hallway in front of Meaghan Keele's office in Eldrich City Hall. With care, she stepped around a tower made from reams of copier paper and yellow legal pads. About three feet high, the stack was capped with a smaller pile of neon-hued Post-It Note pads and surrounded by pens and pencils lying on the carpet with their points facing away, like the petals of a flower.

She peeked into the office next door. Jamie, her deputy city solicitor, sat at his desk with his back to the door, staring out the window—his customary pose since his return. Considering the view from the third floor, looking out the window was understandable, except Meaghan suspected he barely noticed what he saw.

She took a longer look into Jamie's office and stopped short.

There was more to this than misplaced office supplies.

His files were floating about six inches above the glass desktop. Meaghan cleared her throat. The files dropped with a loud thump.

Jamie spun around in his chair, eyes wide with fear, a stapler gripped in his right fist like a club. After a moment, he registered Meaghan standing in the doorway. His face grew red. He placed the stapler carefully on the desktop and stared at it.

"Good morning," Meaghan said with a smile, trying to pretend things were normal. Or at least as normal as they ever were in a haunted city hall surrounded by dimensional gateways to magical worlds. "Would you come out here and take a look at this?"

Jamie followed her into the hall. He stared at the legal pad tower and shook his head. "This wasn't here when I came in."

"When did you get here?"

"Six-thirty," he said.

Meaghan raised an eyebrow, but Jamie, staring at the floor, didn't notice.

"Kind of early," Meaghan said.

"I have keys." He turned and walked back into his office. He sat, turned toward the window, and resumed his vigil. In a moment, the files rose back into the air. The stapler joined them.

Okay, she thought. Time to talk to an expert. Meaghan dropped her purse and gym bag on her desk, and headed out toward the front office to find Natalie Segretti, her office manager and the head witch of the local coven.

It had been quite a shock for Meaghan, at age fifty, to discover that magic was real and that she was impervious to its effects. She thought she'd been moving to tiny little Eldrich to take over her father's job as the city's attorney. In her phone interview, no one had mentioned her father's additional duties—negotiating magical disputes and guarding the human world from magical incursion.

Natalie had helped her quickly find her feet, in both jobs. A tall, curvy woman with a head of unruly copper curls, Natalie was a top-notch administrative assistant. And a powerful witch. At thirty-two, she was young to head the local coven, but no other witch in town approached her in power and skill. In the space of not quite three months, she had become one of the most important people in Meaghan's life.

She found Natalie in the front area of the small office suite, talking with Annie, the mayor's secretary. Somewhere in her late thirties, with shoulder-length blonde hair, Annie had what Meaghan now assumed to be a supernatural ability to know exactly what was going on at any given moment in city hall. Annie wasn't a witch, Meaghan knew. But Annie wasn't a clueless civilian either.

When Meaghan walked up, they turned grim faces to her.

"We've got a problem," Natalie said.

Meaghan sighed. "Would this problem have something to do with the pile of office supplies stacked outside my office and Jamie's floating file folders?"

Annie's eyes widened. "Stacking and levitating? Already?" She turned to look at Natalie. "I was afraid of this after what he'd been through, but I didn't think it would manifest this soon."

It had been a little over ten weeks since Jamie had been kidnapped and tortured under circumstances that, for Meaghan at least, made no sense. The generally accepted narrative was that Jamie had been the victim of a power struggle between his uncle and his father over rule of a dumpy little magical world—now destroyed—known as Fahraya. But Meaghan remained convinced that there had to be more to it.

"Didn't think what would manifest?" Meaghan asked. "What are we talking about and why is it a problem? It's only paperwork. It's not like his desk was floating." She looked expectantly at them. "Oh, and his stapler. That started floating too after I asked him about the office supply sculpture."

Annie's eyes opened wider. "Oh, shit. Definitely a poltergeist. Not good."

"Is that new?" Meaghan asked. "I thought the building was totally haunted already. And how did you know this was going on? Natalie, you got here the same time I did and you haven't been back there yet."

Annie sighed. "Yes, it's new. We have plenty of ghosts, but poltergeists are different. The ghosts told me as soon as I got in this morning and I asked them to let me know when Natalie got here."

Meaghan raised an eyebrow. "The ghosts talk to you? When you're awake?" Meaghan had had her own encounters with the deceased, but only in dreams or under the influence of mystical hallucinogens. And one time when the fabric of reality was unravelling.

Annie looked at Natalie. "I thought you told her."

Natalie shrugged. "I can't remember what I told her anymore." She looked at Meaghan. "Annie's a medium. It's how she always knows who's in city hall and where."

Meaghan nodded. "I wondered about that. Medium, huh? Like on the TV show?"

Annie rolled her eyes. "Not even close. I'm not some kind of post-life therapist, you know? If I tried to solve the problems of every ghost who talked to me, I wouldn't have time to eat or sleep."

"So," Meaghan said. "Tell me about poltergeists. This thing is drawn to Jamie?"

"It *is* Jamie," Annie said. "He's making it happen."

"What—like ESP?"

Annie shrugged. "Sort of. But he's not doing it consciously. Paranormal researchers think it's a kind of involuntary response to stress. Happens a lot with kids in puberty. PTSD will trigger it, too."

Meaghan nodded. "Which Jamie is showing signs of even though he refuses to acknowledge it. Considering what happened to him, I don't know how he couldn't have it. Hell, I'm waking myself up with screaming nightmares a couple times a week and the worst thing that happened to me over there was a bug bite."

Natalie snorted. "It wasn't a bug. It was a giant scorpion." She shuddered. "And it nearly killed you."

Meaghan gave her a look. "Thank you for reminding me. I'm sure I'll sleep much easier tonight."

"Fine," Natalie said, throwing up her hands. "Be a smartass. But denial is killing him and I won't watch you go, too."

To Meaghan's surprise, Natalie's eyes shimmered with tears.

Despite her flippant tone, Meaghan hadn't been lying about the screaming nightmares. The one that had woken her that morning, before dawn, had been the worst one yet. Not the giant scorpion, but Jamie, battered and naked, his throat slashed, blood gushing down his chest, staring at her in reproach. *Too late*, she'd heard him whisper. *You got here too late.*

She couldn't imagine how bad Jamie's dreams must be.

"Natalie, I'm sorry," Meaghan said in a soft voice. "You're right. I shouldn't joke about it. What I suffered was minor compared to Jamie, but I shouldn't minimize it. It makes it too easy for him to do the same."

Natalie nodded, biting her lip to keep the tears in. "And it's so much worse than he's letting on."

At the same moment, as if in response, the stack of paper in Natalie's in-box lifted a foot into the air and burst into flames.

CHAPTER THREE

MEAGHAN LUNGED FOR the fire extinguisher hanging near the door and put out the fire before it set off the overhead sprinklers. Natalie stared at the singed paper and chemical foam covering her desk and burst into tears. Annie guided her to a chair, sat her down, and rubbed her shoulders.

"Can poltergeists set fires?" Meaghan asked, holding the spent extinguisher and surveying the damage.

Annie nodded. "Yeah. Although I've never seen fire this early in a manifestation."

"You've seen a lot of poltergeists?"

Annie shrugged. "Some. There's some paranormal research guys I help out sometimes. Telling them if it's an actual haunting or psychokinesis." Seeing Meaghan's blank look, she added, "You ever read *Carrie*?"

Meaghan nodded. "I saw the movie. So he's throwing stuff

around with his mind? But he's not doing it on purpose, is he?"

"No," Annie said. "Not yet."

Natalie blew her nose loudly. "Not ever. He would never do anything on purpose to hurt us."

Meaghan and Annie exchanged a glance. Meaghan didn't need to be psychic to know what Annie was thinking. They had no idea what Jamie would or wouldn't do. The Jamie they'd all known—happy, generous, kind, a loving husband and doting father—had died in Fahraya. He might get past what had happened to him with time and care, but would never again be the man they had known.

"Okay. Maybe not," Annie said. "But even if he'd never intentionally hurt us, he's still dangerous. We gotta get this sorted out fast. Has anything weird been going on at home?"

"Well . . ." Natalie fell silent.

Natalie had assumed the role of Jamie's big sister since his exile from Fahraya at age twelve. She had followed him to college and law school, never living more than a mile away from him, so she could maintain the amulet he had worn to suppress his Fahrayan DNA and appear human. He no longer needed the amulet, not since a magical explosion had transformed all the surviving Fahrayans into actual humans, but Natalie and Jamie were still a daily presence in each other's lives. They lived two doors apart, Jamie's kids knew her as Aunt Natalie, and his wife was one of her closest friends.

"Natalie," Meaghan said. "I know you want to protect him, but you have to tell us what's going on so we can help him."

"Nothing major. Some doors that won't stay shut, banging noises, some broken dishes." Natalie glared at them, her face red. "He went through hell, okay? He's doing the best he can."

Annie gave Meaghan another meaningful glance.

Meaghan decided it was time to back off, at least for now. To Natalie she said, "Let's just keep an eye on things for now, okay?"

Annie nudged Meaghan and held her index finger to her lips.

A moment later Jamie appeared in the doorway. He glanced at the mess on Natalie's desk a moment, his face expressionless. He walked around them, not making eye contact, on his way out of the office suite. "Running an errand," he mumbled. "I'll be back in a little while."

Meaghan looked at Natalie, who shrugged and said, "I don't know where he's going."

Meaghan turned her gaze to Annie. "City hall's making it worse, isn't it?"

Annie nodded. "This stupid place makes everything worse. It's not only supernatural energy it magnifies. It's psychic energy too."

"And his office is ground zero."

"Right," Annie said. "The center of the vortex. And he's totally human now which means he's vulnerable. Only instead of getting dizzy in there, like everybody else does, he's channeling it."

"Like a magnifying glass focusing sunlight," Meaghan said. "And we're the ants."

"Exactly," Annie said.

Natalie slammed a desk drawer shut with a bang. "I can't listen to this. You don't know him like I do. He won't hurt us."

Glaring at Meaghan, Natalie stomped out of the office and down the stairs.

Annie squeezed Meaghan's arm. "She's having a hard time too. He doesn't need her like he used to now that he doesn't wear the amulet. I'll track her down and talk to her."

"Do I need to get him out of that office?"

"Maybe. I'll talk to Natalie about magical interventions. I assume you know about city hall?

Meaghan nodded. "Yeah. Even I can't be in his office for more than a minute or two without getting dizzy and I'm impervious to magic. I can't believe we didn't think about how it would affect him."

"It doesn't affect everybody the same way. Some people are fine in there. Don't worry. We'll sort it out."

"If he doesn't burn down the place first," Meaghan said.

Annie shrugged. "I'd get some more fire extinguishers if I were you. I'll mention it to Meb. He's got a few stored away downstairs."

Meb was the elderly security guard who sat watch in the main lobby for the occasional visitor. He'd worked in city hall for decades and knew all about its unique features, including ghosts, witches, and the energy vortex on the third floor. He'd lived in the area all his life and was clued in—Eldrich code for being aware of the paranormal—to the supernatural aspects of living in Eldrich and working in city hall.

Meaghan had found out about Eldrich on her first day at work when the city council director, during a heated meeting, started throwing around hexes before tearing off Jamie's amulet. Seeing her deputy city solicitor, the nice young lawyer sitting across the table from her, disappear in a flash of light and reappear eight inches tall with wings had clued Meaghan in fast.

Eldrich had been described to Meaghan as a hole in the fence of reality. Gateways to other worlds, most of them magical in some way, riddled the dark forests, and city hall had been designed to amplify the mystical energy leaking from these worlds.

Staring at the charred contents of Natalie's in-box, Meaghan shuddered. City hall could make whatever was happening to Jamie much, much worse. "Downplay it with Meb if you can, okay? Let's keep this quiet for now. I don't want people being any weirder around Jamie than they already are."

Annie nodded. "If he thinks people are scared of him, that'll ratchet up his stress and make it worse. So far, at least according to the ghosts, he's only affecting the third floor."

"I want to keep it that way if we can," Meaghan said.

Annie tilted her head like she was listening to something. "The mayor's arrived. I have to get downstairs." She headed for the door, then stopped a moment. "Natalie's down in the break room. I'll see if I can catch her on her way back up the stairs. Call me if anything new happens."

"By phone or by ghost?" Meaghan asked as Annie, laughing, walked out the door.

CHAPTER FOUR

ELDRICH'S HISTORIC CITY hall was a fairy-tale castle masquerading as a public building. Built of heavy gray stone, with its high clock tower, four round turrets, and ornate carvings, city hall was lavishly excessive for a town as tiny as Eldrich, which had just over five thousand residents as of the last census.

City hall had been built in the middle of the nineteenth century by Welland Eldrich, the founder and namesake of the town, who had made his fortune in timber and mining. After the untimely death of his much younger wife and stillborn child, he sought comfort through the spiritualist movement sweeping upstate New York.

Soon tired of the charlatans and tricksters he'd encountered trying to contact his wife's spirit through séances, Welland Eldrich began to look for another way to reach her. One day, the story went, he sent a telegram to a business associate and inspiration struck.

Unlike mediums who claimed to have a unique gift, anyone could learn to use the telegraph. Why take the word of a stranger that the spirits had spoken? Why not speak to them directly?

Only thirty years earlier, he reasoned, the notion of sending a nearly instantaneous message across a distance via electricity and copper wire had seemed a fantasy. To ancient man, it would have seemed like magic, like a message from the gods.

So Welland Eldrich set out to build a telegraph to the Other Side.

He abruptly sold his business interests and settled down to build a town in a secluded valley, surrounded by dense forests, in north central Pennsylvania. Long avoided by Indians and European settlers alike, the area was reputed to be haunted. Strange creatures were said to roam through the thick trees, snaring unwary travelers, most of whom were never heard from again.

Unlike most such tales, these were true.

After founding his little town in the middle of a supernatural minefield, Welland Eldrich commenced construction of a lavish city hall that would also serve as his spiritual telegraph.

Meaghan was more than a little fuzzy on the mechanics of it. She'd heard the story from Natalie and Russ, Meaghan's brother, sitting in the Keeles' kitchen one evening about six weeks earlier after one of Russ's routinely excellent dinners and a little too much wine.

Natalie had tried to explain Welland Eldrich's vision using technical terms like *whosit* and *thingy*.

Russ, seeing the look on Meaghan's face, finally interrupted and said, "City hall's like that building in *Ghostbusters*. Some powerful energy doohickies converge on the site, and they did some weird architecture and weird engineering to amplify it, the end result being a big radio tower to the Great Beyond. And some people think it opened up the gateways to Fahraya."

Meaghan said, "But—"

"Take our word for it," Russ said in an exasperated tone. "We don't know how it works either. Something to do with electricity and magnets. I'm a chef, not a physicist. Once you get past the physics of roasting versus steaming, I'm pretty much lost."

"Okay," Meaghan said with a frown. Her understanding of physics wasn't much better. She'd tried reading a Stephen Hawking book once and gave up after she'd read the first few pages several times, once out loud, and still had no idea what it said. "So, what's the deal with the third floor?"

"The clock tower's like a big antenna," Natalie said. "It focuses the power right into Jamie's office. Huge energy vortex in there. It's why people get dizzy and his computer crashes all the time. There's a corresponding spot, not quite as bad, back in the storage room. Great for amplifying spells, but the cell phone reception sucks."

"Why Jamie's office?" Meaghan asked.

"Third floor used to be the attic, right? Welland Eldrich wasn't trying to build a public phone. He wanted to talk to his wife in private, so the building was engineered to funnel everything up there," Natalie said. "We think. What we know comes from his personal papers and he went bat-shit crazy and was shipped to an asylum right after construction began."

"There's a lot more we don't know," Russ added. "A German guy, Bottner, I think his name was. Something like that. He designed the building and supervised construction, but blew town as soon as it was done and took all the notes and plans with him. And the third floor was a big open space back then. Jamie's office was added later."

"But knowing about the vortex, why didn't they put our offices on the other side of the building?"

Natalie shrugged. "No idea. They remodeled the attic in the thirties and it may be whoever made the decision didn't know about city hall. Standard Eldrich denial, you know?"

Denial was a common way of dealing with Eldrich for those not willing to accept its true nature.

"The city solicitor's office was kind of a one-man show back then, right?" Meaghan asked.

Natalie nodded. "Jamie's the first deputy city solicitor we've ever had and Matthew created the position. Partly to give Jamie a job, but also to give Matthew more time to deal with his other obligations. You know."

Meaghan nodded. Having Jamie gone forced Meaghan to do a lot more actual lawyering. She'd even had to go to court a couple of times when Hallam and Associates, the city's outside counsel, couldn't cover something. Meaghan was no litigator and, except for a brief stint as a criminal prosecutor, had spent most of her career trying to avoid the courtroom.

"So, what did they use the office for before Jamie?" Meaghan asked.

"Conference room, I think. I didn't really pay attention. I was a kid when Mom worked for the city. I didn't start working here until we both came back from Philly."

Vivian, Natalie's mother, had worked for Matthew Keele

from the beginning. She had died right after Jamie and Natalie both moved to Philadelphia so Jamie could attend law school. When Natalie and Jamie returned to Eldrich, Natalie took over her mother's role at Matthew's side. It was Natalie who noticed the first subtle signs of Alzheimer's disease in Matthew.

Natalie had been as close to Matthew as she was to Jamie. And to Russ.

Meaghan had no proof they were romantically involved beyond witnessing Russ and Natalie share meaningful glances and seeing Natalie blush a few times when Meaghan had mentioned his name. And considering the nature of Eldrich, there could be explanations other than sex.

But why the secret? They were hiding something. Meaghan already knew about magic and witches and ghosts and wizards and weird creatures from other worlds. She didn't know why they'd keep a paranormal secret from her, but they had plenty of reasons not to tell her if they were sleeping together.

Meaghan had managed to miss the breakups of Russ's second and third marriages, but she'd witnessed every horrible step of Russ's first divorce. She never wanted to do that again.

She wanted Russ to find a good woman and finally get it right. But history was not on his side. And Natalie . . . Natalie was a witch. An actual spell-casting witch. Working with her every day after a breakup with Russ would be bad enough, but what would Natalie do if scorned? Turn Russ into a toad? Talk about an awkward work environment.

Feeling the weight at the end of her arm, Meaghan realized she still held the empty fire extinguisher. She set it on the floor next to Natalie's desk. It wasn't even nine yet and she'd already experienced her first poltergeist, fought a fire, and pissed off the person she depended on most.

Hearing the door creak behind her, Meaghan spun around. Kady Cressley, the fourth and final member of the solicitor's office, walked in. Funny, irreverent, and one of the best legal secretaries Meaghan had ever worked with, Kady was a small slender woman in her early twenties. The youngest child and only daughter of a single father, Kady was also a witch-in-training under Natalie's tutelage. A bit of a late bloomer, she made up for it with raw ability and a can-do attitude.

Kady had become the office's safety valve over the last few weeks. She laughed first when tension needed to be broken, in turns snarky or sympathetic as the situation required. She'd even managed to wring a couple of wan smiles out of Jamie.

"Hey, boss," she said. When she saw Natalie's desk and the fire extinguisher, her smile shifted into a worried scowl. "What happened? Was it Jamie?"

Meaghan nodded. "Yeah, looks like it. I suppose you know about the poltergeist thing?"

Kady dropped her bag on her desk on the other side of the room. "Yeah, and I guess now you do, too." Anticipating Meaghan's complaint, she said, "I know we should have warned you, but you've kinda been dumped with a lot of stuff since you got here, so we figured we'd wait and see if there was a problem and then talk to you. Looks like Jamie beat us to it."

"The files on his desk were levitating along with his stapler. Then he ignited Natalie's in-box and went for a walk."

Part of Meaghan's mind rebelled at the words coming out of her mouth. Even after all she'd seen and done since she'd moved to Eldrich, sometimes a small pocket of rationality recoiled in horror and flooded her mind with denial. She tried to ignore it. "There was also a sort of sculpture of stacked legal pads and pens in the hallway in front of my office."

Kady appraised Meaghan with narrowed eyes. "I need to talk to you about something. How about I meet you back in your office in a minute? I'll bring you some coffee, okay?"

Uh oh, Meaghan thought. *Now what?* "Who'll answer the phones?"

"I'll send them to voice mail." Kady's face broke into a beaming smile. It was like the sun breaking through a storm. "Go. Sit. Don't worry. It's good news for once."

CHAPTER FIVE

As SOON AS Meaghan saw the tea bag in Kady's cup, she knew what Kady wanted to tell her. Kady was normally a black coffee girl.

"You're pregnant," Meaghan said.

"I thought all that psychic stuff had worn off," Kady said, surprised.

Meaghan had received a hefty dose of mind-bending substances in Fahraya. The antidote for the venom of the giant scorpion that stung her had included mushrooms that not only left her stoned off her ass, but gave her powerful—albeit temporary—psychic abilities.

"Please," Meaghan said, smiling. "You're drinking herbal tea. And you're kind of glowing." She didn't add that she'd noticed Kady putting on weight. "I don't need to be psychic to connect those dots. Congratulations."

Kady handed her a mug of coffee. "We wanted to wait to tell everybody until I got along a bit."

Meaghan took "we" to mean Kady and her boyfriend, Jeff. A mechanic, Jeff owned a small garage in town. Meaghan had never heard anything to make her think that Jeff, despite being clued in, had any magical or paranormal gifts.

But he had her cranky, fussy Audi purring, which was a kind of magic as far as Meaghan was concerned. Back in Phoenix, she'd always joked that the Audi was possessed. After two months in Eldrich, it no longer seemed so funny.

Meaghan took a sip of the excellent coffee. Along with being a witch, Natalie loved coffee, a habit she'd picked up from Meaghan's father. The high-end coffeemaker Natalie kept in the file room bubbled all day long. "So," she asked after another sip. "When are you due?"

"March fifteenth is the official date. I'll work right up until I pop and I'll get as much done as I can and organize stuff before I go. And if you need me, I can work from home during maternity leave and—"

"Whoa," Meaghan said, holding up her hand. "Relax. We can figure it all out when we get closer. Nothing we do here is so important that you need to worry about it."

"You're not a typical lawyer, you know that?" Kady said.

"So I've heard."

"When I first got out of paralegal school, I went to work for a law firm down in Harrisburg. They were worse than TV lawyers. The guy I worked for used to brag about how he missed the birth of his first child because he was getting ready for a deposition." She rolled her eyes. "What an asshole."

Meaghan snorted. "I know the type. Matthew wasn't like that, was he?"

Kady flushed slightly. "I didn't start working here until right before he left."

"And he was kind of dotty by then," Meaghan said.

Kady nodded, looking embarrassed.

"It's fine," Meaghan said. "You never really got to know him. It took me spending time with him after he died to really remember how much that sick old man wasn't him. I wish you could have known him better. He would have loved your sense of humor."

Meaghan wished she could have known him better, too. She spent so much time being angry with him when he was alive that she missed most of his life. She got the chance to do what no else could do, to make things right even after death, but it could never make up for the lifetime she had thrown away.

She felt the prickle in her eyes of coming tears, followed by a twinge of disgust at her recurring weepiness. Anything could set her off lately. Time to change the subject. "Have you picked out names yet?"

Kady flushed deeper. "Well, we just started talking about it and we don't know if it's a boy or a girl, but Natalie says it's a boy and she's almost never wrong."

Kady took a breath, then continued, the words coming out in rush. "So, this is the other thing I wanted to talk to you about. Jeff and I are the youngest in large families and our parents' names are already taken and so we were thinking . . . well, I was thinking and I haven't told Jeff this yet, so it's just an idea and we can change it, but I was thinking Matthew." She took another breath, and finally looked up at Meaghan, a cautious look on her face. "Matthew James O'Connell. That's Jeff's last name."

The tears Meaghan had tried to push down now welled up and ran down her cheeks.

A look of horror on her face, Kady said, "Oh, God. I'm sorry. It's too soon. I never—"

Meaghan began laughing through her tears. "No, no. It's okay. It's perfect. Thank you." She groped for the box of tissues on her desk and blew her nose. "Ignore me. I'm such a crybaby these days. I'm blubbering over everything. I spent so many years not feeling anything and now it's all catching up with me."

Unshed tears, Meaghan had begun to realize, were like unpaid bills. They didn't simply go away. They got bigger, as the interest and late fees stacked up. She'd spent years trying not to feel her pain and it was time to pay her tab.

But did she have to pay it all at once? Something innocuous would make her cry, which would be followed quickly by a wave of disgust at what a weepy idiot she had become, which would make her cry even more. It was like being on an emotional hamster wheel.

Maybe you should talk to somebody about that, whispered the treacherous, sensible voice in the back of her head. She ignored it, the same way she had ignored her earlier attack of denial. She didn't need therapeutic handholding. She needed to pull her head out of her ass. People were counting on her.

Kady sighed and relaxed back in her chair. "I'm so glad you like it. There's been so much lost lately, I thought it was time to start . . . I don't know . . . honoring the people we love and moving forward again."

"Good call," Meaghan said. She blew her nose again. "I know wherever Dad is, he'll be pleased."

"Have you seen him since the thing in Fahraya?"

Meaghan shook her head. The last time she'd spoken with her father, he'd been already dead. He'd called in a lot of favors to get to Fahraya to save her, he said, and wouldn't be able to appear to her again for some time, even in her dreams. What those favors were, he hadn't said.

Nobody from the other side had communicated with her since. The dead were cryptic, to say the least. And she still hadn't encountered one of the ghosts that haunted city hall. Even this morning's spooky shenanigans had merely been Jamie working out his issues.

Kady wore a concerned look. "So, you're okay with this?

Meaghan smiled at her. "Absolutely. I think it's a wonderful name and your timing couldn't be better. We need something to look forward to around here."

Soon after Meaghan's chat with Kady, Natalie and Jamie returned. They walked in together, Jamie with a dark expression and Natalie with tear-swollen eyes. Without a word, they parted and Jamie headed back to his office. Natalie cleared the mess covering her desk and Jamie resumed his post staring blankly out the window.

For the rest of the day, nothing levitated or burst into flames. After lunch, Meb, the security guard, dropped by with four new fire extinguishers. He teased Meaghan about too much emergency planning and she merely smiled.

"Safety first," she said.

Meb laughed and went back downstairs. He betrayed no sign that he'd gleaned anything from Annie beyond the agreed-upon explanation.

Meaghan left two extinguishers up front and stowed the other two in the copy room across from her office. *Just in case*, she told herself. *Just in case.*

CHAPTER SIX

MEAGHAN PLOWED THROUGH the few things cluttering her in-box and left at three to hit the pool. It was the Thursday before Labor Day weekend, so no one would miss her. The council took the entire month of August off and things slowed down considerably. Even Emily Proctor, the council director and Meaghan's somewhat hapless nemesis, had slacked off.

For such a tiny town, the Eldrich recreation center was a nice facility, with a good-sized lap pool, basketball and tennis courts, and a well-equipped weight room. It stayed open to the public all day during the summer, but doubled as the high school and middle school gymnasium, and students got first priority during the school year.

Tiny Sylvan County steadfastly bucked the nationwide trend of opening school during August. School started on the Tuesday after Labor Day, so this might be the last peaceful swim Meaghan would get for a while. And she'd have no pool access at all once the swim team began training. She'd need to find something else to do to stay fit.

In Arizona, she'd spent her winters hiking, but she couldn't do that in Eldrich. Not in the forest. Meaghan could be torn apart by teeth and claws like anybody else, and stumbling through the wrong dimensional gateway could land her in one of the many worlds where she wasn't very popular at the moment.

The news of Fahraya's destruction had swept through the magical realms, with Meaghan shouldering most of the blame. But, on the upside, while nobody wanted her negotiating services, her gatekeeper credentials were now well established. *If they don't respect you,* she thought, *better make sure they fear you.*

She tugged at her chlorine-faded swimsuit and plopped down on the edge of the pool to put in her earplugs before slipping into the water. She wrestled on the silicon swim cap, adjusted her goggles, and pushed off from the wall into the lap lane.

The water, cool and soothing, enveloped her and she settled into her routine. Up and back she swam, in alternating strokes, letting her mind wander. But, as usual these days, her thoughts soon settled on the events of ten weeks before.

It still didn't make sense. The accepted reason for Jamie's abduction—the power struggle between Jamie's father, John, and V'hren—had never convinced her.

Why now, after all these years, had V'hren tried to kill Jamie? Meaghan couldn't believe it was merely to consolidate power. V'hren had controlled Fahraya for eighteen years, despite efforts by his son, Jhoro, to mount a resistance. But Jhoro, a fugitive with a handful of ragtag followers scratching out a living in the barren hills, had been no threat.

John, the former king and V'hren's exiled brother, posed no threat either. V'hren had cut John's wings from his back before allowing him to escape Fahraya, and for the next eighteen years, John had lived in a gin bottle, too ashamed to raise his own son. Wings were a big deal to Fahrayans.

Or, at least they had been. Before everyone became human. Now, nobody had wings. John was king again. Sort of. He really didn't want the job, but Jhoro, the logical choice, was as lost in the human world as the rest of the Fahrayans.

Meaghan stopped to catch her breath, her arm aching in the spot where the giant scorpion had stung her. She tried a few careful stretches, but she knew it wasn't a cramp. It was a deep ache that never quite went away.

So she ignored it and went back to worrying about Jamie.

While technically the rightful heir, Jamie hated Fahraya. Five minutes of intelligence gathering would have made clear to V'hren that Jamie had no intention of returning and claiming his lost birthright. Better an average guy in paradise than king of a pre-literate Stone Age dump like Fahraya.

Her heart no longer pounding like a conga drum, Meaghan grabbed her kickboard. She thought about putting on her training fins, but she'd also banged up one of her knees in Fahraya, and using the fins made it hurt again.

I'm too old to be an action hero. With a sigh, she pushed off from the wall and began her leg work.

What bothered her most was that the accepted narrative assumed that V'hren acted out of self-interest, to protect his position and further his ambition. But V'hren was no longer V'hren. Something had consumed him from the inside out, a malevolent force that wore his body like clothing.

The Power. According to Natalie, the Power was a new

player, at least in Eldrich. A non-corporeal entity that lived on fear, pain, and despair—negative emotions—it required a host. Bitter by nature and jealous of his brother, V'hren had fit the bill.

But why did this thing want Jamie? If not to protect V'hren's throne, then why?

And even if the Power was simply trying to eliminate V'hren's competition, that still didn't explain why V'hren's hired muscle manufactured an excuse to drag Jamie back. V'hren had so thoroughly terrified his subjects that he didn't need an excuse and the offense—Jamie changing into his Fahrayan form—by itself didn't violate the treaty.

Meaghan's knee was starting to hurt now, even without the training fins. She considered dumping the kickboard for a leg float so she could concentrate on her arms, but using the leg float made her back hurt.

She abandoned the kickboard at the end of the pool. *Screw it. Back to freestyle.* At least the pain would be evenly distributed throughout her body.

Wizards who called themselves the Order—or as Russ called them, "those gray-robed assholes"—had convinced Emily Proctor, a witch almost as powerful as Natalie, that Jamie was a threat. They juiced her with extra magic and sent her to tear off Jamie's amulet. A week later, three wizards kidnapped Jamie and sent him back to Fahraya.

But why did the Order go to all the trouble? Why not grab Jamie on his way to work or when he was out for a run?

They'd set it up so Emily would force Jamie to change in city hall, the worst place for her stunt because of how city hall magnified the effect, making Jamie stronger and wilder than he would otherwise have been.

And city hall was supposedly a big magic ray gun to the other side, wherever that might be. A big magic ray gun also believed to have opened the gateways between Fahraya and the human world not long after it was built.

Even more sinister, the Order hadn't merely taken Jamie. They'd carved strange symbols—sigils—into his back and chest, symbols that no one in Eldrich could decipher.

Some kind of spell, perhaps? Natalie didn't want to talk about it, but Meaghan could tell the sigils worried her. Jamie's other wounds were healing, and—with the exception of the two lines along his spine where his wings had been cut from his back—would disappear or leave only minor scars.

But the sigils—the skin had closed over them rapidly, leaving raised, ropey lines. Bright red against his skin, each sigil was clearly delineated. Someone who knew the language could read Jamie like a book.

Only no one knew the language. And now Jamie was manifesting poltergeist activity, which city hall amplified into a powerful threat to those around him.

They had to move him out of that office. Meaghan considered cooking up some excuse to get funding to build out more of the attic. But considering that the council approved all funding requests and all funding requests had to be filtered first through Emily Proctor—who would love to see Jamie set Meaghan on fire—that was probably not a viable solution.

Moving him somewhere else in the building might work or it might merely spread the poltergeist activity, albeit a milder form, to the other floors. It was already happening at home when he wasn't anywhere near his office.

There was a third possibility. Maybe Jamie needed more time away. Poltergeists, magic sigils, and paranormally enhanced office space aside, he was barely functional. He stared out the window all day. He rarely spoke. Hallam and Associates wouldn't be handing his cases back anytime soon.

With his short-term disability leave benefits exhausted and no vacation or sick days left, Jamie's only option was the Family Medical Leave Act. But FMLA leave would be unpaid. His wife, Patrice, worked as a nurse at the local clinic, but without Jamie's salary, they'd run into financial trouble before long. The one advantage to FMLA, one that maybe had to be considered, was that Jamie couldn't be fired while taking it.

Meaghan stopped again to catch her breath and decided she was done for the day. She'd do a few easy cool-down laps and head home.

Patrice claimed everything was fine, but the harried shadows under her eyes said otherwise. The kids seemed sad and withdrawn, and Liddy, Jamie's four-year-old daughter, refused to go near him, insisting he wasn't her father.

Not that Jamie noticed. He merely sat, staring out the window.

And now doors were slamming, dishes were flying, and, in city hall at least, things were bursting into flames.

Meaghan finished her final cool-down lap and climbed out of the pool. At least dinner would be waiting when she got home. And Jamie wasn't the only quasi-son she had to worry about. Time to see what sort of trouble Jhoro had gotten into today.

CHAPTER SEVEN

WHEN MEAGHAN GOT home, Russ's car wasn't in the garage and she couldn't smell anything cooking. Since he'd started planning his food truck business, Russ had gotten sloppy about regular mealtimes.

In the kitchen, a woman she knew to be a witch, and her two teenage apprentices, sat at the table watching the open refrigerator, smiles on their faces.

"Hi, I'm home," Meaghan said.

Nobody noticed. She looked around the fridge door.

Shirtless, shoeless, and wearing a pair of tight, low-slung jeans, Jhoro bent, peering into the depths of the refrigerator. He had the kind of body that made even plumber's crack look good. Not the excessive definition favored by Hollywood, but the lean wiry strength of a man who'd spent his life hunting for his food with a bone spear and a stone knife.

He stood up, a covered bowl in one hand while the other hand flipped silky, blond hair out of his face. Another witch,

Marnie, who was a hair stylist, had spent days patiently picking and combing out the mane of matted dreadlocks Jhoro had worn in Fahraya. He shook his head and the golden, newly unsnarled hair spilled to the middle of his back.

The witches sighed in unison.

Meaghan laughed out loud, but still no one noticed her. She appeared to be the only woman in Eldrich immune to Jhoro's sexual charisma. Objectively, she understood his appeal. He was flat-out, drop-dead gorgeous. But when Meaghan had first met him, he'd been grimy with dirt and blood and soot and had body odor that made her eyes water. One of the first things she'd had to do when he moved in with her and Russ was give him a good scrubbing.

And apparently she was the only woman in town who believed he was gay. Finn, his mate, had been killed in the rush to escape the destruction of Fahraya. Despite the mega-watt smile and come-hither looks he gave everyone he met, male and female, Meaghan knew he was grieving for Finn and would be for a long time.

But even if she didn't want to drag him into her bed, Jhoro still affected her in a way she found horribly disconcerting. Not ten years ago, she would have been lusting with everyone else. Now she wanted to make him a cup of cocoa and tell him to clean his room.

Meaghan had a mommy crush.

Her newly awakened maternal instincts had been rebuffed by Jamie, so Meaghan threw it all at Jhoro and he sucked it up like a dry sponge. His own mother had died giving birth to him, and V'hren had never really believed Jhoro was his. John had loved him like a son, but Zhara, John's wife and Jamie's mother, while kind, had never warmed to Jhoro the same way. Jamie, his cousin, had never let him forget it.

He called Meaghan "Mama," and every time she felt her heart swell even as she rolled her eyes and told him not to call her that.

Marnie strolled into the kitchen, wearing a sheer tank top and cutoffs short enough to qualify as panties. Slender with a pierced nose and black hair in a sharp bob, she normally favored ironic T-shirts and baggy cargo shorts. She had cut Meaghan's short silvering hair about a month earlier and done such a good job that Meaghan had scheduled a standing monthly appointment.

Marnie walked up to Jhoro and reached her arm around him. She grabbed his bottom, pulling him against her. He wrapped his hand gently in her hair, pulled her head back, and bent to kiss her.

Meaghan felt the weather change in the kitchen. The trio seated at the table glared. One of the apprentices looked like she was trying not to cry.

Okay, Meaghan thought. Not gay. Clearly, he was comfortable playing for either team. Although not for long, because he and Marnie were about to be blasted into grease spots.

Then—and Meaghan wouldn't have believed it if she hadn't seen it—he lifted his head and gave the fuming witches his movie-star smile. They sighed and smiled back.

So, now, the two men she lived with—her brother and this wild-man surrogate son—were each only one wayward glance, one missed birthday, one wrong word away from pissing off two women critical to Meaghan's well-being.

I'm getting padlocks for their zippers, she thought. *Bastards. Why do they have to sleep with women I depend on?*

Jhoro, at least, had an excuse. Grief made people do stupid things and he'd only been human for ten weeks. A certain allowance had to be made for bad behavior.

But Russ? He knew how much Meaghan relied on Natalie and he knew his own history with relationships. And he'd known Natalie since she was a young teenager, barely out of childhood, which made the whole thing extra creepy.

At least they weren't flaunting it under her nose like Jhoro and Marnie.

Jhoro finally noticed Meaghan. His face lit up. "Mama!" He shoved Marnie aside and wrapped Meaghan in a hug. Marnie and the witches now glared at Meaghan, making her grateful she was impervious.

She patted him in a motherly way and stepped back. "Where's Russ?"

"Roos?" he answered in a deep rich voice.

Meaghan nodded.

Jhoro pantomimed driving a truck, then patted his belly with a smile.

"He's working on his food truck," Marnie said, putting a proprietary hand in Jhoro's back pocket while the other witches seethed.

Meaghan turned to them. "Ladies, I'm sorry, I know we've met, but I forget your names. Are you waiting for me or Russ?" *Or for Marnie to drop her guard?*

The older woman, somewhere in her forties, trim, with carefully highlighted, chin-length brown hair, shook her head slightly, as if to clear it. She wore a sleeveless white polo shirt and pastel plaid capris and looked like she'd just stepped off a golf course. "We're waiting for you. I'm Susan. I've been helping Lynette with the Fahrayans."

Meaghan nodded. Country club Susan. She remembered her now.

Susan had moved to Eldrich after her wealthy husband's death. She had Junior League connections throughout the Northeast, some of whom practiced witchcraft or were otherwise clued in. She'd proved instrumental in gathering supplies to help clothe, feed, and house the Fahrayan refugees now living in Eldrich.

"And you are . . ." Meaghan prompted the other two. Much younger than Susan, they had both adopted what they believed to be appropriate attire for witches. Lots of black velvet and silver jewelry and too much eye shadow.

Real witches, Meaghan had learned, didn't dress any particular way, didn't require mystical accessories, and could improvise spell ingredients from whatever was handy. Meaghan had asked a group of witches once if they were Wiccans. Lynette, an older grandmotherly woman, had sniffed with disapproval and said, "I don't know about the others, but I'm a Presbyterian."

The more flamboyant of the two apprentices, the girl who had seemed the most upset by Jhoro and Marnie kissing, tossed her dark hair over her shoulder and said, "I'm Circe." She pointed at her companion, a round-faced girl with blonde hair, freckles, and far less eye makeup. "This is Cassandra."

Oh, brother, Meaghan thought. *Their real names are probably Debbie and Lisa.*

Susan rolled her eyes discreetly and winked at Meaghan.

"Circe and Cassandra are my apprentices for now, but Circe is about to move on to Gretchen. We're waiting for her here."

Meagan suppressed a laugh. Gretchen, the city's human resources coordinator, looked like a kind, grandmotherly woman, similar to Lynette, until she started talking. Profane, sarcastic, and wickedly funny, Gretchen reveled in screwing with uppity apprentices. She'd knock the Stevie Nicks right out of Circe. If the girl had enough sense to lose her pretensions, Gretchen would hone her into a gifted practitioner.

Susan would keep Cassandra, who had all the earmarks of a follower. Her efforts to dress in the witchy style favored by Circe were half-hearted—jeans, a black velour T-shirt, and a few silver rings—and without Circe bossing her around, she'd have a chance to come into her own.

"So, ladies," Meaghan said. "What's up?"

Before they could answer, Marnie started giggling. Jhoro threw her over his shoulder and, with a final dazzling smile, carried her out of the room. They heard him stomp up the stairs and slam his bedroom door shut.

Susan frowned up at the ceiling. "How long has this been going on?"

Meaghan shrugged. "Don't ask me. I thought he was gay."

"Every woman in town is jealous of you," Susan said with a sigh.

Meaghan snorted. "He calls me Mama. I had to teach him how to use the big boy potty when he kept trying to go in the backyard."

Hearing a moan, Meaghan stared up at the ceiling with a frown. The bed springs began rhythmically squeaking. So much for foreplay. She grabbed the broom from the pantry and walked into the hallway. Banging on the ceiling with the broom handle, Meaghan shouted, "Hey, keep it down!"

The squeaking stopped. Meaghan walked back into the kitchen, met Susan's eye, and they both burst out laughing. Cassandra smiled shyly until Circe gave her a sour look.

"God, he is a magnificent beast," Susan said.

It was Meaghan's turn to roll her eyes. "You got the beast part right. It's like living with a giant horny toddler."

Susan smiled, not fooled a bit by Meaghan's complaints. "You like him too. Only in a mommy way."

Meaghan flushed, then smiled. "Oh, hell. Is it that obvious?"

Susan merely smiled, then her face grew serious. "As much as I've enjoyed the show, Jhoro's not who we need to talk about."

"You're here about Jamie." Meaghan felt her stomach clench. Susan was one of several witches who had spent time at the Smith's house, babysitting the kids and keeping an eye on Jamie while Patrice was at work.

Susan nodded. "Are you familiar with the concept of the poltergeist?"

Meaghan relaxed a little. "Got a crash course this morning. What's been going on?"

Susan sighed with relief. "Oh, thank God. Did Natalie finally tell you? She's . . . well, her devotion to Jamie is not helping right now. She refuses to see what's going on."

"I only heard it from her because I witnessed it firsthand and Annie reported that the ghosts were in a tizzy." Meaghan didn't want to disclose details until she knew what other people had observed. Enough gossiping about Jamie was going on. No need to add to it.

Confirming Meaghan's caution, Circe leaned forward with an eager gleam in her eye. "What did you see?"

Like I'd tell you, Stevie Nicks. "Some office supplies turning up in odd places. A levitating file folder or two."

Not exactly a lie.

Circe looked disappointed, then rallied. "I was nearly decapitated by a flying plate at his house and there are slamming doors and weird smells."

Cassandra snorted. Circe glared at her, but this time Cassandra refused to be silenced. "It was a plastic Little Mermaid plate and it was moving so slow you caught it like a Frisbee. And the weird smell is that patchouli you're wearing."

Atta girl. Meaghan smothered a laugh.

Circe glowered, but had no response.

"So," Meaghan said. "I know all about it. Is there anything else?"

"Let's chat later, when we have more time," Susan said. "I'll give you a call."

Meaghan had come to recognize the *I-have-something-important-to-say-but-not-in-front-of-the-tourists/clueless/newbies* look. Which meant things were worse than Susan was willing to let on in front of the apprentices.

"I'll be home all evening," Meaghan said, a sinking feeling in her gut. "And I should be in the office all day tomorrow."

CHAPTER EIGHT

AFTER THE WITCHES left, Meaghan reheated the small bowl of pasta Jhoro had abandoned in favor of sex, but all it did was sharpen her appetite. If Russ didn't return soon, Meaghan might be forced to cook. No good could come of that.

She found a bag of organic, blue-corn tortilla chips in the pantry—Russ would sooner die than buy a bag of Doritos—and poured herself a glass of wine. She wondered whether she should cut back. She wasn't a big drinker, but Matthew had been an alcoholic.

And then there was John. After eighteen years of being the town drunk, he was going to AA and by all accounts was doing well. She felt her face flush and warmth spread through her body at the thought of him. They'd both agreed they weren't ready for a relationship until John's sobriety was stronger and until the post-Fahraya chaos had calmed down a bit.

Which she was beginning to think might never happen.

Every day it was something else to deal with. It was bad enough trying to feed, clothe, and shelter the Fahrayans, but John also had to protect them from the outside world and from themselves.

First came the leprechauns—not the whimsical little men at the end of the rainbow guarding their pots of gold. No, these leprechauns were foul-mouthed loan sharks, collecting the vig on usurious loans made to the naïve or desperate. They lent out their pots of gold at crippling interest rates—literally. Miss a payment, lose a finger. Or an arm or eye or leg . . . whatever was handy.

They proved no match for the Fahrayans once John explained to his people what they were up to. The leprechauns had been expecting eight-inch-tall fairies. What they got were six-foot-tall humans with lightning reflexes and Stone Age sensibilities. Fahraya had been a brutal place and it had bred brutal people. For people accustomed to hunting enormous snakes and giant scorpions for food, leprechauns—no matter how dirty they fought—were no threat.

But the biggest threat to the Fahrayans were the Fahrayans themselves. They had come from an extremely primitive hunter-gatherer society and had been dumped, without any warning or preparation, into the modern world. They'd lost everything, including their wings and the extra set of vocal cords required to properly speak their language. They hadn't arrived with even the clothes on their backs because of the size difference.

Everything about the human world was alien to them, including their own bodies. It helped that John, once again their king, had suffered a similar dislocation and had lived in the human world for so long. But the transition had nearly destroyed him. The same thing was now happening to his people and John was determined to keep them from making the same mistakes he had.

He turned his property into a refugee camp until permanent housing was found. He helped them quickly learn a pidgin form of their language that allowed them to communicate with human vocal cords. He set up English classes and tried to teach them the basics of life in modern human society.

And in an attempt to save his people from his biggest mistake, John banned alcohol from the Fahrayan camp. But he had no control over the Fahrayans who had been relocated to private homes, and alcohol found its way in. Complicating matters, John had his own daily battle staying sober. He had a hard enough time keeping himself from drinking let alone five hundred grieving Fahrayans.

Even with tight controls and cooperation, it would be a daunting struggle, but not all Fahrayans were inclined to comply with John's directives. Even though everyone called him a king, that wasn't exactly what he was.

"It's not quite a king like humans think," John had told her once, during one of their evening phone calls. "There is not exactly a word in English. The word in Fahrayan means something like 'leader of the hunt who says the last word on stuff.' But that's only so long as there is no . . . what's the word? Complainer?"

"Challenger?" Meaghan asked.

"Challenger," John repeated. "Yeah."

"How's that work?"

"The people decide if they want the challenger to go ahead."

"And then?"

"Fight to the death."

Meaghan gasped.

John chuckled. "Don't worry. I don't have to fight. I can just agree. But I can't quit until a challenge is made by somebody they want."

The challenger, John explained, didn't have to be someone in the same family. Or a man. Women had been kings in the past. John's father could have easily looked outside his family to choose his heir. "If he had done that," John told her, "he would have saved us all this trouble."

The tendency to hereditary succession had developed out of inertia more than anything else. A good leader tended to pass those characteristics on to his or her children.

"If it ain't broke, don't fix it," Meaghan said.

"Something is broken? Are we still talking about kings?" John had been speaking English for nearly two decades, but sometimes he could be annoyingly literal.

Fights to the death notwithstanding, being a Fahrayan king was more like at-will employment than a divine mandate to rule. V'hren had attempted to rule like a human king and the Fahrayans wanted no more of that. Heredity was not in John's favor on this. After all, he was V'hren's younger brother. If one brother went bad, so could the other.

It was only a matter of time until a new leader rose. Or several. John was seeing the growth of several factions and it worried him. But whoever ended up as the new king, it wouldn't be Jhoro. Heredity wasn't helping him either. He had originally seemed like the logical choice to succeed his father, but the very fact that he was V'hren's son now made the Fahrayans mistrust him.

It was so bad that Jhoro had almost no contact with his people, including those who had fought with him in the hills and who had been so loyal to him in Fahraya. Meaghan had initially thought he wanted to live with her and Russ to protect her, and that was part of it, but basically he had nowhere else to go.

Another stray. Another lost boy. Which probably played no small part in spurring Meaghan's mommy crush.

For now, a fragile peace existed and nobody had been killed or hurt. Yet. But John could only protect them for so long. The modern world beckoned, terrifying but enticing.

Meaghan's stomach growled loudly. Where the hell was Russ? It was almost seven. She eyed the phone book. A pizza maybe? She liked a little place downtown that Russ eschewed because they used dough conditioners in the crust and didn't use hand-crafted mozzarella.

Sometimes she wanted to hit him with a Happy Meal, he was such a food snob. She opened the refrigerator to see if she could find any salsa for the chips. She'd give Russ ten more minutes and then she was calling for that pizza.

Meaghan found the salsa and poured herself another glass of wine, took a sip, then set it down on the counter. She knew that John's sobriety didn't require her to abstain too, but she didn't want to rub his nose in it. She liked wine, but she liked John a lot more. Even if the thought of being with him scared her to death.

They'd both been celibate for many long years, too wounded in their respective ways to let anyone near them. Even the scant emotional intimacy they had already shared had required serious effort. If it hadn't been for their ordeal in Fahraya, they'd both still be blushing and stammering, unable to make eye contact. John would be too timid to approach her and Meaghan would be too shut down to let him in.

They had agreed that neither was ready to start a physical relationship, but they talked on the phone daily. It may have kept them from physical temptation, but if John's dreams were anything like Meaghan's . . . when she wasn't dreaming about giant scorpions attacking her, she was dreaming about attacking John. In all sorts of creative ways. Dream Meaghan and Dream John were getting busy all over town.

Everyone, including Meaghan and John, assumed they'd hook up eventually. Unless . . . Meaghan hated how her feelings for John reduced her emotional age sometimes to about sixteen. What if he'd met somebody else? He was surrounded by Fahrayan women every day. John had been celibate since his exile from Fahraya eighteen years earlier. He'd only ever been with Fahrayan women. Tall, fierce, beautiful. And—at least until they'd become human—without body hair.

Which launched her into a whole new anxiety cycle. She was fifty years old. Fifty! She knew she was a young, vibrant fifty, but still. The last time she'd had sex, only women waxed away their body hair, and only on their legs and bikini lines. Now everybody waxed everything, sexual attractiveness apparently requiring skin as smooth and hairless as a baby's bottom. And this would be what John considered normal, since the only hair Fahrayans used to have was on their scalps.

The thought of waxing her nether regions gave Meaghan the heebie-jeebies.

She snorted in disgust and picked up her wine glass. With everything else going on in her life—poltergeists and evil wizards and murky nefarious plots fueled by black magic—she was worried about pubic hair.

Sex. As if the paranormal wasn't bad enough, now she might have to deal with sex again, too. Life in Phoenix had been simpler. Stultifying, lonely, and despair-inducing, but simpler.

CHAPTER NINE

MEAGHAN HEARD MARNIE and Jhoro roll out of bed again, then the sound of the shower in the hall bath, along with boisterous laughing. Apparently the language barrier wasn't a problem, but then, Meaghan supposed, based on what she'd seen and heard since she got home from work, they weren't spending a lot of time talking.

As she picked up the phone to order a pizza, she heard a car horn blare in the driveway. A few short blasts and then a long honk. Russ was finally home.

"About goddamn time," she muttered. She walked out to the driveway and saw an old, rusted delivery truck, one of the big square ones. She waited until he climbed out. "So, you're really gonna do it."

"I sure am," Russ said. "Isn't she beautiful?"

"She's a piece of shit," Meaghan said. "Where's my dinner?"

Russ waved his hand dismissively. "You have no imagination. Dinner's on the way. Natalie's bringing it."

"Natalie? Since when does Natalie do our cooking?"

Russ walked around the truck, smiling and gently patting it. "Come here. Let me show you what I'm gonna do." Meaghan's question finally registered. "I pit-cooked some pigs out at John's house for the Fahrayans. Natalie grabbed some ribs and a shoulder for us."

She felt a quiver down her spine when she heard John's name, followed quickly by a flutter in her gut. "So . . . how's he doing?"

"Why do you want know?" Russ asked, smirking and waggling his eyebrows.

Her face turned red. "Shut up."

Russ rolled his eyes, then gave her a wicked grin. "Meaghan's got a crush on John," he said in a sing-song tone. "John and Meaghan sittin' in a tree, k-i-s-s-i-n-g."

Meaghan stared at her toes. Blushing furiously, she said, "Just answer the question. How is he?"

"You talk to him all the time," Russ said, eyes roaming lovingly over the rusted truck.

"On the phone. I mean, how does he look?"

"Ooh," Russ said in falsetto. "He's so dreamy."

"Russ, I'm right on the edge here. I haven't had any dinner yet, remember?"

Russ laughed. "He looks good. Healthy. His face isn't as puffy as it used to be. He smiles more. A lot more, actually. I've never seen him this happy." He tore his gaze away from the truck. "Feel better?"

"What about the drinking? Is he sober?"

Russ sighed heavily. "He appears to be. Why don't you ask him?"

"Do you know anything about his sponsor?"

"No. It's Alcoholics *Anonymous*. I don't even know who his sponsor is."

"But you suspect, don't you?" Meaghan asked.

"Maybe. But it doesn't matter because it's none of our business. The sponsor gets to be anonymous too, you know."

"Nobody's anonymous in Eldrich. Not if you're clued in. You can't keep secrets for long." She looked at him to see if he got the hint.

Russ looked back, his face carefully neutral.

It was an expression she knew well. He was a lousy liar. If she wanted to find out about him and Natalie, this would a good time to ask. "So, Russ, um . . . about Natalie . . ."

At that moment, Natalie screeched into the driveway in her ancient Subaru wagon and stopped inches from the rear bumper of the truck.

"Aaaah," Russ cried, a stricken look on his face. "Don't smash my truck," he yelled at her as she climbed out of the car.

With a dismissive wave similar to the one Russ had just given Meaghan, Natalie said, "Relax. The thing's built like a tank." She glanced at Meaghan, then looked down, a slight flush on her face. She and Meaghan hadn't spoken since Natalie had stormed out of the office that morning. "Hey, boss."

"Hey, administrative goddess, where's my dinner?"

Natalie looked up and smiled broadly, relieved. "In the back. Help me carry it in."

Jhoro ran out of the house, back in his skin-tight jeans and now wearing a snug white T-shirt, his hair still wet from the shower. "Nat-a-lie," he roared and picked her up off the ground in a big hug. She giggled and slapped his arm lightly, but didn't tell him to put her down.

Marnie walked out on the porch, eyes narrowed, glaring at Natalie, who stared right back, with a defiant half smile.

Meaghan felt a flash of anger. While she didn't want Natalie sleeping with her brother, she didn't want her cheating on him either. What next, Russ and Marnie? No sexual triangles—quadrangles, she corrected herself—in my house, she thought. Time to be mommy.

"Put her down, you big oaf," she said to Jhoro, smacking him on the arm, much harder than Natalie had.

He gazed down at her, puzzled.

"Put Natalie down." She pointed at the ground. "Down." She waited a moment. "Now."

With a dazzling smile, he obeyed her. Meaghan grabbed him by the arm and dragged him to the Subaru. "Dinner." She pantomimed eating. "Help me carry it into the house." She popped open the unlocked tailgate and pulled out a heavy cardboard box filled with warm, foil-wrapped packages, and plopped it in his arms. "C'mon."

On her way to the back door, Jhoro following behind like an oversized duckling, Meaghan gave Natalie and Marnie a warning look. The first jealous witch who started blasting spells was getting her ass kicked. Both women, knowing that Meaghan was the only person in Eldrich who could make good on that threat, refused to meet her eye.

Once inside the kitchen, she pointed at the counter. "There."

Jhoro set the box down and looked at her with a worried expression. She sighed and patted him on the arm. She couldn't stay mad at him. He really didn't mean any harm and she knew the grief that was fueling it. If Finn walked through the door right now, Jhoro would never look at a woman or another man again.

But Marnie and Natalie were another matter. If they wanted to stalk around each other like a pair of wet cats, they could do it on their own time. And if either used magic against Russ or Jhoro, Meaghan would take them apart like a pissed-off grizzly bear. *No goddamn soap operas in my world. Don't I have enough shit to deal with as it is?*

Natalie and Marnie both stayed for dinner and glared at each other. Jhoro, happily oblivious, a dish towel stuffed in the collar of his T-shirt like a bib, ate with abandon. Ribs suited him. He still struggled to use a fork, so food he could eat with his hands made mealtime more pleasant for everyone.

After he'd polished off a rack of ribs, he pulled off the dish towel, leaned back in his chair, and stretched like a cat while sucking grease off his fingers. Marnie and Natalie stared, wide-eyed.

Marnie leaned into him, whispered something in his ear, and pulled her car keys out of her pocket. His eyes lit up. He took their plates to the sink, squeezed Russ's shoulder, kissed Meaghan on top of the head, and he and Marnie were out the door.

Natalie, her face red, stared down at her empty plate, then took it to the sink.

Russ merely smiled.

Time for a chat, Meaghan decided. "So, now that it's just the three of us, there's something I'd like to know. What's the big secret you two are keeping? If you're sleeping together . . ."

Russ spat out his sip of beer and started coughing.

Natalie dropped the plate with a crash. Both stared at her, incredulous.

After a long silent moment, Natalie said to Russ, "You wanted to wait to tell her until the right moment. I think this is it." To Meagan she added, "I wanted to tell you right away, but he said it was too soon."

"Look," Meaghan said. "It's a little awkward, but if you're both happy, I'm happy for you. But I don't want to have to take sides if things go wrong."

Russ started coughing again.

Natalie walked over and thumped him on the back and said, "We aren't sleeping together. Ewww. Russ, if you don't tell her right this minute, I will. She thinks we're . . . *ewww*."

"Meg, Natalie's not my girlfriend," Russ said, his face still red from his coughing fit. "She's my . . . sister." He waited a moment to let it sink in. "*Our* sister."

Meaghan stared at him. Sister. Natalie was her sister. Which meant Matthew and Vivian . . .

"Oh," she finally said, eyes wide.

CHAPTER TEN

"WAIT A MINUTE," Meaghan said. "You're my . . . *what?*"

"Sister," Natalie said. "I'm your sister. Half sister. Matthew was my dad. I'm sorry we didn't tell you sooner. Russ thought we should wait."

"How long have you known about this?" Meaghan asked, glaring at Russ.

He rubbed the back of his neck. "A while."

"How long a while?"

"A fairly long while," Russ said.

"Russ, goddammit, how long?"

"Twenty years or so. Since I moved here the first time."

"Twenty years?" Meaghan said. "You've known about this for *twenty years* and you're only telling me now? Oh, look, another big secret we can keep from Meaghan. Another kid Matthew replaced us with. He even got the birth order and ages right."

The anger at her father that Meaghan thought she had shed came roaring back. "Why fix things with Meaghan and Russ when he's got Natalie and Jamie? And here I am feeling guilty because I didn't fix things with him sooner and he's gone and gotten himself a new daughter. So, what, the only reason he wanted me back was because I was impervious and could take over his fucking job?"

"I'm sorry. I'll go. I'm sorry," mumbled Natalie, her face wooden. She stumbled out the back door and a moment later her car roared into life and screeched out of the driveway.

"*Nice*," Russ said. He shook his head, his eyes narrowed. "This is why we didn't tell you. Do you always have to be such a bitch? Does it always have to be about you?"

Meaghan's face flamed, her anger replaced with shame.

"Dad didn't replace you," Russ continued. "He never even claimed her as his. She grew up thinking she didn't have a father, that he'd died before she was born. I only figured it out watching the three of them together. I knew years before she did."

Meaghan stared at her feet. Finally, she asked, "When did she find out?"

"Right before she moved to Philadelphia with Jamie. Vivian had cancer and she knew she didn't have long and wanted Natalie to know."

"Why wouldn't Dad claim her? Did he know?" She stared at her feet, still unable to meet Russ's gaze.

"He knew. It was too dangerous for anyone else to know. At least until she got powerful enough to protect herself." Russ sighed. His anger spent, he began clearing the table. "I always meant to tell you. Once things settled down a little. Which they haven't yet."

Meaghan had no reply. She sat as Russ puttered around the kitchen, both avoiding each other's eyes. She thought of Natalie, of how much she'd liked her the first moment she'd met her, of how much she depended on her. And instead of embracing the news that she shared an even deeper bond with this woman who had become so central to her life, Meaghan had attacked her.

Finally she said, "You're right. I am a bitch. I find out I have a sister and the first thing I do is send her running for the door. I have to fix this." She rubbed her eyes and realized how tired she was. She hadn't been sleeping well lately. Too many nightmares. "Did she go home, you think?"

Russ nodded. "Yeah, probably."

"So, why the danger? Is it the war I've heard mentioned before? Which I haven't found anywhere in Dad's journals, which is kind of weird."

It was more than weird. Events had been excised from the record, leaving gaping holes in the narrative. It was obvious to Meaghan that scrubbing the record had not been Matthew's idea, otherwise he would done a much better job of it. His ham-handed editing was a purposeful red flag to the reader that a significant cover-up had occurred.

"I don't know much about the war myself," Russ said. "You want more wine?"

Meaghan shook her head. "I've got to drive over to Natalie's. Tell me what you know before I go."

Russ sat down at the table. "It's been going on a long time. Not everybody is happy about magic losing sway over humanity. They want the old days back. And by old days, I mean pre-Iron Age. Before the magic started fading."

"Jamie and Kady looked confused when I asked Natalie

about it my first day at work. I only knew about it because Mom told me in that dream the day after I got here."

"What did Natalie tell you?"

"Nothing. She said it was something different from Fahraya and they didn't talk about it and I didn't press it."

"So, what did Mom tell you?"

"That Matthew didn't try to keep in touch with us after we moved to Arizona because the war had started and it wasn't safe."

Russ snorted. "And because she wouldn't let him near us without a court-appointed babysitter. Even dead she's still got the selective memory." He got up and grabbed another beer from the fridge. "Sure you don't want anything?"

Meaghan ignored the urge to defend her mother. Not the right time. She'd never noticed before that Russ held a grudge against Mom. "I'm sure. But the war was part of it too, right?"

Russ sat down, twisted off the cap, and took a long swig. "Yeah. I guess it was. He never told me much. When I asked, he'd change the subject. 'Bad stuff' was all he'd say."

"So is it over now?"

"It's never really over from what little I got out of Dad. It's like the Cold War, but it heats up sometimes."

"So why it isn't it in his journals?"

Russ shrugged. "Hell if I know. Maybe there's something out in the garage. Did you check?"

Meaghan nodded. "I started going through his file cabinets a couple of weeks ago, after I got through the boxes, but I haven't found anything out there either."

The day Meaghan had learned about Eldrich, Russ had brought over several boxes of journals and files Matthew had prepared for her before he'd gotten too sick to function. After she'd worked her way through those, she started going through the bulging file cabinets in the garage, but so far all she'd found was further evidence of Matthew's deliberately clumsy scrub job.

Russ nodded and said nothing.

"Plus," Meaghan said, "it appears things have been redacted. The war isn't mentioned, but there's an obvious hole in the story." She watched him carefully to detect any signs of lying. "Any ideas why the war would be edited from his journals?"

He gave her a puzzled look and shrugged. "Not a clue. Like I said, he wouldn't talk about it with me. There was a lot he didn't tell me."

Meaghan nodded, reasonably satisfied that he was telling her the truth. "So, if it's not the war, any other reasons Natalie might be in danger?"

"Well, yeah." Russ leaned back in his chair. "Think about it. She's the child of an impervious man and a powerful witch. Nobody knew if she'd have both traits or only one. Can you imagine? An impervious witch? She'd be unbeatable. The bad guys would want her taken out before she got enough power to be a risk."

"Or they'd want to turn her into a weapon for their side," Meaghan said. "Which is why Dad and Vivian had to hide her until they knew." Meaghan sighed. "Which makes me feel even shittier. I gotta get over there and try to fix this."

"Yeah, you do," Russ said. "She's always wanted to tell you, even though she thought you might respond like this. She said we owed it to you. We're her only family, Meg. And now that Jamie doesn't need her anymore, she's feeling abandoned. You aren't the only one whose life got hijacked by Dad's destiny."

"I guess not," Meaghan said. "Who else knows?"

"Only you, me, Jamie, and Patrice. Some people may suspect, but Matthew and Vivian did a good job hiding it."

Meaghan nodded. "While we're being honest, is there anything else I need to know? Somebody who I thought was human who isn't? Somebody else I work with who you're dating?"

"I think you've got the scoop on our immediate circle and if you haven't heard something, it's just an oversight. Same thing with the rest of the town. Natalie was the last big secret I had." He blushed. "You know Annie?"

"The medium?"

"Yeah. I'm not dating her, but I'm thinking about asking. She's been helping out at John's house and I really like her. I know my record sucks, so I'm not rushing into anything. No more whirlwind romance crap." When Meaghan didn't respond, Russ added, "I know you work with her, but not directly, and in a town this size that's the best I can do."

Meaghan smiled. "I can live with that." Her smile faded. "Before I go, any advice on how to deal with our baby sister?"

"Don't yell at her. That would be a good start."

"Russ, be serious."

"I am being serious. Nothing's changed between you, except now you have another word to describe her and then only to a few of us. And the good news is you don't have to worry about us sleeping together." He gave her an encouraging grin. "She wants you to be okay with this. Show her you are."

CHAPTER ELEVEN

NATALIE'S HOUSE LOOKED like a storybook cottage inexplicably dropped into a middle-class neighborhood. Eldrich was full of charming little houses like Natalie's. Jamie's house, around the corner, was a Tudor Revival straight out of an Agatha Christie novel.

Painted a warm buttercup yellow, the cottage squatted in the middle of a riot of wildflowers, herbs, and vegetables. A stone path wound through the garden leading to a small front porch containing a battered rocking chair. Wind chimes clanked softly in the twilight breeze.

Meaghan pulled into the driveway and parked behind Natalie's Subaru. She hadn't called first. This conversation had to be face to face. Taking a deep breath to steady her nerves, Meaghan climbed out of her car and picked her way through the overgrown yard to the front door.

Despite the mess, it all worked somehow. Like Natalie.

The effect wasn't neglect, but freedom, a warm sustained chaos full of joyful life.

And here comes bitchy big sister to crash the party. Meaghan climbed the front steps onto the porch and knocked on the wooden screen door. She could hear music—Patsy Cline, it sounded like—drifting from the kitchen.

"Natalie?" Meaghan pulled open the door and stepped into the living room. The chaos continued inside, still homey and comfortable. Stacks of books sat on the floor next to an overflowing bookshelf. Framed photographs covered the walls and mantel. Meaghan recognized Vivian—who looked remarkably like her daughter—Jamie at various ages, Jamie's kids and his wife, and a few photos of a younger Russ.

But no photos of Matthew. He was as absent from Natalie's life as he had been from Meaghan's.

Is that the price? Does this gift, burden, whatever the hell it is, force you to live apart, to push everyone away? Meaghan had done that all her life. Not many happy family photos of her floating around either. Or was it something about her and Matthew? A shared coldness that had nothing to do with the ability to repel magic?

"Natalie?" Meaghan moved into the kitchen. An iPod in a docking station sat on the windowsill, blaring into the backyard. Turning down the volume a bit, she called again. "Natalie?"

"Out here," a muffled voice said.

Meaghan pushed open the screen door and stepped onto the small enclosed patio. Natalie's cottage sat on an oddly shaped corner lot. Most of the yard was out front, with the cottage crowding the lot line. The patio consisted of a concrete pad with a solid board fence, and a gate to the driveway and the overgrown alley behind the house. But Natalie had filled even this tiny barren space with colorful pots of herbs and flowers, and a string of twinkly Christmas tree lights.

Natalie lay on a webbed, aluminum chaise lounge, her arm over her face. An empty wine glass and a half full bottle of chardonnay sweated on the small plastic table next to her.

"I'm a bitch," Meaghan said, sitting in a rusted metal chair.

Natalie said nothing.

"I'm a lousy excuse for a sister," Meaghan continued. "And . . . well . . . I suck. There's no other word for it." She waited a moment. "Please forgive me." Another silent moment passed. "At least yell at me or something."

Natalie sighed. With her arm still covering her eyes, she said, "We've had a super great day, you and I, haven't we? That's why I wanted Russ to tell you when you got here. Then if you wanted to fire me you could have done it right away before we got used to each other."

"*Fire you?* Where in the hell . . . You know damn well I couldn't fire you, not if you had any interest in keeping your job. I'd never make it past the first post-termination hearing. My whole world would fall apart without you. That's why I was so freaked out about you and Russ dating. I thought you'd break up with him and dump me, too."

"Really?" Natalie asked in a small voice.

Meaghan sighed in exasperation. "Yes, really. I liked you the first moment I met you. I felt comfortable with you. Now I know why."

Meaghan sat and Natalie lounged, both silent, listening to Patsy Cline sing about her aching heart.

Meaghan finally broke the silence. "Please say you forgive

me or tell me to go to hell. Something. So I know where I stand."

Natalie sat up. "I never once called him Dad."

"I know. Russ told me."

"I was more pissed at Mom than him at first. And then she died and Jamie and I moved back and I had to deal. He was right there and he needed me. But we never . . . he never felt like a father. A mentor, someone I liked and respected, yeah. But never a father."

"And that didn't bother you?" Meaghan asked.

"Well, yeah, of course it did. But not in the same way it bothered you to have him leave. I was pissed about the deceit, although I get why they did it, but I never knew him as Daddy. You know?"

Meaghan nodded. "I know. Got another wine glass? I could use some of that."

Natalie stood up. "You okay with some ice cubes? This cheap crap really needs to be cold to be drinkable and the bottle's been out of the fridge for a while."

"Ice is fine. I always used to put ice in white wine back in Phoenix, but stopped when I got here. Russ—"

"He makes that face, right? He does the same thing to me."

Natalie fetched a glass and some ice and poured them each some wine.

"So," Meaghan said. "I'll ask again—am I forgiven?"

Natalie nodded. "Of course you are. I'm sorry I was such a weepy ninny."

"Please," Meaghan said. "I yelled at you. I'm glad you didn't throw something at me."

Natalie's mouth twitched into a grin. "I really wanted to for a second there."

Meaghan smiled back, relieved. "With magic or muscle?"

Natalie laughed. "Both. If there'd been a piano handy, you'd have been toast."

"Good thing we aren't out West. Then you could have used a big boulder like Wile E. Coyote."

"My Acme bitchy-sister-destructo-ray—except the coyote always gets his ass kicked. I think I'd better stick with pianos."

They laughed until they both started coughing and had to stop to blow their noses.

"So," Natalie said, wiping her eyes with her arm. "Now what?"

"Shit, I don't know," Meaghan said. "I never had a sister before. I'm guessing you didn't get the impervious gene from Matthew?"

Natalie shook her head. "I'm all Mom. So far, at least. I can get zapped like everybody else if I don't watch out." She sipped her wine. "You're calling him Matthew again, instead of Dad. Don't be mad at him, okay? He really regretted not having you around all those years and only kept his distance because he didn't know how to fix things, but mostly because he didn't want you to get stuck with all this. It's why it took us so long to do what we did."

Meaghan nodded, her eyes filling with tears. Natalie and Kady had cast spells on the people around Meaghan to help nudge her into coming to Eldrich. She would have been fired from her job in Arizona eventually, because she hadn't been able to hide how disgusted she'd become with her boss's flexible ethics, but the magic hastened it.

"I . . . it surprised me how mad I got at him when you

guys told me," Meaghan said, pushing her tears back down. "I really thought I'd gotten past it." She finished her wine in a large gulp. "If you ever do get past it."

"You get past it," Natalie said, "when you decide to. You got ambushed tonight. You'll get there. And nothing's really changed between us. You're still my boss and I'm still here to help you navigate both jobs. But please don't tell anybody. The risk if I am carrying the impervious gene—you'd think that and my magical skill would be mutually exclusive—but if they aren't . . ."

Meaghan nodded. "A lot of bad guys might get interested. Either to get rid of you or exploit you."

"Don't think that hasn't kept me up nights."

"So people really don't know?" Meaghan asked.

"As far as Russ and I can tell. Although you're the first who ever thought we were . . . ewww. You know. How did you ever reach that conclusion?"

Meaghan shrugged. "I could tell you were hiding something. The big magic secrets had already been spilled, so I figured it had to be about sex."

"Well," Natalie said with a smile. "You were half right, I guess." She held up the empty bottle. "You want me to open another?"

Before Meaghan could answer, the world exploded.

CHAPTER TWELVE

A THUNDEROUS BOOM AND the sound of breaking glass echoed from the direction of Jamie's house.

Natalie ran to the gate accessing the tiny overgrown alley between the houses. Jamie's house sat around the corner, his back gate only about twenty feet away.

Meaghan grabbed Natalie and pointed to her bare feet. "Glass. Get some shoes and I'll meet you there." Natalie nodded and ran into the house.

Meaghan dashed down the alley to Jamie's back gate. A high board fence surrounded the backyard. She threw herself at the wooden gate and heard a padlock rattle in its hasp.

The six-foot fence was too high to climb, so Meaghan ran back to Natalie's house. There she found Natalie comforting Patrice. Natalie caught Meaghan's eye, her face grim, eyes wide with shock.

"Look at this," Natalie said, her voice tight. She gently tilted up Patrice's chin. A fresh bruise covered Patrice's left eye and cheek. Blood trickled from her split lip. Angry red marks, finger shaped, covered her bare arms.

Feeling a sick knot in her gut, Meaghan, already knowing the answer, asked, "Who did this, Patrice? Where's Jamie?"

Patrice's eyes welled up. "He . . . he's . . ." The remaining shreds of her self-control evaporated. Her face screwed up like a child's and she dissolved into racking sobs. "He hit me."

"Where are the kids?" Meaghan asked Natalie.

"Lynette's. To give them time to be alone," Natalie said, her face pale and rigid. "You . . . I can't see him right now. I'll do something I can't take back." Patrice sobbed in her arms. "That bastard," Natalie continued. "I'm done protecting him."

"I'll go," Meaghan said. "Stay with Patrice."

"Be careful," Natalie said. "He blew out the windows when she left."

The neighbors were already out, trying to see what had happened. She walked past them without a glance, through the gate in the white picket fence and into the yard.

Glass lay everywhere in jagged shards. Someone standing in the yard—or, Meaghan thought with a chill, running from the house—could have been killed.

She stepped through the open front door, grateful she'd changed from flip flops to heavier sandals before driving to Natalie's.

"Jamie?" Her voice shook, fear and anger fighting for control. Meaghan wasn't sure she could save him this time. The young man she had known before he'd been taken never would have harmed his wife and never would forgive himself for hurting her now.

Meaghan found him standing in the kitchen. The sigils etched into his back glowed a deep angry red. Below them, like the trunk of a tree, ran long scars along his spine where his Fahrayan wings had been cut away. He gripped a shard of glass in his right hand, blood dripping from his fingers.

"You should have let them kill me," he said, his voice flat.

"Jamie, put the glass down." Meaghan crept closer. "Please. Put it down and tell me what happened."

"I hit my wife," he said in the same flat voice. His fingers dropped the bloody shard and curled into a ball. "I made a fist and slugged her. Like this." He hit himself hard on the side of his head. "And like this." He punched himself in the mouth.

He fell to his knees in the broken glass. "Like this," he shouted, now enraged, and pummeled his head with both fists. His fury spent, he hugged himself and rocked back and forth, sobbing. "Why didn't you let them kill me? Why?"

She placed her hand gently on his shoulder. "Jamie, I . . ."

He scrambled away, leaving bloody handprints on the floor. "Don't touch me. I'm wrong. I'm bad." His tears came in painful gasps that echoed Patrice's sobs. Still on his knees, he curled into a ball, his arms over his head.

Meaghan pulled her phone from her pocket. Jamie needed help she couldn't give him. He needed to be in a hospital, in a psych ward. But she had to get him calm before help arrived. No suicide-by-cop scenarios could be allowed to unfold.

"9-1-1 dispatch," a young female voice answered. "What is your emergency?"

"This is Meaghan Keele—"

"Meaghan? This is Dana—I mean Cassandra—I was at your house today?"

Meaghan felt a stirring of hope. A witch was working dispatch. "Dana, I need to keep this to the clued-in as much as possible."

"Got it. Are you at Jamie's?"

"Yeah," Meaghan said, surprised. "How did you know?"

"The calls are rolling in. I've got a couple of clued-in cops—"

"City cops? Not county?"

"Yeah. And paramedics. It's handled."

"Dana—or is it Cassandra?"

"Dana," she said firmly. "Cassandra was Circe's idea."

"Whatever your name, you're a lifesaver," Meaghan said, feeling a wave of relief.

"If there's anything else you need, call me," Dana said. "I know how bad this stuff is. My dad, a long time ago . . . let me know if I can help, okay?"

The increasingly familiar maternal instinct stirring within her, Meaghan said, "You got it, kiddo. I owe you on this one. Thanks. How soon until they get here?"

"Cops are about two minutes. The EMTs are going over to Natalie's first to take a quick look at Patrice, so expect them in about five. Is that okay?"

"Yeah," Meaghan said, looking at Jamie huddled on the floor. "He's cut up, but it looks superficial."

"I'll try to keep the spectators away. Susan's working on it with me. Official story's a gas leak."

"Thanks again for this."

"You're welcome. Keep us posted, okay?"

Meaghan hung up. Jamie still hunched on the floor, his

sobs replaced with quiet weeping. She crouched near him and stroked his back. She avoided the angry red sigil, feeling a deep aversion in her gut at the thought of it pulsing under her fingers.

He didn't pull away this time, which she took as a good sign. "Jamie," she said. "Let me help you."

He sat up and finally met her gaze. She tried not to gasp. Circles like bruises stood under each eye. His once bright blue eyes were dull and bloodshot. Hopelessness etched his face, his skin so pale it was nearly gray.

"You can't help me," he said, his voice thick with tears. "No one can help me. They marked me. I tried to cut it out, but it won't go."

He patted his chest. Horrified, Meaghan realized he'd been using the glass shard to try to carve away the sigil located above his heart. The tattered flesh oozed blood, but the sigil remained, like an island rising above a thick red sea.

"Jamie," she whispered, tears in her eyes. "Oh, Jamie."

"I can hear them," he said, "whispering in my head, telling me to do bad things. I try to fight, but it blows out of me and hurts someone else. They won't even let me kill myself. I tried and I can't. They stop me."

"Who are they, honey? Do you know?" she asked. "Is it that thing from Fahraya? That thing in your uncle?"

He shook his head. "Worse," he whispered. "So much worse. They come in my dreams. I try not to sleep, but then I do and they come and they . . ."

He turned away from Meaghan. She felt his body shudder and knew he was weeping again.

"They tell me to hurt her and . . . Oh, God, I did. I hit her and now they want me to kill her and the kids." He turned and clutched at Meaghan. "Put me down. Blow my head off. Before I hurt them again. Please."

"No," Meaghan said. "We can figure this out. We'll keep them safe. Patrice is with Natalie, and the kids are with Lynette."

He calmed slightly. "Natalie?"

Meaghan nodded. "And Lynette. And you're no match for either one. Your family is safe. I promise you I will keep them safe."

He stared in her eyes for a long moment, then nodded.

"The police are coming," she said. "Don't resist in any way. We'll figure this out."

He nodded again. Meaghan kissed him on the forehead. He clung to her a moment, like a small child, his body shaking.

"Stay here," she said. "I'll handle this."

Meaghan walked into the living room, raised her hands, and waited. Two police officers entered, guns drawn. In a loud commanding voice, the first cop, middle-aged and stocky, said, "Who else is in the house?"

Meaghan knew she needed to stay relaxed and not add any energy to the situation. "Jamie's in the kitchen. He's not violent or resisting. He needs medical attention and a psych evaluation, but he's calm."

"Who are you?" The cop still had his gun raised.

"Meaghan Keele, family friend. I was nearby when it happened."

The officer lowered his gun. He motioned to his companion. "She's Matthew's daughter."

She stepped closer and in a low voice said, "Something

bad—magically bad—is happening and he's scared. The sooner he's sedated and out of here, the better."

Both cops nodded and holstered their guns. The first cop pulled a hex bag from inside his shirt, gave it a squeeze, and muttered something.

Meaghan led them into the kitchen. The officers saw the sigils carved into Jamie's back and winced. Approaching slowly, they spoke in low soothing voices.

The second cop, nearer Jamie's age, approached Meaghan, eyes wide with shock. He had a receding hairline and a round, plain face. "I went to high school with him. What the hell happened? Is this from the Fahraya thing?"

Meaghan nodded. "Partly. Plus—"

"Some kind of spell, right?"

Meaghan shook her head slightly, taken aback.

Noting her reaction, the cop said, "I'm Brian Cressley. Kady's my baby sister."

Meaghan smiled for a moment. "Kady's a good kid. Yeah, a spell, but nobody can decipher the symbols."

Brian looked at the shattered windows. "Poltergeist, right?"

Meaghan nodded. "Did Kady tell you what's going on?"

"No, but I've seen it before on domestic calls. Where's his family?"

"His wife's around the corner at a friend's house and the kids are staying somewhere else." Meaghan noticed Brian's eyes flicker.

"The friend around the corner," he said. "Is that Natalie Segretti?"

"Yeah. You know her?"

Brian looked away, blushing. "Big crush on her in high

school." He took a deep breath and got back to business, pulling a small notebook from his shirt pocket. "Wife is Patrice, right? A nurse at the clinic?"

Meaghan nodded.

"Her condition?"

Meaghan hesitated.

"We won't recommend charges unless she wants us to," Brian said. "Those things on him are heavy black magic. I can't even begin to explain that to the district attorney. We'll look out for Jamie. Don't worry."

Meaghan sighed. Normally, cops covering for batterers infuriated her, but this was different. It always was when magic was involved. "She has a black eye and a cut lip, but no serious injuries. Natalie will take care of her. The kids are with another witch, Lynette Coffey. You know her?"

"Yeah, I do," Brian said with a smile. "She and my mom were best friends. We can leave social services out of it."

They heard someone enter the house and a paramedic walked into the kitchen. "Wife's okay. We checked her out first." He looked around the room. "What happened?"

"DV with poltergeist," Brian said. "Bad shit."

"Magic?" the paramedic asked.

"Yeah."

The paramedic shook his head in disgust. "Always with the magic." He spoke into his radio. "Hector, grab the hex bags off the truck." He clipped the radio onto his belt. "Which one's the dabbler?"

"Neither," Brian said. "It's Jamie Smith. That shit back in June."

The paramedic grimaced. "I heard about that."

While the paramedics worked, Brian Cressley tried to

control the growing crowd. A friend from the fire depart-ment inspected the house and declared, in a loud voice, that it looked like a gas leak. The spectators quickly backed away.

Russ showed up right after the fire inspector. "Go help Natalie," he said in Meaghan's ear. "I'll go with Jamie and make sure we get the right doctors."

Meaghan nodded, gripped him in tight hug, then walked back to Natalie's house.

CHAPTER THIRTEEN

B Y THE NEXT morning, everyone agreed that until they could figure out what was happening to Jamie—given his claims that something was ordering him to kill his family—Patrice and the children needed to be somewhere else.

Patrice, it turned out, wasn't as rootless as Meaghan had thought. Raised in the foster care system down in Harrisburg, Patrice had stayed in touch with her last set of foster parents. By the time she'd gotten to them, in high school, she was far too cautious to let them take the place of parents in her heart, and wisely they hadn't forced it. But Patrice looked to them as friends and mentors, and she and the kids were headed down to Tyrone to stay with them until things settled down.

Her eye swollen shut, standing in front of her shattered house beside her packed-up minivan, Patrice looked even smaller than she was and—for the first time since Meaghan had met her—vulnerable.

"Don't argue with me," Meaghan said as she handed

Patrice a check. "Neither of you can work right now. You don't need to be worrying about money on top of everything else."

"Meaghan, I can't," she said, shaking her head.

"Yeah, you can. Matthew took good care of me and Russ. Plus, I get paid well and where the hell am I going to spend it in Eldrich? Take it. Let me help." Meaghan pushed down the tears that threatened to spill. "Let me do something. This shit is magical and I let it happen and—"

Patrice cut her off with a furious glare and a hug. "You did not. They did this to him. Find out why. If you love him, find out why." She let go of Meaghan and climbed into the minivan.

"You're going to the bank with that check, right? If you don't deposit it, I'll get Natalie to magic it in there somehow."

Patrice gave Meaghan a wan smile. "First stop is the bank, then out to Lynette's to pick up the kids."

Meaghan waved as Patrice drove away. She wiped away a stray tear and then turned her attention back to the house where a couple of workers were boarding up and measuring the windows. Meaghan hadn't told Patrice, but she planned to buy them new insulated windows, with safety glass, rather than merely repair the old ones.

Kady was minding the office while Meaghan and Natalie helped Patrice pack. Now Natalie walked up with a mug of coffee, which she handed to Meaghan. "I put a tracer spell on her and Lynette's got the kids. To make sure they're okay."

"You know any witches down there?"

Natalie nodded. "A few. But Tyrone is close enough I can keep track of her myself."

"You hear anything about Jamie?" Meaghan sipped her

coffee. She needed the caffeine. Between learning that Natalie was her sister and worrying about Jamie, Meaghan had slept very little the night before, even less than normal. But on the up side, no sleep meant no nightmares.

"He's still in the hospital down in Williamsport," Natalie said. "The doc's clued in. He dummied up a quarantine order to keep Jamie away from prying eyes and to keep him from having a psych eval on his records. It would raise too many questions."

"How long will they keep him?"

"A few days at most or the state health department or CDC will start paying attention."

"And that would be bad?" Meaghan asked.

"What do you think?"

Meaghan nodded. She couldn't see the feds being able to wrap their brains around black magic as suitable grounds for a quarantine. "So where's he staying when he gets out of the hospital?"

Natalie sighed. "Well, with me, of course. I'm furious with him for what he did to Patrice, but I still love him. And I'm powerful enough to protect us both."

"You didn't see him last night. He beat himself up far worse than he did Patrice. It's not him doing this."

"I know it's not him. It's those bastards screwing with him." Natalie shook her head. "I've never seen Patrice scared like this before. She and Jamie were solid. They hardly ever disagreed about anything. If they can make him hurt Patrice, none of us are safe."

"Will you be safe?"

Natalie's face grew grim. "If Jamie tries anything on me,

I'll kick his ass so hard he won't have an ass left to kick. Double for those Order freaks."

"Well," Meaghan said, "at least now we don't have to worry about finding him new office space. Thank God for FMLA."

The estimator from the window company walked up. He was from Williamsport and not clued in, but Buzz Hallam trusted his boss. "Got my measurements. I'll run up some estimates for you at a few different price points. What happened, by the way, if you don't mind me asking?"

"Gas leak, they think," Meaghan said.

"Nah, there'd be signs of fire damage if there was a gas explosion. Has Homeland been out? This looks like some kind of bomb to me."

Meaghan glanced at Natalie, who nodded slightly and muttered something under her breath.

The estimator's eyes closed. He shook his head slightly, opened his eyes, and looked at Meaghan. "Yeah," he said. "You got to watch out for gas leaks in these old houses. One spark and boom, no windows." He handed Meaghan his card. "I'll get you that estimate by this afternoon."

"You have my business card?" Meaghan asked.

He patted his breast pocket. "Right here. Is email okay?"

"Perfect," Meaghan said with a broad smile.

He smiled back, then walked to his truck. He waved as he drove past.

"That's a nifty little spell," Meaghan said.

"The last thing we need is a bunch of out-of-town law enforcement sniffing around," Natalie said. "Not everybody's as amenable to getting their thoughts nudged."

"But it's not like they'd believe it was magic that did it," Meaghan said.

"That's the problem. Denial won't let them accept the real reason, so they'll have to come up with something else instead. And before we know it, Jamie's a suspect in something, and he's not exactly here legally."

Meaghan nodded. "And if they can't accept poltergeists, they really won't be able to handle Fahraya."

"Exactly."

"Do you think they know?" Meaghan asked. "The government? At any level?"

Natalie shrugged. "The truth is out there? Will Smith in black-tie? Maybe. What do you think?"

"I think the feds leave really big footprints, and the conspiracy buffs give them way too much credit."

Natalie nodded. "You've heard the rumors about the missing Fahrayans and the European gateways?"

Only about half the population of Fahraya survived the destruction of their world. Most of them arrived through the Eldrich gateway, with a handful showing up in England. The remaining gateways in Germany, France, and Romania had signs of the same wind damage as the Eldrich gateway, but no Fahrayans.

It had long been rumored in the magical worlds that several Fahrayans, presumed dead after flying through a gateway right into a World War II battlefield, had instead been captured by the Germans and taken to a secret lab in Berlin. The rumor mill now assumed that a similar fate had befallen the five hundred missing Fahrayans.

Meaghan rolled her eyes. "The one where NATO grabbed them?"

"I heard the Russian mob."

Meaghan almost spit out her coffee. "Russian gangsters? Seriously?"

"There's also the version where they were grabbed by a big biotech firm. Or pharmaceutical maker. I've heard both."

"Unbelievable." Meaghan's coffee was now cool enough for her to drink rather than sip. "We only had a few minutes to escape while the place was tearing itself apart. The real mystery is how anybody managed to survive at all. The missing Fahrayans are dead." She drained the coffee mug with one last gulp. "I think. That's the most likely explanation."

"So the feds aren't clued in?"

Meaghan shrugged. "They might be, but not in a large-scale way. The only way to keep a big secret in government is by not telling anybody. You have to keep it in-house and limited to a very few people."

"Which means there's probably not much they could do to help us with the Fahrayans even if they did know," Natalie said.

"Probably not," Meaghan said. "But, one crisis at a time, right? We've got whole *days* before the weather turns on us."

"Maybe we'll have a long autumn. It's only the end of August."

Meaghan handed Natalie the empty coffee mug. "We're not that lucky."

"Did Kady talk to you about her big news?" Natalie asked.

Meaghan smiled. "She did. She wants to name him after my . . ." She looked around. Nobody was close enough to hear, but she lowered her voice anyway. "*Our* father. Does Kady know about that?"

Natalie shook her head. "No. She doesn't even suspect it. Russ only figured it out because he spent so much time with all three of us, and you know how he is—Mister I-know-you-better-than-you-know-yourself."

"He does that to you, too?"

Natalie smiled. "Oh, yes. All the damn time."

Meaghan laughed, for the first time in about fourteen hours she realized. Which brought the horror of the previous night back into the front of her mind. Her laughter evaporated.

"Oh," Natalie said. "I forgot to tell you. Kady called while I was getting you the coffee. There's a leprechaun waiting for you at the office."

"Wonderful," Meaghan said, all remaining shreds of good humor gone. "As if we don't have enough shit to deal with already."

CHAPTER FOURTEEN

T HE LITTLE MAN, whom Meaghan assumed to be the leprechaun, stood on the third floor landing, outside of the solicitor's office, talking loudly to himself. "I don't care about that. No more bullshit. Get it done."

He spoke with an American accent. Not a trace of a brogue. He tapped his ear with an index finger and whirled around.

Meaghan saw a Bluetooth earpiece under his carefully tousled dark hair. About four feet tall, he wore a dark business suit, impeccably tailored, and carried a leather folio in his left hand. He walked toward her, right hand extended. This was definitely the guy Kady had described, but . . . the size was right for a leprechaun, but nothing else about him was.

"Ms. Keele?" He flashed a perfect smile, a rakish twinkle in his sea-green eyes.

If he were six feet tall, he'd be a menace to all womankind, Meaghan thought. Even at four feet tall, he had the potential to be devastating. She suspected that he had no difficulty attracting women. Or men, she corrected herself, thinking of Jhoro. Or both.

Meaghan didn't take his hand. Shake a leprechaun's hand, Russ had told her, and you had to count your fingers to make sure you got them all back. You might be sealing a deal you never intended to make. "Whatever you're selling, I'm not interested."

"Ah," he said, dropping his hand. "I see you've met some of my less advanced brothers. May I ask?"

"Jimmy Sweeney," Meaghan said. "And his band of little thugs."

A pained look crossed the leprechaun's handsome face. "I heard something about that. Please accept my apologies." He smiled. "If it helps, you made quite an impression on them."

"Yes, I expect I did."

"As did the king."

Now it was Meaghan's turn to smile. "That was something, wasn't it? I think my favorite part was when he had Jimmy by the throat and the red-headed one—what's his name?"

"Fergus."

"Yes, Fergus. When he had Jimmy by the throat and Fergus by the ankle and hoisted them both into the air. John's English skills are not the best, but he has developed a remarkable facility with profanity."

The leprechaun laughed. "They were also quite shocked to discover that the Fahrayans were human-sized instead of pixie-sized."

"They had recovered from that particular shock by the time I arrived," Meaghan said. "It was business as usual. Hence John's displeasure. But what I found most interesting was that, even with John's outburst, they seemed more frightened of *me*."

The leprechaun grimaced. "Yes, well, you do have a reputation. Destroying a world will do that."

"Hmm," Meaghan said. "From my perspective I was saving all the other worlds."

"From my perspective," he answered, "you did the Fahrayans a favor. That world of theirs was a dump. Time for them to come home."

"I'm not sure they see it that way."

"Some of them never will. But they're finally human again. Which is one of the things I'm here to see you about." He stepped closer and lowered his voice. "Is there somewhere we can talk? Privately?"

"My office is nearby."

He frowned. "Is Natalie Segretti around today? I hear she's even more talented than her mother, and Vivian cast a mean barrier spell."

"You knew Vivian?" Meaghan asked, intrigued.

A sad look crossed his face. "Yes. And your father. I have some information you might find useful. But I really don't want to say anymore out here."

Meaghan stared at him for a long moment. She still didn't trust him, but the least she could do was hear him out. He knew about the Fahrayans' human origins and he'd known her father. Maybe he could give her some details about the war or at least help her figure out what had been redacted from Matthew's journals.

"Natalie's taking the day off, but if we need her I can call her," she said. "And she's not the only witch in the building if we need additional security, Mr.—I'm sorry. I never gave you an opportunity to introduce yourself."

"Owen Finnerty." This time he didn't offer his hand.

"Mr. Finnerty, why don't you come in and have a seat. I suspect Natalie has a barrier up already, but if we need more privacy, I'll ask her to come in." Natalie maintained a sturdy magical firewall around the entire solicitor's office to keep Emily Procter at bay, but Meaghan didn't mention that. She pushed open the door and held it for him.

With a nod, he walked past her into the reception area, where Kady sat.

"Mr. Finnerty and I are going back to my office," Meaghan said.

Kady glared at the leprechaun. "If you need my help with anything, I'll be right here."

Located in one of city hall's four turrets, Meaghan's office was small and round. Almost perfectly round. Unlike Jamie's office next door—spook central—Meaghan's office felt warm and inviting.

Owen Finnerty could feel it too. Nodding, he surveyed the room. "Nice space. Well protected." He pulled himself up onto one of the chairs in front of her desk.

Meaghan noticed that his feet didn't touch the floor. *Good*, she thought. She felt a momentary stab of shame, then reminded herself that he wasn't a little person. He wasn't a human man who had been born a bit different. Owen Finnerty was a leprechaun, and leprechauns were not the whimsical wee folk of legend guarding their pots of gold. They were hard-boiled thugs and petty criminals who used magic to torment humans. Owen Finnerty may have had a more polished exterior than Jimmy Sweeney, but that likely only meant he was a better class of criminal. *Let his feet dangle.*

"Do you still want Natalie to put up an additional barrier?" Meaghan asked.

"No. She's done a good job shielding this space, which I suppose isn't surprising considering the mystic geyser that's spewing next door." He pinned her with his gaze, looking at her with an intensity that he had lacked in the hallway.

He knows about city hall. I wonder what else he knows. Meaghan stared back, letting her brows knit into the hawk-like glare she'd inherited from her father. She knew this game. She'd stared down enough $1,000-an-hour hotshot attorneys over the years. She had a law school friend who called it the sheepdog stare. Now it was merely a matter of learning which one of them was the sheep.

Eventually Owen Finnerty wilted and looked away. He plucked an invisible hair from his silk tie and cleared his throat. "I am not your typical leprechaun, Ms. Keele."

"You certainly don't look like the ones I've encountered," Meaghan said. "From what I've learned about leprechauns, Jimmy Sweeney does seem a bit more representative of your race. But just because you look different doesn't mean you are. Why are you here, Mr. Finnerty?"

He grinned at her. "You don't like to sugarcoat things, do you?"

"I'm too old. Sugarcoating ups my diabetes risk. Mr. Finnerty, why are you here?"

"Owen. Please call me Owen. Do we need to be so formal?"

"We do, until I know why you're here."

"Well, then, Ms. Keele," he said, with an even wider grin, "I'm here to offer assistance."

Meaghan snorted. "And what will it cost me? An arm? A leg? I may be new to this job, but I'm not a complete idiot. I'm a lawyer, remember? I don't trust anybody, let alone magical loan sharks."

Owen Finnerty grimaced. "Fair enough. My people have an unsavory reputation for valid reasons. But you don't know the whole story, Ms. Keele. That's the other reason I'm here. I want to offer assistance with the Fahrayans in exchange for your services as a negotiator."

Meaghan raised an eyebrow. "Me? Negotiating? Haven't you heard? I destroyed Fahraya. Nobody trusts me either."

Owen Finnerty shook his head. "Not true. You didn't destroy Fahraya. That *thing* did. And it's still out there." He shuddered. "There are plenty of us who trust you even more than we trusted your father. And that's got a lot of the old guard very upset."

"The old guard?" Meaghan asked. Was she finally going to get some details on the mysterious war?

"The races who like their humans fearful and easily hexed. Those who want a return to the old ways."

"My brother mentioned something about that. Pre-Iron Age was what he told me. But after all this time—what, three millennia?—they surely don't think they can push us back to the Bronze Age."

"A millennium isn't as big a deal if you're immortal." He sat back in his chair. "How old do I look to you?"

Meaghan sighed. "About thirty-five, but I'm betting the number's a bit higher."

"Try a hundred times higher."

"You're thirty-five hundred years old?"

Owen Finnerty shrugged. "Give or take a few hundred. It's

hard to keep track after a while. It becomes a big blur. Been there, done that, done it again. And again. And again. Can you imagine how tedious that is?" He shook his head. "Of course you can't. Human lives zip by so fast you don't have time to get bored. Not like immortals can get bored. And when magical immortals get bored, they tend to cause trouble."

"And if humans lose their susceptibility to magic, these magical immortals lose their favorite toys."

"Exactly."

"So, is this the war I keep hearing hints about?"

Owen Finnerty glanced around the room and took a deep breath.

He's scared, Meaghan thought. *Like Natalie was the first time I asked her about it.*

"How do you even know about it?" he asked. "Matthew had to lock up those files to keep . . . there's . . . how do you know?"

"My mother told me in a dream the day after I arrived in Eldrich."

Owen Finnerty nodded. "Was this before or after your father died?"

"Before."

"Well, that's something in our favor, I guess. Makes it harder to argue that he coached her to slip you the info. That would violate the truce. But I'm not sure they'll see it that way."

"Who?" Meaghan asked. "What truce? Will you just tell me what's going on? *Who* won't see it that way?"

Owen Finnerty stared at her a moment, his face grim. "The gods. The gods won't see it that way."

CHAPTER FIFTEEN

M EAGHAN STARED AT him. "The . . . *who?* Did you say gods? Actual *gods?*"

"Well, that's what they call themselves, but they are prone to exaggeration." Owen Finnerty rubbed his small hand over his handsome face. "It doesn't make them any less dangerous, though. The fair folk are basically energy suckers who can also shift. And they have hefty inborn magical skills to boot. They're basically what humans think of as elves." He sighed. "I assume you know what I'm talking about?"

Meaghan still couldn't keep the names straight, but magical species tended to fall into four broad categories. The first two—informally called shifters and suckers—were inherently magical, but not necessarily practitioners. Shifters could change shape at will, while suckers drained life energy, either psychic or physical. Some of them could contaminate victims and make more of their kind, but those created in this manner held much lower status, being little more than slaves.

The third group were the species created or sustained by magic, like the Fahrayans had been, who didn't have any special magical abilities. The fourth group, at the bottom of the status pile, didn't require magic to exist, but had the inborn skills to use it. And among those bottom dwellers, humans who used magic were considered the lowest of the low.

Humans with no magical skills were considered livestock.

By far, the most dangerous of magical species were sucker-shifter hybrids who could also manipulate magic. Like these fair folk.

Meaghan sighed. "Yeah, I know what you're talking about. So they aren't deities?"

Owen Finnerty snorted. "No. They just think they are. Anytime in the folklore you find an otherwise sensible god acting like a jerk, they were likely involved. You can find examples all over the world."

"So, how does that work?" Meaghan asked. "They're the source of human myth? Gods are really energy-sucking shape-shifters?"

Owen shook his head. "No, no. Not at all. The fair folk don't create the beliefs or even initially personify them. They merely exploit existing belief systems and co-opt their gods. They don't have enough imagination to come up with it themselves."

"Believers create their gods?"

"Yeah, to a certain extent. People striving for the divine, trying to put names and faces on something vast, something they can feel, but can't articulate." Owen gave her a wistful smile. "Humans do love their stories."

"And then the fair folk come in—"

"And run it into the ground," Owen finished for her.

"They suck all the wonder out of it and make it a hollow shell of what it was originally."

"And this happens in every religion?"

He seesawed his small hand in the air. "To some degree. Genuine yearning for the divine is a delicacy for them, because they get so little of it. Either they consume it quickly or it flees from them. Their primary food sources are dogma and judgment and fanaticism. And it's not always religion. They've found some success diversifying into the entertainment industry. Take promising but troubled young kids and turn them into flaming train wrecks. Some survive it and get their lives back. Most don't."

Meaghan grimaced. "And the stupid humans eat it up with a spoon."

"And the fair folk eat that up with another spoon," Owen said. "Nothing generates fascinated condemnation like a once-loved entertainment idol running amok."

Meaghan fumbled in her desk for some ibuprofen to quell her soon-to-be-pounding headache. As if things weren't weird enough, now she was pissing off wannabe gods.

"You mentioned a truce," she said. "Let me guess. Humanity started fighting back and the fair folk had to call a truce, but didn't want to go public about it."

The leprechaun nodded. "Yeah. Being egotistical jerks, they agreed to a truce only if all references to the war in human folklore and history were magically expunged. They didn't want word getting out that the monkeys stood up to them."

"Did Matthew negotiate the truce?"

"Yeah, but not as a neutral mediator. He tried to stay above the fray, but the fair folk never trusted him. They couldn't bewitch him and he could see their true faces. As vain as they are, they hated him for it."

"Their true faces?" Meaghan leaned back in her chair. She was starting to warm up to Owen Finnerty. She couldn't imagine ever trusting him, but he was actually answering her questions without all the cryptic hemming and hawing.

"They aren't much bigger than me and skinny with pointed teeth and ears. And bad skin. They always use a false face. It's one reason why there's so many different manifestations of elves in the folklore. They can use magic to make themselves appear any way they wish. Big, little, beautiful, terrifying, whatever."

"So what about leprechauns? Are all small magical races really these fair folk?"

Owen's look darkened. "No. The rest of us are slaves. Or were until we started fighting back. In the case of leprechauns, we were their bagmen. Enforcers. We were small and beaten down, and like many abused groups, when we got a little bit of power, we used it to beat down a group even more pitiful than we were. Humans." He sighed and stared out the window behind her. "We were little shits. Some of us still are."

"I'm aware," Meaghan said. "But humans do exactly the same thing."

"Yeah, I suppose they do. God help the poor bastards at the bottom."

"They brutalize each other. So, do these fair folk have an actual name?"

Owen nodded. "Yeah, but it requires special vocal cords and it's like thirty syllables long. Magical types may lack imagination, but they're big on pretension. It translates as something like 'the glorious wonders who are better than you.'" He rolled his eyes. "You know. Flaming assholes."

In spite of herself, Meaghan laughed. "I know the type. So why do these particular flaming assholes want to shove us back to the Bronze Age?"

"The fair folk survive on dogma and blind devotion, right? With a side helping of awe and fearful wonder. They use magic to keep the food flowing. Before the Iron Age, humans had very few defenses against magic. But like you, iron is impervious to magic. Once humans started working iron and began to understand its protective properties, the fair folk had to work harder." Owen flashed a grim smile. "And humans started changing. They got less susceptible."

"I thought being impervious was really rare."

"Well, fully impervious like you, yeah. But, there are degrees."

Meaghan nodded. "Some people will believe anything. Others are harder to persuade."

"And there's more of the second type every day. The Enlightenment dealt them a killing blow, but they don't know it yet because the pickings are still so good in certain parts of the world. Immortals have a hard time adapting to new conditions. They don't like change."

"Yeah, I bet they don't." Meaghan leaned back in her chair and gazed out one of the narrow windows that circled her office. City hall was the tallest building in Eldrich and she could see the north end of town and the forest that rose up behind it. Isolated patches of yellow and orange already dotted the thick green canopy. *Winter won't wait until we get our shit together. He knows we need help with the Fahrayans, but what's it gonna cost?*

She turned her gaze back to Owen Finnerty. "The war references that got expunged from my father's journals—were they destroyed?"

Owen smiled. "They were supposed to be."

"Which means they're stored somewhere. I don't suppose you know where?"

"I do. That's where the negotiation comes in. The keepers don't trust me. But if *you* make the case . . ."

"And do these keepers mistrust leprechauns in general or have you given them specific cause?"

Owen fidgeted in his chair and looked away. "Both, I suppose. The keepers have long memories. I stole something from them a long time ago, but I gave it back. No harm done. I don't see what their problem is."

"You're a leprechaun."

Owen scowled. "That's racial profiling. Which is a violation of my civil rights."

Meaghan snorted. "Leprechauns are not a protected class under the law." She had another Eldrich moment. *I'm arguing civil rights law with a thirty-five-hundred-year-old leprechaun.* The moment passed. "Get over it."

"You know there was a time when no human would dare mouth off to a leprechaun like that. I do have some powerful magical abilities of my own."

"To which I'm impervious. So, what do you get out of this? What's in the journals that you need?"

"The same thing you need. Information. You want to know about the war and whether it has anything to do with what's happening to Jamie Smith. So do I."

"Why?"

"Either the fair folk are up to something or there's a new

player in town. Either way, I need to know more. That shit that went down in June in Fahraya made no sense to me." He stared at her, considering his next words. "And I don't think it made sense to you. Am I right?"

Meaghan shrugged. "I have questions, yeah. So, assuming I can get Matthew's missing notes, what are you willing to give in exchange?"

"Resources to help the king care for his people."

"Which you couldn't offer directly or the king would snap you in half. He really doesn't like you guys. He said he has history."

Owen sighed. "Eamon O'Malley—slimy little sod, even by leprechaun standards—tried to horn in on John's honey business about ten years ago. Eamon and his moron crew were crawling all over John's place threatening to smash his hives if he didn't agree to pay them half his net revenues as protection money. Instead they got chased off by the swarm. I don't know how John does it, but those bees really like him."

Meaghan smiled. "Yeah, they do."

"You really like him, too," Owen said with a sly smile.

Meaghan's smile evaporated. "Not a topic you and I are going to discuss. What specific resources are you offering?"

Owen opened the leather folio he'd brought with him and pulled out a spiral-bound report, which he placed on her desk. "My proposal. Resources, deliverables, and timetables."

Meaghan picked up the report, impressed in spite of herself. It might be bullshit, but it looked good. "I have to confess. I wasn't expecting something this thorough."

"I'm a businessman, Ms. Keele. I haven't been a criminal in quite a while. I make more money legitimately than all my thuggish brethren combined."

"So, why aren't they in business with you?"

Owen flashed his perfect smile. "Fear, Ms. Keele. They don't like change any better than their former masters do. Look through my proposal and I'll give you a call tomorrow." He held out his small hand across the desk.

This time Meaghan shook it. "I'm not promising anything here. We have not reached an agreement and no deal has been made."

He raised an eyebrow, then smiled. "Nice disclaimer. You've done your homework. No, I know better than to try to lure an impervious attorney into a leprechaun's deal. Until we put something in writing, you don't owe me anything. I can find my way out. Thanks for your time."

Once he was gone, Meaghan breathed a sigh of relief. Despite her flippant comments to Owen Finnerty, leprechauns scared her. They were sometimes helpful, sometimes malicious—but always unpredictable and often dangerous. Owen Finnerty couldn't hurt her with magic, but he could hurt everyone around her. The trick of dealing with leprechauns was figuring out which version you were getting and why.

It's probably some kind of con, she thought as she opened the report. *Don't get your hopes up.*

CHAPTER SIXTEEN

MOMENTS AFTER OWEN Finnerty's exit, Kady knocked softly on Meaghan's office door. "Hey, boss, got a minute?"

Meaghan looked up from the leprechaun's report. "What's up?"

Kady walked in and sat down. "That leprechaun guy, he just left—did everything go okay?"

"As far as I can tell. He's offering help with the Fahrayans." She gestured at the report. "It might be bullshit. I need to do more research."

"Speaking of Fahrayans, do you know where Marnie and Jhoro are?"

"What do you mean? Are they missing?"

"Yeah, they seem to be." Kady looked grim. "Did they stay at your house last night?"

"You know about them?"

Kady rolled her eyes. "Who doesn't? Marnie's flaunting it all over town." Her eyes narrowed to slits. "What a *slut*."

Meaghan frowned. Kady wasn't a gossip and, as far as Meaghan knew, she got along well with Marnie.

Kady seemed surprised as well. She shook her head, as if to clear it. "Sorry. I don't know where that came from. Must be baby hormones or something. Marnie blew off her nursing home clients this morning. She didn't even call. She loves setting those old ladies' hair. I can't imagine her bailing on them without a word unless something was really wrong. When did you see them last?"

Meaghan thought about it for a moment. "Dinner. The last time I saw them was dinner. They left right after in her car. Jhoro's like a dog. He likes to hang his head out the window while you drive."

"Did they come back last night?"

Meaghan thought some more. "You know, I have no idea. With all the shit going on with Jamie, I didn't even notice. Have you talked to Russ?"

Kady nodded. "He was at the hospital all night. They weren't there when he left to go to Jamie's or when he got back this morning."

"What about her place?"

"Not there either. Lynette swung by and checked for me a little while ago. And she's not answering her cell. Could they have left before you woke up?"

Meaghan thought about it. Had Jhoro's door been shut when she got home last night? She had been in such a daze she hadn't even noticed. "I got about ten minutes sleep last night worrying about Jamie. I never really did more than nap. If they were there, they must have been awfully quiet. I assumed he was at her place."

"If you remember anything, let me know. I'm going to call around some more and see if anybody's seen them." Kady got up to leave.

"Don't worry," Meaghan said. "I'm sure they're fine. Marnie's just a little . . . distracted right now."

Kady's eyes narrowed again. "Distracted? Trampy is more like it."

Before Meaghan could comment, Kady was gone. *What's got her so pissy?* Maybe it was baby hormones. It certainly wasn't her normal behavior. Meaghan had never heard Kady say a negative thing about any witch but Emily Procter.

Meaghan yawned deeply. Coffee. She wouldn't make it through Owen Finnerty's report without more coffee and nobody had made any this morning. Rather than try to figure out Natalie's high-end Italian coffeemaker, Meaghan decided to walk over to Eldrich Brew. Her safe little office suddenly felt very lonely without Jamie next door.

With Owen Finnerty's report tucked under her arm, Meaghan made her way out of city hall and across the town square. The coffee shop was on Washington Street, which ran along the north end of the square, next to the food co-op. Natalie's coffee-making notwithstanding, Eldrich Brew was usually full of city employees. Without city hall, Sally and Nate, the Brew's young, tattooed proprietors, would be out of business. Meaghan liked to pop in a few times a week to see everybody and be seen. It was too easy, especially lately, to hide up on the third floor all day.

But the Brew was empty. Meaghan looked at her watch. It was only one thirty. The place was normally winding down the lunch rush by now. Granted, it was the Friday before Labor Day, but she'd never seen it this deserted.

"Finally," Sally said as Meaghan approached the counter. "I expected it to be slow today, but you're the first person to walk through the door. Did everybody stay home from work?"

"I guess," Meaghan said.

"You want lunch? I've got plenty of food."

"Surprise me," Meaghan said, realizing she was hungry. She held up the report. "And a cup of dark roast before I slip into a coma."

Sally laughed. "Have a seat and I'll get your coffee. Nate," she called through the window back into the tiny kitchen. "Salad special." She looked back at Meaghan. "Chicken salad, okay?"

"Perfect." Meaghan sat down at the counter.

Sally set a steaming cup of black coffee and a small pitcher of cream in front of Meaghan. "Hey, I don't want to pry, but I heard about the thing at Jamie's house last night? They okay?"

Sally wasn't magical, but she and Nate were both clued in and knew about Fahraya. Meaghan gave her an abbreviated version, leaving out the domestic violence and glossing over the uglier details of Jamie's mental state.

"What a shame. I heard a little about the poltergeist stuff. Not surprising considering what he went through over there. So . . . how are the Fahrayans doing?" Sally glanced toward the kitchen, then leaned forward, smiled, and whispered, "How's Jhoro doing?"

"Um, okay, I guess," Meaghan said, surprised by the question. Sally had only met him once or twice as far as Meaghan knew. Maybe Marnie had brought him in.

"Speaking of which," Meaghan continued, "have you seen him or Marnie today?"

Sally scowled. "She's pathetic the way she follows him around. Like a dog in heat."

"You don't like him?"

Sally looked shocked. "Of course I like him. He's . . . I mean." Her face grew red. "He's . . . *him*."

Meaghan had never seen Sally flustered before. And what was the deal with Jhoro? Sally and Nate were self-described soul mates and clearly in love with each other. And she and Marnie were good friends. *First Kady, now Sally? Has every woman in town lost her mind?* "Sally, have you seen Marnie? No one seems to know where she is."

Sally stared at the counter, embarrassed. "I'm sorry. I don't know what that was. I haven't seen her since the day before last. What's the problem?"

"Kady said she blew off her nursing home clients."

Sally looked up, startled. "She what? She didn't call or anything?"

Meaghan shook her head.

"She loves those old ladies," Sally said. "Has anybody tried her cell?"

"Yeah," Meaghan said. "No answer."

Nate appeared at Sally's elbow with a large plate covered in salad greens. "Chicken salad special." He set the plate down in front of Meaghan and glared at her and Sally. "What are you talking about?"

"Have you seen Marnie today?" Meaghan asked.

"No," Nate said, his voice sullen. He walked back into the kitchen.

Her voice low, Meaghan asked Sally, "What the hell is going on? What's up with Mr. Smiley?"

Normally, Nate was as bubbly and effusive as Sally. He exuded goodwill and optimism from every tattooed pore. Meaghan had never seen him unhappy.

Sally rolled her eyes. "I don't know." She raised her voice so he could hear her. "Some bug up his ass. Like I care." She leaned forward, a concerned frown on her face. "Is Jhoro missing too? Please tell me he's okay."

"Haven't seen Mr. Frickin' Perfect either, thanks for asking," Nate growled from the kitchen.

Okay, something weird—Eldrich weird—was going on. Trying to sound casual, Meaghan said, "Sally, I'm such a dope. I forgot I have to be somewhere in about ten minutes. Can you wrap this up to go?"

"Sure," Sally said, a dazed look on her face. "I . . . I'm sorry. It's been a weird day."

"There's a lot of that going on. Sounds like you and Nate could use some time off."

"Yeah," Sally said. "I don't know . . ." She trailed off. Her eyes looked unfocused for a second and then she came back. "Tell you what." She pulled a piece of plastic wrap off a roll sitting on the prep counter behind her. "I'll put some plastic over this. Pay me later. And bring the plate back whenever." She poured Meaghan a fresh to-go cup of coffee. "I think we're closing up early today."

"Good idea," Meaghan said. "Call me if you see Marnie or Jhoro, okay?"

Sally nodded and locked the door behind Meaghan.

CHAPTER SEVENTEEN

BETWEEN THE REPORT, the salad plate, and her cup of coffee, Meaghan didn't have a free hand to use her phone. She headed for the nearest bench in the town square and called Natalie.

"Where are you?" Meaghan asked.

"At home, clearing out the spare room for Jamie. What's up?"

"Have you heard that Marnie and Jhoro are missing?"

Natalie gasped. "What? Please tell me he's okay."

Meaghan shut her eyes and groaned. "Not you, too."

"Not me too what?"

"Natalie, listen carefully. Something weird is going on. Something magically weird. Is there any way you can trace Marnie and tell me where she is?"

"If that bitch hurts him, I'll kill her." Natalie's voice shook with anger. "She's using him. She doesn't really love him."

"Natalie," Meaghan said in a low calm voice, "please listen. Take a deep breath and try to clear your head. Something stranger than normal is happening. Nobody knows where Marnie and Jhoro are. You and Sally, over at the Brew, both appear to be much fonder of Jhoro than you were yesterday and everybody suddenly hates Marnie. What the hell is going on?"

"Sally better stay away from him, too," Natalie said in a shrill tone Meaghan had never heard her use before. "I'm the only one who really loves him. Marnie's only using him for sex. She doesn't understand him like I do. You saw him last night. He couldn't keep his eyes off me."

Okay, Meaghan thought. Definitely magic. At mealtime, Jhoro only had eyes for his plate. "Natalie, does anything about this conversation seem odd to you?"

"Yes, you just told me the man I love is missing and you don't sound panicked," she said in a rush. "Unless . . . unless . . . *you* did something to him. I've seen how you look at him."

"Oh, for hell's sake, Natalie." Meaghan's patience was fraying. "I'm probably the only woman in town who hasn't been looking at him that way. Think. You're under some kind of spell. How we do we find Marnie?"

"Forget Marnie," Natalie said, nearly in tears. "We have to find Jhoro."

Meaghan shook her head. Time for a new strategy. Natalie was off the rails and headed for crazy town. Meaghan wouldn't get any useful information unless she followed her. "The best way to find Jhoro is to find Marnie. Can you do a locator spell on either one?"

"I can try. But if Marnie's trying to steal him from me, she'll already have thought of that and hidden him."

"Let's hope not. You need to try to find them. But just locate them. Don't try to confront Marnie, okay?"

"You can't have him either."

"Natalie, I don't want him. I like him in a mommy way only. Trust me on this. I'm on your side."

"You are?" Natalie asked suspiciously.

"Absolutely. You're the girl for him. I knew it the moment I met him." Meaghan rolled her eyes. She hadn't been aware that Natalie had any interest in him at all until last night, but whatever.

"You promise?"

"I swear. You find Marnie, but let me deal with her. We don't want to tip her hand that you're on to her, okay?"

Natalie agreed and they said goodbye. Meaghan picked up the cooling cup of coffee and took a big slug. She now had a fairly strong suspicion about what was going on. Marnie had tried to cast some kind of love spell on Jhoro and the spell had gone sideways.

"As if I don't have enough bullshit to deal with," Meaghan mumbled. She drained the coffee cup. She needed to find Marnie before a jealous, love-crazed witch did. And judging by Nate's jealous reaction to Sally's fawning, Jhoro wasn't safe either.

Meaghan also needed to determine how far the contagion had spread. And how it was affecting people. City hall was in the crazy-making zone, and judging by Natalie, so was her neighborhood a few blocks west. And it seemed to be affecting the magical and non-magical alike.

The first number on her speed dial was Russ's cell.

"Yeah, Meg, what's up?"

"You know where Jhoro and Marnie are?"

"Haven't seen him. Or *her*." There was a growl in his voice Meaghan didn't like.

"Why did you say it like that?" Meaghan asked.

"Say what like what?"

"You kinda snarled when you mentioned Marnie. I thought you guys were friends."

"I snarled?" Russ sounded genuinely surprised.

"Yeah, you did. Something weird is going on and it involves the two of them. Think. When's the last time you saw them?"

"Uh . . . dinner. When they took off right after dinner."

"Any idea where they might have been going?"

"For a ride in the car is my guess. Jhoro's eyes always light up like that when he gets in a car." Russ giggled like a teenage girl. "He loves it. Sticks his head out, that long blond hair streaming behind him. He's so gorgeous."

"Russ, will you listen to yourself? Since when are you hot for Jhoro?"

"Hot for . . . God, I did get kinda giddy over him right there. I . . ." He trailed off. "Am I gay?"

"You like girls. You always have. My gaydar has you pointed at true hetero. Something magical is going on. Kady called Marnie a slut—"

"Which she totally is. Did you see—"

"Russ! Get a grip. I was just over at the Brew, and Sally and Nate are fighting over her sudden love for Jhoro. Nate was downright grumpy."

That got Russ's attention. "Nate was grumpy? *Nate?* Are you sure?"

"Yes, I'm sure. And Natalie is referring to Jhoro as the man she loves and she's ready to tear Marnie apart."

"There was a little bit of that going on between them at dinner," Russ said.

"Well, there's a whole lot more going on now. Trust me. Things are not normal and if it's magical, you're being affected, too."

"So I'm not gay? Because I'm feeling really attracted to him right now. Because I'm . . . he's . . . well, you've seen him. You know."

"Yes, I know. And if I wasn't impervious, I'd probably be drooling all over him too. You aren't gay, you're hexed."

"I mean not that there's anything wrong with being gay, only it's so . . . sudden. Could that be why I keep getting divorced?"

Meaghan snorted. "You keep getting divorced because you let your pecker pick your wives. Where are you?"

"Home."

"Stay there, okay? I have to figure this thing out. If you see or hear anything about Jhoro or Marnie, call me on my cell."

Okay, she thought as she hung up. That was weird. The two straight men she'd talked to were having different reactions. Nate was jealous of Jhoro and angry at his wife's sudden attraction. In contrast, Russ was ready to come out of a closet Meaghan knew he'd never been in.

She had to get back to the office, but couldn't summon the energy to stand up. Lack of sleep was catching up with her despite the jolt of caffeine. Poltergeists, leprechauns, magical refugees, secret wars, a new sister, domestic violence—wasn't that enough to deal with?

Sex. It always came back to sex. As did quite a lot of crime and violence. A runaway love charm could go very wrong very quickly. *And the only person who isn't affected is too tired to drag her ass off this park bench.* Time to get back to the office and sort this out. She needed to find Jhoro and Marnie. Most of all, she needed to find someone not lovesick to help her clean up this mess.

Meaghan immediately thought of Owen Finnerty, but she couldn't be sure he hadn't created the mess in the first place. Screwing with humans in unexpected ways? Classic leprechaun behavior.

But what would it get him? She couldn't see the advantage for him, at least not in the context of what he claimed he wanted from her. But that was the problem. He was a leprechaun. She couldn't trust anything he told her without knowing more about him. She needed the dirt on Owen Finnerty. If he was as old as he claimed, there'd be plenty of it.

Time to call the Troon.

CHAPTER EIGHTEEN

The TROON, LIKE humans, were not particularly adept at using magic. They didn't need it. What they could do was even better.

They translated.

The Troon had four sets of vocal cords. The result was a language so complex that most other languages were laughably easy in comparison. The magical realms were full of complicated dialects and no shared language, making the Troon indispensable.

They also gossiped relentlessly. They would keep a secret if required, or if it was to their benefit, but recognized no general right of client confidentiality. If you wanted to know who was who and what was what in the magical worlds, you talked to a Troon.

The problem was finding one if they weren't currently in the human world. Short of driving to their gateway in the woods and shouting, Meaghan had no idea how to contact the three Troon she knew—Melanie, Wally, and Sid. Even if she knew where to look for them, Troon was another world where she wasn't welcome at the moment.

She didn't know their Troon names and even if she did, they were unpronounceable with human vocal cords. As far as she knew, they didn't have human last names, but then she supposed they didn't need them. It's not like they needed to forge papers or anything. There were no magic amulets that could make a Troon look human and one look was all it took to realize they were from somewhere very far away indeed.

The Troon had blue skin and hair. About the size of ten-year-old children, they had small orange eyes, porcine noses, and tusks. They were also hermaphrodites, bearing both male and female sexual organs. Culturally they seemed to recognize gender roles, but, as far as Meaghan could tell, the distinctions were quite fluid.

Melanie, for instance, reminded Meaghan of her mother. Meaghan always thought of Melanie as "she." Yet, even though Meaghan knew Melanie was Sid's parent, she wasn't clear on whether she was Sid's mother or Sid's father. Or possibly both.

Normally, Meaghan would have asked Natalie to get in touch with them for her, but Meaghan wasn't sure she wanted Natalie to know what she was doing. An extremely powerful witch, Natalie could wreak havoc even on Meaghan. She couldn't hex her directly, but she could hex everything around her. Being impervious wouldn't protect Meaghan from Natalie dropping a desk on her or setting the room she was in on fire. And, at the moment, Natalie had all the rationality of a lovesick teenager. A magically super-charged, love-sick teenager.

Meaghan headed back to the office and forced herself to eat her lunch even though she wasn't hungry anymore. All coffee and no food wouldn't do her any good. She tried to read Owen Finnerty's proposal while she ate, but quickly gave up. She couldn't concentrate on the proposal because her mind was too busy coming up with nightmare scenarios of lovesick witches battling in the streets. And if the non-magical were affected, as her encounter with Sally and Nate and the phone call with Russ suggested, then casualties were likely.

Without Natalie, Meaghan was blind.

Unless . . . she did have a phone number for Sid, even though Troon was way out of either of their service areas.

She'd only seen Sid once since they'd come back from Fahraya. He'd taken a knife to his chest, but Troon were tough and, after a highly dramatic "death scene," he bounced back within a few weeks. He made an unannounced visit to let everyone know he was okay and then, she assumed, he'd headed back to Troon.

Meaghan hadn't heard that he was in town, so it was a long shot, but nothing ventured, nothing gained.

He picked up on the second ring.

"La Meg!" he cooed. "How's my favorite ass-kicker?"

"Where are you?"

"At your house."

"What are you doing there?" she asked, surprised.

"Your brother sent me an SOS. He thinks he might be gay."

"Oh, hell. How'd he contact you?" Russ had no magical power that Meaghan was aware of.

"A special little hex bag Natalie whipped up for him for emergencies. He gave it a little squeeze, said the magic words, and poof! Here I am."

"Poof? You can materialize like the witches?"

"All right, you got me. We got here right after you talked to Russ. I hitched a lift with John. We were headed your way already. Speaking of John . . . you might want to get home. He's kinda hot to see you. Somebody's been messing with the love magic, am I right?"

At the mention of John, Meaghan felt her face grow hot. "I'm not sure seeing John right now would be a good idea. I think Marnie did a love charm on Jhoro that's gone viral somehow."

"So I hear the J-Man is playing with girls now? Good for him. I told him he needs to stay away from guys while he's grieving. All he'll do is try to find a new Finn and that never works."

"Um, yes, it appears he's bisexual."

"*Bi*sexual? Honey, that boy is omnisexual." He giggled. "Trust me on this. I have personal experience."

"Sid. You didn't."

"I did." Sid sighed, then giggled. "During my last visit. When you were at work and Russ was off doing . . . whatever it is he does. That was a night—well, technically an afternoon—to remember. Those Fahrayan guys are . . . wow. You know."

"No, Sid, I don't know. What do you know about love charms?"

"You and John haven't," his voice dropped to whisper, "*done it yet?* What are you waiting for? How many years has it been?"

In Fahraya, during a fit of anger at John, Meaghan had disclosed to Sid how very long it had been since she'd had sex. "Sid, I . . . we . . . this is not the time to talk about this. We have a crisis."

Sid sighed. "Meggy, this is Eldrich. There's always a crisis. Think how much calmer you'd be dealing with this mess if you got laid first. John would be thrilled to help you out with that."

"Oh. My. God." Meaghan face grew so hot she felt like she was about to burst into flames. "I am not having this conversation with you. How the hell do we stop this thing?"

"You're not the only woman who's got her eye on John," Sid said, concern in his voice. "Don't wait too long."

"Sid," she said through gritted teeth, "the love spell. Are you affected? What do you think about Marnie?"

"Lovely girl. Of all the witches circling, I'm glad he picked her."

"You're not jealous that she's with Jhoro?"

"Jealousy's a human thing. Relax, Meg, I'm not hexed. John, however—"

"Sid," she said, trying to control her anger. *But it's not really anger, is it,* the sensible voice whispered. *It's fear. Why are you so scared to get close to him?* "Drop it. This isn't about me and John. How do we fix this mess?"

"Fine," he said oozing exasperation. "First, we find Marnie and Jhoro and get her to tell us the specific spell she cast. Then we figure out what's amping the magic up and try to shut it down. But in the meantime, we need a better idea how this is affecting people."

"Natalie claims she's the only one who really loves him," Meaghan said, "and that Marnie's only using him. Kady called Marnie a slut but expressed no specific opinions on Jhoro."

"And your straight brother's all gay for Jhoro while John only has eyes for you." Sid paused a moment. "Please don't yell at me."

"I'm not going to yell at you," she snapped. Before Sid could respond, she added, "Sally and Nate over at Eldrich Brew are on the verge of divorce."

"They both want him?"

"No, only Sally. Nate's really jealous."

Sid hissed. "Oh, shit. I was hoping we were only getting the lovey-dovey. If there's a jealousy component, this could get bloody real fast."

"No kidding." Meaghan needed to get home and search Matthew's files to see if he'd ever dealt with something like this, but the last thing she wanted to do right now was be around John. Her resolve to wait until his sobriety was stronger was fragile at best. If he kissed her again, she wasn't sure she could say no.

Maybe that's not a bad thing, the sensible voice chimed in again.

Sometimes Meaghan really hated her lawyerly ability to argue both sides, particularly when she was arguing with herself.

Meaghan wanted to ask Sid about Owen Finnerty, but it could wait until she saw him. "I need to check in with some folks here to see how they're being affected and then I'll head home. Try to keep Russ from proposing to John."

"John's in your room, hugging your pillow. I think he's ready to start without you."

"Sid," she warned. "We're not talking about this."

"Relax. God, you're uptight." Sid giggled again and hung up.

CHAPTER NINETEEN

MEAGHAN HAD NO appointments on her calendar. She planned to check in with Kady and then head home. But she couldn't find her.

She called Annie in the mayor's office, but the phone went right to voice mail. Sarah in the council office failed to answer. Gretchen, down in human resources, likewise didn't pick up. All the receptionists were gone. Meaghan couldn't even summon up Meb down at the front desk or on the phone he wore clipped to his belt.

Not good.

Even on the Friday afternoon before Labor Day, Meaghan knew there should be somebody in the building answering the phones.

Kady's purse was gone and the solicitor's office phones were set to voice mail. Meaghan wrote her a note in case she came back and locked the office door behind her.

Heading down the stairs, she finally found someone.

Emily Proctor stood outside the council office looking bewildered. She saw Meaghan and gave her a beaming smile. "Meaghan! It's so good to see you."

Here was a new wrinkle on the spell. Even when Emily acted friendly, her smile never reached her eyes and her syrupy sweet inflection oozed insincerity. But right now, Emily looked genuinely happy to see her.

"Um, yeah. Hi, Emily. What's going on?"

"Well, I don't know. Nobody's here. And I just got the oddest call from my husband." She giggled, her face turning pink. She leaned forward conspiratorially and said in a low voice. "It was kind of *naughty*, if you get what I mean. I think I'll head home early."

Meaghan stared at her, nonplussed. She could have more easily imagined Emily uttering a death threat. "You do that, Emily," Meaghan said, in what she hoped was a soothing voice. "Take the rest of the day off."

"Only if you take the day off, too." She giggled again. "You should go out and see John. He's quite a handsome guy now that I think about it. And he really likes you. I can tell."

Only ten weeks before Emily had referred to John as a "filthy insect man." Any lingering doubts Meaghan had about the magical origins of the odd behavior she'd witnessed now evaporated. Only magic—powerful magic—could make Emily act like this.

"Okay, I'll do that," Meaghan said. "Only I need to check on a few things on my way out."

Emily handed her a key ring. "Here are the front door keys. Lock up on your way out, 'kay?" She waved her fingers and bounced down the steps. "Bye!"

"And that's gotta be one of the signs of the end of the

world," Meaghan muttered. She headed for the mayor's office, hoping Annie was still around and still in her right mind. Maybe the ghosts knew something.

She found Annie back in the mayor's private office, sitting at his desk, tears streaming down her face. When she saw Meaghan, she spun around and faced the wall. "I'm sorry. I . . . But it's so sudden and I really liked him."

"Really liked who?" Meaghan asked, dreading the answer. "Jhoro?"

"*Him?*" Annie shrieked, spinning back to face Meaghan. "That . . . that . . . boyfriend stealer?"

"Oh, God." Meaghan slumped down into one of the armchairs in front of the desk, exhausted again. "Who did he steal?"

"He stole . . . he stole . . ." Annie's chin wobbled and she burst into tears. "He stole your brother," she wailed. "Russ called and told me he thought he was gay and didn't want to lead me on until he knew for sure."

"Unbelievable," Meaghan growled. "Annie, get ahold of yourself. Russ is not gay. He told me only last night how much he likes you. He's hexed. And it sounds like you are, too. What are the ghosts telling you?"

"That there's something magical going on." Annie wiped her tear-stained cheek with the back of her hand. "That somebody cast a spell."

"Well, there you go. See?"

"I thought they were only saying that to make me feel better."

"And how often do they lie to spare your feelings?"

"Well . . . never, now that I think about it. The dead don't really have any filters. They don't care about my feelings."

"The inconsiderate dead?"

This drew a small smile from Annie. "Well, they're not exactly evil and they certainly aren't grateful. So who cast this spell?"

"Marnie, I think, trying to cast a love spell on Jhoro that's gone wild. Everybody's reacting a little differently. How do you feel about Marnie?"

"Poor thing. Does she know Jhoro's stringing her along while he tries to turn Russ gay?"

Meaghan buried her face in her hands with a groan. "Annie, listen to yourself."

"Oh! That was the spell, wasn't it?"

"Yes, Annie," Meaghan said as calmly as she could. "That was the spell. Trust me. Russ is straight as an arrow. And he wants to ask you out, but he doesn't want to rush things and screw up like he has before."

"If you say so," Annie said. "The ghosts tell me to listen to you."

"Good. Do they have any other insights?"

Annie cocked her head, listening. "One at a time . . . shut up and let him finish what he's saying."

It took a moment for Meaghan to realize Annie wasn't talking to her. This was how Sid must have felt when Meaghan was talking to her father's spirit in Fahraya.

"They don't know anything about a love charm, but they say some big magic is at work. That yesterday was only a taste of what's coming."

"Yesterday?" Meaghan's heart sank. "Jamie? This is about Jamie?"

"Not the love spell part. They don't know what that's

about, but say it might be related. Jamie's energy could be boosting the spell."

"But Jamie's in Williamsport."

Annie cocked her head again and listened. "Oh, shit. No, he's not. He's on his way in the front door . . ."

She jumped to her feet, ran around the desk, and grabbed Meaghan, pulling her behind a large storage cabinet.

A huge boom rocked the building and the windows exploded.

Her face grim, Annie pulled Meaghan into a large closet next to the cabinet and locked the heavy wooden door behind her. She yanked open another door, this one steel, dragged Meaghan into the dark, and slammed it shut. Meaghan heard her turn a heavy deadbolt and then a few metallic clunks.

"Hang on a sec, let me find the flashlight," Annie said.

A moment later, a narrow beam of light filled the space. They were in a small room with brick walls. Runes and symbols that Meaghan had seen Natalie use were spray-painted on the walls and floor. Several leather pouches—hex bags, Meaghan realized, but larger than she'd ever seen—hung from the beams above their head. In addition to the deadbolt lock, three heavy bars secured the door.

"What is this place?" Meaghan asked.

"Safe room. We're insulated from the building's effects in here. It should protect us from Jamie or whatever's using him."

"Does the mayor know this is here?"

Annie shook her head. "Tony doesn't have a clue. You know how he is. I told him this was a utility room and he never questioned it. Utility rooms are for lesser mortals."

They heard another loud boom. The hex bags swayed slightly. "Is that Jamie?"

"Yeah." Annie frowned up at the ceiling. "He's on his way to the third floor. The ghosts say we have to get out of here now. Before he gets settled in and realizes we're here."

"He'll hurt us?"

"Not him. The things . . . riding him? Does that make any sense to you?"

"Yeah, it does. They're controlling him somehow. Through those nasty sigils on his back and chest, I think. He told me those things, whatever they are, are telling him to kill his family. We have to go get him."

Annie shook her head. "Absolutely not. Whatever he is right now, you and I don't have the power to fight him. We need some witches."

"Who are all hexed at the moment. Goddammit. This wasn't a coincidence. It's those damn wizards again."

Annie tilted her head as if listening. "Are those the guys in the gray robes? They're outside blocking the doors."

"Shit. Natalie told me they'd put up a barrier around town to keep them out. The love spell must have knocked it out somehow. So, how do we get out of here?"

Annie flashed a grim smile. "What good's a safe room if it doesn't have a secret exit?" She pressed one hand into the middle of a wall rune and the other onto the side of the nearest hex bag. She muttered something and a small section of the brick wall trundled backward, leaving a dark hole about the size of a large doggie door. "C'mon."

With Annie leading the way, Meaghan crawled through the hole into the dusty space beyond. A narrow wooden staircase descended into the darkness. With the help of the flashlight, they crept carefully down the stairs.

"Where do these go?" Meaghan whispered.

"Sub-basement crawl space," Annie whispered back. "From there, we can access a tunnel that will take us a few blocks away. My car's in the employee lot across the street."

Meaghan took a deep breath, trying to quell her fear. She was afraid for Jamie, but, more immediately, the words *sub-basement, crawl space,* and *tunnel* filled her with dread. "You got your keys?"

"Oh, *shit,*" Annie hissed. "No. They're in my purse under my desk."

"I've got mine," Meaghan said. "But I'm parked right outside the front door."

"Wizards are crawling all over the front steps. We'd never make it."

"Okay," Meaghan said, trying to keep her voice from shaking. The space was dark and narrow and cramped, and she was in it, and there was no option but to keep moving. "One problem at a time. Let's get out of here first."

After what seemed hours, but was actually about ten minutes, Annie led them to a ladder beneath a locked trapdoor. A relatively new combination lock secured it. Meaghan held the flashlight, while Annie opened the trap and, within moments, dust-filtered light shone down into the tunnel.

Meaghan poked up her head. The trapdoor opened into what looked like another basement. Sunlight shone in several of the narrow windows. After the suffocating tunnel, the basement looked like a convention hall.

She climbed up, then gave Annie her hand and helped her through the trapdoor. "Where are we?"

Annie brushed cobwebs off her now filthy white blouse. "The basement of the Eldrich Historical Society."

Meaghan looked at her blankly.

"You know," Annie said. "The big yellow Victorian on Iron Street? Two blocks west of the square?"

"Where the town museum is?" Meaghan kept meaning to stop in, but hadn't gotten around to it.

"Yeah. Welland Eldrich's house. The guy who built city hall. The tunnel and the safe room weren't on the original plans, so nobody knows if that was to keep them secret or if they were added later."

Meaghan shuddered. "I don't care who built it so long as I never have to go through that tunnel again. I *really* don't like small places. I'm sure you could tell."

"You're claustrophobic?" Annie asked. "You're kidding. You acted like that was a stroll in the park. Russ is right. You are a stone-cold badass."

Meaghan had to smile at that. "Russ called me a stone-cold badass?"

"His exact words. Okay, boss, now what do we do?"

"Something badass, I suppose. But right now what I really want to do is wash my hands. And figure out what the hell is going on."

CHAPTER TWENTY

IT DIDN'T TAKE long for the love spell to reassert itself over Annie. They snuck up the stairs and found the museum empty, a closed sign on the door. In the tiny employee bathroom, Annie took one look in the mirror and burst into tears.

"Look at me. How am I going to make Russ forget Jhoro looking like this?"

To Meaghan's eye, Annie looked great for having crawled through a sub-basement and a dank tunnel. Her shirt and skirt were trashed and her hair was a little mussed, but otherwise, she looked fine.

"If Russ weren't currently addled with magic, he wouldn't be looking at anybody but you," Meaghan said. "Trust me. You're totally his type, and prettier than his ex-wives. The only reason he hasn't asked you out yet is that he likes you too much to risk you becoming ex-wife number four. He doesn't have a great track record and he's scared of screwing up again."

"Really?" Annie asked.

"Really," Meaghan said. Annie had acted like a seasoned commando getting them out of city hall. Now she was falling apart again, but only after the immediate danger had passed. So maybe, Meaghan thought, her usual allies weren't as useless as she feared.

"So, now what?" Annie asked.

"Fortunately for us, I have my phone in my pants pocket along with my car keys. Let's see what's going on."

"Have you found him?" Natalie asked, breathlessly, after one ring.

Meaghan didn't bother to ask who she was talking about. "Not yet. But we got a bigger problem. Jamie's back, along with a bunch of those Order assholes."

"That's impossible," Natalie said, sounding indignant. "The coven helped me put up a spell barrier all the way around town to keep wizards out."

"Well, the barrier's down and they've staked out city hall. Which currently has no windows, by the way, thanks to Jamie."

Natalie sucked in a sharp breath. "Jamie did that?"

"Yeah. We only got out of the building because Annie knows about the secret exit."

"The one in Tony's office?"

"Yeah," Meaghan said. "We're hiding out in the town museum right now. We can get to Annie's car, but she doesn't have her keys. I've got my keys, but we can't get near my car. Come get us. We need to get out to my house."

"I'll be right there."

"Any word on Marnie?"

Natalie growled, actually *growled.* "Not yet. But she can't hide from me forever."

"Whatever. Get here as fast as you can. And avoid city hall."

Meaghan spent the next few minutes trying to assure Annie that Russ was straight without throwing all his ex-wives and ex-girlfriends in her face. But the parade of women seemed to reassure her.

"He sure doesn't sound gay," Annie said.

"Because he's not. He's hexed."

"So, why's it playing out that way for him? Why isn't he hot for Marnie?"

Meaghan shook her head. "I don't know." She thought a moment longer. "Because magic is treacherous and love is treacherous and mixing the two is a really bad idea."

"John's hot for you, I bet," Annie said with a sly smile.

Meaghan blushed. What was everybody's fascination with her and John?

Annie laughed. "Look how red you are. He's a cutie-pie. What are you waiting for?"

At that moment, somebody pounded on the front door, saving Meaghan from having to either answer or hit Annie over the head with something.

Meaghan peeked through the window and saw Natalie standing on the porch. An Eldrich police car, light bar flashing, sat on the lawn. Meaghan unlocked the front door and pulled it open.

"Who called the cops?" Meaghan asked.

"It's Kady's brother. He came to check on me." Natalie leaned forward conspiratorially. "You need to help me let him down easy. Brian's always had a thing for me and it's sweet, but he's no Jhoro."

"You mean he's not a sleazy man-stealer?" Annie bristled behind Meaghan.

Natalie's look grew dark. "Who are you calling sleazy, you bleach blonde tramp?"

"He likes *men*, you cow, not overfed witches. And don't you dare call me out on hair color from a bottle, little Orphan Annie. You think you're fooling anybody with those copper curls? No way that color came from nature."

Natalie began muttering and waving her hands.

"Knock it off," Meaghan said. "Natalie, you try to throw a spell and I'll kick your ass. Both of you, shut up, before I crack your heads together."

In the police car, Meaghan discovered that Brian wasn't doing much better keeping it together. He was sick with love for Natalie. Brian was off shift and in plainclothes, but he had his gun with him. He wasn't saying anything threatening, but the look in his eyes when Natalie gushed over Jhoro worried Meaghan.

The first challenge was figuring out who sat where. On the drive over, with Natalie in the front seat, Brian had been so distracted he'd dinged the police car on an abandoned truck in the middle of the road.

But if Meaghan sat up front, that would leave Natalie and Annie in the backseat and judging by their initial comments, they'd kill each other. If Annie was upfront, she and Brian could commiserate with each other, but that would merely fan the flames of their resentment and could endanger Jhoro.

Judging Brian and Natalie to be the most dangerous members of the group, Meaghan decided keeping them apart was the best option. She climbed into the backseat and dragged Natalie in with her. Fortunately, the cruiser wasn't equipped with a barrier between the front and backseat, so Meaghan could keep an eye on everybody.

"Sit up here with me, babe, please?"

"I'm not your 'babe,' Brian, and I never have been," Natalie said dismissively. "We made out a couple times in high school. Get over it. You know Jhoro and I are deeply in love and plan to build a life together."

Brian scowled into the rearview mirror. "When I get my hands on that son of a bitch, I'm taking him apart. Nobody steals my girl."

"I'll help," Annie chimed in. "He stole my man."

"What man?" Natalie asked, eyes narrowed.

"He's trying to turn Russ gay."

"That's impossible. He loves me. Only me."

Brian stared into the mirror, his face red. "And I love only you, Natalie. Why can't you see that? I've always loved you. He wasn't even *human* ten weeks ago."

"Well, I don't love you," Natalie said, with a flip of her copper curls. "Quit whining and get us out to Meaghan's house."

"We find him," Brian said, his face hard, "and I'll kill him. I'm the only one around here with a clear head."

"Brian," Meaghan said, "can I borrow your gun?"

"My gun? Why?"

"I need to check something inside the museum and I want to make sure I'm protected."

"I'll go in. You stay here," Brian said.

"You need to stay out here and keep Natalie safe,"

Meaghan said. "Evil wizards are crawling all over town. And they hate witches."

"I'm not giving you my gun. I don't have a shotgun in this car. My sidearm is the only weapon I have."

Meaghan leaned closer and put a motherly hand on his shoulder. "You know you're the only one who can protect Natalie," she whispered in his ear. "If I go in there and something happens to me because I can't defend myself, you'll either have to leave her here at risk or bring her inside, where she'll also be at risk. And if you leave her, she's so crazy right now she might run off to find Jhoro. You don't want that."

Brian thought a moment. "You know how to use a Glock?"

"Absolutely," Meaghan lied. She knew how to use a shotgun, but had only shot a pistol once before. "Give it here. I'll be right back."

Reluctantly, after making sure she knew how to work the gun's safety, he complied. Meaghan got out of the car and holding the gun like she'd seen on TV, crept onto the porch, and into the museum. Once she was inside, she dropped the act. *I can't believe he fell for that.* Holding the gun carefully, she headed down to the basement.

Meaghan examined the trapdoor that led down into the tunnel. There was a hasp on both sides, and Annie had left the combination lock lying open on the floor. That would work. She double-checked that the safety was on, then dropped the gun into the darkness. She clicked the padlock shut and twirled the dial. Annie knew the combination, but appeared to be a bit more rational than Brian, so Meaghan hoped she wouldn't tell him.

Meaghan returned to the car.

"Where's my gun?"

"Locked away safely." Meaghan glared at Brian. "You're hexed. Think like a cop for a minute, okay? What will happen if you shoot Jhoro?"

"I'll go to jail," he said in a sullen tone.

"Exactly. You told me last night that you couldn't explain black magic to the district attorney. You think a magic-induced jealous rage would be any easier to sell?"

"No." He banged his hand against the steering wheel. "But if I see that son of a bitch, I'll knock his lights out. I don't need a gun to do that."

"Fine," Meaghan said. "Have at him, as long as you do it with your fists. Throwing a punch gives you more time to think. With that gun, one squeeze and you're both screwed." She slumped back into the seat, exhausted. "Now get me home."

"But, Jhoro won't be . . ."

Meaghan silenced Natalie with a glare. "Not one word."

"Will Russ . . ."

"From any of you," Meaghan said to Annie. "Brian, drive. Eyes on the road. If I see you sneaking so much as one peek at Natalie in the rearview mirror, I will smack you in the back of the head with one of my shoes. Do you understand me?"

"Yes," Brian growled. "We better be able to find my gun when this is all over."

"If we can't, I'll buy you a new one. Now shut up and drive."

CHAPTER TWENTY-ONE

ELDRICH APPEARED DESERTED. Except for the occasional abandoned vehicle, they saw no signs of life. And no signs of the Order. Whatever the dark wizards were up to, it seemed to center on city hall.

That didn't make Meaghan feel any better. If they were using city hall to amplify whatever they'd already done to Jamie when they carved those cryptic sigils into his flesh, the whole town could be at risk.

And even without the magical boost from the vortex on the third floor, Jamie had been able to blow out the windows. There was no telling how much damage he could cause at the center of a magical geyser with the collective power of the Order behind him. Or what torment they were subjecting him to while they were using him.

As dangerous as Marnie's love spell had the potential to become, it was ultimately a distraction. To fight the wizards, she needed her troops united behind her. Instead they were acting like a bunch of horny teenagers.

Jhoro and Marnie. They had to be found.

As it turned out, Owen Finnerty had already solved half that problem for her. When they got to the Keele house, Meaghan saw Owen sitting on the front steps of her neighbor's house.

He walked over, pulled her aside. "I found your Fahrayan houseguest."

"He's inside?" Meaghan whirled around to see Natalie rushing into the house with Brian and Annie glowering behind her. "*Shit*. Brian wants to kick his ass."

"No. He's next door with Edna. She grabbed his ass a few times, but I think now she's settled down into Mrs. Robinson mode. Trying to be sly."

Edna McGinty was eighty-five and had buried three husbands. Meaghan had caught her sneaking peeks, with binoculars, at Jhoro through her lace curtains. Suddenly, it wasn't so amusing, especially after Sid's comments about Jhoro's omnivorous sexual appetites.

"Oh, God. What's he doing?"

Owen sighed. "He's weeping. It appears he's no longer able to screw his way around his grief."

"Where did you find him?"

"Lying on top of his dead lover's grave. I assume you know what's going on?"

Meaghan nodded. "Got a good idea. Love spell gone wrong?"

"Yeah. Maybe that closed gateway hasn't quite lost all its mojo. By itself, I don't think it could have made the spell go free-range, but it could have been a contributing factor."

Jhoro had insisted that Finn be buried in the stone circle that marked the now-defunct dimensional gateway to Fahraya. "How'd you get him to go with you?"

"I took him by the hand and led him to my car. He's such a hot mess at the moment he didn't resist."

"Was there a woman with him? A witch with black hair?"

Owen shook his head. "Not that I saw. She's the one who conjured up this disaster?"

"Yeah, I think so. I don't suppose you speak Fahrayan?"

Owen snorted. "Do I look like a Troon?"

Meaghan pointed at her house. "There's one inside. Does anyone in there know you're here?"

"No. Well, I suppose they do now unless the pack you arrived with were too love crazy to notice me. You want me to introduce myself?"

Meaghan shook her head. "God, no. John's in there along with my brother and neither one are fond of leprechauns. Hang on." She pulled out her phone and called Sid.

"Where are you?" he hissed. "Annie and Natalie are about to claw each other's eyes out. Unless they turn on Russ first."

"I'm in the driveway. I need you to translate. Make a quiet exit and get out here."

Meaghan slid the phone back in her pocket. To Owen she said, "So why aren't you all gaga? Or are you just playing it cool?"

Owen rolled his eyes. "Please. Love charms? Give me a break. That's kiddie magic." He paused a moment. "So, you had a chance to look at my proposal yet?"

Meaghan glared at him. "What do you think? How did you find Jhoro anyway? What made you go out there? And how did you know to come here?"

"Checking a hunch. I can feel magic gone wrong even if it's not affecting me. And I had to take him somewhere. I figured you'd show up eventually, and Edna and I go way back. The Order's skulking around town, by the way."

"Yeah, I know. They showed up at city hall with Jamie."

Owen's eyes widened. "Oh, shit. That can't be good. What happened?"

"He blew out all the windows and then the mayor's secretary dragged me into a magical safe room and we escaped through a secret tunnel."

"He was in his office when he did it?"

Meaghan shook her head. "No. He did that coming in the front door. We have to get this love-spell crap dealt with fast. As dangerous as it might get, it's still only a sideshow."

Sid trotted up, in his usual assortment of trendy boys' and girls' clothes. Today it was plaid cargo shorts, orange Chuck Taylor high-tops, and a powder blue T-shirt featuring a glittery butterfly and ruffled shoulders. On top of his blue head sat a pair of neon green sunglasses. "Sorry that took so long." He looked Owen up and down and with a sly smile said, "Who's your handsome friend?" He stuck out his small blue hand. "I'm Sid."

"I'm a leprechaun," Owen replied.

Sid pulled his hand back like he'd been burned. "Uh . . ." He glanced up at Meaghan. "You know this guy?"

"Owen Finnerty, meet Sid. Sid, Owen Finnerty. Yes, we met earlier today. He's not the typical leprechaun."

As soon as Sid heard Owen's name, he took a big step backward. "Owen Finnerty? Oh, dear." He nodded at Owen. "Mr. Finnerty, I'll skip the handshake. You understand."

At least now I don't have to ask Sid if there's any dirt on

Owen, Meaghan thought. *All I need are the details. Which I don't have time for right now.* She decided to trust Owen on a provisional basis until she had evidence otherwise.

Owen sighed. "Screw up one time and it's like you're radioactive." He looked up at Sid. "I haven't struck a single leprechaun's deal since my little misadventure. Don't believe everything you hear. I'm a legitimate businessman now."

"Yeah, you and Michael Corleone," Sid said. "Meg, do you know anything about leprechauns?"

"Yes, Sid. I do," Meaghan said. "Enough to know that whatever Owen may have done or may currently do, he's not a typical leprechaun. That doesn't mean I trust him." She gave Owen a pointed look. He rolled his eyes again. "But it does mean I'm willing to listen to what he has to say. And, in case you haven't noticed, the three of us appear to be the only persons in Eldrich not under the influence of magic. So, no drama, please. We've already got more than we can handle."

Sid frowned but dropped it. "Who am I translating for?"

"Jhoro. He's next door."

"Jhoro?" Sid squeaked. "He's *here?* Do you have a mirror?"

"A mirror?"

"Yes. Look at me. I haven't seen him since, well, *you know,* and I need to look my best."

Owen laughed. "Oh, you're one of *those* Troon. Relax. He's in such a state I doubt he'll notice."

Sid looked glum. "Because he's all hot for Marnie now?"

"Oh, for God's sake," Meaghan said. "C'mon. We need to figure this out." She marched over the lawn to Edna McGinty's front door with Sid and Owen in tow.

She knocked on the screen door before stepping inside the foyer. "Edna? It's Meaghan."

Instead of Edna McGinty, Jhoro hobbled into view. Owen hadn't lied. Jhoro was a mess. Eyes swollen from weeping, he wore the same clothes, now muddy and torn, that he'd left the house in the previous evening. Angry red scratches covered his arms and his bare feet.

"Mama," he choked.

Meaghan opened her arms, and he went to her. She hugged him while he sobbed into her shoulder. She felt her own tears try to well up again and she shoved them back down. *Not the time*, she told herself sternly. For once the sensible voice stayed quiet.

When he'd calmed a bit, she steered him into Edna's living room, and led him to the sofa. "Sid, ask him what happened."

Hiccupping like a child from too much crying, Jhoro choked out his story as Sid translated.

Marnie had taken him for a drive in her car, as Russ has suspected. She drove them into a clearing about a half mile from the spot where Finn was buried, although she took a roundabout route and Jhoro didn't realize at first where they were. She pulled a blanket from her trunk and spread it on the ground. While Jhoro lay down to look at the stars, Marnie puttered a bit and then appeared with a plastic shopping bag.

He pulled her down on the blanket and they kissed a bit. Then she said some words, moved her hands, and that was the last thing he remembered until he woke up later, alone.

The remains of a small fire smoldered a few feet away. A sweet, cloying scent hung in the air. Marnie's car was there, but there was no other sign of her. He felt a bit dizzy at first, but otherwise normal, until he heard a small pop from the fire.

Flames flared up and belched a cloud of smoke, this time acrid, and when the smoke cleared, Finn was standing before him.

"Or at least the image of Finn," Sid explained. "But he was still Fahrayan. He had his wings. When Jhoro tried to touch him, his hand passed through him. Then Finn turned, unfurled his wings, and started to fly. That's how J got so cut up. Running barefoot through the trees trying to follow."

Edna appeared with a pitcher of lemonade and plate of cookies. Jhoro slouched listlessly beside Meaghan on the sofa, his head on her shoulder.

"Watch it, girlie," Edna said. "Don't you steal my new boyfriend. I've had my eye on Blondie for a while."

"Yes," Meaghan said. "I've noticed. That's a nice pair of binoculars you have, by the way."

Edna threw back her white head and laughed. "And lately there's been a lot to see." She leered at Jhoro. "Owen here told me that he suspects a love charm gone awry?"

Meaghan raised an eyebrow. "You're aware you're being hexed?"

"Honey, I'm feeling things right now I haven't felt in years. No way this is natural. I'd be comforting him in a totally different way if I didn't have bones like Cheetos. One good thrust and he'd crack me in half. But what a way to go."

"Edna," Owen said, in mock condemnation. "You naughty girl. You're making me blush."

"Ha, as if I could, you little stinker." Edna turned her attention back to Meaghan. "Never trust a leprechaun, particularly one as charming and handsome as this wee bastard."

"Can we resume our story?" Sid said, frowning at Owen. "Still have a crisis on our hands, remember?"

"Yes, Sid," Meaghan said. "You're right. So, Jhoro was running through the woods. Then what happened?"

Sid buzzed something to Jhoro. With a shuddering sigh, Jhoro slumped deeper into the sofa cushions, a look of despair on his face, and began to speak.

"He says that Finn finally landed and he realized that he was standing on Finn's grave. He had no idea how close he and Marnie had been to it." Sid listened intently for a moment and then grimaced. "We've got big trouble if we can believe what the Finn apparition said. Finn told him that the witch had tried to use magic to make Jhoro forget his grief and then the wizards came. The wizards in the gray robes. They took her."

CHAPTER TWENTY-TWO

"THE GOOD NEWS," Owen said, "if you can call it that, is she's still alive or the spell wouldn't still be going."

"How do you know that?" Meaghan asked.

"Love charms are personal magic."

"But this has blown way past Marnie and Jhoro," Sid said.

"No, it's merely been amplified," Owen replied. "Someone talks into a microphone and everybody hears it. But if the speaker shuts up, then the sound stops, you know?"

Sid gave Owen a sullen look. "Not if it's recorded."

Owen ignored him. "Love charms are about creating an intimate emotional connection with someone. But it's not real, at least not at first. It's basically a magically induced crush. Sometimes it can grow into real love. But the magic dies when the spell caster does."

Meaghan nodded. "Edna, you still want to jump Jhoro's bones? More than you did before today?"

Edna smiled. "Yesterday, he was mere entertainment.

Today—if I was forty years younger . . ." She giggled as her face grew pink. "Oh, what I wouldn't give for an estrogen patch and denser bones. I think it's safe to say I'm still under the influence."

Jhoro stared at the ceiling, bereft, tears leaking out of his deep blue eyes.

Meaghan leaned away from him toward Owen. "This," she gestured back at Jhoro, "is being caused by the spell, too?"

Owen shrugged. "Hard to say. If her intent was to make him forget, she clearly didn't accomplish that. But love magic is fussy stuff. Lots of ways for it to go wrong—as you already know. Maybe all Marnie did was force him to finally feel his grief instead of trying to screw his way around it."

"Which I bet wasn't her intent," Meaghan said. She leaned back against the sofa. Jhoro slumped over and put his head on her knee like a small child. Even curled in a ball, he was so tall his feet hung off the end of the sofa. She stroked his hair distractedly.

"So," Meaghan said, "what happens if we take him to my house? Edna seems to be able to control her impulses."

"It's not control, honey," Edna replied. "It's physical infirmity. If I could do him, I would. I'm not sure you'll be able to pry the youngsters off him."

"And if he rejects them," Owen chimed in, "which he will because he's sick with grief for his dead boyfriend, things will turn ugly. Hell hath no fury, right? And that's regular women. Natalie Segretti could turn him into hamburger with a few words and a wave of her hand."

Meaghan sighed. "Only if Brian doesn't beat him to death first."

"In which case, Natalie will turn Brian into hamburger. We have to keep Jhoro with us and under wraps." He turned to Edna. "Sorry, doll. But you can't be trusted, either."

"Don't I know it, sugar pie. You better get tall, blond, and handsome out of my house. I'm close to stripping down and doing the hootchy-kootchy for him, and nobody wants to see that, not even me." She glared at Meaghan, eyes narrowed. "I'm also feeling like I want to tear your hair out, dear, you being so close to him. You ever taken him out for a test drive?"

"Edna!"

The old woman snorted. "Don't act all innocent with me. He's a short tiptoe away from your bed every night. You can't tell me you haven't thought about it."

Meaghan started to answer but stopped. Had she thought about it? And if not, why not? And why had everyone else been so giddy? "I fell into mommy-mode with him the moment he got here. But the witches . . . they went nuts about him. More nuts than you'd expect even for a guy this handsome."

Owen nodded. "I see what you're getting at. Maybe there was some magic at work before Marnie's charm was cast."

"Exactly. I found a trio of witches in my kitchen yesterday, watching him and they were mesmerized. Then Marnie came in and he kissed her. I thought the witches were gonna blast them both into cat chow, but then he smiled at them, and the witches sighed and smiled back. They didn't even notice I was there until Jhoro saw me, and the looks I got when he hugged me made me very glad to be impervious."

Owen took a long look at Jhoro. "Maybe that's why Marnie's spell went wrong. Somebody else took a shot at him first. So, what do we do next?"

"Find Marnie," Meaghan said. "Even if she's still alive, the Order hates witches and there's a lot of ways they can hurt her short of killing her."

"So where do we look?"

"City hall's a good bet. We know there are wizards there."

Sid rejoined the conversation. "There's also a lot of broken glass, and Jamie manifesting big poltergeist activity. We need to get him back, too."

Jamie. Meaghan had been so distracted by all this other crap she hadn't had time to worry about him. She felt a bloom of panic in her gut. "I know. But I don't think we can do that until we get everybody's head clear. I need Natalie in her right mind."

"But we can't shut this mess down without Marnie," Owen reminded her. "And if she's with the wizards, we're going to have to deal with Jamie, ready or not."

Everyone was looking at her, waiting for her to figure out what to do next. What she really wanted to do was crawl into bed and sleep for twelve hours. She wanted to hide. Instead, she took a deep breath and tried to ignore her fear.

"Okay," Meaghan said. "We have to treat this as the same problem then, but I'm not leading us into city hall blind. We need to talk to Finn—if the thing Jhoro encountered really was him—and see if he knows anything. If Finn's a ghost, Annie's our best bet. She hates Jhoro at the moment because she thinks he's trying to steal Russ, but on the plus side, she can't hurt him with magic."

"How do we get her here?" Sid asked.

Meaghan stared at him.

"Oh, no. I'm not going back in that house with the love-crazy witch, the jealous cop, and your sexually confused brother. Russ kept asking me how to be gay. How should I know, I told him. Troon don't think that way. Gay, straight, male, female—those kind of labels are a human thing."

Meaghan sighed and pulled out her phone. "Fine. Let's do it this way."

Russ picked up immediately. "Where are you?" he hissed. "Natalie keeps threatening to hex me if I don't give up Jhoro. I keep telling her it's not my fault, I was born this way, but she won't listen."

"You weren't born this way, Russ. You didn't even wake up this way. Now, shut up and put Annie on the phone."

Russ sighed. "I know she's hurt, but I can't pretend to be something I'm not."

"Whatever. Put her on the phone."

"What?" Annie snapped at her. "Your brother's going to get hexed by Natalie and it will serve him right. Lying rat bastard pretending to like girls."

"He's already hexed," Meaghan said. "As are you and Natalie and Brian. I need you to get your shit together, like you did getting us out of city hall. Come over to Edna's house. We need your help."

"Should I bring Russ before Natalie turns him into something? Why does he keep calling her 'sis'?"

"I have no idea," Meaghan lied. "Leave him there. Tell him I need your help and you'll be back soon. Then get over here."

She called Natalie's phone next. "Don't hex Russ," Meaghan said before Natalie could say hello. "Or Brian."

"Like I'd waste the magic on either of *them*. What about Betty Bleach?"

"Annie's leaving. When she's gone, go lock yourself in Jhoro's room and leave the boys alone."

"Don't let her hurt Jhoro," Natalie said.

"I won't." On impulse, Meaghan added, "And put up a barrier around the house. Nobody gets in, nobody gets out."

"But what if Jhoro comes home?"

Meaghan rolled her eyes. "If he shows up, you can let him in. But we need to keep you safe from the wizards, okay?"

"All right. Bring him home safe, okay? I can't live without him."

Meaghan slapped her hand quietly against her forehead. "I promise. Now do what I asked you."

She ended the call and heard a couple of gentle knocks on the screen door. "Wait here," she said to the others. "Let me head her off."

Annie had changed into a pair of Russ's jeans and one of his T-shirts. "Boyfriend jeans," she said with a wan smile. "A girl can still hope, right? That's not too pathetic, is it?"

Meaghan pulled her into a quick hug. "It's not pathetic at all. Trust me. You can do more than hope. As soon as this thing is over, you'll be the only one Russ has eyes for, I promise."

"You sure?"

"Absolutely. But until then, I need you to be the strong, sensible woman you were getting us out of city hall. There's somebody here you aren't going to want to see."

Annie stepped back. "*Him?* That yellow-haired, over-sexed, man stealer? Here to gloat?"

Meaghan shook her head. "No, not to gloat."

Jhoro stepped into the hallway. Meaghan grabbed Annie before she could lunge at him.

But Annie merely gazed at him, taking in his scratched arms, his muddy clothes, and his tear-swollen eyes. "He's been crying?"

"Yes," Meaghan said. "This is what Marnie's spell did to him. Or maybe it's not even the spell. He's grieving for someone he lost when Fahraya was destroyed."

Annie nodded, her rage spent. "The guy with the dark hair. The one buried in the forest." She stared at the space around him. "But it's not only him he's crying for. There are others here with him. He's grieving for all of it."

Please let it be this easy. "Finn—the guy with dark hair. Is he here?"

Annie shook her head. "No. These aren't ghosts I'm seeing. They're . . . memories? I've never seen anything like this. It's like his memories are so strong, he's manifesting them." She shivered.

"Still mad at him?"

"God, no. There's no room in there for Russ. Or Natalie, or anybody else." She nodded. "I can feel the hex now. I still feel jealous, but it's . . . I can feel it isn't real." Now her eyes filled with tears. She opened her arms. "Come here."

Jhoro let her hug him.

Meaghan drew in a sharp breath waiting to see what would happen.

After a few moments, Annie patted him on the arm, stepped away, and dug a tissue out of her pocket. "Waaah. Now he's got me going. I'm usually only a little empathic, but he's radiating grief like a forest fire. I feel like the world just ended."

"Like it did for him. You aren't going to get all mushy about him instead, are you?"

Annie shook her head. "No. Not now."

Meaghan sagged against the wall. "That's a relief. You think seeing him like this would be enough to break the spell for Natalie?"

"I don't think so. I'm . . . like I said, something about him is amping my psychic radar off the charts. I haven't been this empathic since I was a kid. And even with that, I can still feel the spell nibbling at me, trying to find a way in. Have you found Marnie yet?"

"No, but we think the wizards took her. At least that's what something that looked like Finn told Jhoro."

"And if it was Finn, you need me to see if I can talk to him."

Meaghan nodded. "It's not a great plan, but right now it's all I got."

CHAPTER TWENTY-THREE

OWEN'S SLEEK BMW convertible was too small to carry them all, so they commandeered Edna's enormous Crown Victoria. Sid and Jhoro didn't know how to drive and Owen could only drive with the adaptive equipment he had in his own car. That left Meaghan and Annie, but Meaghan felt so exhausted she wasn't sure she'd be safe behind the wheel. She climbed into the backseat with Jhoro and Sid, leaving Owen and Annie to navigate.

Jhoro was big and warm and solid next to her. She put her head on his shoulder and said, "Let me shut my eyes for a minute."

When Meaghan woke up, she found herself alone in the car. She looked out the window for the others, but couldn't see anyone. Trees crowded around the small clearing where the car was parked. She vaguely recognized her surroundings, but it definitely wasn't the clearing where Finn was buried.

Then she saw a shimmer on the other side of the clearing

and within it a distant figure walking across a barren plain. That's why the place looked familiar. She wasn't awake. She was dreaming. Someone from the other side wanted to chat.

She stepped out of the car. While she hoped to see her father, she wasn't surprised when the figure resolved into a young man with dark brown dreadlocks. And wings.

Finn.

He smiled and raised his hand. "It's good to see you again."

"You speak English?"

"No. Is that what you're hearing? I'm speaking Fahrayan."

"But I'm hearing English."

"Yet I hear you speak Fahrayan. Even without the requisite number of vocal cords."

"Curious," Meaghan said.

"Not really," he said in a soft voice. "Death tends to erase such differences. We aren't really speaking to each other in any case. This is happening in a dream."

"Yes, I'm aware. Which means you don't have a lot of time to say what you've come to say."

He shook his head. "No. Is he well?"

Meaghan knew he meant Jhoro. "At the moment, no, not particularly, but I'm not sure that's a bad thing. Ignoring grief only makes it worse. As much as he hurts now, he'll be better for it."

"You take good care of him. Like a mother. Thank you."

"You miss him."

Finn nodded. "They say that passes, but it hasn't yet."

"I'm so sorry you had to die."

He shrugged. "It was my time. Nothing could change that."

"It must be hard to see him with Marnie."

"Unexpected, certainly." Finn smiled for a moment, then

grew serious again. "But death takes all that away. Resentment, jealousy, disappointment—it all fades."

"All of it?"

"Everything but the love. The love stays." He looked away, his face sad. "The love stays." He turned his attention back to Meaghan. "There isn't much time. You have questions to ask."

"You saw the wizards take Marnie?"

Finn nodded. "I did."

"Do you know why?"

"A sacrifice. To bring something evil into this world."

Meaghan frowned. "Jamie's not the sacrifice?"

"No, he's the conduit."

"So, the Order isn't going to kill him?"

Finn shook his head. "They don't need to. He won't survive their passage."

"Whose passage? The Order?"

"No. The wizards serve what's coming."

"That thing inside V'hren?" Meaghan shuddered involuntarily.

"No. Things long trapped that want to break free."

She waited for him to say more. *I don't have time to play twenty questions.* When Finn failed to fill the silence, she sighed and asked, "Trapped where? How?"

"A place between the worlds."

"Where that thing inside V'hren went? Is he one of them?"

"He serves them, but he's only a shadow of his masters."

Meaghan felt a stab of fear. "So these things are worse?"

Finn nodded. "Much worse."

She shuddered again. Her first encounter with the Power, when she'd had her drug-induced psychic skills, had been bad enough. "So do those sigils they carved into Jamie summon them?"

"They don't need to be summoned. They've been waiting for millennia. But they need a way in. The sigils are the spell needed to open the way."

"But why now? And why Jamie?"

"The fulfillment of a prophecy."

Meaghan scowled. "Prophecy is nothing more than hindsight and good guessing. I don't believe in prophecy."

Finn smiled. "As was prophesied. Prophecies are tricky things, though. Your father told me to tell you to use your head and find the . . . loopholes? Am I saying that correctly?"

Now Meaghan smiled. "Good old Dad. Once a lawyer, always a lawyer. Yeah, you're saying it correctly."

A prophecy, she thought. Great. More cryptic, mystic nonsense. She didn't bother to ask him the details. He'd merely smile enigmatically and tell her he couldn't talk about it. "You see my father a lot?"

Finn didn't disappoint her. "I only spoke with him once, not long after I died. I can't really tell you more than that."

"Of course you can't. Any suggestions on how to get Marnie back?"

"Help is coming. But you have work to do before it arrives."

"Help from where?"

Finn looked over his shoulder and then turned back to Meaghan. "My time is up. I wish I could tell you more, but . . ." He shrugged.

"Yeah, I know. No peeking beyond the veil. That would make it too easy."

"Keep him safe," Finn said.

The dream dissolved into the sound of gentle tapping.

Meaghan jerked awake and saw a face smiling at her through the car window.

A woman about Meaghan's age, with wild black curls threaded with a few white hairs, stood outside the car. Meaghan, still fuzzy with sleep, gazed at her, confused. Where the hell was she?

Annie appeared behind the woman and waved.

Meaghan opened the door and climbed out of the backseat.

They were in the clearing where Finn was buried. Owen and Sid stood on either side of Jhoro, who sat by the stone at the head of the grave with his face in his hands. Sid had his small, blue hand on Jhoro's shoulder.

"No luck," Annie said. "There's no sign of him." She gestured at the woman with the curly hair. "This is Ruth Greene. Ruth, meet Meaghan."

Meaghan stared a moment, her head still fuzzy with sleep. "Sorry," she finally said. "I fell asleep and I'm not waking up very quickly." She didn't want to say anything about her dream until she knew who this woman was. "Um, Ruth, I don't mean to be rude, but . . . who are you and why are you here?"

"Owen didn't tell you?" Ruth sighed. "He told me you knew all about us. I'm here to help you with the Fahrayans. Owen didn't tell you any of this?"

That was fast. But Finn had also said they had work to do before the help arrived, so he probably hadn't been talking about Ruth Greene.

"He gave me a proposal this morning, but I haven't had a chance to read it. You know what's going on here?"

"Love is in the air, and it's starting to stink. There's a missing witch?"

"Yeah," Meaghan said. "Sorry to be so blunt, but who are you? Who do you work for?"

Ruth shrugged. "It's complicated."

"Simplify it for me."

"Basically I work for an agency that deals with magical . . . stuff."

"Seriously? Is this a government agency? The feds are trying to hide the existence of magic?"

Ruth rolled her eyes. "Please. You don't believe in that *X-Files* crap, do you?"

"I've worked in the public sector for over twenty years. What do you think?"

"I think you know how rare it is for government to get its shit together enough to pull off a competent conspiracy."

"So who do you work for?"

"It kind of depends on who you ask. Everybody thinks we work for the other guy."

"You're double dipping?"

"More like quadruple dipping. We get funding from several levels of government under several different names."

Meaghan raised an eyebrow. "Fraud?"

Ruth laughed. "Big time. But what else can we do? It's not like we can submit budget requests for what we really do."

Despite everything else going on, Meaghan was fascinated. "You know, that sounds a lot like a government conspiracy."

"Ha! You got me. But there's only five of us so it's a lot easier to pull off. And we're conspiring to con the government, so the conspiracy's on the other foot." She squinted a moment. "Or something like that. But we're small potatoes, so we get away with it."

"So, no super-secret lairs or fancy equipment?"

"Like what? Invisible flying aircraft carriers?" Ruth snorted and shook her head, her dark curls bouncing. "I should have such a budget." She pointed over her shoulder with her thumb to a blue minivan parked on the other side of the clearing. "We could barely afford the magic bus."

Meaghan wondered if she was still dreaming. "So, what do the governments funding you think you're doing?"

"Weather-stripping. Promoting energy efficiency through better use of weather-stripping. Research, advocacy, and weatherization grant programs."

"Do you really do that?"

"Hell, no. We tried to pick something that sounds vaguely useful and really boring at the same time. You should see how quick a legislator's eyes glaze over when you start talking about R-values."

Meaghan nodded. "So they rush you along and approve whatever you ask for as long as you don't ask for too much."

"And then they can say they voted for a conservation program that benefits homeowners, but not so much that they can be accused of being enviro-bunnies." She laughed. "You know the drill. But it looks like you got bigger problems at the moment."

Annie finally broke in. "Ruth didn't get into town until after the spell was cast so she doesn't seem to be affected."

"Also, I like girls," Ruth said. "Let's get that out there right from the start. So you know you don't need to worry about me."

Meaghan raised an eyebrow. "We all thought Jhoro liked boys and look how that worked out."

Ruth shrugged. "It's a continuum, they say. He's pretty, I'll grant you, but he's got the wrong parts for me. I prefer indoor plumbing. I don't like . . . big hoses lying on the porch. Doesn't look right to me."

Meaghan had no response to that. "So, um, Ruth, are any more of your people here?"

"My wizard should be here soon. Not evil, by the way."

"Is Owen part of the team?"

"More like an angel investor. On our own, we don't have the resources to help relocate five hundred people. But we do have the expertise. Owen bankrolls us from time to time."

"And how did you know to come here?"

"Owen called me. Led me in. The magic bus has some nifty upgrades. Kind of a magic-based GPS capability. I'd be lost in a second if I had to find my way around in these woods on my own."

"Hang on a sec," Meaghan said. "I'll be right back." She walked over to Finn's grave. "Owen, is she who she says she is? You know her?"

Owen nodded.

"Why ask him?" Sid's tone was petulant. "I know her, too. I've worked with her. She's legit."

Meaghan—surprised—frowned at him. "A fact you've managed not to mention until right now despite knowing how badly we need help with the Fahrayans. I think you and I need to have a talk. About prophesies."

Sid's eyes widened. "How do you know about that?"

Meaghan tilted her head toward the grave. "Had a chat with a dead man."

CHAPTER TWENTY-FOUR

MEAGHAN RETURNED TO the car. "Ruth, have you been over to see the Fahrayans yet?"

"I stopped by. I was supposed to meet Sid there. But he was gone and I didn't see anybody else."

So that's what he was doing at John's, the little shit. Secrets from Owen she could live with. But Sid? He was supposed to be helping her, not hiding things from her.

Meaghan took a deep breath. Sid might be annoying at times, but she couldn't believe he'd betray her. If he was hiding stuff, he must have a reason, but she didn't have time right now to pry it out of him.

For the moment, she'd let it go. "The Fahrayans weren't around?"

Ruth grinned. "Oh, they were around, but they were all . . . busy."

Meaghan was sure she didn't want the answer, but asked anyway. "Busy doing what?"

"Judging by the sounds, busy making little Fahrayans."

"Oh, God. No jealous rages? No violence?"

Sid had finally wandered over. "Fahrayans don't mix sex with violence like humans do. They can't. Or at least they couldn't."

Ruth nodded. "The second jaw. Right."

"Fahrayan men," Sid said, with a giggle, "have a special incentive not to skimp on the foreplay. Fahrayan men are dynamite in the sack because they have to be. Or," he sliced one small blue hand through the air, "thwack. Hello, Mr. Pain." He shrugged. "At least that's how it used to be, and I suspect the ladies have not bothered to inform the menfolk about their new plumbing."

Meaghan shut her eyes and shook her head. The nap hadn't refreshed her. It had only made her feel punchier. "Do I want to know? About any of this?"

He sighed. "Meggy, if you would head home and unclench, John would be happy to show you some of those fancy moves."

She felt the blood rush to her cheeks. "Sid, I swear to God, if you don't drop this, I'm going to drop-kick you all the way back to Troon. What the hell are we talking about? What's the second jaw?"

Ruth gave Sid a look. "Let me handle this one, okay?"

Sid shrugged and walked away.

"See, here's the thing. Fahraya is—sorry, *was*—a tiny little place, right?"

Meaghan nodded.

"So, overpopulation would be a big problem if procreation hadn't been very tightly controlled."

"Yeah. John said something about how Jhoro and Finn being together let another couple have a second baby."

"Exactly. A couple of the things I really like about Fahrayans. All their kids were wanted and nobody got fussed about same-sex relationships."

Meaghan frowned. Considering how brutal the Fahrayans could be, she suspected a very dark cloud surrounding at least one of those silver linings. "So, there's a lottery or something?"

"Yeah. That's where John came from. His parents won the baby lottery and got to have a second kid."

"I thought it was because his father was the king."

"Nah. No special privileges on procreation even for the bigwigs."

"But even the best birth control can go wrong. What happened to the accidental babies? Nothing good, I suspect."

Ruth grinned. "There were no accidents. Truly, every kid was wanted."

"No accidents? Give me a break. How is that possible?"

"Magically induced adaptation happens a whole lot faster than natural selection. And in this case, it was way more precise."

A realization stirred in the back of Meaghan's mind. "The second jaw?" She burst out laughing. "Fahrayan women had an extra set of teeth, down *there*?"

"Not teeth. A bony protuberance about halfway in they could shut at will. Forcefully, if need be."

Meaghan shook her head. "The ultimate barrier method."

"That, plus—you remember a little while back that idiot politician who claimed that women's bodies can shut down conception during rape?"

Meaghan snorted. "Yeah. What a moron."

"Well, Fahrayan women can . . . *could* do exactly that. They could ovulate at will, as well as flush their systems with hormones to neutralize conception. Very useful adaptations for a world that couldn't support more than a thousand people. The jaw was an additional form of contraception. Plus, it didn't take Fahrayan women long to learn that it was also an effective male behavior modification tool."

Meaghan let that one sink in. "No . . . rape? At least not intercourse?"

"No sexual violence of any kind. Because of the critical need to control population, the taboos against forcing sex were so deeply ingrained in their culture that it was nearly unthinkable, with either gender, and regardless of the sex act involved. And for the rare few who tried, well . . . you know how fierce Fahrayans are."

"An attacker would have to get past the stone knife and killer instincts before the second jaw even became an issue." Meaghan shook her head. "Wow. I can barely wrap my brain around that. How do you know so much about this?"

"Alex, our anthropologist. He's a little obsessed with them to be honest. The only reason he's not here now is because he's out in the field somewhere. In Asia. I think. He never tells me where he goes until he wants me to reimburse him for his expenses."

Meaghan nodded. At least she could stop worrying about the Fahrayans for the moment. It was the rest of the town that was in trouble. And Jamie. How was she going to save Jamie this time? She could feel her alertness beginning to slip away again, oblivion preferable to panic. "So, Ruth, you mentioned a wizard. Where do we find him?"

Ruth glanced at her watch. "Probably at your house by now."

"Then that's where we need to go. Would you take Sid with you? If he starts in again about my sex life, I'm gonna kill him."

Ruth snorted with laughter. "Gladly." She put her fingers in her mouth and whistled loudly. "Yo! Time to head out. Mr. Blue, you're with me."

"Where are we going?" Owen called.

"My house," Meaghan called back.

Owen gave her a skeptical look. "All of us?"

"All of us. I don't have time to chaperone the junior prom. If there's trouble, you can take Jhoro back to Edna's."

"Eliot can help keep the peace," Ruth said to Meaghan.

"Eliot's your wizard?"

"Yup. Nice guy, but scary when he needs to be. Very powerful. Vodun background."

Meaghan looked at her blankly.

"You know," Ruth said. "Voodoo?"

"Oh, great. My brother can lecture him about why he should sacrifice only free-range chickens."

Ruth chuckled. "I wouldn't say that in front of him. He's a little sensitive about the . . . um . . . inaccurate cultural stereotypes associated with his training. And whatever you do, don't mention zombies."

"Other than me? I feel like a walking corpse right now. I gotta get some more coffee. Okay, no zombies. You know how to get to my house?"

"It's programmed into the magical GPS." Ruth motioned to Sid to follow her.

Owen and Annie led Jhoro to the big Crown Vic, followed by Meaghan. Annie drove them home in silence. Meaghan, her head on Jhoro's shoulder, again drifted off as soon as the car started. After what felt like a moment, she jerked awake as the car came to a stop in front of her house. Ruth pulled in right behind them.

A slender man of medium height, his arms folded across his chest, leaned against the rear bumper of Brian's police cruiser, still parked in Meaghan's driveway. Simply but elegantly clad in tailored tan trousers and a white collared shirt that accentuated the dark caramel of his skin, he smiled when he saw Ruth climb out of the minivan.

"I'm trying not to get a complex about this, Ruthie." He patted the police car. "You invite me to this lily-white town and this is what's waiting for me?"

Ruth smirked. "Like it? It's been kind of a weird day around here."

"No kidding. I couldn't get any closer to the house because of the spell wall somebody put up. There's so much sexual energy flying through the air in this town that it's about to start raining Viagra.

Meaghan frowned. "You didn't run into any magical barriers trying to get into town?"

He shook his head. "Was I supposed to? Trying to keep wizards out?"

Meaghan nodded. "Yeah. No offense."

The man grinned. "None taken. I heard you had some wizard trouble a little while back, but whatever you had up is gone. Those Order freaks are crawling all over the city hall building." He grinned broadly. "But whomever or whatever's guarding it against them is kicking ass quite effectively. You know how much I enjoy watching them get their asses kicked."

Meaghan stepped forward. "Guarding it? You mean the wizards aren't holding it?"

"Heh. Not even close."

"Do you have any idea what's in there?"

"Something with some big power. And it's pissed off at the Order in a major way."

Relief swept through Meaghan. "They don't have him. Annie, did you hear that? They don't have Jamie. He's keeping them out." She turned back to the man. "That's the best news I've heard all day. I'm Meaghan, by the way."

The man smiled. "I know who you are. You've been upsetting magical folks big time." He held out his hand. "Eliot Milton. Government wizard."

Meaghan shook his hand. "Is that your official title?"

He laughed. "No. It's not. Officially, I'm a community grant implementation specialist. Ruthie told you about us?"

Meaghan nodded. "Yeah, but I don't think you're here to inspect the weather-stripping."

"All joking aside," Eliot said. "We better get indoors. I've been attracting some attention from the neighbors." He gestured toward Edna's house. "We're being watched."

Meaghan shook her head. "That's Edna. She gets bored. And she only has eyes for him right now." She pointed at Jhoro who now stood next to her, staring at his feet. "Love charm gone wrong."

"No kidding. He's the object of affection?" Eliot scrutinized him. "He looks awful. Why so sad?"

"Misses his dead boyfriend," Ruth said. "Despite his live girlfriend's best magical efforts. But the results aren't consistent. Some people love him, some people hate him, some people are getting busy with whoever's handy. The girlfriend's missing by the way. Last we heard the Order has her. It might get dicey inside. Be ready."

"Please tell me whoever drove this here," he patted the police car again, "doesn't have a gun."

"He doesn't have a gun," Meaghan said. "I locked it up. My father had a gun cabinet up in the attic, but my brother got rid of it right after the funeral. But my brother does have high-grade professional cookware."

Eliot looked puzzled. "Cookware?"

"I beat up an Order wizard with a saucepan back in June."

Eliot grinned. "Oh, I'm gonna like working with you. You got style.

CHAPTER TWENTY-FIVE

UNAFFECTED BY NATALIE'S barrier spell, Meaghan banged on the front door and shouted, "Hey, it's me. I'm coming in."

Cautiously, she stuck her head in the front door, then entered the hallway.

Brian sprawled on the living room sofa, staring empty eyed at the ceiling.

"Where's Natalie?" Meaghan asked.

"In love with another man," Brian said. "Forever out of my reach."

Meaghan rolled her eyes. "I meant geographically. Is she upstairs?"

"I dunno." Brian put his arm over his eyes. "She's not with me. That's all I know. She'll never be with me."

"Oh, God. Where's Russ?"

"Kitchen."

Meaghan found him at the table, surrounded by books.

"Hi," he said, not looking up. "I've found some great ideas in these old cookbooks of Mom's."

"Ideas for what?"

"The wedding."

"Whose wedding?" Meaghan asked, sure she wouldn't like the answer.

"Well, mine and Jhoro's, of course."

"Of course. Silly me."

Russ looked up at her, beaming. "I think I'm finally getting it right this time. This will be the most beautiful gay wedding anyone's ever seen."

"Russ. You can't have a gay wedding."

"Why not?"

She threw up her hands in frustration. "Because you're not gay. Where's Natalie?"

"Upstairs in your bedroom. With John. She's giving him relationship advice. About you."

Meaghan ran for the stairs. She heard Natalie's voice clearly through the open door. "She's scared she won't measure up. That you won't find her desirable."

She heard John groan. "How could she think that? I have been . . . desiring her all day."

"Did that potion help?"

Meaghan could practically hear him blush. "Uh . . . yes. Thank you. Things are . . . calmer down there. They will stay that way?"

"Yeah, it'll wear off in a day or so and normal function will come back. It's not good to be that way for too long, but we caught it in time."

Now Meaghan was blushing. "Natalie?" she called. "Would you come out here, please?"

She heard a loud thump and then John was standing in the hallway.

"Hi," he said. "You . . . hi."

Russ had been right. John looked great. His dark blue eyes were clear and bright. Every feature of his face seemed more sharply delineated, making him even more handsome than she remembered. And he was smiling. Not the shy smile he used to wear but an open grin that made the years drop away. It had only been eight weeks or so since she'd seen him, but the difference was striking.

"Hi," was all she could manage to say back. She couldn't take her eyes off him. *He looks like a god and I've been crawling through sub-basements.* She felt a moment of despair.

Natalie now appeared. "Did you find Jhoro?"

"Yeah," Meaghan said. She couldn't take her eyes off John. "He's outside."

Natalie tore down the hall.

"There's a bunch of people with him," Meaghan shouted after her. "Let them in, too." She turned her attention back to John. "I need to get downstairs. Before they all kill each other. You know what's going on, right?"

"Love spell," he said and then swept her up in his arms.

In addition to his reputed Fahrayan sexual skills, John was a great kisser. Meaghan felt a rush of heat through her body. Rational thought stopped, replaced by desire.

After a few moments, he broke away. "Woo. That's . . ." He looked puzzled a moment, shifted his leg, and then nodded. "That potion works. Good. I . . . I don't want to try to convince you to do something you don't want to do." He paused a moment and gave her a hopeful smile. "Yet?"

"Just hold me a minute. It's been a really weird couple of

days." Head spinning, she clung to him. Without any emotional prelude, she burst into tears. She couldn't hold them back any longer.

John held her close and let her cry. When she began to calm down a little, he scooped her up in his arms and carried her into the bedroom. He placed her gently on the bed, then stepped away.

"Oh, hell," she sniffled. "Get me the box of tissues from the bathroom, will you?" She pulled herself up into a sitting position. "And then get over here and sit with me. Please?"

He beamed at her and ducked into the bathroom. A moment later, he reappeared with the tissue box. Meaghan plumped up the pillows against the headboard and leaned back, patting the bed next to her.

John snuggled in beside her. He held his arm out and she curled up against his chest. She grabbed a tissue from the box and blew her nose.

"I guess I should be grateful for this stupid love spell," Meaghan said. "I must look like crap. I didn't sleep last night, and I had to crawl through a mucky tunnel, and my nose is all runny and . . ."

"You look beautiful."

"That's the magic talking."

"Nah. I always think that. The magic has been doing . . . other things to me." He laughed and his cheeks grew pink. "You heard me talking to Natalie?"

Meaghan giggled, feeling a bit better. "Yeah, I think I got the general idea."

"I'm better now. Tell me what is happening before we go downstairs."

"Did Natalie tell you about last night?"

John sighed. "All she talks about is Jhoro. And my . . . problem. I didn't know there was anything between them. He likes men."

Meaghan snorted. "Turns out he likes everybody. But there's nothing between him and Natalie. It's Marnie he's been sleeping with. She's the one who cast the love spell to try to get him to forget Finn and love her instead."

"The witch who cuts hair? Did it work?"

"Yeah, the witch who cuts hair. And no, it didn't work. At least not the way she wanted. He's so heartsick over Finn, he's falling apart."

"Good. He needs to feel his pain and get past it. Or he'll end up like me. Drinking his life away for years and years." John pulled her closer. "I'm going to AA every day."

"Even today?"

"Morning meeting. I promised Terry."

"Is he your sponsor?"

John nodded. "Yeah. He's away from here today. He and his wife are on the motorcycle somewhere."

"Do I know him?"

"I don't know. He fixes things. Big guy, red hair, beard?"

Meaghan thought about it a moment. "He does repair work?"

"Yeah, whatever needs to be done."

Meaghan nodded. "I think I've seen him working around city hall."

"You'll see more of him soon. Terry and Steph—his wife—they bought the house across the street a couple of weeks ago. They move in when they get back from the motorcycle ride."

She felt warm and safe chatting like this with him, but

she had to stay focused. "Did Natalie tell you about Jamie? About last night?"

He stiffened. "What? What has happened?"

"You know he's been having a really hard time."

"I talk to Patrice all the time. She wants him to talk to me, but he won't. Those marks the wizards put on him, they frighten her."

"With good reason. He beat her up last night."

John sat upright and stared at Meaghan in shock. "He did *what*? Did he hurt her bad?"

"Black eye, cut lip, some bruises on her arms. But he hurt himself a lot worse. Do you know what a poltergeist is?"

John shook his head.

"It's a . . . like a ghost, but it's not. I don't know how to explain it. Basically, the stress of what happened, stress he's not dealing with, is causing him to throw stuff around with his mind. He's also breaking windows and setting things on fire."

"Does he mean to do this?"

"No. No, it's an involuntary reaction. We think it has something to do with the effects of city hall and those things they carved on him."

John buried his face in his hands. "My poor boy. I should have tried harder to make him talk to me."

Meaghan put her arm around John and held him. "It's not your fault. It's those damn wizards. Whatever it is they did to him."

"Where is he now?"

"They took him to the hospital in Williamsport."

John tried to stand up. "My truck's outside. Let's go."

She pulled him back down. "He's not there anymore.

He's in city hall. But there's good news. At least I think it's good. We thought the wizards were keeping him there, that they had control of him. They don't. He's keeping them out. He's fighting them. And doing a really good job of it, from what I've heard."

"We need to get to him."

"Yeah," Meaghan said. "I agree with you. But first we have to get everybody's head straight and see if we can confirm that Jamie's . . ."

"Still Jamie," John said.

Meaghan nodded. She was so exhausted she could barely think straight.

He brushed his hand across her cheek, worry in his eyes. "You need to rest. Stay here. I'll go downstairs and find out what we need to do."

"I don't have time to—"

"Only a nap," he said. "I'll wake you before too long." He smiled at her. "Trust me."

CHAPTER TWENTY-SIX

WHEN MEAGHAN WOKE, the room was dark. She fumbled for the clock. It was after ten. She'd been asleep for almost six hours.

She stretched, climbed out of bed, and went into the bathroom, still groggy but feeling better.

The seat was up and she nearly fell into the toilet. Swearing, she put the seat back down where it belonged. It had been so long since she'd shared a bathroom with a man she never checked anymore.

No nightmares for once. This time Meaghan could only remember one dream. Featuring John. She felt her cheeks grow hot. This time they were in the backseat of Edna's Crown Vic, steaming up the windows.

Good thing he didn't try to wake me up then, she thought. *So much for only a nap. That liar.*

Unless he hadn't been able to get back upstairs.

Suddenly wide awake, Meaghan made her way with care

to the door and eased it open. There was a glow of light coming from the stairs and the murmur of voices. No yelling. It sounded like a convivial family gathering.

Meaghan crept down the hall. She heard Russ laughing and then Natalie joined in. Whatever was going on, it didn't sound like a crisis. She exhaled the breath she'd been holding.

She stopped in the hallway bathroom and looked in the mirror with a grimace. With wet hands, she patted her hair down a little, then gave up. She followed it with a swish of mouthwash. She'd have to take John at his word that he always found her beautiful because this was as good as things were going to get under the circumstances.

Maybe they sorted everything out while I was asleep. Even as she thought it, Meaghan realized how unlikely that was. But she felt clearer and stronger. Time to find out what had actually happened.

"There's our Sleeping Beauty," Russ cooed when she walked into the kitchen. The table normally sat six, but Russ had brought in folding chairs from the garage and somehow squeezed ten people around it. And they all seemed to be getting along with each other. Even Jhoro was smiling.

Meaghan made eleven. "What's going on?"

Russ, who was sitting next to John, stood up and offered her his chair. "Dinner. I'll get you a plate."

"Thanks, but I meant what's going on with everything else?"

"Sit down and we'll tell you." Russ moved to the stove.

Meaghan took John's hand. "You said you'd wake me up."

John smiled. "I lied."

Meaghan looked around the table. Several people had

wine glasses in front of them. Dropping her voice, she said, "You okay with the drinking going on?"

"So far. But I never liked wine that much. If they start drinking gin, we may have a problem." He grinned. "Don't worry. If it gets bad I can call Terry."

She nodded. Addressing the full group, Meaghan said, "So, tell me what's going on."

"I'll go first," Russ said. "You were right. I'm not gay."

Everybody laughed.

"How'd you figure that out?" Meaghan asked.

"I helped him with that," Ruth said. "First I asked him, 'Have you had sex with men?' and he said no. Then I asked him, 'Do you want to have sex with men?' and he said no. And then I said, 'Honey, you're not gay. It's not like catching a cold or deciding to be a vegetarian.'"

Everybody laughed again, Russ the loudest.

Russ nodded. "That was all I needed to hear."

"So, is the spell gone?" Meaghan asked.

"No," Russ said. "It's still there, but we all can kind of see around it now. Something Eliot did. I still think Jhoro's a total hottie, but in a straight, aesthetic sort of way. I can appreciate him without . . . you know . . . wanting to do him."

He brought Meaghan's dinner to her—one of her favorites, meatloaf with bacon on top—and then nudged Annie. "Move over, cutie. Let me get a cheek in."

Annie giggled while Russ squeezed in next to her on the chair. "Good thing you got such a tight little bottom, mister."

"The spell's still working," Eliot said, "but, around here at least, it's more appropriately directed."

Meaghan nodded. "Annie, if he asks you to marry him, say no. He's been busy planning his big gay wedding."

Now Brian laughed the loudest, then choked on his wine. Jhoro reached over and thumped him on the back. Natalie was sitting on the opposite side of the table. She wasn't laughing, but she wasn't giving Brian the stink eye or Jhoro the come-hither looks anymore, either.

"Thanks," Brian said to Jhoro when he finally caught his breath. "Russ wanted me to be best man. I said only if I could kick the other groom's ass first." Brian looked at Meaghan, now serious. "Thank you for taking my gun away. This could have ended very badly."

"You're welcome. What about Marnie and Jamie?"

Eliot shook his head. "No word on your lost witch yet. I can . . . *feel* her out there somewhere, but I can't get a fix on her."

"Can you tell if she's okay?"

Eliot's face screwed up in frustration. "She's alive. I know that. But, there's . . . *something* blocking the signal."

Meaghan felt a cold lump in her gut. "Something that feels wrong."

"Yeah," Eliot said, nodding. "I wish could be more precise than that, but yeah."

"You're not close enough to it," Meaghan said, glancing at Sid. "The Order calls it the Power."

If it was possible for someone with royal blue skin to turn pale, Sid managed it.

John's eyes narrowed. He gripped Meaghan's hand tighter. "That thing that took my brother. Now it wants my son."

Meaghan pushed her plate away, her appetite gone. "The Power is merely the warm-up act. It works for things that are even worse that are trying to get into our world. Finn told me in a dream I had when I fell asleep in the car out in the forest. He said Marnie's the sacrifice and Jamie's the conduit."

At the sound of Finn's name, Jhoro perked up. He leaned over to Sid, who whispered something to him. Jhoro nodded, his smile gone.

"Why didn't you tell us this earlier?" Natalie sounded more like herself than she had all day.

"I didn't get the chance. I woke up and there were new people and then we got home and . . . I was so tired I couldn't think straight."

"You weren't the only one not thinking straight." Natalie stared down at her plate, obviously embarrassed. "Can you think straight now?"

Meaghan nodded. "What do we know about Jamie? Is he . . . still Jamie?"

John smiled. "That's the best news. We spoke with him."

"You . . . How the hell did you do that?" Meaghan glanced at Eliot. "Some kind of spell?"

Natalie shook her head. "We called him. On the phone." She looked sheepish. "The cell service was all screwed up from the magic even if he had his phone, which he doesn't, but I was so . . ."—she rolled her eyes—"*stupid* it never occurred to me to try the landline."

"Where did you find him?"

"It took a while, but he's in Emily's office. I called around the building until I got lucky. He recognized the number on the caller ID and picked up."

"What's he doing in there?" Meaghan asked.

"Emily has so many protection spells around her office that when he blew the windows on his way into the building, her windows stayed intact. Plus she's got a nice comfy sofa in there." Natalie laughed. "He knows how much it will piss her off when this is all over, which amuses him."

"But last night . . ." Meaghan shook her head. "You didn't see him. He was out of his mind with fear. Suicidal. He beat himself up way worse than he did Patrice. What changed?"

"They shot him up with lorazepam," Eliot said. "It's commonly used in hospital settings for short-term treatment of severe anxiety, delirium, aggression—for short-term sedation. It usually makes the patient dopey, but in rare cases, it can have paradoxical reactions."

"Meaning even more anxiety and aggression?" Meaghan asked.

"Anxiety, aggression, loss of impulse control, restlessness, violence, manic behavior . . ."

"How's it affecting Jamie?"

Eliot grimaced. "In Jamie's case . . . magic and pharmaceuticals don't mix well. The magic they're trying to manipulate him with amped up some of the drug's paradoxical effects and—"

"He's freaking Superman," Russ said. "Psycho-kinetically, at least. And he's really—"

"Tweaky," Natalie finished.

"Tweaky?" Meaghan asked.

"Speedy," Brian said. "You know. Like a jackrabbit on meth. A really talkative jackrabbit on meth."

Meaghan nodded. "I'm getting a mental picture. But is he okay? How long will this drug keep working and how long can he handle its effects?"

Eliot frowned. "He's okay for now. On his way out of the hospital, he used his brand new superpowers to bust into the drug room and grab a couple of bottles and some syringes. I told him what I knew about dosage, although who knows how the magic will affect that. But he can't keep going at this pace for more than a couple of days. Even a young man's heart will falter under too much strain."

"So we can't wait out the Order," Meaghan said, feeling the worry rush back in. "And we still don't know how to neutralize those sigils in a way that won't eventually cause a heart attack. Or a drug overdose."

Eliot nodded. "The good news is the lorazepam seems to be interfering with the black magic—they aren't controlling him at the moment—but we need a better solution."

Owen finally spoke up. "I've got some feelers out to see if we can figure out what the Order's up to. They came for Jamie at the hospital and chased him all the way back into town."

"How'd he get back here?"

"Stole a car," Brian said.

"*Borrowed* a car," Natalie said, giving Brian a look.

He smiled at her. "Thanks for the clarification. Jamie borrowed a car."

"Why'd he pick city hall?" Meaghan asked.

"The poltergeist activity he'd been manifesting was a lot stronger in city hall," Annie said. "And he said a Fahrayan came to him in a vision and told him to get there as fast as he could. To make his stand."

"Finn?"

"Yeah," Russ said, glancing at Jhoro who was staring at his plate.

No one spoke for a long moment. Meaghan sighed. Everyone, she knew, was waiting for her to come up with a plan. *I'm the least powerful person here, but I'm supposed to have all the answers.*

"So," she finally said. "What's happening to the rest of the town, love spell wise?"

"Good question," Ruth said. "Anybody want to go for a drive around town and see what's happening?"

"Can we get near city hall without alerting the Order?"

Ruth nodded. "If we take the magic bus. Eliot's tricked it out with all kinds of protective magic. They'll only be able to detect us with their eyes, and to them, we'll look like harmless civilians. That might be our way into city hall. Somebody makes a distraction and I can pull up right—"

"Why don't we use the secret entrance?" Annie asked. "We'll go back in the way Meaghan and I got out."

"You are such a clever woman," Russ said, with a big grin on his face.

Not the tunnel. Meaghan tried not to cringe. The wizards would be preferable to that damn tunnel. "Let's go for a ride in the magic bus and see what's going on before we go busting into city hall. But first, I want to talk to Jamie."

Natalie handed her the phone. "Hit star sixty-nine. That will take you to Emily's office."

CHAPTER TWENTY-SEVEN

JAMIE PICKED UP on the second ring. "Nat?"

"It's Meaghan."

"Meaghan?" He took a ragged breath and said in a rush, "I'm sorry I've been such an asshole since we got back." Before she could say anything, he continued. "I never thanked you for saving me. You came and got me. You said you would and you did and I never said thanks because I was so busy feeling sorry for myself and it wasn't only you—"

"Breathe, okay? You're welcome. You're forgiven. It's all good."

He took another ragged breath. "No. It's not all good. I . . . how do I make things right with Patrice? After what I did to her?"

"You get better," Meaghan said, feeling her eyes fill with tears. The phone was corded—the only corded home phone Meaghan had seen in years—to better function in the presence of big magic. "Hang on a sec." The long cord stretched enough to let her move into the powder room in the hall and shut the door if she sat on the floor. "Okay."

"Where are you?" he asked. "It sounds like a party."

"Late dinner with a lot of people very relieved you aren't being screwed with further by our wizard friends."

"For now," he said. "I've still got this shit all over my chest and back and the things in my head aren't gone, only drowned out by this other shit in my head, which is loud, I gotta tell you." He took another breath. "Sorry. I know I'm talking really fast. Do you know where my family is?"

"Jamie, I'm not sure that's a good idea—"

"Agreed. It's better I don't know. I just want to make sure you do. Natalie said she'd talked to Patrice and she's safe and the kids are safe and they're all away from here." He paused a second, then plunged on. "How do I get them back? How do I fix this?"

"Honey, you get better."

"But we don't know what the sigils—"

"I'm not talking about the sigils. We'll figure that out. I'm talking about the trauma. I think you have PTSD."

"Oh, *that*," Jamie said.

"What do you mean 'oh, *that*'?"

"Well, I figured that would, you know, work itself out if I didn't have all this other shit to deal with."

"Like it worked itself out for your dad?"

"Yeah . . . but . . ." He sighed. "Shit. So I have to deal with that, too?"

"Well, yeah, dopey," Meaghan said with a small laugh. "What did you think? It's not the sigils and the energy vortex in your office that are causing you to go all Carrie-at-the-prom. It's the trauma."

He was silent for a long moment, then said, "Hang on. I've got wizard trouble."

She heard the phone clunk on Emily's desk and then Jamie shouting, "You want another gargoyle dropped on your heads? I got plenty more. See?" She heard a wrenching noise and a loud crash. "You aren't getting in here, assholes. Give it up."

He picked up the phone. "You there? Had to drop some masonry on them. Speaking of which, I sort of . . . blew up the solicitor's office."

Meaghan let that news sink in a moment. "Blew up how?"

"Uh, well, it's . . . kind of . . . gone. Not gone exactly, but there's a giant hole where my office used to be and your office isn't exactly round anymore. Or totally indoors. And the ceiling is on top of the floor. The beams are still there, I didn't get that crazy, but it's a mess. Sorry."

Her office. Meaghan loved her round office. She let herself feel a moment of grief before moving on. "We'll deal with it. And at least now I don't have to worry about finding you a new non-mystical office."

"Well, actually you do, along with everybody else . . . did you hear what I said?"

"Yes," Meaghan said. "But now I can get money from the council to rebuild the suite and we can design around the vortex and—"

"We have to plug the vortex. Even if it means I have to blow up the whole building. I'm the only thing standing between us and *them*. I think I'm some kind of key or password to access something really bad. I think that's why they wanted Emily to make me change in city hall. It triggered something. And why they came after me in the hospital.

They didn't count on me fighting back. And if they get past me . . . if it comes to it . . ."

She heard him take another ragged breath.

"They need me alive to make this work. If it comes to it, I'll bring the whole building down on top of us. Right now I think I'm strong enough to do it."

Meaghan's heart dropped. "Jamie, you can't."

"Yeah, I can, and I will if I have to. Did you feel like you had a choice when you came after me in Fahraya?"

"No." She gripped the phone tightly, knowing what she was about to say. "I knew I wouldn't be able to live with myself if I didn't bring you home or die trying."

"Same situation. If I don't keep these things out, none of us will live. None of us. Except these wizard shitheads who are trying to make this happen. Why the fuck is everybody in such a hurry for the world to end?"

Meaghan could hear the rising panic in his voice. "I don't know, honey."

"This isn't suicide talk like last night. I want to live."

"Then," Meaghan said, trying to hide her own panic, "let's put these bastards down. Is there a way you can . . ." She was about to ask him to commit murder. She took a deep breath. "Is there a way you can end them without ending yourself?"

"I almost killed one," he said. "They're easy enough if you get them one at time. But, then I thought what if he was like that kid they sent after you in June? Being used by remote control? What if I killed some abused kid who didn't choose to be here?"

The wizard Meaghan had vanquished with the saucepan had turned out to be a terrified, half-starved, twenty-year-old boy with no memory of how he'd gotten there. Caleb had spent almost his entire life with the Order, which had brutalized him along with other children in its control in order to feed their pain and fear to the Power.

Possessed by a powerful wizard, Caleb had broken into Meaghan's house and tried to hex her. When it didn't work, he was abandoned, bleeding on her kitchen floor. All it had taken was a little food and kindness to flip him to their side.

"Oh, God," Meaghan said. "You're right." Her mind was churning. They needed a plan. First things first, she decided. "Do you have any food? How long can you hold out?"

Jamie snorted. "There's enough junk food stashed in the council break room to open a minimart. I can hold out for a week if I have to."

"Okay." What next? "Do you know about the secret exit?"

"The what?"

"The magical safe room with the secret exit out of the building. It's in the mayor's private office."

"Is that the little room behind the steel door in the closet? Natalie showed me that a while back. I didn't know it had a secret exit."

"Yeah," Meaghan said. "That's how Annie and I got out of the building when you first arrived. We were in that office at the time."

"Oh, shit, I didn't hurt you guys, did I? I tried to blast the glass outward at the wizards."

"No, we're fine. The ghosts warned Annie you were coming in the front door and she dragged us in there. It goes to an internal stairwell that leads down to the basement and a tunnel over to the historical society house."

"The big yellow one?"

"Yeah. But the safe room's locked from the inside and—"

"I'm not leaving," he said, his voice firm.

"I know that, but it might be a way we can get in." She shuddered. She'd rather face the wizards head on than crawl back through that tunnel and up those narrow dusty stairs. "So we can back you up. Without the Order knowing. We have our own wizard now, by the way."

"Yeah, I heard. Can we trust him?"

She thought a moment. Owen seemed to trust Eliot, but Owen, despite having proved himself helpful so far, was a leprechaun, and Meaghan knew she shouldn't trust him, even if she wanted to.

Sid also trusted Eliot, but Sid was keeping secrets from her. But she couldn't bring herself to believe he'd betray her. Not after Fahraya. If she started mistrusting everyone, she'd end up alone. Again. "Yeah, I think we can."

They were silent for a long moment.

"Are you sleeping with my father?" Jamie asked.

Meaghan choked. "Really? You want to talk about that *now*?"

"Yeah. I do. I'm really weirded out by it, but if you . . . please be careful, okay? I don't want you to end up like my mom."

"If you were anybody else, I'd tell you to mind your own goddamn business. No, I'm not sleeping with your father." She took a deep breath. "Yet. I'm being very careful, but I really . . . I'm being careful. You really need to talk to him. You need to give him a chance to be there for you."

"I . . . Let me save the world first, okay? Then I'll talk to him."

"Don't wait too long," Meaghan said. "Like I did. Even

though I got to make things right with Dad after he died, I missed his life. And I will regret that forever." She felt the tears well up again. She reached over and grabbed a wad of toilet paper. "Don't make that mistake."

"I wo—"

The phone went dead. And then the lights went out.

CHAPTER TWENTY-EIGHT

MEAGHAN SCRAMBLED TO her feet, the phone receiver clattering on the tile, and pressed her ear against the bathroom door. The laughter and chatter had turned to shouts of alarm. She pulled open the door.

The entire house was dark. Then she saw a dim white light—a flashlight, it looked like—appear from the kitchen. "Relax," she heard her brother say. "It's probably a fuse. I'll run downstairs and—"

"Don't," Meaghan shouted. "The phone's dead, too."

Everyone stopped talking.

Meaghan fumbled her way down the hallway toward the living room and peered out the window. Holly Lane, which was a dead-end street, was dark but she could see lights in the houses on Sycamore. It could be merely downed lines some-where, but Meaghan knew in her gut it wasn't. The Order was paying them a visit.

Sid appeared at her side. Troon had night vision far

superior to humans, and Sid's eyes didn't require time to adjust to the darkness. He peered out the window. "There," he said a moment later, pointing toward the street. "And there." His hand began to tremble. "I see five of them so far. We're outgunned."

"The hell we are," Meaghan answered, feeling anger bubble up inside her. This was the second time the bastards had attacked her in her own home. "We've got a witch, a wizard, and a leprechaun. As well as three big, strong men with excellent fighting skills and a powerful medium."

"And we've got you. And your temper," Sid said, his voice now shaking. "What about me?"

"Night vision. You can see better than any of us right now, including the wizards if they start throwing flashy spells around."

Sid took a deep breath and, his voice steadier, said, "Okay, boss. What do we do?"

They were all calling Meaghan "boss" now. She'd never thought of herself as a leader, but in Eldrich, even surrounded by people and beings far more powerful than she, Meaghan had developed an easy authority to which everyone responded. She wasn't in charge—not officially—of anything but the solicitor's office, but as soon as things got dicey, magically or not, everyone started looking to her for answers.

Which really freaked her out sometimes. But now, under attack, she had no time for doubt. Time to lead the troops. "First thing, magical barriers."

Natalie crept up beside her. "Done. Eliot's watching the back door. And John and the boys are closing and locking all the windows and looking for weak spots where they might be able to get in."

"What's Owen doing?"

"I'm behaving myself," she heard him say behind her. "I really wish you'd trust me."

"That's not why I asked," Meaghan said. "You said in my office that you had powerful magic. What can you do to help us here?"

"Uh, well, I might have exaggerated a little bit."

Meaghan snorted. "And you wonder why people don't trust you. Can you do anything to help us?"

"Yeah, I'm not completely useless. I've got certain . . . I'm really good at hiding—"

Now Sid snorted. "Our hero. You're even more useless than I am."

"Watch it, Blue," Owen said. "I don't know what your problem is, but—"

"Shut up, both of you. Now." Meaghan turned to Owen. "Is there anything else you can do?"

"If I'd been allowed to finish," Owen said in a haughty tone as Sid snorted and stomped back to the kitchen, "I would have told you that I'm really good at hiding in plain sight. If I don't want to be seen, you won't see me. And with a little magical boost from Red here, the person with me will be just as hard to spot."

Natalie giggled. Owen grinned at her.

"That might be very useful," Meaghan said. "Can you hide all of us?"

"Not at once. But I could sneak us out of here one at a time. Everyone but you, of course. My magic won't work on you."

A blinding flash of green light knifed through the window accompanied by a loud sizzle.

"Gah." Meaghan shook her head. "There goes my night vision. What the hell was that?"

Natalie peeked over the window sill. "My spell wall doing its thing." She extended her middle finger at the wizards outside and shouted, "How you like chick magic now, assholes? Effective enough for you?"

The Order believed that women were incapable of doing *real* magic, whatever that was, and shouldn't be allowed to use it. It appeared to be a sore spot with Natalie.

"Don't taunt them," Meaghan said, even as she wished she'd been the one to flip them off.

"Why not?" Natalie slumped down next to Meaghan.

"It tells them our position in the house. We need to get back to the kitchen and make a plan. If we can't outgun them, then we might need to let Owen escort you all out. C'mon. Stay low."

Crouched, they stumbled back to the kitchen. Meaghan, her eyes still not recovered, tripped over someone right inside the door.

"Ow. Watch it," Russ said.

"What are you doing down there?"

"Looking for that saucepan. The wizard beater."

"Ha, ha," Meaghan said. "Not a great time to be a smartass."

"No, I mean it. Eliot," he called. "Tell her."

"Iron is impervious, right?" she heard Eliot say from the other side of the kitchen. "Like you. Means you're our best shot at taking out these idiots."

"You expect me to fight wizards with a saucepan?" Meaghan moved next to him and looked out the window. She still couldn't see a damn thing.

Eliot shrugged. "You've done it before. Brian will tell you that you should never draw a weapon you don't know how to use. You've already shown what you can do with that saucepan."

"But—"

"Look," Eliot said. "They're not getting through our defenses right now, but we can't attack them without dropping the wall. Which turns this into a siege. I thought you were bullshitting me about the saucepan, but Russ says it's true, and since you and the pan are both impervious, you can stroll right through both our barriers and start swatting."

"That was a skinny kid. If they sent the muscle, they won't need magic to stop me. Those guys who took Jamie were huge." She looked around the room. She could see several figures, but couldn't tell who was there. "Is everybody okay?"

"Yeah," she heard Ruth say. "I think."

"Is everybody here?"

"No, the Fahrayans and the cop are upstairs shutting and locking windows."

There was a clatter of feet on the stairs and John and Jhoro entered the kitchen, followed by Brian. "The upper stories are secured," he said, all business now. "Is the perimeter in place?"

"Yes, sir," said Natalie. "You're kind of cute when you're being the Man."

Brian ignored her. "Do we have a plan yet?"

"Working on it," Meaghan said. "Any suggestions?"

"We either stay put or get out. Do we know how many we're dealing with?"

"I saw five," Sid said.

"Out front?"

"Yeah. Do you want me to check again? I've got the best night vision."

"How good?"

"I don't need to adjust between light and dark."

"All right," Brian said. "You're reconnaissance. Get us a head count—front, back, and sides of the house, and anything else you notice."

"Check how big they are," Meaghan said. "They're not all half-starved like Caleb was. See if they sent the big guys."

"On it," Sid said as he started looking out the kitchen windows.

"We're safe here for now?" Brian asked. "Magically?"

"For now," Eliot said. "But if enough of them show up, they'll eventually out-hex us."

"But they won't want to siphon too many from city hall," Meaghan said. "That's their primary goal. They need to get inside and they need Jamie alive and under their control to do whatever it is they want to do."

"Any thoughts on how we can get out of here?" Brian asked.

"If they're the skinny, starved wizards," Meaghan said. "I can take out at least one or two with my trusty saucepan. If they're the big guys, no. But Owen's got the power to hide in plain sight, and with a magical assist, he can get the rest of you out of here one at a time. But I don't know where we go then. The cars are all in the driveway or out front."

"Not all of them," Russ said, with a sigh. "My food truck's in the alley space, behind the garage."

"What kind of truck?" Eliot asked.

Russ sighed again. "Big boxy delivery truck."

"Can we all fit?"

"Yeah," Natalie said. "The thing is huge."

"And it's made of steel, I bet," Eliot said.

"Yeah," Russ said morosely. "And I just bought it. I had to go all the way to Scranton to get it. Please don't blow it up."

"Don't worry," Annie said taking his hand.

"Okay," he said with a goofy grin, his concern for his truck forgotten.

Meaghan had almost managed to forget the love spell in all the excitement. "Marnie's spell—Eliot, you said you had it handled *here*. What about out there? What are we driving into?"

"Yeah," Eliot said. "That's a problem. Hopefully everybody's getting it on in the privacy of their own homes, but we probably should keep Jhoro under wraps until we know for sure. We don't need a mob of the lovesick trying to kill each other to get to him."

"Under wraps magically?" Meaghan asked.

"I was thinking more along the lines of a ponytail, ball cap, and baggier clothes. There's enough magic flying around him as it is."

Meaghan nodded. "Not sure about the bigger clothes. Russ?"

"There's a bag of stuff somebody dropped by for the Fahrayans I haven't looked at yet. Let me see what we've got." He grinned at Annie. "C'mon, you. Let's go shopping."

"You cook me dinner and then you want to go shopping?" Annie giggled. "You're the perfect man."

"Find clothes for Jhoro," Meaghan said. "Save the canoodling for when the world isn't about to end."

CHAPTER TWENTY-NINE

"WE NOW HAVE undeniable proof that those tan walking shoes with the Velcro straps are bad on everyone," Sid said. "If he can't make them look good, nobody can."

Jhoro stood before them in the clothes Russ had managed to find for him. A loud Hawaiian shirt—black, orange, and lime green—several sizes too large, baggy khaki shorts that hung to his knees, a red Phillies cap, black socks, and the offending shoes.

"What do you think? Is he effectively camouflaged?" Russ looked at him proudly. "Anybody still find him attractive?"

"Hell, no," Sid said. "Woof. He looks awful."

Natalie stared at her feet.

Brian smiled. "Well, I'm feeling better looking all of a sudden. Does everybody know what they're supposed to do?"

Sid had identified seven wizards outside, all robed, but none of more than average height. They circled the house loosely, with most of the firepower out front—assuming that the only escape was in one of the cars parked on the street or in Brian's police cruiser.

Eliot and Natalie had cooked up a diversion out front to keep their attention. When the magical fireworks commenced, Meaghan would go first, armed with her saucepan, and take care of anyone who remained in the backyard. If she needed backup, Eliot and Natalie would drop the spell wall and come after her, but the plan was for her to get to the truck and back it up as close to the house as she could get. Only then would Natalie and Eliot drop the barrier and lead everybody out.

Edna, Meaghan thought. We forgot all about her. "What about Edna next door?"

"I'll head over and stay with her," Owen said. "I doubt they'll bother her, but I can hide her if they do. And this way you don't have to go into battle wondering whether you can trust me."

"And as soon as we're gone, he'll tell the wizards what we're up to," Sid said, glaring at Owen.

"I bet you can hex me, so I can't tell them a thing," Owen said to Natalie. "Your mother did a wicked silencing charm."

Natalie nodded. "I can do that." She waved her hands and muttered. "There. So where are we going?"

"You're going . . . to . . ." He coughed. "Uh, it feels like somebody's trying to strangle me."

"You believe that?" Sid asked Natalie.

"You don't believe I can do that spell?" Natalie waved and muttered again. "So, Sid, where are we going?"

"To . . . out . . . I want to say it, but I can't. Fine. I surrender. Give me my voice back."

With a smug look at Sid, Natalie reversed the spell. To Owen, she said, "But we'll need to drop our spell wall to let you out."

Owen shook his head. "No, you won't. That's part of the hiding thing. I can slip through magical barriers."

Natalie gave him a surprised look. "Really? I never knew leprechauns could do that."

"That's because I'm the only one who can," Owen said. "Long story. I'll tell you about it next time I see you."

Natalie nodded. "Okay. Take good care of Edna. Be careful."

"All of you be careful too. Even you, Sid." With a grin, Owen slipped out the backdoor and was gone.

"Wow," Sid said, looking out the window into the backyard. "I'm actually impressed. I can't see him anywhere. One minute he was there and then he sort of melted away."

"You can trust him," Ruth said. "We've known him for years and he's never pulled any leprechaun crap on us."

"He's never pulled any *malevolent* leprechaun crap on us," Eliot said.

Meaghan didn't ask. "So, everybody ready?"

"Give us a second to make some noise out front," Eliot said. He took Natalie's hand. Eyes shut in concentration, they chanted something, then Eliot lifted his hand.

A loud boom was followed by flashes of light.

"There they go," Sid said. "Running around to the front of the house."

Meaghan gripped the saucepan and patted her pocket to make sure she had the truck keys. "I'm up."

"Go . . ." Eliot made another hand gesture. Another loud boom shook the house. "*Now.*"

Meaghan darted out the back door. No wizard in sight. She took about five steps into the yard and felt a hand grab the back of her shirt.

"No, you don't, bitch," a gravelly voice said.

"Yes, I do, shit-for-brains," Meaghan snarled. She twisted out of the wizard's grasp, and, gripping the handle in both hands, swung the saucepan. She felt it make contact and heard the man exhale with a gasp as she started to run.

He tackled her, bringing her hard to the ground on her stomach. The saucepan bounced out of her grasp. Meaghan felt his hands go around her throat. She could hear a voice roaring from behind her. Reflexively, she jammed her elbow back and felt it connect with the man's face.

He rolled off her. She scrambled to her feet, breathing in panicked gasps. She saw John running towards her, shouting. Eliot was behind him.

Meaghan stomped on the wizard's groin before he could hex John. The wizard howled in pain and curled into a ball. She kicked him hard in the kidneys and ran for the truck, Eliot and John now on either side of her. When they reached the alley, Eliot shoved John and Meaghan into the truck and turned to battle the trio of wizards that now ran toward them.

"Get in," Meaghan shouted to Eliot, "and hang onto something." She started the truck and jammed it into reverse. The yard was dark and she couldn't see much behind her, so she accelerated backward in the general direction of the house.

Meaghan heard a scream and a thump, then the back porch loomed in the side mirror. She stomped on the brakes.

John and Eliot opened the back doors and the rest of the group poured into the truck.

"Putting the barrier back up so they can't get in the house," Natalie shouted. There was another flash of light and more shouting.

Eliot yanked Natalie into the back of the truck and shouted, "Meg, go!"

Meaghan slammed the shifter into drive and sped out of the yard into the alley, heading toward Sycamore. When she was close enough to see the glow of the lone streetlight ahead, someone stepped into the mouth of the alley.

One of the big wizards. He waved his hands over his head, sparks flying, as he threw spells at them.

"Get down," Meaghan shouted as she drove faster. The wizard's spells had no effect on Meaghan or the body of the truck, but one hex tore the windshield from its frame. The blast of air in her face caused her to swerve and she nearly lost control.

She steered the truck back into the middle of the alley and pushed the gas pedal to the floor. In the high beams, she could see fear flash over the big wizard's face when he realized she didn't plan to stop. At the last moment, he dove out of the way.

Meaghan screeched onto Sycamore, again almost losing control of the boxy truck as it rounded the corner. After a couple of blocks, she turned onto Main and roared south toward downtown.

The streets were deserted. She ignored a couple of stop signs, but had to stop about a mile down Main because she began shaking so hard she couldn't drive anymore.

John was immediately at her side. She threw her arms around his neck and clung to him, shuddering. Now that she had a moment to breathe, the fear hit her the way she'd tried to hit the wizard in the alley.

"Give me that," she heard John say. He pulled back and dabbed her cheek with a soft cloth. "There, not too bad. Only a little scratch." He pulled her close again. "I saw his hands on you, and I wanted to kill him."

"But before you could, Meg neutered him," Russ said, moving next to her even as John held her. "For a while at least. Nice shot, sis. He was puking when I ran past him."

Meaghan had started to calm down a bit. "Good. He tried to choke me, the bastard."

"That big one in the alley will need to go home and change his pants," Ruth called from the back of the truck. "I bet he shit the ones he was wearing. You're a badass, sweetie. I am impressed. A round of applause for Meaghan, huh?"

Everybody clapped for a moment, then Eliot spoke up. "I hate to be a nag, but the Order won't be far behind us. We need to keep moving." He motioned toward the empty hole where the windshield used to be. "Give me a boost, Red."

After a moment, Eliot said, "Done. Now you won't get bugs in your teeth while you're driving. You okay?"

Meaghan stepped away from John. It wasn't easy. She wanted to stay in his arms, where it felt safe, for the next week or so. "Yeah. I'm okay. Where are we going? I assume the sneaky drive-by plan is no longer on the table."

"Maybe," Ruth said, "we could double back and get the minivan."

A blast rocked the truck.

"Oh, shit," Eliot said. "Probably not. Go. Go!"

Meaghan jumped behind the wheel and they took off again, the wizards in hot pursuit. In Ruth's minivan.

"Those sonsabitches stole the magic bus!" Ruth shrieked. "No," she added when she saw Natalie raise her hands. "Don't hurt it. It's the only nice thing we got. We don't have the budget to replace it."

"It won't work. It's really well shielded," Eliot shouted. The truck hit a pothole and threw everyone to the floor.

Brian struggled to his feet and made his way to the front. "Let me drive. I'm a better driver."

Meaghan had known enough cops to not doubt him. Cops spent most of their work day behind the wheel. The average driver didn't have a hope in hell of outrunning them. "How do we do this?"

Brian reached around her for the seat adjustment lever. "Keep your hands on the wheel and I'll slide under you. Hang on." He slammed the seat back, slid neatly under Meaghan, kicked her foot off the gas pedal, and grabbed the steering wheel with his left hand. "Let go."

She dropped the wheel and Brian dumped her off his lap onto the floor. John caught her and dragged her back into the cargo area.

Brian cut the headlights and took a sudden left at full speed. The tires screeched, and it felt like they went up on two wheels for a moment. He shouted, "Somebody take out the tail lights."

There was a pop and sizzle as the spell shattered the bulbs.

Meaghan knew she couldn't have made that turn without rolling the truck. They were in a shadowy alley she'd never seen before. Another sharp turn and they were in a dark parking lot. Brian screeched across it into another even darker parking lot.

The minivan had fallen behind, its driver flummoxed by Brian's sudden turns in the darkness. Brian moved from parking lot to service alley to parking lot, avoiding the street. He finally veered into an open garage, screeched to a halt, and shouted, "Shut the door. Get it shut."

John dove out the back of the truck and pulled the aluminum door down.

Eliot waved his hands over his head in a complicated maneuver, chanting in what sounded like French. "There. Everyone shut up. Not a sound."

The only sound was the metallic ticking of the cooling engine. After a tense minute, they heard the crunch of tires driving slowly through the alley behind them.

"And now . . . they're . . . gone," Eliot said. He leaned back against the truck wall, his eyes shut, and slid to the floor. "Can I throw up now? Nice driving, officer. Where the hell are we? And how did you know there'd be an open garage back here?"

"Back entrance to Jeff's garage. Kady set up this charm for me." He pulled a fat key ring out of his pocket. "It's like a magical garage door opener. So I can get in whenever I want if the cruiser gets a flat or I need the bathroom or something."

"Jeff and Kady?" Eliot asked, eyes still shut.

"Kady's my witchy baby sister and Jeff's her boyfriend. So, now what?"

Meaghan couldn't believe how calm Brian was. Natalie had conjured up a dim light source so they could see each other in the dark garage without turning on the lights and attracting attention. Meaghan looked around the cargo area. Everyone looked as queasy as Eliot. Except Jhoro. He had a big stupid grin on his face. He buzzed something to John, who smiled, too.

"He says that was almost as much fun as flying and he wants to do it again," John said.

"No," said everyone else in unison.

CHAPTER THIRTY

"WE NEED SOMEWHERE to hide," Meaghan said. "Any ideas? And where the hell are we anyway?"

"We're right behind Eldrich Brew," Brian said.

"Nate and Sally converted the second floor to their apartment," Russ said. "They'd hide us."

"But it's only one big room," Natalie said. "It's all lofty. Is that a good idea for us all to jam into one big room?"

"Last time I saw them, Sally was in love with Jhoro and Nate was not pleased," Meaghan said. "Eliot, can you do anything about that?"

"I'm kind of straining as it is," Eliot said. "If I try to refocus too many people, I'll lose control of all of you."

"We need Natalie functional," Meaghan said. "Any other ideas?"

"Why not here?" Brian asked. "It's not terribly comfortable, but it's got a bathroom. And a table and chairs and a sofa in the break room.

"Plus they already missed it," Eliot said. He looked around the garage. "He do any bodywork? Any sheet metal around."

"No," Brian says. "Only maintenance and repairs. It's a small operation, just Jeff." He pointed at a large roll-up door in the cinder block wall. "He rents out the other bay to that blacksmith guy. He might have some sheet metal."

"Terry," John said.

"There's a forge in here?" Eliot grinned. "Perfect. No place safer from magical attack."

"Terry's a blacksmith?" Meaghan asked John.

"He makes things," John said. "Special tools, things for the yard, swords for playing." John wore the same purposefully blank expression that Meaghan saw on Russ's face whenever he lied to her.

John had told Meaghan back in June that his sponsor was a good fit because he'd "once been a big deal to his people, then not anymore." And he was clued in and surrounded himself with iron. She wondered who this Terry had pissed off and what John was trying to hide.

Secrets. They were driving her nuts. Everybody still hid stuff from her. Hadn't she proven herself yet?

No time to worry about it now. She filed the mysterious blacksmith away with her questions about Owen Finnerty— what had he done centuries ago that still upset people? And the prophecy, she reminded herself. Don't forget about Finn's cryptic comments about a prophecy.

"All right," she said, putting the brakes on that train of thought. One magical mystery crisis at a time. "We stay here. Can we get into Terry's forge?"

John sighed. "I have a key." He pulled an amulet from his pocket. "Here."

"A magical lock?" Eliot said, eyebrow raised. "Who is this guy?"

"My AA sponsor," John said. "Nothing more."

Meaghan rolled her eyes. John was a terrible liar. He had no skill at all. "Where's the bathroom?"

Brian pointed toward a dark doorway on the far side of the garage. "Last door on the right."

"Can I turn the light on?"

"Don't," Brian said. "It'll be visible from the street. There's a flashlight around here somewhere."

"I've got a flashlight app on my phone. I'll only use it if I have to."

Meaghan didn't need it. There was enough light coming through the plate glass window in the front office to light her way and the bathroom had a small window. Besides, what she really wanted to do was be alone for a few minutes to pull herself together.

The dark of the garage had hidden her shaking hands. Everything hurt from her fight with the wizard. She dropped the cover down on the toilet and sat down. The small room began to whirl and she leaned over with her head between her knees until it stopped.

"I'm too old for this shit," she murmured to herself, not for the first time.

When Meaghan had to go to Fahraya to rescue Jamie, she had thought the waiting was the worst part—that it would have been easier to simply be dumped into the situation.

She'd been wrong about that, she now realized. It had felt like a constant onslaught since she'd encountered Jamie's poltergeist-constructed tower of office supplies. She thought of a quote she'd seen somewhere about how fear was peeing your pants and courage was doing what you had to do with wet pants.

What she really wanted was a moment to put on dry pants. But if the last two days were any indication, she wouldn't get the chance.

She washed her hands and took a few deep breaths. She decided not to ask John about Terry, the mysterious blacksmith. He'd be evasive and she wasn't sure she had the patience right now to deal with it.

What Meaghan needed was a plan. They were seriously outgunned by the Order wizards. Natalie and Eliot would need reinforcements if they wanted to do something besides hide. Odds were good that the other witches were as addled by Marnie's spell as Natalie had been before Eliot interceded. If they could get to Marnie and reverse her love spell, they could recruit the other witches.

But they didn't have any chance at all of getting to Marnie without the witches. And Eliot couldn't redirect the spell in anyone else without potentially losing control over everybody. Which would leave Meaghan without Natalie once again.

Unless they came at the problem from a different direction. The strongest one of them right now, by far, was Jamie, assuming he hadn't already reduced city hall to rubble and they could get to him. Which meant the tunnel. More metaphorical pants-peeing. But she didn't see any other way.

Meaghan opened the bathroom door, stepped into the hallway, and saw a pulse of red and blue light. The large plate glass window fronted on Elm Street, one block north of the square. Two gas pumps sat out front with a small parking area for garage customers.

An Eldrich police car, light bar flashing, blocked the entrance to the parking lot, hemming in Ruth's minivan.

A traffic stop. A cop had pulled the wizards over. The cop stepped out of the cruiser and walked slowly to the minivan, gun drawn. Meaghan recognized him as the officer who'd accompanied Brian to Jamie's house the previous evening. Lyons, she thought, remembering the name tag on his uniform shirt. Meaghan crept up to the front counter and crouched behind it to get a better view.

"Sir," Lyons shouted toward the minivan. "Stay where you are. Stay in the van."

The large wizard Meaghan had nearly run over stepped out of the driver's seat, holding up his hands, seemingly in a placating gesture, then shouted something. Lyons flew backwards against the cruiser, hitting it hard enough to dent the door panel. He crumpled to the ground and didn't move.

The wizard walked over to Lyons, checked his pulse, then unbuckled Lyons's utility belt and handed it to one of his gray-robed companions. The wizard conjured a small hovering ball of light that dimly illuminated the parking area. He pulled off his gray robe to reveal black paramilitary clothing and poked around Lyons's still form with his foot, then bent to pick up something.

Lyons's gun. The big wizard took back the utility belt, pulled out the spare clip, and dropped the belt in the bushes next to the driveway. He tucked the gun in the back of his waistband and shoved the clip in his pocket. In the dim light, Meaghan recognized him as one of the wizards who had kidnapped Jamie back in June. Not Cooper, the malevolent ringleader, but the one who had waited in the SUV with a knife to Jamie's throat. The one who most likely had carved the sigils into Jamie's chest and back.

Meaghan felt her temper rise, now sorry she hadn't tried harder to mow him down with the food truck.

With a grim smile, the wizard turned back to Lyons and kicked him hard in the gut. Lyons groaned and curled into a ball.

Not dead, Meaghan thought, relieved. The wizards dragged him to the back of the minivan and shoved him into the cargo area. The big wizard climbed into the police cruiser and backed up to let the minivan exit the lot. She could see him talking to the wizards in the van. He pointed toward city hall and they drove off.

Meaghan thought he was going to follow the minivan. Instead he cut the light bar and headlights and, in darkness, pulled into the parking lot and down the driveway towards the back of the garage.

Meaghan ran down the hall. "We got trouble," she shouted. "The big wizard in a police car headed straight for us."

"Shit," Brian said. He stood outside the door to Terry's forge. "I need my gun."

"Won't do any good," Eliot answered, grabbing Brian's arm. "Everybody in the forge. *Now.*"

Meaghan made it to the forge a moment before the police cruiser rammed through the closed garage door.

And smashed right into the back of Russ's truck.

The truck bumped up a few inches and that was all. The police cruiser absorbed the remaining shock, crumpling like an aluminum can as the airbags deployed with a loud bang.

Natalie had been right, Meaghan thought. That truck was built like a tank.

For a moment, everyone stood silent in shock. Brian moved first, but Eliot held him back. "Stay here. Big magic." He motioned to Natalie. "C'mon, Red. You hold him, I'll stun him."

They didn't need to do either. When they got to the shattered cruiser, they found the wizard trapped in the wreckage, barely conscious. Eliot motioned to the group. "Meaghan, come over here. The rest of you stay back, okay?"

Meaghan felt a savage joy, which ended abruptly as she neared the mangled car. Eliot had deflated the air bags and Meaghan could see that all they had done was give the wizard behind the wheel a few extra moments of life. Blood bubbled from his nose and mouth with each wheezing gasp. The lower half of his body was encased in the remains of the car. A piece of jagged bone jutted from his upper arm.

Up close she saw how young he was, no older than Jamie. As much as she hated him for the things she knew he had done, she felt a pang of shame at her initial delight. *He's somebody's son*, she thought. *Once upon a time, a woman gave birth to him.*

Meaghan's eyes filled with tears. She didn't want to feel compassion for this man, this monster, as he lay dying, but she couldn't help herself. He no longer seemed huge and menacing, but small and fragile, smashed beyond repair.

"What's your name?" she asked.

"Not . . . telling . . . you," he gasped. "They're almost here."

"Who's almost here?"

"Them . . . they . . ." He groaned and spit up a wave of fresh blood. "You'll all burn . . . soon."

Even with his threats, she couldn't hate him anymore. "What have you done to Jamie? What are those things you carved into him?"

"The rift will . . . open. You . . . you . . ." The defiant look in his eyes vanished, replaced with fear. "It hurts . . . I . . . hurts." He looked at Meaghan, a plea in his eyes. "Please . . . I . . ." He let out a final shuddering breath and was still.

The three of them stared down at him, silent for a moment. Natalie broke the silence. "How do people get so wrong?" She turned to Meaghan, tears in her eyes. "I can't even hate him. I should. What he did to Jamie was vicious and evil, but . . . look at him."

Meaghan put her arm around Natalie and pulled her close. "I know. I can't hate him up close either." She looked past Natalie to Eliot. "Whatever these things are, they need Jamie to help them get here and he told me he'll pull the building down on top of himself and the Order to keep that from happening. We have to get inside city hall and help him."

Eliot was staring at the dead wizard. "Oh, shit. They didn't."

Meaghan followed his gaze. "What?"

"They rigged him." He shoved her and Natalie hard. "Go!"

Meaghan and Natalie ran, Eliot behind them. She heard a soft whoosh and felt a wall of air shove her from behind, then the world went dark.

CHAPTER THIRTY-ONE

MEAGHAN HEARD SCREAMING. And voices. But she couldn't tell what they were saying.

She lay on her stomach on the gritty concrete floor. Hands touched her back and legs. *Go away*, she thought. She felt the hands shake her gently. *Go away and let me sleep.*

The hands moved to her neck and head. She heard a voice, close to her, calling her name.

Why's Natalie calling me?

"No major injuries that I can feel," she heard Natalie's panicked voice say. "Help me turn her over."

More hands rolled her body face up. She couldn't see. After a moment of panic, Meaghan realized that her eyes were closed. She opened them and saw John's worried eyes. She smiled, reached up a clumsy hand, and stroked his cheek. "What's going on?"

John, trying not to cry, took her hand and kissed it. "I thought I'd lost you."

He helped her into a sitting position. Meaghan shook her head, hard, trying to wake up. She glanced around. Russ crouched next to her, a relieved smile on his face. Everyone else clustered around something out in the garage. She heard the rough hiss of a fire extinguisher.

The police car. She remembered the crash. And then . . . the memory rushed back. "That wizard, his body, it exploded?"

"Yeah," Russ said. "You scared the shit out of us."

"Natalie? I heard her talking a minute ago."

"She's fine. You broke her fall. Which is how you ended up face first on the floor."

Eliot had been behind them. Meaghan's stomach clenched. "Eliot?'

"Over there," John said, looking at the knot of people. "He's hurt."

"Help me up. I need to see him."

With John's help, she walked with unsteady steps into the garage. Everyone stepped aside. She slumped back to the floor next to Eliot.

He smiled up at her. "How you doing?"

"I'm fine. How about you?" Gently, she took his hand. Blood streaked his face and his clothes hung in shreds, but the real damage was to his leg. A twisted chunk of steel jutted from his thigh. Someone had torn away the blood-soaked trouser leg, and used strips of cloth to secure the object in place.

"I'll live, so long as nobody pops the cork." He gestured at his leg. "Impervious damn shit. Goes right through a protection spell. I gotta get me to the hospital."

Meaghan squeezed his hand. "We're on it." She looked up and said in a loud voice, "We need a car."

"On my way," Brian said. "Unless anybody else knows how to hot-wire a vehicle?"

"Take Red," Eliot wheezed. "In case those shithead wizards are still roamin' around." He smiled up at Meaghan. "Whee. Your girl did something to ease the pain. Making me high. My bayou voice is coming back." He grew serious. "You lean in close, Meg. We gotta talk."

She bent closer.

"I can't help you anymore, but you'll be okay. You don't need me."

"But you have power," she said in a small voice. "I don't."

"Shit, you don't have power," he rasped. "You're the only one here whose head they can't screw with. Whatever's coming at us, you're the only one who'll be able to see its real face. Just because it looks big and scary to everybody else, doesn't mean it is. You remember that." His eyes fluttered shut for a moment. "Wooh, I'm off to dreamland here. Where was I?"

"Why you think I have power," Meaghan said.

"Why I *know* you have power. You see the world the way it really is, not the way these magical bastards want you to see it. That's power. Don't let anybody tell you otherwise . . ." His eyes fluttered again. "That's why they're so scared of you. Ooh, I think I'm going sleepy-bye for a while. Ruthie'll take care of me. You take care of the rest of them."

His breathing grew deeper as he lost consciousness.

Meaghan looked up at Ruth. "You're taking him to the hospital?"

Ruth nodded. Her eyes were red and swollen in her pale face.

"Is everyone going to get stupid again with him gone?" Meaghan asked.

"Maybe. Maybe not. Eliot's had some help." She pointed

at Jhoro, who was examining the remains of the police cruiser. "This one has some power of his own. Not magic. Something else."

Meaghan glanced over at Jhoro. Even in his baggy mismatched clothes and ball cap, he still drew attention.

She remembered the utter devotion she'd felt in his followers when she was on her psychic high in Fahraya. And how easily he had read her intentions when she had tried to communicate with him mentally. It was Jhoro who had mixed up the hallucinogenic antidote to the scorpion bite and the foul-tasting drink that dialed Meaghan's high back enough so she lost the giddiness but retained all the psychic benefit. Jhoro had assured her she would still "see whole" and not lose her connection to her dead father.

"Annie said something," Meaghan said to Ruth. "Something about how his grief was so strong it was manifesting memories. Like ghosts, but not. She said she'd never seen anything like it. And she said her empathic skills around him were goosed way beyond normal." She turned to John. "What's the deal with Jhoro?"

"He's a . . . what's the word I hear used for ones like him? Shaman. A seer. Trying to be at least. He had to teach himself because V'hren killed the ones who would teach him."

Ruth nodded. "That might explain it. A self-taught Fahrayan shaman. Alex will go nuts over that."

John looked at Ruth. "Who is Alex?"

"Our anthropologist. He works with me and Eliot."

John looked at her blankly.

"Somebody who studies different cultures," Meaghan said.

John nodded.

There was nothing to do now but wait for Brian.

Meaghan, remembering Lyons's dropped utility belt, sent John out to look for it. The gun was gone, but there would probably be pepper spray and maybe a collapsible baton.

And handcuffs.

Meaghan watched her brother work his way around the room. Russ, falling back on his instinctive response to stress, was handing out sodas and snacks he'd found in the small fridge under the front counter. He had even less power than she did, but he'd follow her into hell whether she wanted him there or not. Eliot had said a forge was the safest place to be during a magical attack. The handcuffs would make sure he stayed there.

Brian appeared at Ruth's elbow. "The car's outside. I can't get it in here. We're going to have to carry him out."

Meaghan almost told him about Lyons, his kidnapped fellow officer, then stopped. Brian couldn't help Lyons now. All he could do was get himself killed or turned into a weapon for the wizards.

Brian, John, and Jhoro popped the hinges on the bathroom door and used it to carry Eliot to the big SUV parked outside.

Annie laughed when she saw it. "That's Tony's Escalade. You stole the mayor's car."

Brian grinned. "He gave it to me. He lives a couple blocks north of here. He was home getting freaky in his living room with his latest girlfriend. And some of her friends. Nat and I told him we needed his car, he gestured at his pants, I took his keys, and here we are. Speaking of which . . ."

He pulled Natalie into his arms and kissed her. She resisted for only a moment. When the kiss was done, Brian brushed the red curls off Natalie's face and smiled at her.

"Something to remember me by in case you get stupid for Blondie again."

Natalie, looking dazed, simply nodded.

Brian held out the car keys to Ruth. "You know how to get to Williamsport?"

Ruth shook her head. "Not without the magic bus I don't. I don't have a great sense of direction in normal landscapes, let alone the haunted forest out there. No way I can drive out of this valley at night without a navigator."

Meaghan felt relief. Ruth's refusal to drive would save her an awkward conversation with Brian, who was even less likely than Russ to voluntarily stay behind. She dragged him away from the others so they couldn't hear her. "Brian, you need to go with them. Eliot's no help right now and Ruth needs you."

Brian looked at her, eyes narrowed as he gestured at the wreckage in the garage. "I don't suppose you have any idea where that police cruiser came from."

Shit.

"From somebody you can't help right now. I need you to think strategically here, not heroically. You can't defend us against magic. Even if you had your gun, it wouldn't do you any good. And they could hex you, turn you against us." She shook her head. "Get Ruth and Eliot out of here. Keep them safe. If we live through this mess, we still have to deal with the Fahrayans before winter and they're our best resource."

"But, I can't leave. Natalie—"

"Has a lot more power than you do in this situation. And if she gets all love addled for Jhoro again, you really want to stick around and watch that?"

Brian sighed. "No. But running away sure won't win me any points."

"First person who says that's what you did is getting his or her ass kicked. I need someone I can trust to do this. Eliot's out cold and, as far as I can tell, Ruth's a civilian. You need to get them out of town as fast as you can and stay with them until this is over."

"What about your brother? And John? They don't have any more power than I do."

Now it was Meaghan's turn to sigh. "Yeah, and they won't go with you or stay behind willingly. I need somewhere safe to stash them."

"Like the forge," Brian said. He dug into his back pocket and pulled out another set of handcuffs. "Take these."

She smiled. "My thoughts exactly."

CHAPTER THIRTY-TWO

"AND THEN THERE were seven," Sid intoned, in a sepulchral voice as the Escalade pulled away.

Meaghan motioned to Annie to wait while everyone else drifted back into the garage. "Soon it will be five. I need your help with something."

"Russ," she said. "We need to keep him out of harm's way."

Meaghan nodded. "And John."

"They won't leave just because we ask them."

"That's why I have these." Meaghan showed Annie both pairs of handcuffs—the set Brian had given her and the set John had found in Lyons' abandoned utility belt.

Annie giggled. "Ooh, you naughty girl."

Meaghan rolled her eyes. "If the forge is as safe as Eliot claims—"

"It is. Ruth was telling me about it. Something to do with all the iron molecules getting into everything and making it super-impervious."

"But this forge has a magical lock."

"Yeah, but that's outside."

"That makes a difference?"

Annie shrugged. "Apparently. Don't ask me to explain this crap. I don't understand it any better than you do."

"So, do you know this Terry guy? What's his deal?"

"He and his wife moved here right before you did. They've been renting a place on the east side, out by the river."

"Not anymore," Meaghan said. "According to John, they bought the house across the street from me and are about to move in."

Annie raised an eyebrow. "Interesting. I've seen him around, but I don't know anything about him. He's John's AA sponsor?"

Meaghan nodded. "John told me he's clued in and he used to be a big deal to his people, but isn't now."

Annie snorted. "Well, that narrows it down. That only describes practically every leader ever."

"Except this guy has pissed off somebody magical. Or he's magical himself."

"Or both." Annie glanced at the handcuffs Meaghan held. "You want to lock Russ and John in the forge for their own safety and you want me to help you."

"Yeah. Any suggestions?"

"Go find something to cuff them to and I'll round them up. Provided Russ isn't drooling over Jhoro now that Eliot's gone."

"You're not going to get stupid on me again?"

Annie shook her head. "No, whatever power Jhoro's got, it's stronger than Marnie's spell. With me at least."

She smiled at Meaghan, winked, and walked toward Russ and John.

Meaghan slipped into the forge to take a closer look. It wasn't merely iron molecules that would protect them. Around his workspace, Terry had constructed a large cage out of galvanized steel chain-link fencing. The chain-link fabric was lined on the inside of the forge with steel screen mesh.

Along one wall of the cage, metal pipes had been constructed into what looked like a tool rack. Two vertical pipes had been bolted into the concrete floor, with horizontal piping between them bracing the structure.

The pipes were still shiny and the hooks welded into the cross bars were empty, making her think it had been recently installed. The top of the rack was firmly attached to the ceiling of the cage. She gave it an experimental tug and felt no movement at all. Even with their combined strength, she didn't see Russ and John pulling it down.

The run of vertical piping from the floor to the first crossbar was long enough to let them sit or stand without stretching the cuffed arm into an awkward position. It wouldn't be comfortable, but she could drag in the cushions from the break room sofa and leave them water and food. The trick was getting them in here and cuffed to pipes before they figured out what she was up to.

Annie appeared at the door. "They're coming. Got a plan?"

Meaghan nodded. She trotted over to the door and handed Annie a pair of the cuffs. She pointed at the tool rack. "The vertical pipes, under the first rack."

"So they can slide the cuffs up and down," Annie said, nodding. "Perfect."

"We can bring them some drinks and snacks and the cushions off the sofa."

"And something to pee in."

Meaghan nodded. "But first we gotta cuff them."

"I'll take Russ, you take John. Follow my lead."

Meaghan's heart pounded. She knew John would be furious and she wasn't sure she was smooth enough to pull this off.

Annie grabbed Russ by the hand and pulled him into the forge. "We need to talk to you guys. Before things get crazy again. John, you too."

She maneuvered Russ to the far end of the tool rack. Meaghan motioned to John and he came over to where she stood on the other end.

"Russ, honey, I know the love spell might make you get all crazy for Jhoro again," Annie said. "So, before that happens I want to remind you how straight you are." She threw her arms around his neck and kissed him hard.

"Um, me too." Meaghan pulled John to her with one hand. With the other she cuffed his wrist.

"What—" was all he had time to say before Meaghan attached the other cuff to the pole and stepped back fast. A quick look confirmed that Annie had done the same to Russ.

"No," John roared as he pulled on his cuffed wrist. "No. I want to stay with you."

"I know," Meaghan said. "But you can't help me with this." She heard Russ banging on the tool rack. "Either of you. All you can do is get yourselves hurt or killed. This way I know you're safe."

"I thought you were into me," Russ said to Annie in a hurt voice.

"I am, honey. That's why I don't want to see you get dead."

"Oh, ho ho. What's going on here?" Sid walked into the forge. He waggled his blue eyebrows at Meaghan. "Meggy, I never saw you as the kinky type."

"Shut up," Meaghan said. "Better yet, go get Jhoro to help you bring in the sofa cushions and some drinks and food. And a couple of buckets or trash cans."

"Meaghan, you can't do this to me," John shouted. He pulled at the pipe with both hands. Already his cuffed wrist was red and chafed from pulling. "You need me."

"I need you alive. When this is over. This is the safest place in town right now."

"But—"

"Jamie needs you alive."

He glowered at her but said nothing.

"What if you don't come back for us?" Russ asked, in a petulant tone. "What if you get killed? We'll starve to death."

Meaghan pulled out her phone. Service in Eldrich was notoriously spotty, but she had a strong signal. "You got a phone?"

"I do," John growled.

"Then call Terry and tell him to come let you out."

"I'll call him right now."

"Fine," Meaghan said, exasperated. "You do that."

He pulled his battered flip phone out of his back pocket, punched the number, and held it to his ear. "Is me . . . Nuh, I'm not drinking . . . Magic trouble . . . Yeah, the evil wizards . . . something in city hall with my boy . . . no, no, you don't need to come right now, but Meaghan is handcuffing me to your forge to keep me safe."

He listened for a few more moments, his look darkening.

"No, this is not a good idea . . . no . . . but . . . all right." He held the phone out to Meaghan. "He wants to talk to you."

"Slide it over on the floor," Meaghan said.

"You don't trust me?"

"Not right now I don't."

Grumbling something in Fahrayan, John set the phone on the floor and slid it over to her.

Meaghan grabbed it and put it to her ear. "You still there?"

A deep, booming voice said, "Yeah. So, you got our buddy John locked up tight, huh?"

"Yeah."

"Good."

Meaghan had been prepared to argue with this man. "You're okay with this?"

"I built that space to be magic proof. Plus, the door has a special lock. It'll keep the bad guys out. John's still got the amulet key?"

"Yeah, but I don't think I can get it away from him."

Terry laughed. "You don't need to. Shut the door until you hear the double click. If the key's inside, it works like a safe room. Time lock. That baby won't open for twelve hours. On a scale of zero to apocalypse, how bad is this thing?"

Meaghan shook her head. "I wish I knew. From what John's son told me, probably closer to apocalypse."

"Well, shit," Terry said. "I think me and Steph will start heading home a little early. Put Johnny back on the phone, okay?"

"Will do. Thank you." She slid the phone back across the floor to John. "He wants to talk to you."

John glared at her as he picked up the phone. He turned

away, mumbled something to Terry, and then shoved the phone back into his pocket. "I still don't like this."

"Too bad," Meaghan said. *Our first fight*, she thought.

Annie had gone in search of Sid and Jhoro and now all three appeared carrying supplies.

"Don't get too close to them," Annie said. "They aren't very happy about this."

Sid buzzed something to Jhoro, who laughed. John snarled something in Fahrayan. Jhoro flashed him an innocent smile and pointed to Meaghan while responding. She didn't need Sid's translation to know Jhoro was saying, "Don't look at me. It was her idea."

John gave one more desultory tug on the handcuff and then sat down, his back turned to them.

Jhoro gave Meaghan a sympathetic pat on the shoulder.

"He'll get over it," Sid said.

They tossed the sofa cushions over to John and Russ. Using a push broom, Annie pushed two plastic shop buckets filled with bottled water and whatever food she could find in the break room close to them.

"Well," Meaghan said. "I guess that's it."

John turned to face her. "How can you do this? If you are hurt, I will never forgive myself."

"Likewise, which is why you're staying here."

"I'm gonna tell him about every embarrassing thing you've ever done," Russ said. "All dirt will be revealed."

"Fine. Shovel away," she said, then turned to Annie. "We ready to roll?"

"I guess. Roll where?"

Meaghan sighed. "City hall. I think. Come on."

CHAPTER THIRTY-THREE

"WHERE'S NATALIE?" MEAGHAN asked. There was no sign of her in the garage and Meaghan hadn't seen her since Brian had left with Eliot and Ruth. "Oh, shit. Please tell me she's still with us."

"The bathroom," Sid said.

"They put the door back?"

Sid nodded. "She's meditating. She's trying not to get all giddy about Jhoro again."

"Is it working?"

Sid shrugged. "She's not out here wrapped around him. That's a good sign, I guess."

Meaghan banged on the bathroom door. "You ready to get out of here?"

Natalie cracked the door open and peeked out. "Is Jhoro going with us?"

"Is that going to be a problem?"

Natalie sighed. "God, I hope not." She pulled the door

open, then stared down at her feet without moving. "I'm . . . I was kind of into him before all this happened."

"Yeah," Meaghan said. "I figured that out on barbecue night."

"I have to confess something." She looked up at Meaghan, then looked away quickly. "Marnie wasn't the only one messing with love magic." In a rush she added, "He's so hot and I was lonely and I should have known better but . . ."

Meaghan sighed. "So how much of this insanity did you cause? And what can you do to fix it?"

Natalie chewed on her lip a moment. "I don't know. I don't think my spell is the one that went wild. I cast it like three weeks ago."

"And it didn't work?"

"Oh, it worked. Sort of. I made him hot for a woman—which took some big magic, let me tell you—only it was the wrong woman. I didn't factor in all the time Marnie spent with him combing out his dreadlocks." Natalie groaned. "You saw them at dinner the other night."

"He was more interested in the ribs than either you or Marnie," Meaghan said. She decided not to mention what Jhoro and Marnie had been doing before dinner. Better Natalie fawning and lovesick than scorned and vengeful.

"Yeah, but I still came in a distant third." Natalie sighed again.

"What happened to your spell?"

"I shut it down as soon as I heard they were together, but he's still with her, so Marnie must be casting her own spells. Like last night." Natalie shook her head. "I don't know what I was thinking."

Meaghan relented a little. "Honey, you weren't thinking.

At least not with your brain. That's the problem with love, at least at the beginning. We've all been there. But, I really need you to keep it together now. Jamie needs you to keep it together."

Natalie buried her face in her hands. "It didn't help," she said, her voice muffled, "that Jhoro looks so much like Jamie."

Meaghan gasped. Here was a wrinkle she hadn't anticipated. Everything she'd seen and been told about Natalie and Jamie's relationship led her to believe that they were like brother and sister.

"I know," Natalie said, running her hands through her tangled curls and looking back at Meaghan. "It surprised me, too. I've never had those feelings for Jamie. At least I don't think I ever have. Patrice is my friend and I'd never try to get in between them. But he's my best friend and he doesn't need me anymore. Even if we get him better, without the amulet to maintain, what am I to him?"

"Family. You're family. Hell, my dad—*our* dad—helped raise him. And I'm . . . doing whatever it is I'm doing with his father. And I'm your sister."

"Which makes John my brother-in-whateve-it-is -you're-doing."

"Exactly," Meaghan said. "Which makes me Jamie's not-quite-stepmother."

"Which makes him my . . . not-quite-step-nephew?"

"Yeah, I guess it does."

Natalie grinned. "I'm totally gonna lord that over him." She grew serious again. "If he survives this. If any of us survive this."

Meaghan grabbed Natalie's hand. "You're our best shot at

making sure that happens. I need you on deck. You need to remember what's real and ignore the hex. Can you do that?"

She nodded. "I'll try, but if I start getting stupid again, hit me with something, okay?"

"Gladly. Now let's get out of here."

They found Annie, Sid, and Jhoro out in the main bay of the garage, standing outside of the forge's still open door. Sid turned toward them and smiled. "Oh, the *profanity*. English and Fahrayan. They are not happy boys."

"I know," Meaghan said. She pushed the door closed without a word to John or Russ and waited for the second click. "There. Time-locked for twelve hours. Nobody's getting through that door but Terry."

"So, boss," Sid said. "Now what?"

"City hall by way of the historical society. Unless somebody has a better idea?"

Nobody did.

"I'd like to get a look at city hall if we can sneak up," Meaghan said. "See what we're dealing with on the outside so we can tell Jamie—" She stopped short and looked around in panic. "Has anybody tried to call Jamie? I can't believe I'm only thinking of this now."

"Yeah, because nothing else was going on," Natalie said. "Relax. I called him when you were in the bathroom."

Meaghan looked at her blankly.

"Right before the police car crashed through the door and the wizard exploded."

"Oh, right. Sorry." Meaghan laughed and then abruptly stopped when she felt the hysteria well up. "Jamie's okay?"

"Fine," Natalie said. "City hall's a mess, though. We'll need new office space."

"One crisis at a time. What's the best route to get there?"

Eldrich's town square was more accurately a rectangle, bordered on the west by Main Street and on the east by Eldrich Avenue. Eldrich Brew fronted on Washington on the north end. At the south end, across the aptly named South Street, sat city hall.

The historical society house was located on Iron Street, about two blocks west of the square. Iron intersected with Main about halfway down the square. From there they could get a closer look at city hall. If they ran into trouble before Iron they could double back and take the side streets.

Meaghan expected to see robed wizards, but instead saw a crowd, about a hundred people, milling around the south end of the square, their attention focused on city hall.

"We need to get closer," she said. "Any ideas?"

"Yeah, hang on a sec." Natalie stared intently at the light poles on Main while muttering a spell, then turned her focus to Eldrich Avenue. The street lights didn't go out. Instead they slowly dimmed and the pools of light contracted and faded. The lights were still lit, but the north end of the square had been plunged into darkness.

"Nice," Meaghan said, impressed. Every time she began to take Natalie's power for granted, Natalie did something amazing.

"If we shut off the lights, they'd notice. This way, it's almost as dark and nobody's the wiser."

"Where'd you learn that?"

Trying to sound nonchalant, Natalie said, "It's a little something I came up with on my own."

They stayed on the other side of Main and worked their way slowly down the street, hiding behind parked cars, ready to bolt into the darkness at the first sign of the Order. They stopped at Iron, where Natalie dimmed a few more street lights, and then crept closer to city hall.

The Order had constructed barricades on either end of South Street, blocking access to city hall. As they crept closer, Meaghan realized that the barricades were made mostly of overturned cars. One car, in particular, looked familiar.

"My Audi," Meaghan whimpered, as they stopped to crouch behind a low hedge. "The bastards smashed up my Audi. I love that car."

"You've never driven around here in winter," Annie said. "Trust me. You would have been trading it in for an SUV after the first snowstorm." She pointed to a knot of people, mostly women but also a few men, on the green lawn in front of city hall. "We've got bigger problems."

The smaller group was stacking up a pile of what looked like firewood and junk from people's garages—odd-sized pieces of two-by-fours, sheets of plywood, cardboard boxes, a few old doors, broken pallets. The pile was built around the base of one of the twelve-foot tall decorative street lamps dotting the city hall grounds. Loops of heavy steel chain hung from one of the lamp's arms.

Several small gas cans sat next to the pile. The very combustible pile, Meaghan realized.

She looked at Annie, eyes wide with shock. "Is that what I think it is?"

"Yes," Natalie hissed in her ear. "Gee, who do you think they're planning to burn? A witch maybe?"

Meaghan felt sick. "Marnie. Oh, God, no. We have to find her now."

Jhoro crept up next to Annie. Meaghan heard the hiss of

his sucked-in breath, then heard him whispering something in Fahrayan. Sid whispered back furiously.

"What?" Meaghan asked. "Sid, what's he saying?"

"He says we need a diversion. Something to clear the crowd out a little. Natalie, he wants to know if you still feel Marnie's spell."

Carefully avoiding looking at Jhoro, Natalie nodded. "Definitely."

"Do you think the mob's affected?" Meaghan asked.

"It's mostly women up there," Natalie said. "Some of them are witches. What do *you* think? Why else would they be participating in this?"

Sid relayed everything to Jhoro in Fahrayan. He nodded and reached around Annie to give Meaghan's arm a gentle squeeze. Then he stood up and sprinted toward the group assembling the bonfire, yelling in Fahrayan.

As he got closer, he pulled off the ball cap, letting his long blond hair stream free. He stripped off his oversized Hawaiian shirt, whirled it around his head, and threw it. Finally he dropped his baggy shorts. Clad only in snug jersey boxer briefs, he let the crowd get a good look at him before running into the darkness on the east side of the square.

Meaghan heard shrieks as the crowd realized who it was. The pile was abandoned as a stream of people followed Jhoro into the night.

"If they catch him, they'll tear him apart," Natalie said, as she began to rise to her feet to give chase.

Meaghan, Annie, and Sid yanked her back down.

"You need to stay here. I'll go," Sid said. "So at least he'll have a voice if he needs it. Plus, I'm the only one here besides Marnie who's actually slept with him."

"You *what*?" Natalie lunged at Sid as Meaghan and Annie tried to hold her back.

Before she could reach him, Sid was on his feet. He stuck out his blue tongue at Natalie, then grinned and ran after the mob.

"I'm going, too," Natalie snarled as she tried to wriggle out of their grasp. She hissed something at Annie, and Annie was thrown back several feet.

Meaghan smacked Natalie hard across the face. "Knock it off. You promised me you'd keep it together. Annie, you okay?"

"Fine," Annie said with a groan. "Mostly fine."

Natalie shook her head, hand on her cheek. "Ow. That hurt. You can be a real bitch sometimes, you know that?"

"You told me to hit you if you got stupid again. Is your head clear?"

"I didn't think you'd really do it. Yes, thank you, my head is clear," Natalie said petulantly. "*Bitch*."

The wizards were moving across the street and into the square calling to each other.

Looking for us, Meaghan thought. "We're not getting in that way." She shuddered. "Back to Iron Street. We're taking the tunnel.

CHAPTER THIRTY-FOUR

MEAGHAN, FOLLOWED BY Natalie and Annie, crept back up Main Street, hoping none of the wizards saw them.

When they hit Iron, they ran, trying to stay on grass to muffle their footsteps. The decorative lamp posts on the street, similar to the ones outside city hall, cast a feeble glow that created shadows but no useful illumination.

The historical society house sat at the end of the second block. With its ornate trim and cheerful yellow paint, in daylight it looked like a lemon frosted wedding cake.

At night, in the dim shadowy light of the street lamps, the sunny clapboards were bled gray. The ornate structure loomed in the darkness, hulking over the smaller houses that surrounded it, like a child's nightmare.

And it's only gonna get worse, Meaghan thought, with a shiver. Better a haunted mansion than a dark cramped tunnel.

They stepped onto the shadowy porch.

"Well, it's about goddamn time," a male voice said from the darkness.

The three women screeched in unison.

Owen Finnerty stepped into view.

Hand over her pounding heart, Meaghan said, "You scared the shit out of me, you little bastard. What are you doing here?"

"Waiting for you. What took you so long?"

"You're supposed to be with Edna."

Owen gestured dismissively. "Edna's fine. Sound asleep, probably having X-rated dreams about Blondie. Where is everybody?"

Natalie grabbed Meaghan's arm. "We need to have this conversation inside. Anybody got a key?"

"It's open," Owen said. "I took a look around while I was waiting. Come on."

Once inside, with the door locked behind them, Meaghan and Annie slumped to the ground. Natalie stood near the front window, putting up a protection spell and watching the street.

"I'm too old for this shit," Meaghan announced, lying on the hallway floor.

"Me too," Annie said.

Owen snorted. "I'm a hundred times older than both of you and you don't hear me complaining."

"That's because you haven't done anything yet," Meaghan said. She pulled herself into a sitting position.

"Because I've been waiting for you. Where the hell is everybody?"

"Brian, Ruth, and Eliot are on their way to the hospital in Williamsport," Annie said, "and—"

"*Hospital?* What happened?"

From over by the window, Natalie said, "A wizard blew up. After he crashed a police car into the garage."

"But—"

"Long story," Meaghan said. "We'll fill in the details later. Eliot got a chunk of steel through his thigh and Brian and Ruth are civilians so I got them out of here. John and Russ are locked away safely, and Jhoro and Sid ran off into the darkness a few minutes ago to draw the mob away from the square."

"And we're going to get into city hall through the secret entrance in the basement," Annie added.

"That's what I thought," Owen said. "The Order's brought in reinforcements. You aren't getting in the regular way." He paused, then sighed. "And you've seen the mob. That's got potential to get really bad. They're building—"

"A bonfire to burn Marnie on," Meaghan said. "Yeah, we saw it."

"Not for her," Owen said. "I did some eavesdropping. It's for Red here."

"*Me?*" Natalie stomped over from the window. "Why *me?*"

"Because you've got the most power. And Meaghan relies on you so much. And because . . . they know about Matthew and your mom."

Even in the dim light, Meaghan could see Natalie flinch.

"What about Matthew? What are you talking about?" Annie looked back and forth at the others. After a moment, understanding dawned on her face. "Oh. So that's why Russ kept calling you sis. Which, now that I think about it, isn't really surprising considering how much time Matthew and Vivian spent together. Why should the Order care about that?"

Meaghan looked at Owen. "It's the impervious witch thing, isn't it?"

"Well, partly," Owen said. "But it's more about the prophecy."

Natalie sank onto the stairs, her face in her hands, and moaned. "Oh, God, that is what it means. They told me it didn't mean me, but who else could it be?"

Meaghan threw up her hands. "*What* prophecy? Will somebody tell me what the hell this is all about?" She could feel a rant building. Suddenly furious, she didn't try to suppress it. "Why all the secrets? Everybody keeps telling me how powerful I am and how I'm even better at the job than Matthew and how scared the magical bad guys are, but you're all still hiding shit from me."

Annie, in a meek voice, said, "I'm not hiding anything. I don't know what they're talking about either. Unless . . ."

Meaghan glared at her. "Unless what?"

Annie wilted. "Nothing. Thinking out loud. Never mind."

Meaghan turned on Natalie. Part of her mind registered how terrified Natalie was at the moment, but the fuse had been lit and Meaghan couldn't hold herself back. "Does Russ know about this? Is he still lying to me? Or is it only you? It's pretty fucking pathetic that the only one who's been straight with me is a damn leprechaun."

Natalie, eyes wide with fear, backed away, shaking.

"Leave her alone," Owen said, anger in his voice. "Your brother doesn't know about the prophecy. Your sister has had to carry this particular bucket of shit all by herself. And maybe if you hadn't been off in Arizona all those years feeling sorry for yourself because daddy went away and pissing on Matthew every time he tried to reach out to you, all of this wouldn't be such a surprise now."

Owen's angry words quenched her fury like a bucket of water thrown on a fire. Meaghan tried to respond, but the words wouldn't come. The stress of the last few hours—the last few months—hit her like a sledge hammer. The room started to whirl. Her breath hitched in her lungs and her heart pounded in her chest, anger replaced with gut-twisting fear.

She hadn't been this scared since Fahraya, since her first encounter with the Power, when all she'd wanted to do was turn and flee. Meaghan wanted, desperately, to be anywhere but here.

Because Owen was right, everything he'd said was right. She'd pushed her father away and now everyone she loved was going to pay for it.

Like Jamie had already paid for it.

His face, the one from her nightmare, battered and bloody, rose up in her mind, his dead lips whispering in reproach. *You promised you'd save me, but you let me die. You failed. This is your fault.*

And then a new image appeared in her mind's eye. Natalie, screaming in agony as flames engulfed her. Meaghan's heart pounded harder in her chest, and her legs gave way. She dropped onto the staircase behind her, clutched her knees, and curled into a ball.

They were all going to die. Jamie, Natalie, Russ, John— the people she loved were going to die because she was weak. Because she couldn't stop crying. Because she had failed.

"Meg," she heard Owen say in a gentle voice, as a small

hand touched her shoulder. "I'm sorry. That was harsh. What do we—"

She pulled away from him and shook her head. "You don't get it. I don't know . . ." Her voice rose. "I don't . . ."

Somewhere in the back of her mind, her calm, rational self tried to regain control, but it was too late. The wave of guilt and self-loathing swept over her, followed by the hated tears.

"I don't know what the hell I'm doing. People are getting hurt," she gasped through her sobs. "People will die and you all keep looking at me like I have the answers. I don't have any power and I don't have any answers and I can't stop crying and everybody's keeping secrets from me because nobody can tell me what's really going on because I'm such a fuck-up they don't dare."

Meaghan felt arms around her. Natalie, it was Natalie. Meaghan tried to pull away, but Natalie held her tight.

"I know," Natalie murmured in her ear. "I feel the same way all the time. You're not a fuck-up. Not even close."

Meaghan resisted for a moment longer, then let go. Aching from injuries old and new, exhausted from weeks of broken sleep, Meaghan clung to her newly discovered sister and let the tears flow.

After a minute or so, Meaghan felt the storm begin to pass. She realized for the first time that Natalie was crying, too.

"I think maybe I need to talk to somebody," Meaghan whispered in Natalie's ear. "A professional. About Fahraya. About all of this."

"Ya think?" Natalie squeezed her tighter. "You're as messed up as Jamie, only without the special effects."

"You're squishing my ribs," Meaghan said, "and I need to blow my nose."

"I know," Natalie said, releasing her grip. "I can hear it bubbling."

Meaghan gave a weak laugh. "Hang on." She dug a raggedy tissue out of her pocket. One tentative blow and the tissue disintegrated.

"Here." Annie appeared at her elbow with a roll of toilet paper. "I'm making tea back in the break room. We need a time-out."

Meaghan and Natalie rose to their feet and pulled Annie into a hug. There was more crying, this time including Annie, but it was punctuated with the occasional giggle.

"Oh, my God," Owen said. "Are we done yet? Or are we waiting for Oprah and Dr. Phil to arrive?"

"Shut up," Meaghan and Natalie said in unison. This made them laugh again.

"Humans," Owen said in withering tone that didn't match the look of relief on his face. "You live five minutes and waste four of them crying."

This time, Meaghan ignored him. She blew her nose again. "Come on. I need that cup of tea."

"I found cookies, too," Annie said. "Those fancy chocolate-covered, foo-foo Pepperidge Farm ones."

"Even better," Meaghan said. "And while we have our tea, Owen's going to tell me all about this prophecy." She glared at him. "Right?"

"The world is about to end, and she wants to have a tea party." He shook his head. "*Humans.*"

CHAPTER THIRTY-FIVE

ANNIE HAD ALSO found an apple and some cheese, which she'd cut up and placed on a paper plate. She'd even fanned out the apple slices to make them look nice. Meaghan smiled when she saw it. Annie and Russ really were perfect for each other.

The small room had no windows, so they could actually turn on the lights instead of stumbling around in the dim light from the street.

"We don't have time for this," Owen growled.

Meaghan, calm again, handed him the plate of cookies. Her eyes and nose were still leaking a bit, but the fear was gone. At least for now. "Shut up. We mortals need to recharge for a few minutes here and there, and you need to tell me more about this prophecy."

"I thought you wanted me to shut up."

"Don't be difficult. Have a cookie."

Owen sipped the mug of tea Annie had handed him and

munched on a mint Milano. "It's a long story, so understand this is going to be an abridged version, and if I don't tell you everything, it's not because I'm lying, but because we have other stuff to do so the world doesn't end."

"I understand," Meaghan said, nibbling on a slice of cheddar. "Abridged is fine."

"I guess the easiest place to start is telling you where the prophecy came from. Have you ever wondered about the irony of this town being called Eldrich?"

"What irony?" Meaghan asked. "It's named after the guy who founded it."

"Yeah, but the other meaning, the i-t-c-h spelling."

Meaghan shook her head. "I have no idea what you're talking about."

Owen frowned at her. "What sort of stuff do you like to read?"

"What's that got to do with anything?"

"You read any horror, fantasy, that kind of stuff? Any Lovecraft?"

Meaghan wrinkled her nose. "Bleh. I had a friend in college into all that crap. He convinced me to read a Lovecraft story, but it was so overwrought and racist I couldn't finish it."

"So, let me guess," Owen said. "You prefer realism."

"I prefer nonfiction. How is this an abridged version?"

Owen rolled his eyes. "Lovecraft used the word eldritch—i-t-c-h—a lot in his stories."

"It means eerie, spooky, sinister, that kind of thing," Natalie said.

"Okay." Meaghan nodded. "I get the irony now. But what does that have to do with this prophecy?"

"I'm getting to that. Using the word eldritch to mean

spooky is from the early sixteenth century. Scottish. Some linguists think the derivation comes from 'elf' but it doesn't. It comes from a name."

Meaghan's eyes widened. "Eldrich. Our boy Welland had a spooky ancestor?"

"He had many. But it was Alastair Eldrich, his great, great—" Owen stopped to count on his fingers. "I don't know, a lot of greats, grandfather who wrote down the prophecy."

"Made it up, you mean," Meaghan said.

"No, had brain-pounding, insanity-producing visions that he put down on paper before he set himself on fire in the village square with a jug of whiskey and a lit taper, screaming 'thou shalt not suffer a witch to live.'"

Meaghan set her mug down with a grimace. "Ouch. How do you know about this?"

"I was there," Owen said. "I'm the one who shoved him in a horse trough to put out the flames. Too late, of course. Nobody had the medical knowledge back then to deal with burns like that. And no opiate painkillers. I tried to help him when nobody else would go near him, but after a few hours of listening to his moans, I put a pillow over his face."

Natalie gasped. "You killed him?"

Owen shook his head. "He was as good as dead. All I did was put him out of his misery."

Meaghan, her horror overruled by hunger, reached for a chocolate-covered cookie. "Is that the thing you did that got you in trouble?"

"No." Owen shook his head. "That was something else. But it was why I was living in Scotland in the late fifteenth century posing as a human dwarf instead of living as a leprechaun."

"You got banished," Meaghan said.

Owen seesawed his hand in the air. "Sort of."

"For stealing something, right?"

Owen nodded. "Yeah, but I gave it back. So no harm done."

Meaghan gave him the sheepdog stare.

"Fine, not *much* harm done. I'll tell you that story another time. When we aren't fighting a horde of asshole wizards. I thought you wanted to hear about the prophecy."

"I do. Was Alastair crazy before all this happened?" Annie asked.

"No . . . well, not *that* crazy. But the Eldrich family all had something odd about them. They knew things, felt things. Alastair, especially."

"They were psychic?" Meaghan reached for another cookie.

"Psychic plus," Owen said. "The use of their name to describe something spooky started before Alastair, but he's the one who made it stick. There was occasional grumbling about witchcraft, but, fortunately, they didn't live in the Highlands. They were a lowlands family with English ties and wealth and land so nobody got burnt. Until Alastair, that is."

"They never went after those people," Natalie said. "Only the poor and friendless. Little old ladies who knew about herbs, that kind of stuff."

"Yeah." Owen nodded. "And who didn't have any power. Real witches only got burnt if other witches—"

"Or wizards," Natalie added, shoving away her mug and half-eaten cookie.

"Or wizards," Owen repeated, "were involved."

"Like right now," Natalie said. "Please don't let them do

that to me. If it comes to it, shoot me or something. I . . ." She shuddered. "Not fire."

"Nobody's shooting anybody," Meaghan said. "And nobody's burning anybody either. Not in my town. So, what's this prophecy gotta do with Natalie? Or with me? Or Jamie? Finn mentioned the prophecy in relation to both me and Jamie."

"Well, the thing is a big rambling mess, as you can imagine. No tidy Nostradamus-like quatrains for Alastair."

"Don't tell me Nostradamus was for real." Meaghan snorted. "You can make that vague crap mean anything you want it to."

Owen laughed and shook his head. "No. Nostradamus was a total bullshit artist. If he were still alive, he'd be laughing all the way to the bank. Honestly, humans will believe anything."

Meaghan raised an eyebrow.

"Okay, not all humans," Owen said. "I know, you're a lawyer, you don't trust anybody, blah, blah, blah."

"Tell me what Alastair's prophecy says," Meaghan said.

"The key part for you two—" He pointed at Meaghan and Natalie, "involves an impervious man and a witch who have two daughters."

"Which is why they told me it didn't refer to me," Natalie said. "Because they only had one daughter."

"But what about the burning?" Meaghan asked. "Why do they want to burn Natalie?"

Natalie moaned and put her head on the table. Annie rubbed her back.

Owen sighed. "Because the prophecy talks in a few places

about the need to purify witches with fire. How the burning will open the door to humanity's new masters."

"But they already have Marnie," Meaghan said. "What about her? Finn told me Marnie was the sacrifice."

Owen grimaced. "Oh, trust me. They have plans for her, too. But in one of the references it talks about the daughter witch. And how they need to burn her to . . . stop you."

Meaghan noticed the hesitation. He'd almost said something other than stop. *Kill me, maybe?*

"And," Natalie said, her voice shaking, "here I am."

"But the prophecy says two daughters," Annie said. "Matthew and Vivian only had you. Meaghan has a different mother."

Owen shook his head. "You're being too literal. They did have two daughters. Just not together."

"Which is why Matthew and Mom tried so hard to hide me from everyone." Tears glistened in Natalie's eyes.

Meaghan reached over and took her hand. "And why Dad was so reluctant to bring me into all this."

"He tried to find somebody else to do the job in your place, but finding impervious people is tricky to say the least." Owen rubbed his face. "I need a shave."

"Why is it tricky?" Meaghan asked.

"You can't use magic," Natalie answered, her voice steadier. "At least not efficiently. You can hex groups of people and look for the one still standing, but . . ." She shook her head. "It's the needle-in-a-haystack thing, only in this case, the needle is invisible."

Owen said, "There's also some stuff in the prophecy about the kings of the lost tribe."

"John and Jamie," Annie said.

He nodded. "And wizards using beacons to heaven to free something evil."

"City hall is the beacon to heaven," Annie said. "Right?"

"Well, not necessarily," Owen said. "Here's the thing—Alastair might not have been a con artist, but he was even less clear than Nostradamus. He was a raving lunatic. The guy set himself on fire, for God's sake. The prophecy is inherently untrustworthy. Not through any intent by Alastair to deceive, but because he was nuts. So, who knows?"

Meaghan snorted. "Which means this prophecy is a load of crap like all the others."

Owen shrugged. "They aren't all crap."

"Yes, they are. I don't believe in prophecy."

"Of course you don't. One of the daughters is described as having a mind like granite, a tongue like a knife, and the gift of plain sight. According to Alastair"—Owen shifted into a thick Scottish brogue—"'she will refuse to heed these words.'"

Natalie snorted back a giggle. "That does kind of sound like you."

Meaghan smiled, relieved to hear Natalie laugh. "What does it say about you? Magic skills, hair like flame?"

"Um." Natalie stared at the table. "I don't think Alastair knew about Clairol."

Annie grinned. "I knew it."

"Don't start with me," Natalie said. "I'm having a really bad day. Wizards want to burn me."

Annie giggled. "Because you turned one of them into a newt?"

Natalie giggled back, and said, in a fake British accent, "I'm *not* a witch. This isn't my nose, it's a false one!"

The women laughed.

Owen rolled his eyes. "Where's the bathroom?"

"Down the hall," Annie said. "First door on the left."

When their laughter subsided, they sat silent for a long moment.

"Why am I joking about this?" Natalie's voice shook. "I'm so scared."

"That's why," Meaghan said. "I do the same thing. So does Russ."

"Promise you won't let them burn me."

"I promise. And as long as Jamie's still on his feet, I don't see how they think they can do it. If he doesn't squish them with a chunk of city hall, he'll blow a hydrant."

"Or one of the sprinkler pipes in the lawn," Annie said. "You'll be too soggy to burn."

"You think?" Natalie asked, her face worried.

Meaghan nodded. "Of course he will."

Natalie sighed. "Don't get mad," she said to Meaghan. "Do you think Jhoro is okay?"

"Is the spell still working?"

"Yes," Natalie and Annie said in unison.

"Annie?" Meaghan didn't need them at each other's throats again. "Keeping it together?"

"I'm fine. But you have to admit that thing with the shirt—"

"Was really hot," Natalie finished, "and he really looked good in those undies."

Annie sighed. "You could see everything. And the hair. He has really great hair."

"Yeah," Natalie said. "And the whole hero thing makes me all . . . melty."

Meaghan smiled. "Brian may not have the hair, but he's got the hero thing down cold."

Natalie looked thoughtful. "You know, I do prefer to be the pretty one in the relationship. Jhoro's . . . I'm not sure I'm confident enough to be with a man that beautiful."

"I know," Annie said. "Brian's not a looker, but . . ."

"He's a surprisingly good kisser," Natalie said. "He's had some practice since high school."

"You've both had some practice since high school." Owen poked his head into the break room. "If you're done doing each other's nails and talking about boys, can we please go save the world now?"

CHAPTER THIRTY-SIX

ANNIE SPUN OPEN the combination lock on the trap-door leading into the tunnel.

"I threw Brian's gun down there," Meaghan said. "We need to find it."

Owen frowned. "You can't use a gun against the wizards."

"I know that. But I promised Brian I'd get it back for him. I'll leave it down there, but I don't want anybody to step on it."

Nobody moved.

"Fine," Owen said. "I'll go. Point the flashlight at the ladder so I can see where I'm going."

Meaghan held the flashlight. She pointed it as directed.

"Meg," Owen said. "Why's your hand shaking?"

"She doesn't like small places," Annie said.

"You're claustrophobic?" Owen asked.

Meaghan nodded. "A bit."

"How big a bit?"

"Oh, pretty big," Meaghan said. She took a deep, shaky breath. "But, if I have to do it, I'll do it."

"She was a trouper coming through the other way," Annie said.

"But now she's had to time to think about it." Owen looked at Meaghan. "I can help you with that."

"How?"

"You know magic doesn't work on her," Natalie said.

"This isn't magic." He asked Meaghan, "You ever been hypnotized?"

"No," Meaghan said, suspiciously. "What are you proposing?"

"Simple little relaxation exercise. Should take about ten minutes. Once you're under, I'll give your subconscious a pep talk and a way for you to remind yourself to relax when we're in the tunnel."

Meaghan hesitated.

"Annie and Natalie are here to make sure I don't do anything weird, okay?"

"You're a leprechaun," Meaghan finally said. "I still don't totally trust you."

Owen nodded. "Understood, but you trust Red and you know she'll blast me into chunks if I try something hinky."

"In a heartbeat," Natalie said. She looked at Owen. "Nothing personal."

Meaghan frowned, still not convinced. "How do you know hypnosis?"

"Something I picked up along the way," Owen said.

Now Natalie was frowning.

"For strictly non-nefarious purposes," Owen said in defensive tone. "Geez. I started grinding my teeth in my sleep from stress, all right? I went to a hypnotherapist when I started getting migraines and it worked so well, I took some classes."

Meaghan nodded. "Okay. That sounds reasonable. I doubt it will work, though."

She was wrong. A few moments listening to Owen's measured voice telling her to breathe deeply and relax and Meaghan was out. When she opened her eyes a few minutes later, she felt great, like she'd woken up from a restful nap.

"If I start clucking like a chicken, I'll kick your ass," she said to Owen, but she was smiling. "I feel great. What did you do?"

"Nothing major."

"He reminded you how tough you are," Natalie said. "Can I tell her the rest?"

"Sure."

"And that when you feel the walls closing in, you'll remember a sunny open place where you feel safe."

"The desert," Meaghan said. "Cool. Let's go."

Once down the ladder, they found Brian's Glock. Natalie tucked it carefully into a corner and put a protection charm on it so only Brian could pick it up.

They headed down the tunnel. Meaghan was amazed at the difference. By now, she should have broken into a cold sweat. But this was a stroll in the park. Whenever she felt the fingers of panic try to work into her, an image of the desert meeting the bright blue Arizona sky filled her mind.

Whatever else Owen had done, he'd turned her from skeptic to true believer in hypnosis. "So my claustrophobia is cured?"

"Well, no, you'd need more sessions for that and even then you'd need the occasional tune-up."

"I may have to look into it. Normally I need a whole lot of Valium to do something like this. Can you use hypnosis for other stuff?"

"Sure. Whatever you want to get a handle on. You have to want to make the change, though."

"Hmm." There were certainly things she'd like to change about herself. And others. "Would it work on . . . say . . . alcoholism?"

"You mean would it work on John?"

"Well, yeah." If she could be sure John wouldn't drink again maybe she wouldn't be so scared to let things move forward with him.

Owen sighed. "Probably not. I mean it might be able to help with cravings, but . . . it's kind of like a love spell."

"But it's not magic."

"No, but remember what I said about love spells creating an artificial emotional connection? Sometimes it can lead to a genuine relationship, but only if that chemistry is already there. Or could be there. You can't use magic to make someone fall in love with you unless they want to. Otherwise the infatuation ends when the spell does."

Meaghan thought about this for a moment. "Hypnosis won't work unless you really want it. And alcoholics, on some level, really don't want to stop drinking. That's their struggle."

"Exactly."

Meaghan sighed. "It was a nice thought."

"But it seems to me," said Owen, "that the problem isn't with John."

"It's with you," Annie said. "I'm sorry. I don't mean to

eavesdrop, but it's not like I can give you any space down here. You want to be with John. He wants to be with you. You're both scared, but you're more scared."

Meaghan felt the need to retort, but couldn't find any words. Because Annie was right. She was absolutely right. "God, you really are perfect for my brother. First, you pull a Martha Stewart with the stolen break room snacks and now you're doing the know-me-better-than-I-know-myself routine."

"You're not mad?"

"Well, a little, but I'm so chilled out from whatever Owen did to me, it's not worth fussing about."

"If we survive this," Natalie said, "we're bringing Owen on as staff hypnotist. You should be ripping Annie's head off right now."

"Really? I'm not like that, am I?"

"Where John's concerned," Natalie said, "um, *sex* with John to be perfectly accurate, yeah, you are. We've all been tiptoeing around you since you got back from Fahraya."

"I thought I'd gotten mellower."

"About some stuff," Annie said. "Not about that."

"Is this why Sid keeps telling me I need to get laid?"

"Yes," Annie and Natalie both said.

Owen laughed. "Oh hell, that's the Troon response to everything."

"Really?" Meaghan asked.

"Oh, yeah," Owen said. "They're notoriously promiscuous. They think the whole male-female, gay-straight thing is kind of silly. And limiting. They think humans would be a lot happier if you didn't try to categorize everything by genital plumbing and fashion sense, and focused on the person instead."

"Yes," Meaghan said. "That does sound like Sid."

"Did he really sleep with Jhoro?" Natalie asked.

Owen laughed again. "Troon are also notorious liars when it comes to sex. I'm sure Sid *tried* to sleep with him."

Now Meaghan laughed. "That sounds even more like him."

"So," Annie asked. "He's only been sleeping with Marnie? I'm still confused by that. He spends his whole life with a man and his rebound relationship is with a woman? That doesn't sound right to me. His grief for Finn is enormous . . . soul-shattering—and the first thing he does is switch teams? *That* sounds like a love spell to me."

Owen nodded. "Yeah, you know it does. This can't be the first spell Marnie cast on him."

"Then why did this one go wrong?" Annie asked.

"I don't know," Owen said. "Maybe this was the first one Marnie cast out in the woods near Finn's grave and the residual gateway magic amped it up somehow."

"Or, maybe," Meaghan said, "somebody else cast their own spell first."

"I told you that in confidence," Natalie said in a small voice.

Owen stopped short.

Annie bumped into him, too amazed by Natalie's admission to wonder why he stopped. "You hexed him first?"

"Owen," Meaghan said from the back of the line. "What's going on?"

"Not us," Owen said. "Get up here and look at this."

Meaghan squeezed past Natalie and Annie. "What am I looking at?"

"Up ahead," Owen said, handing her the flashlight.

She peered over Owen's head and pointed the light in front of her. A tangle of debris snarled the corridor about twenty feet ahead. "Shit. We need to get closer and see if we can get through that."

"Through what?" Annie asked.

"Some kind of cave-in, it looks like," Owen replied.

"Let me see." Annie squeezed close behind Meaghan. "Crouch down a little so I can see over you."

Sandwiched between Owen and Annie in the dark, cramped tunnel, Meaghan closed her eyes and imagined walking through the desert. The sun shone down on her. A slight breeze blew. *This hypnosis shit is amazing*, she thought.

"We're under city hall," Annie said. "That's the entrance to the stairway. We aren't getting in that way."

Meaghan took a deep breath, her calm fading a bit. "Annie, switch places with me, okay?"

They squeezed around each other and Meaghan found herself next to Natalie, who took a close look at Meaghan's face in the dim light and took a big step backwards. "Let me give you some space. You okay? Hypnosis still working?"

Meaghan nodded, her heart pounding. "Mostly. That just got a little close in there."

"*You* aren't getting in that way," Owen said. "But I might. Shine the light up there. The hole. On the left." He shook his head. "I can't tell from here. Let's go take a look."

Annie followed him down the corridor, leaving Meaghan and Natalie alone.

"I'm sorry I outed you about Jhoro," Meaghan said.

Natalie sighed. "I'll live."

"Do you think Marnie knew you'd hexed him?"

"I think she suspected it. Which is why she did her spell."

"To make him forget you? And Finn?"

"Yeah. And to keep liking girls. No wonder it went wrong. I'm such an idiot."

"Well," Meaghan said. "You aren't the only one. I'm betting a few other witches did exactly the same thing."

"Me too. Do you think maybe he . . . I don't know . . . contributed to it?"

Meaghan laughed. "By being too hot to resist?"

"No, I mean something about him hexed us all first. I thought Fahrayans didn't do magic, but he's got some kind of power."

Meaghan nodded. "Yeah, Ruth said something similar and John told us Jhoro had been training himself to be a shaman before he got here. Which is why he knew how to mix up the stuff he gave me that took me on my little psychic trip."

"Trippy drugs and shamanism do kind of go together. You think he's been taking the stuff, too? That's why he's manifesting all the weird stuff Annie's seeing?"

"It didn't have any lasting effects on me, but I only took it that one time."

"And you're impervious."

"Hmm. Good point." Meaghan nodded. "They're coming back."

Owen and Annie made their way through the tunnel.

"It's blocked," Annie said.

"On purpose?" Meaghan asked.

Annie shook her head. "Nope. Looks like a cave-in of

some sort. Maybe from all the damage Jamie's doing to the building."

Meaghan looked at Natalie. "Can you clear it?"

She shook her head. "The tunnel is warded against magical sabotage. Built right into the bricks. I'd bring the whole building down on top of us. We can't get in that way."

"But I can," Owen said. "I'm small enough to crawl through the gap in the pile. The stairs look undamaged. I can get to him while you find another way in."

"He doesn't know you," Meaghan said. "He could crush you like a bug right now."

"And so could the wizards. And whatever the hell they're summoning. If it's the same things Alastair saw in his visions, crushed might be the best-case scenario."

Meaghan shook her head. "Owen, this isn't your fight."

"Bullshit, it's not. I was there, remember? I saw what those things did to Alastair." He looked up at Meaghan. "What they're trying to do to Jamie. Those symbols they carved on him? I've seen them before. Alastair wrote them in his own blood on the front of the village church right before he set himself on fire." He shook his head, his face grim. "Not again. Not if I can do anything to stop it."

CHAPTER THIRTY-SEVEN

THEY SAID THEIR goodbyes.

Owen took Meaghan through a very quick hypnosis session to reinforce his earlier work. "It should be enough to get you back through the tunnel." He said. "We can do more later if you're interested."

With all the magic, nobody's phone worked, so they couldn't call Jamie to tell him about Owen. Instead, Natalie told Owen something only she and Jamie would know to help prove he was on their side, then Annie boosted him through the hole in the pile again. He took the flashlight with him.

With the help of a little ball of light conjured by Natalie, the only magic she could manage without activating the tunnel's existing protection spell, they followed the tunnel back to the historical society and cautiously opened the trapdoor. The house remained dark and silent.

"Okay," Meaghan said as she climbed out of the tunnel, "that's that last time I'm going in there tonight. Gah."

"You're still really calm," Annie said.

"Yeah, but I wouldn't have been for much longer." She laughed. "Yes, Natalie, I know I'm a talented bullshit artist just like Dad."

"I never said that." Natalie was the last one out of the hole. She closed the trapdoor behind her, but didn't lock it.

"No, but you might as well have," Meaghan said. "Seriously, though, I'm surprisingly good."

"So what do we do now?" Annie asked.

Meaghan shook her head. "I don't know. Let's get outside and see if we can call Jamie. Maybe he can create a diversion, and we can sneak in the back way, but we can't risk them getting hold of Natalie."

"And if we can't sneak in?"

"No idea," Meaghan said. "But I can't shake the feeling that I need to be in there. Why, I don't know. I don't have any power."

"What was it Owen said about the prophecy?" Natalie asked. "The daughter with the gift of plain sight? They can't baffle you with magic. You can see their true faces."

"Owen said something similar the first time I met him." Meaghan nodded. "Eliot, too." She sighed. "But these things are strong. I doubt seeing what they really look like will make any difference. Look what they're doing to Jamie. And what they did to poor Alastair Eldrich."

"With magic, which doesn't work on you." Natalie said. "And Jamie's fighting back and winning."

"For now," Meaghan said, "but only because the drug he's taking is goosing his psychic abilities."

His psychic abilities . . . she thought about what Matthew had said to her in Fahraya when she had been tripping on Jhoro's hallucinogenic scorpion antidote. "Psychic isn't magic, it's organic."

"What?" Natalie looked puzzled.

"Something Dad said when I was high in Fahraya. Explaining to me why being impervious wouldn't interfere with the psychic effects of the drug." Meaghan thought a moment. "There's . . . I think there's a connection here somewhere. Like maybe it goes both ways?"

"What the hell are you talking about?" Natalie asked, a worried look on her face.

"I'm not exactly sure," Meaghan said. "Being impervious doesn't prevent me from accessing occasional psychic abilities, right? And Jamie's supercharged mind skills are blocking powerful black magic right now. And Jhoro—"

"Is manifesting psychic crap I've never seen before," Annie said.

Meaghan nodded. "And it seems to be messing with the magic. What if . . . We know psychic ability isn't magical. I'm impervious and I can use it. Magic can amplify it, otherwise Jamie wouldn't have—"

"Superpowers," Natalie said.

"Right, but magic doesn't seem to be able to control it, at least not well. And these psychic skills of Jamie's and Jhoro's also seem to have some capacity to mess with magic. The Order uses magic as a weapon and shield against us. Maybe we can do the same thing against them with psychic energy."

Natalie nodded, staring into the distance. "Like maybe activating enough psychic ability could make people . . . impervious?"

"Yeah," Meaghan said. "Sort of. But, that's only half of

it. What if somebody could learn to use psychic energy as a weapon as well as a shield?"

"And," Natalie said, her voice trembling, "somebody like you, with the inborn trait, would only have to learn the weapon side. If you could wield psychic energy like Jamie currently can, only without the magical interference, you could be . . . unbeatable."

Meaghan nodded slowly. "The impervious witch scenario, only without the witch."

Natalie, eyes wide, took a shaky breath. "You're the one they should be scared of."

Meaghan snorted. "In theory, yeah, assuming I'm right about this. But Jamie only has psychic skills because the drugs and magic aren't working well together and I don't have any psychic abilities at all."

The three women stared at each other for a long moment, then Meaghan shrugged. "I know, Annie, but where am I going to get Fahrayan peyote?"

Annie looked at Meaghan in shock. "How did you know what I was thinking?"

"What? About the peyote?"

Annie nodded, her face pale in the dim light.

"You didn't say that out loud?"

Now Natalie looked shocked. "No. She didn't." She scrutinized Meaghan's face, then understanding dawned on hers. "We were under city hall."

"What are you talking about? Quit looking at me like that. You're freaking me out."

"The hypnosis," Natalie said. "It woke up something."

Annie nodded, eyes wide. She said to Meaghan, "What am I thinking?"

"Um . . . I don't—"

"Don't think about it. Blurt it out. What am I thinking?"

"You're wishing I'd locked you in the forge with Russ because you're scared, and you're not sure how much more running around you can take," Meaghan said in a rush. "You keep flashing back to the image of Jhoro ripping his clothes off, and you're wondering if that's the spell or because it's been a while since you've been with anyone. Not as long as me, but still a decent while. And your feet hurt, and you'd really like a glass of wine and a hot bath."

Annie and Natalie stared at her, their mouths open.

"Oh, shit," Meaghan said. "I must be having a flashback or something."

They were silent a moment until Annie said, "Well, that's not a bad thing, is it? You were worried you didn't have any power. Now you do. Maybe a whole lot more than we think."

"Sounds good," Meaghan said, "except you don't really believe that. You're trying not to freak out at the implications of me with big psychic skills and trying not to admit to yourself that you're a little bit jealous because now you aren't the only special one." She looked at Natalie. "So are you. Sorry. So, the hypnosis—wait, this isn't some leprechaun thing, is it? Did he do something sneaky?"

Natalie shook her head. "I've been reading up on them since the thing out at John's house and nothing's mentioned about them making people psychic. This is something else. How long have you been noticing it?"

"I haven't," Meaghan said. "Not until right now." She thought a moment. "The last little bit of hypnosis, what did he say? I went right under."

"Um, that all the courage and strength you needed you

already had within you, and you could handle whatever came your way," Natalie said.

"Oh," Annie added, "and something about how harnessing the power of your own mind would make you strong."

Meaghan nodded. "And he said all that while we were standing under city hall. A great big magnifier of magical and psychic energy, which is now gushing all over the place instead of being channeled neatly into Jamie's office."

The three women stood in silence for a long moment.

"Well, shit," Meaghan finally said.

"I don't suppose the psychic mojo is helping you come up with a plan," Natalie said. "Sid said in Fahraya you were totally confident that you'd have a plan when you needed it."

"Yeah," Meaghan said. "Some plan. I planted a big sloppy kiss on John to push the bad guy's magic out of his head."

"I told you so," Annie said to Natalie. "You owe me five bucks."

Meaghan looked at Natalie. "You made a bet?"

"Um, is this really the time to worry about that?" Natalie looked sheepish. "Are you going to start yelling at us again?"

Meaghan rolled her eyes. "No. Geez. Have I really been doing that?"

"Yes," Annie and Natalie said.

"I was tripping pretty hard in Fahraya. I got way less confident as the drugs wore off."

"And the psychic stuff faded with the high?" Annie asked.

Meaghan nodded.

"But how do you feel now?" Natalie gazed at her intently. "Are you high again?"

"Honestly, I'm too damn tired to feel anything right now," Meaghan said. "I feel like I'm on Xanax or something.

Kind of flat. Not anxious or confident or happy or sad. I'm—"

A cold spike of pain slammed through her forehead and down into her stomach. She felt herself falling until Natalie and Annie caught her arms and lowered her to the floor. She pulled herself onto her hands and knees and threw up on the cold cement.

"Jamie," she gasped. "He's . . ." She crawled away from the steaming puddle of vomit and curled into a ball as another wave of nausea struck her. Deep in her mind she could hear screaming, an electric shriek of fury and pain. "I think they got in. The Order . . . Jamie." Now a wave of terror and pain struck her. "And Marnie. I feel Marnie." She burst into tears as the full force of Marnie's emotions struck her. Even stronger than her fear was her shame. "Oh, God. They . . ."

"They what?" Natalie asked. "What are they doing?"

"They hurt her. They hurt her so bad and now they're going to burn her. It was you they were trying to get in the first place, but they'll settle for Marnie." Meaghan tried to shove Marnie and Jamie's emotions aside enough to let her think. "For now. They'll settle for her for now."

"Did Owen sell us out?" Natalie asked, her voice grim.

"I don't . . ." Meaghan closed her eyes and tried to slow her breathing. "Let me find him." She tried to reach out with her senses like she had in Fahraya. Jamie and Marnie were so loud, their presences so huge, that Meaghan couldn't get around them. "Too much. Jamie and Marnie. It's too much. I don't know where he is."

"Hiding in plain sight maybe," Annie said, nodding. "If we can get close enough, maybe I can talk to the ghosts in city hall and find out what's going on. One in particular, I think."

Meaghan had never heard Annie differentiate between them before. She wiped her eyes and croaked, "Who?"

"I never knew his name until today." Annie pointed at the ceiling. "His portrait's upstairs. We're in his house. Welland Eldrich. He never left city hall."

CHAPTER THIRTY-EIGHT

"WAIT," NATALIE SAID. "Bat-shit-crazy Welland Eldrich?"

Annie nodded. "Help me get Meaghan upstairs."

They both pulled Meaghan to her feet and half-dragged, half-carried her out of the basement.

"Let go of me," she said when they got to the top of the stairs. "I'm not an invalid."

"Right now you are," Natalie said. "Annie, let's get her into the break room. Clean her up a little."

"Clean me up?" Meaghan looked down at her black V-neck T-shirt, now splattered with vomit. "Aw, shit."

"No, sis," Natalie said. "That's puke. Please tell me you didn't crap your pants, too."

"Bite me," Meaghan gasped. "Bitch."

"Atta girl," Natalie said with a wan smile. "You can always tell she's feeling better when she starts swearing."

They settled Meaghan into a chair, and Natalie handed her a wet paper towel. "Here."

Meaghan dabbed ineffectually at her fouled T-shirt.

"Take that off," Annie said. "I'll rinse it out and get you a clean shirt."

Meaghan nodded and pulled her shirt over her head. At least her bra was still dry. The cannon blasts of emotion had receded, leaving Meaghan numb. She'd failed. She hadn't saved him this time. Or Marnie. What advantage was there to being psychic again if all it let her do was hear their final agony?

She looked up at Natalie. "I don't know what to do."

Natalie plunked a plastic cup half full of a clear liquid in front of her. "Drink this."

"What is it?"

"Drink it. Throw it back. Don't sip."

Meaghan drank as instructed. Liquid fire engulfed her throat and stomach. The taste was pungent, almost antiseptic. The fog in her brain boiled into steam and evaporated. Eyes watering, Meaghan coughed convulsively for a moment, then caught her breath. "Holy hell. What is this shit?"

"Moonshine. I found a jar of it stuffed in the back of a cabinet."

"Moonshine? Really?"

"Yeah. I know the folks who make it. Way back in the woods."

"Human?" Meaghan asked before dissolving into another coughing fit.

"Mostly," Natalie said. "Feel a little clearer now?"

"Yeah. Like a window sprayed with glass cleaner."

Natalie smiled. "Nah. This is stronger than glass cleaner."

"I get now why they call it white lightning," Meaghan said. "Yikes." She looked down at her dingy bra and bare stomach. "I had to put on this bra? I gotta die in this bra?"

"No. Nobody's dying," Annie said. "At least not on our side." She handed Meaghan a red T-shirt. "It'll probably be a little big. All they had in the gift shop was kids' sizes and men's XXL."

Meaghan held it up. A drawing of city hall with the words "City of Eldrich" above and "Founded 1844" below it covered the front. She pulled it over her head. The sleeves hung to her elbows and the hem hung at mid-thigh. The fit wasn't the least bit flattering, but at least it wasn't stained with vomit.

"Here," she heard Natalie say, then Annie started coughing.

"Hoo-whee," Annie said. "The Millers?"

Natalie nodded. She poured herself a shot, screwed the lid back on the Mason jar, and put it back in the cupboard. "If we survive this, we need to bring by a fresh pint and a couple of bags of Pepperidge Farm cookies." She held up the cup. "Cheers." She threw it back, then stomped her foot hard a couple of times. "Damn." She coughed. "Damn."

"We also need to pay for this shirt," Meaghan said. "Should we leave a note?"

"Forget the note," Annie said, her voice sounding strained. "Forget the cookies. What are we going to do now? Owen's missing, Jamie's been taken, and they're about to kill Marnie. We didn't have much of a plan before, but without Jamie, we've got nothing."

Meaghan buried her face in her hands and slumped into her chair. "Let me think a minute."

But no thoughts came. She had no idea what to do next. Every plan she'd come up with had been blocked. Her troops had been injured and scattered. The power of plain sight, and now psychically charged sight, was less than useless if all it showed her were the people she loved—people she'd pledged to protect—being hurt and killed.

Under the blankness, panic began to bubble once again. Annie and Natalie were staring at her and she still didn't know what to do.

Through the roiling fear, a memory rose clear and fresh in her mind. She was sitting at the kitchen table in the Tarrytown house, when Matthew was working for the law firm in Manhattan, long before his breakdown and their move to Arizona. Meaghan was so small her feet didn't reach the floor. Duke, her childhood dog, still young himself, slept next to her chair.

She squinted at a math workbook, a fat pencil in her small fist, frustrated and nearly in tears.

Matthew sat next to her, his arm around her. "Don't worry about the answer yet," he said. "We'll get there. Remember how I said to solve one problem at a time? Well, each problem is really only a set of smaller problems. Solve the smaller problems, one step at a time, and the answer will take care of itself."

Meaghan took a few deep breaths and felt the panic evaporate. Smaller problems. Solve the smaller problems. She pushed down the wave of emotion that was trying to follow the memory. She'd spent so much time over the years focusing on negative memories of her father that she'd forgotten she had any good ones.

"Okay," Meaghan said. "We still need to try to get into

city hall. But first we need more information. I felt strong emotion, but I don't know what it means. We need to figure out if we've lost Jamie or if he can still help. And we need to find out if Owen is still in play."

"And Sid and Jhoro," Natalie said. "We have no idea what happened to them."

"And Jhoro's got some power of his own," Annie said, sounding calmer. "And while the love spell's still working, he's a powerful diversion." The strain crept back into her voice. "Assuming he's still alive. He and Sid."

"Something else we need to figure out," Meaghan said, pushing down her worry for Jhoro. "I watched Sid take a knife to the chest in Fahraya. Him I'm not worried about. He's a lot tougher than he looks. What time is it?"

"A little past four," Natalie answered. "It should start getting light in another hour or so."

"Which gives us another hour of cover." Meaghan stood up. "Time to go. We need to get a look at city hall and the square. See what's going on outside. We'll have to create our own diversion." She looked at Annie. "You think the ghosts can help us if you get close enough to talk to them?"

Annie got to her feet, a wan smile on her face. "Only one way to find out." She turned to Natalie. "C'mon, Little Orphan Annie. Shake those orange curls. We got wizards to fight."

They left an IOU on the fridge and headed out into the night, Meaghan in the lead. Once she'd recovered from the blast she'd gotten from Jamie and Marnie, Meaghan realized that whatever psychic power she had this time was merely an echo of what she'd experienced in Fahraya. She could feel strong emotion around her, but she couldn't pinpoint it.

Which made her feel better about her ongoing inability to sense Jhoro. In Fahraya, he'd felt like a roaring fire, but, assuming he was still alive, his energy was now lost in the crowd.

"You feel anything?" Natalie asked in a whisper as they crept down Iron Street toward the square.

Meaghan shook her head. "It's only noise. No help at all."

"That blast from Jamie and Marnie . . ." Natalie grabbed Meaghan's arm to stop her, a look of cautious hope on her face. "Is there a chance you got it wrong?"

From the back of the line, Annie whispered, "Got what wrong? Why are we stopping?"

"Jamie and Marnie," Natalie said. "Are you sure about them?"

Meaghan sighed. "I'm not sure about any of this. But, as much as I wish I was wrong, I wasn't. That blast was clear. I think whatever Owen did to me was temporary and it's already wearing off. So now I have no power again."

Annie scowled. "Yes, you do. They can't bullshit you, remember?"

"Not with magic, no, but I'm as flammable as anybody else." Meaghan began moving down the sidewalk. "C'mon. We need to get in there before the sun comes up."

CHAPTER THIRTY-NINE

T HEY MADE IT halfway to Main Street. The dimly lit square lay a block ahead.

Then hands reached out of the darkness and yanked them to the ground.

Meaghan felt a rough palm clamp over her mouth. She felt a flare of panic followed immediately by a wave of rage. With adrenaline-fueled strength, she kicked out hard, making contact with flesh. Her attacker rolled off her with a groan.

She scrambled to her feet, then heard a male voice gasp, "Dude, we're on your side."

Meaghan looked around. She saw Natalie lying on top of somebody, kissing him frantically. Annie was crouched by the sidewalk, her hand over her heart, nodding at the small figure standing next to her.

Meaghan looked down at her attacker.

Nate, the tattooed co-proprietor of Eldrich Brew, lay curled in a ball on the grass, trying to get his breath back.

"Nate? What are you doing here?" Meaghan crouched next to him. "You okay?"

"No," he whimpered. "You got me right in the 'nads. Gimme a minute." He drew in another ragged breath. "God, that hurt. Never sneaking up on you again."

"What are *you* doing here?"

Meaghan jumped at the sound of the annoyed voice behind her and turned her head.

Sid stood with his hands on his hips. His clothes were torn and dirty, but he looked otherwise unharmed. "Why aren't you in city hall? Didn't you get to the historical society?"

"We did," Meaghan said. "The tunnel was blocked. Owen got through, but we had to turn back."

"The *leprechaun?*" Sid hissed. "*He's* in there with the wizards? You showed him the way in? You can't trust him. Why can't you see that?"

"Can't trust *him?*" Meaghan's rage, barely abated, rose up again. "He's the only one lately I do trust. The only one who's not keeping secrets from me."

"Oh, he's got secrets. Did he tell you why he's such a different type of leprechaun, why the rest of them won't have anything to do with him?" Sid looked furious.

"No," Meaghan said. "He hasn't told me the details yet because we haven't had time. But he hasn't tried to hide it from me."

Sid shook his head. "You still don't get it."

"No, Sid, I don't get it. Because no one will tell me the complete truth. Owen at least admits things are being kept from me. Which is more than you've ever done. And he's answered every question with a minimum of bullshit."

Shaking with anger, she turned back to Nate. She took a deep breath to calm herself. "Can you stand up?"

He nodded and she helped him to his feet.

"What's going on?" Meaghan peered over at Natalie, who was still kissing somebody on the ground. It was too dark to make out who it was. "Please tell me that's not Jhoro."

Nate shook his head. "Brian. Jhoro's—"

"*Brian?* What's he doing here?"

"Got his people copacetic in Williamsport and cruised back to help."

"So where's Jhoro?"

"Gone," Sid said behind her, his voice shaking. "The mob took him. There were too many of them. Emily did her best to—"

"*Emily?* Did her best to what?" Meaghan grabbed Sid's shoulder. "Kill him? Is she leading that mob?"

"No," a soft voice said at her elbow. "I understand why you'd think that, but I tried to save him."

Meaghan spun around and there stood Emily Procter, hater of all things Fahrayan and Meaghan's nemesis.

"Em's been great," Nate said with a beaming smile. "Kicking ass and taking names."

Emily gave him a nervous smile. "I put up some shield charms to make us a little less visible, but we need to keep our voices down and stay in the shadows." She turned her attention to Meaghan. "You have no reason to trust me, I know."

"You hate Fahrayans," Meaghan hissed. "Remember? You started this whole mess."

Emily nodded, her eyes shiny. "I did."

Meaghan took a deep breath, trying to regain her composure. Emily *had* started the whole mess by helping the Order take Jamie, but she'd had her reasons, it turned out.

Adopted from foster care at age four by a couple who soon conceived another child, Emily had been eight years old when a band of rogue Fahrayans, still tiny and winged, had flown through the Eldrich gateway to raid. Seeing what he thought were fairies, Emily's three-year-old brother followed them into the trees. Emily ran after him and found Toby being brutally attacked by a swarm of tiny flying men. She saved him, screaming and throwing rocks at the Fahrayans until they withdrew, but when her father arrived, all he saw was Emily standing over her bloody brother, a stone still in her hand.

Her story—that Toby had been set upon by vicious fairies and she'd chased them off—had been dismissed as a fantastical lie to cover up a violent jealousy-infused assault. When she stuck, adamantly, to her story, mental illness was assumed.

Emily's terrified parents—faced with the prospect of raising a violent, mentally ill, adopted daughter who had already attacked their biological son—abandoned her at the hospital she'd been sent to for evaluation. Soon after, they terminated their parental rights and Emily was returned to foster care.

In Emily's mind, the Fahrayans had stolen her family from her. She'd nursed a grudge for over thirty years. When Jamie came to work at city hall, Emily finally had a single focus for her rage and pain. For a long time, she limited her revenge to trying to make his work life miserable.

Until the Order approached her with warnings that Jamie intended to seize control of Fahraya and resume raiding in the human world. When they asked for her help in stopping him, she gladly agreed. Not only had she torn off his amulet in city hall, forcing his conversion to his Fahrayan form, but she'd helped the wizards kidnap Jamie from his home.

Emily hadn't appeared particularly chastened by her role in Jamie's ordeal, but neither had she gloated. Meaghan had given her a wide berth, partly out of caution, but more out of the knowledge that if Emily pushed her, even a little, Meaghan would explode into rage and say or do something she couldn't take back.

Like she might right now, except for that tiny voice of reason in the back of her head. *Get a grip on yourself. Hear her out.*

With heroic effort, Meaghan forced herself to take a few deep breaths before saying, through gritted teeth, "You expect me to believe you'd help Jhoro? Why would you do that?"

To her credit, Emily met Meaghan's furious glare and didn't look away. "I helped him because he helped me. He showed me . . ." Her eyes filled and a tear slipped down her cheek. "He showed me what his people really were. And what they've lost. What I helped take from them."

Meaghan's rage evaporated. She'd seen enough of Emily faking friendly feelings to be able to tell she was now sincere. How long it might last was anybody's guess, but at this moment she was an ally. Maybe it was a mistake to trust her, but Meaghan needed all the help she could get right now. Even if it came from a backstabbing witch and a leprechaun with a shady past.

"Okay," Meaghan said. "Good. I'd rather have you helping us than helping them." Or helping yourself, Meaghan thought, but reminded herself that Emily had never been *truly* evil. She'd done an evil thing, handing Jamie over to the Order, but she'd had her reasons, however misguided they were. Emily could be petty, controlling, and occasionally malevolent, but she was motivated by fear more than cruelty.

They'd never be friends, she and Emily, but for now they were on the same side.

Meaghan looked around the small group. "Fill me in. What do we know?"

Nobody spoke.

Solve the small problems first.

Meaghan turned to Brian, who was now on his feet, Natalie at his side. He wore a glowing smile and had an arm wrapped protectively around her.

"What happened to Eliot and Ruth?" Meaghan asked him. "I told you to stay with them."

"I called a buddy in Williamsport to keep an eye on them. He's former military and the son of a witch. He pulled some strings at the hospital and got Eliot rushed into surgery with a minimum of questions. They're in good hands." Brian brushed a red curl off Natalie's forehead. "I couldn't leave my best girl behind. She might forget all about me."

Natalie wore an adoring smile. "Never."

Meaghan rolled her eyes. "What happened to Jhoro?"

Sid, his voice tight, refused to meet Meaghan's eye as he answered. "The mob we saw on the square, they chased us until we ran into *them*." He gestured at Nate and Emily.

"We were hunting," Nate said. He rubbed his nose and stared down at his feet. "For Jhoro. We thought he'd done all this and if we stopped him, then everything would be okay."

"You thought that," Emily said, patting his arm. She sighed. "I was still looking for revenge."

"Yeah, well, me and the guys wanted that, too," Nate said. He looked back at Meaghan. "We wanted to kick his ass for stealing our wives. The spell . . . you know. You saw it this afternoon at the Brew."

Meaghan nodded. "You said the guys?"

Nate grinned. "Oh, yeah. There's a bunch of us."

"We're not all guys," said a woman now standing behind Nate. "My husband thinks he's gay now. We'll be having a big talk when this is all over."

Several men laughed quietly.

Meaghan looked around. More figures had arrived out of the darkness. A few she recognized from around town. Others she'd never seen before. Several, she knew, were not clued in. Or at least hadn't been until very recently. Meaghan recognized the woman who had spoken as someone she'd seen in the Brew, but she didn't know her name.

To the woman, Meaghan said, "My brother got all gay, too, but he got over it."

Annie snorted back a giggle. "I'll say."

The new arrivals were armed with baseball bats, golf clubs, and garden rakes.

"Any guns?" Meaghan asked.

"No," Brian said. "Fortunately, I hooked up with them before they ran into Jhoro. Got rid of the guns as fast as I could. I remember how I felt when the spell had me. I use a gun professionally, and I could barely control myself. No way am I letting untrained, magic-addled civilians have them."

"Good. So, how's the angry husband club doing now?'

"And wives," said a male voice behind, followed my more soft laughter.

"All we want to do now," Nate said, "is get our wives—*spouses*, sorry—back before they do something crazy."

"Like burn a witch?" Natalie asked, her voice an octave higher than normal.

"Yes," Emily said. "And they won't stop with Marnie. There are hexed witches in that mob, and they'll be next. I've worked with the Order, remember? They won't be satisfied until every witch in Eldrich is dead."

CHAPTER FORTY

N O ONE SPOKE for a long moment.

Smaller problems, Meaghan thought. But even the smaller problems suddenly felt huge. With a sick feeling in her gut, Meaghan asked, "What's the mob planning for Jhoro?"

Emily answered. "They didn't take him so much as he led them away from us. The mob is made up of those who got hit with the attraction part of the spell. Right now they all love him, but that could change."

With a quick glance at Natalie, Meaghan said, "This spell is unstable, isn't it?"

Emily frowned. "I think it's more than that. It seems like several spells interacting. My husband and I—" She stared at her feet, obviously flustered.

Meaghan smiled. She couldn't help herself. "Yes, I ran into you in city hall yesterday, remember?"

Nate leaned toward Emily and nudged her with his elbow, a

knowing smile on his face. "You and the mister, huh? I notice he's not here. You wear him out?"

Emily spluttered a bit and then said with a giggle, "Well, yes. I think I did. He's home asleep."

Meaghan was struck by how different Emily looked, with her face softened into a genuine smile. Seeing it made Meaghan realize how tight and rigid Emily normally appeared, how *scared* she always looked. Meaghan had always read fear in Emily, but now realized that what she'd perceived as insecurity mixed with arrogance was more accurately terror and gut-wrenching anxiety.

What an awful way to live, Meaghan thought. *No wonder she's so bitchy all the time.* She felt the last shreds of resentment melt away. This was an Emily she might actually be able to like rather than merely tolerate.

"Okay," Meaghan said. "We've got multiple spells." She carefully avoided looking at Natalie. "We've been thinking the same thing. Would that explain the varying reactions?"

"Maybe," Emily said. "But Marnie's spell appears to be the one that's gone wild. If we can get that reversed, things should calm down a bit. Then we can unravel the rest of it."

Meaghan thought a moment and decided to err on the side of trust again. Emily seemed to be dealing fair with her so she'd return the favor. "Do you know about Jamie? And what the Order is trying to summon?"

Emily frowned. "Jamie? What's he got to do with this? I'd heard he was in the hospital in Williamsport."

Meaghan shook her head. "Jamie's in city hall. He's why the wizards are here in the first place. They followed him here from Williamsport, but he wouldn't let them get inside."

Emily's eyes widened. "He did all that damage?"

"Yeah. He's been trying to keep the wizards out because they want to use him to open a mystical door to let in something very, very bad. We don't know what exactly, but we do know it's a huge threat to all of us. End-of-the-world kind of threat."

Emily's smile was gone, replaced by fear. "What . . ." She wiped at her cheek. "What are they doing to him? Are they hurting him again?"

Meaghan realized with a start that Emily was crying. "We don't know. For a long time, he was fighting them. But I think they took him."

"No," said a voice from the shadows, "they didn't, the assholes. They got into city hall, they woke up these fucking things on my chest again, but they didn't get me."

Jamie walked into the dim light of the street lamp. He wore grubby blue hospital scrubs, his feet bare. The sigils stood out clearly on the faded blue cloth and when he came to stand in front of Meaghan, she saw they were scorch marks as if the scars had burnt the cloth. A manic grin stretched across his sweaty, flushed face. His blue eyes were preternaturally bright, the circles underneath even deeper and darker than they'd been the last time Meaghan had seen him.

"Wow," Jamie said. "I can see right through your hiding spells. It's like magical X-ray vision."

"Let me see your eyes," Meaghan said, pulling him close. She grabbed his chin and tilted his head in the dim light. "Your pupils are enormous. You look like a sad-eyed puppy in one of those tacky black velvet paintings."

"It's dark out," he said. "Everybody's got big pupils."

"Not that big," Meaghan said. She threw her arms around him and hugged him fiercely. "You're high as a kite, you little shit. I'm so glad to see you. I thought they got you."

"They tried. They got in the building. Had me cornered in Emily's office."

"My office?" Emily squeaked.

Jamie stepped back, glanced at Emily, and then glared at Meaghan. "What's *she* doing here?"

"She's helping us," Meaghan said. "She went after Jhoro, and when she caught up with him, he did his woo-woo shaman thing on her, and she's very sorry, and now she's on our side."

"He did his what?" Jamie scowled.

"We don't know what he's doing, but it turns out he's got some big psychic mojo of his own."

Jamie snorted. "Of course he does. Anything I do, he's gotta do better. He was like that when we were kids. He hasn't changed a bit." He flipped invisible blonde hair out of his face and gave Meaghan a huge cheesy smile. "Ooh, look at me. I'm Jhoro. I'm too sexy for this world. Everybody wants me."

"Nice," Meaghan said. "The world is ending and we gotta deal with this? Stow the sibling—*cousin*—rivalry. How did you get out of city hall?"

"Oh, that." Jamie scratched his arms absentmindedly. He could barely stand still. "That was kinda cool. I sort of *floated* out the window and down to the lawn. I couldn't bring down the building like I thought, but I can fly . . . well, not fly really, more like fall slowly. It's sort of like flying, but only in one direction."

Natalie shoved Brian aside. She seemed angry. "How the hell did you do that? You've never been able to do that. I can't even do that."

Jamie smiled at her. "Nat!"

She shoved him away when he tried to hug her. "Don't you Nat me, you tweaker. How much of that lorazepam stuff have you taken?"

He sighed. "Don't be pissy. I'm fine."

"How much?"

Jamie rolled his eyes and started walking in a tiny circle in front of her. "I tried cutting back, but when I heard the wizards coming I knew that was a mistake, so I jammed a nice full needle into my vein before they broke the door down." He stopped circling and tried to stand still, but within moments, he was bouncing up and down on the balls of his feet. "I can handle it."

Natalie snorted. "The hell you can. Eliot said too much of that shit would kill you. Give you a heart attack." She punched him hard on the arm. "If you die, I'm gonna be so pissed at you. I'll hold daily séances so I can tell you what an asshole you are."

He grinned at her, rubbing his arm where she'd hit him. "I love you too. You can drag me to rehab when this shit is over, but now we've got wizards to fight." He looked over at Meaghan, still grinning. "Where's this Eliot guy anyway? I'd like to meet him."

Brian stepped to Natalie's side. "Injured. In the hospital in Williamsport."

Jamie squinted in the dim light. "Brian? What are you doing here?" He stared at him a moment. "Wait. You were at my house. When I . . ." He shut his eyes, the manic energy draining from his face. "When I . . . did what I did. Oh, God. I'm . . . it's . . ." He looked back at Natalie. "I lied. I'm not fine at all. If I live through this, I'll do whatever it takes to make it up to her. And to you. To all of you."

Natalie grabbed him into a fierce hug. "Shut up. Nobody's dying tonight. Except those damn wizards."

Jamie let himself be hugged for only a moment before pulling away. He looked at Meaghan. "What are you doing here? Is my father here?"

Meaghan shook her head. "We locked him and Russ away somewhere safe."

Jamie giggled. "I'm guessing John didn't agree to that."

"No. He's pretty angry with me right now."

Jamie gave her a small smile. "He'll get over it. He really likes you." He took a deep breath. "So, what's going on out here?"

Sid finally stepped up. "Did the leprechaun sell us out?"

"Sid!" Jamie gave him a beaming smile, then looked puzzled. "What are you talking about?"

"You didn't see a leprechaun in city hall? He was supposed to find you and help you."

"There was nobody there but me and the wizards."

"I knew it," Sid said, his voice grim. "I knew we couldn't trust him."

Meaghan glared at him. "You know nothing. You don't even have circumstantial evidence. For all we know, the stairs collapsed under him and he's lying dead at the bottom of the tunnel. Give it a rest."

"But—"

Meaghan silenced him with a furious look. "Enough." She turned back to Jamie. "Did you see Marnie? Was she with the wizards?"

Jamie shook his head. "No. Not that I noticed, but it was crazy in there. But I did see the bonfire the mob was building. Whether that was for me or Marnie, I don't know."

"What about the wizards who took you in June? Or that thing that was inside your uncle? Are they involved in this?"

Again Jamie shook his head. "I didn't see them, but I heard somebody calling for . . ." He shivered and for a moment looked small and lost. "Cooper. The one in charge. The one you confronted at the gateway. And if he was there, then the other two—" He squeezed his eyes shut, but not before a tear slipped down his cheek. "That big one, the one who . . . cut me . . . he . . ."

Natalie drew in a sharp breath through her gritted teeth.

"He's dead," Meaghan told Jamie. "We watched him die."

Jamie sagged with relief. "He's dead? Really? He's dead? Oh, thank God."

Meaghan put a supportive arm around him and he clung to her. She could feel his body shaking. She gave him a moment to calm down, then asked. "That . . . thing in your uncle. The Power. Is it involved?"

Jamie nodded but seemed calmer. Of the two, Meaghan would have expected him to be more afraid of the Power. "It's . . . I could feel something, but I don't know if it was that or the other . . . *things* that are trying to get through. I think they're related somehow."

"The things the wizards are trying to let in?" Meaghan asked.

Jamie nodded.

"But Cooper can't let them in without you, right?" Natalie looked back and forth between Meaghan and Jamie for confirmation.

"Wrong," Annie gasped from the periphery as she slumped onto her knees in the grass, holding her head. "They've got a replacement."

CHAPTER FORTY-ONE

"**I**S THIS WHAT you felt in the basement?" Annie asked. "When you got sick?"

Before Meaghan could answer, Annie vomited onto the grass. Meaghan rushed over to her and pulled back her hair as she vomited again.

Annie rubbed her mouth with her hand and grimaced. "Ewww. I wish I hadn't eaten all those cookies."

Meaghan stroked her back. "What happened?"

"Someone stabbed me in the forehead with an icicle dipped in acid." She crawled away from the puddle and then curled in a ball on the grass. "Gah. That was awful."

The group stood silent, staring at Annie, while Jamie crouched down next to her. "Who's my replacement?"

Annie smiled faintly. "Don't get jealous. Your cousin. They took your cousin from the mob."

Jamie squeezed her shoulder gently and smiled. "Of course they did. That show-off. Where did they take him?"

"Inside. The vortex." Annie shut her eyes tightly and seemed to be listening to something.

"What are they doing to him?" Meaghan asked.

"Hang on a sec." Annie, eyes still shut, nodded. "I can hear the—" She curled into a ball and cried out in pain. "Oh, they . . . it's the blood. They're going to use his blood."

"But, I thought they needed Jamie," Natalie said.

"No," Annie said. "They're far enough along that painted sigils will do. Jhoro's blood is close enough to Jamie's to work."

"Oh, shit," Natalie said. "They'll use his blood to draw them. Like Alastair did."

Meaghan nodded. "The conduit and the sacrifice. That's what Finn told me. Blood and fire. The symbols and blood must be the conduit and they'll burn Marnie as the sacrifice. Only whatever Alastair summoned scared him so badly he set himself on fire."

"Who's Alastair?" Jamie asked.

"So Alastair torched himself as a sacrifice to these things?" Natalie said. "That doesn't make any sense. Those things didn't get into our world then or we wouldn't be here now."

"Who's Alastair?" Jamie asked again. "When did you talk to Finn?"

Meaghan scowled. "Maybe he did it wrong. Maybe it didn't work because he burned himself instead of somebody else. Who knows? But we've got the same scenario unfolding here and we can't allow it to happen."

"Who the hell is Alastair?" Jamie asked, frustration in his voice.

"Scottish guy," Annie said, still curled in a ball on the ground. "Welland Eldrich's many times great grandpa. Nuttier even than Welland. Barbecued himself after painting bloody sigils all over the church wall. Owen knew him."

"Who's Owen?" Jamie asked. "Who are all these new people?"

"Owen's the leprechaun," Meaghan said distractedly. "The one who was supposed to join forces with you in city hall."

"I'm so confused." With a heavy sigh, Jamie slumped down next to Annie. Even in a reclining position, he couldn't stay still. His legs twitched and he shuffled his feet restlessly in the grass.

Annie reached out a hand and patted him clumsily on the head. "You aren't the only one." She pulled herself awkwardly into a sitting position and looked at Meaghan. "So, what do we do now?"

Meaghan flashed suddenly on a memory from her first year of law school. A professor had grilled her about a concept she didn't understand, badgering her for an answer despite her obvious confusion. When he had asked her in exasperation what she would tell her client, she had replied, in tears, "I'd tell him to find a real lawyer."

For a moment, Meaghan wanted to throw back her head and wail, "Find a real leader." Instead she took a deep breath to steady herself and said, "Let me think."

Smaller problems. Meaghan shoved aside her worry for Jhoro and Marnie for the moment. Rushing in unprepared wouldn't help them.

She did a quick mental inventory. She now had two witches on her side as well as Jamie and his current abilities. And she thought she could trust Emily for now.

As for Jamie—at the moment he was firmly on their side, but for how long? His ability to fight the influence of the sigils was pharmaceutically induced and she had no clear idea how long she could count on it. He was fidgeting like a strung-out junkie. When the magically supercharged lorazepam wore off, what would happen? Would he merely fall back under the sigils' influence or would something more dramatic occur? Worse, could he go from ally to enemy without anyone noticing? Provided he didn't have a heart attack first.

For now, she'd ask Natalie and Annie to keep an eye on him. That was the best she could do in the circumstances.

Owen was on the missing list—he might still be in play, but without knowing more, Meaghan couldn't count on his assistance. She had been surprised by her furious reaction to Sid's accusations about Owen. Sid wasn't saying anything she hadn't said herself only yesterday. She knew she shouldn't trust Owen, but somehow she did. Whether that was wise or foolish remained to be seen, but Meaghan didn't want to believe that he'd sold them out.

And then there was Sid. She didn't want to be angry with him. He'd been a brave, loyal companion in Fahraya and he'd nearly given his life helping her get Jamie back.

If it was only his mistrust of Owen, she could deal with it. But Meaghan knew he was hiding things from her. She knew him well enough to believe that he was trying to protect her, but somehow that made it worse. Sid was keeping things from her that he didn't think she could handle. What if he was right? What if he and everyone else could see what she herself believed in her deepest heart—that she was too weak and too powerless to fill her father's shoes?

How was she supposed to believe in herself if nobody else did?

She sighed and shoved down her insecurities. For good or

ill, everyone was looking at her for answers. She didn't have time for self-doubt.

Smaller problems . . . could she count of either of the mobs circulating through Eldrich?

From what Meaghan could tell, most of the band following Nate were non-magical. Witches seemed drawn to the mob building the Order's bonfire. But why? That made no sense. Why would the witches want to burn another witch? Why was the spell so strong when it came to the witches?

Meaghan glanced around to see what everyone was doing. Nearby, Emily stood alone on the sidewalk, staring at her feet, trying to avoid Natalie and Jamie, who were sitting together on the grass whispering to each other and glaring at her.

Meaghan knew that asking them to trust Emily was impossible. The best Meaghan could hope for was to avoid outright mutiny. Nate and Emily's companions were also getting restless, some pacing, others whispering in small groups.

Meaghan needed to get a handle on things fast or there'd be trouble. She grabbed Sid and Nate and pulled them aside. "Let me get the chronology straight," she said in a low voice. "We were on the square and Jhoro took off to lure the mob away and you followed him."

Sid nodded.

"And then the wizards headed to the square to find us, so we headed over to the historical society," Meaghan said.

"Which was where I figured you'd go when I saw the wizards cross the road." Sid laughed nervously. "Hey, that sounds like the start of a joke. Why did the wizard cross the—"

He wilted under Meaghan's glare.

"What happened then?" Meaghan asked through gritted teeth.

"Uh, well, we ran around a bit, letting the mob chase us. Mobs don't move very fast, by the way. You'd think they would, but—"

"Sid," Meaghan said. "Not a great time to be cutesy. What happened?"

"We tried to lure the mob away from the square and ran smack into his bunch."

Sid pointed at Nate, who nodded and took up the story. "They grabbed Jhoro, then Brian pushed to the front of the pack and tried to shield him from Emily, who wanted to blast him into chunks right there."

Meaghan nodded. "Yeah, that's what I thought. What happened next?"

Nate shook his head. "If I hadn't seen it, I wouldn't believe it. Hell, I did see it and I can barely believe it."

"Jhoro did something?"

"He smiled at her," Nate said. "He nudged Brian aside, and took hold of Emily's hand. She was so stunned she didn't resist. They stared at each other for a long moment, then Emily began to cry. Big, sobby, weepy crying. She gave him a big bear hug and then turned around and told us to knock it off, that Jhoro wasn't the enemy, and our job was to help him keep our loved ones from doing something stupid that they'd all regret."

"What did everybody else do?" Meaghan asked. "Emily got them to back down?"

"No," Sid said. "Jhoro got them to back down. It was . . ."

Nate stared into the darkness. "I'm not sure I can even describe it."

"What did he say?"

Nate shook his head. "He didn't *say* anything. He . . . *showed* us. It was like . . . well, like doing 'shrooms. Ya know?"

Meaghan nodded. "I know. Believe me. I know."

Annie had wandered up while Nate was talking. "Did you see the memories?" she asked. "Like ghosts but not? I'm sorry to be so imprecise. I can't really describe it, either. Ghosts are the closest thing I can think of, but that's still completely wrong."

"I suddenly had all these memories and feelings that weren't mine," Nate said. "I could . . ." He grimaced. "It was like for a moment I knew everything about everything and then it was gone."

"You saw whole," Meaghan said.

His face lit up. "Yeah. Saw whole. I like that. I can't exactly remember what it was I saw, but I can feel it. Only I can't find the words to explain it."

"It sort of *transcended* words," Sid said. A moment later, he shook his small blue head. "No. That's not right. It didn't transcend words because it wasn't . . . *of* words." Sid looked at Meaghan. "I'm sorry. I can't describe it either."

"Did everything seem clearer and brighter afterward?" Meaghan asked.

"Yeah. Yeah, it did."

Meaghan smiled. "Same thing happened to me in Fahraya. After drinking a concoction brewed up by Jhoro. John said he was teaching himself how to be a shaman."

Nate nodded. "Shaman. Cool. That makes sense. So, then Em did some kind of counter hex to the love spell and we all got sane again."

Emily had joined them. "And then the *other* mob arrived," she said. "The one with all the witches. That's when things got weird."

CHAPTER FORTY-TWO

"*THAT'S* WHEN THINGS got weird?" Jamie bounced to his feet and walked over to Emily. "At the beginning of the summer, you handed me over to those Order fucks so they could torture me to death, and now I'm supposed to trust you? You really expect us to believe you went from hating me and the rest of my species to being all warm and fuzzy because my super awesome cousin held your hand?"

"You have no reason to trust me," Emily said in a soft voice. "None at all, and it's my fault. I did a terrible thing to you and asking for forgiveness now is beyond presumptuous. That level of forgiveness has to be earned." She looked around the crowd. "I know it's hard to believe, but it's what happened."

Jamie glared at her. "You bet it's presumptuous. If I live through this, which is far from certain, I'll carry the scars of what you did to me for the rest of my life. I've lost my family. I'll share the blame with you on that one, but I doubt it makes any difference to my wife, who's never coming back, and who can blame her?"

Natalie shook her head. "Jamie, you don't know—"

"Yeah, I do. Now shut up." He pinned Emily under his furious glare. "I don't know who I am anymore, but I'm not the guy she married. He died in Fahraya and you helped kill him. I think you're an evil, conniving bitch, and this little performance is more of your bullshit. Nothing is forgiven. You try to betray us, and I won't need that bonfire to burn a witch." He tapped his temple. "Right now I can do it with a thought."

Nate stepped toward Jamie. "Yo, dude, that is so unfair."

Jamie glared at him. "What the fuck do you know about it, *dude?*"

Emily stepped between then. "Nate, it's all right. God knows, it's the least I deserve." She looked up at Jamie, who towered over her. "Do what you have to do. I don't know who I am now, either. I want to believe I won't betray you, but even I don't know that."

"Knock it off," Meaghan said, pulling Jamie away from Emily. "We don't have time for this shit." She glared up at Jamie, then turned to Emily. "What happened when the mob arrived?"

"They were wild. Like those films of early Beatles' fans. Screaming and crying. I thought they were going to tear him to pieces along with anybody else who got in their way."

"Was Marnie with them?" Meaghan asked.

Emily shook her head. "Not that I saw."

"I don't think she was there," Nate said.

Meaghan sighed. "That means the wizards still have her. So, then what?"

"I got everyone behind me and tried to put up a barrier," Emily said, "but I was so outgunned it was impossible. I told them to run and then I felt a hand on my shoulder. It was Jhoro. He smiled at me, and then walked past me toward the mob."

Meaghan nodded. "And then he smiled at them, right? And they all stopped and smiled back?"

Emily looked startled. "Yes. How did you know that? I still can't believe I saw that happen."

"The same thing happened in my kitchen a couple days ago. It was only three witches, but I could barely believe it either. Then what happened?"

Jamie snorted with disgust and walked away.

"He led them away from us," Emily said. "We were about to follow when we heard the wizards running up the street."

"So we all ran up this way and dove into the bushes to hide," Nate said, "and then Sid told us what you guys were trying to do, so we decided to try to come find you. Before we could go any further, you almost stepped on us." He grinned at Meaghan. "And you kicked me in the nuts."

"Yeah," Meaghan said. "Sorry about that."

"No, I get it. Good fighting technique. Always go for the soft bits." He looked back and forth between Meaghan and Emily. "So, now what do we do?"

Emily looked at Meaghan. "Yes, now what?"

We find a real leader, Meaghan thought. Out loud, she said, "Well, I think it's safe to assume, based on what Annie told us, that the wizards found Jhoro and the witches right after they left you. We still need to find Marnie and we have to try to rescue Jhoro. And we have to stop the wizards opening the door to whatever's on the other side. We still need to get inside city hall."

"We could do a locating spell," Emily said.

"We already tried that," Natalie said, her voice cold. "I'm with Jamie on this. Why are we trusting her? On her word that she's had some kind of mystic conversion experience? This is only a more clever variation of the Pollyanna fake-friendly crap she pulls all the time."

"Meg's big lately with the misguided-trusting thing," Sid added from the shadows. "That leprechaun sold us out. I know he did."

What if they're right? What if I've killed everybody by trusting the wrong people?

Annie stepped into the silence, shaking your head. "Sid, you're wrong about Owen. He may have an agenda we don't know about, but he's on our side."

"How do you know?" Natalie said. "He's not dead, is he? It's only dead people you talk to."

Annie glared at her. "You should shut up once in a while. You don't know as much as you think you do."

Natalie growled and began waving her hand.

"Babe," Brian said, stepping between Natalie and Annie. "Calm down."

"Don't you 'babe' me," Natalie snapped at him. "You aren't my boyfriend. Stop acting like you are."

Brian's eyes narrowed. "Oh, it's like that again, huh? Good old Brian. There when you need him, like a faithful dog. I'm done chasing you. You aren't worth it."

"Fine," Natalie said. "You aren't him and you're never going to be him."

Meaghan groaned. Without Jhoro's psychic influence, the spell was reasserting itself.

Nate snorted. "Let the wizards have him. Maybe now I can get my wife back. All we need to do is take care of that bitch Marnie. She's the one who started this mess." He looked around the crowd. "Come on. Before it's too late."

Before Meaghan could stop him, Nate ran off into the darkness followed by most of the crowd. She glared at Emily. "Is this your doing?"

Emily shook her head, eyes wide. "No. I . . . no. If you want me to go I can, but I'd like the chance to help you. I've got a lot to atone for."

"No kidding," Jamie said. He looked at Natalie. "Can you believe this shit?"

"Not in the least," Natalie said, lifting her hand again to cast a spell. "I think it's time for some payback."

Meaghan stepped in front of her and slapped her face hard.

"*Bitch,*" Natalie hissed. "Watch it or I'll—"

"You'll what?" Meaghan snarled back. "Hex me? Go for it. Because we've got so much time to waste right now tearing each other apart." She looked over at Emily. "For what it's worth, I think you've had a genuine change of heart, but . . ."

Emily nodded. "I'm a distraction. The best thing I can do for you right now is be somewhere else. I'll try to find Marnie and protect her." She took a last sorrowful look at Jamie, then ran into the darkness.

"And off she runs, like the coward she is," Natalie said, with a smug smile.

Meaghan resisted the urge to slap her again. *It's the spell,* Meaghan reminded herself.

"What are you looking at?" Natalie glared at Brian. "Aren't you supposed to be in Williamsport? Aren't you supposed to be—" Natalie made air quotes with her fingers—"*protecting* Eliot and Ruth?"

"What's that supposed to mean?" Brian glared back.

"Oh, I think you know," Natalie said with a sneer. "Meaghan sent you off to get you out of the way. So you don't get hurt. Why don't you go find some safe place to hide while those of us who can actually do something get back to work?"

Brian stared at her for a long moment, his face unreadable, then he nodded. "I'm going after Emily."

Natalie refused to look at him. "You do that, *babe.*"

Brian nodded again and disappeared into the night.

"Nat," Jamie said. "Geez, why are you being such a bitch? Emily needed to leave, yeah, but Brian could have helped us."

"It's Marnie's spell," Meaghan said, her voice tight. She could feel the anger bubbling up inside her trying to burst out. "Ignore her."

Natalie glared at her. "You're just jealous. Because I have real power. And I'm younger."

Seeing the look in Meaghan's eye, Sid grabbed Natalie's arm. "Whoa, there, sweetie, let's go over here a second, okay?"

As they walked past her, Annie said. "At least Meaghan has an actual human hair color." She turned back to Meaghan. "So, what do we do next?"

"Are you still with me? Have you lost your mind again, too?"

Annie shook her head. "Not totally. But Natalie is getting on my last nerve. The way she treats Brian is inexcusable."

Meaghan shrugged. "That's the spell."

"No," Jamie said. "It isn't. She's always been awful to him. Poor guy. He's loved her since high school. She gives him enough to keep his hopes up, but no more. He'd marry her in a minute if she'd have him."

"Maybe not anymore," Meaghan said, remembering the flat, dispassionate tone in his voice when he said he was leaving. "Not that it matters if we don't get into city hall soon." She sighed, aware again of how exhausted she was. But that didn't matter. She had work to do.

Jamie and Natalie were by far the strongest of the group, but both were increasingly unreliable. Every moment took Jamie closer to when the lorazepam finally wore off and the black magic of the sigils reasserted itself. Or he had a heart attack.

Natalie was now acting like the stereotypical high school mean girl, with the exception of being able to hurl hexes along with insults.

Annie seemed to be keeping it together better and she could talk to the ghosts in city hall, true, but she had no defensive abilities. In a confrontation with the wizards, she'd be helpless to protect herself.

Then there was Sid, who still didn't trust Meaghan enough to tell her what was going on, but seemed to have no problem criticizing her judgment.

The person she most wanted by her side right now was John. But he was locked behind a magical door that couldn't be opened for hours. And she'd tricked him into being locked behind that door.

Jamie touched her arm and smiled at her. "Don't worry. John will get over it. You made the right call."

Meaghan frowned at him. "You can read minds now, too?"

He laughed. "No. That one I could read on your face. I better go talk Natalie off the ledge before she turns Sid into a frog." He gave Meaghan a sideways glance. "No matter what happens between you and John, I'm not calling you Mom."

Meaghan smiled, feeling better for a moment. "I can live with that."

CHAPTER FORTY-THREE

WITH EVERYONE LOOKING to her for answers and no better options, Meaghan decided to stick with the original plan. They would get as close to city hall as they could without being detected, so Annie could try to talk to the ghosts, Welland Eldrich in particular.

The wizards must have all headed back inside after grabbing Jhoro. Meaghan couldn't think of any other reason why they hadn't been attacked yet. Even with Emily's protection charm, they hadn't exactly been quiet.

But they were running out of time if they wanted to sneak up under the cover of darkness. The blackness now had a charcoal-gray quality to it. Birds were singing.

"Let's move, people," she hissed. "Dawn's almost here."

"The wizards aren't out," Jamie said. "Only the mob and the—"

"Mob-ette," Sid offered. "The husbands barely qualify as a full-fledged mob."

"Whatever," Meaghan said. "Quit talking and move. We don't want to run into either group."

"I'm not going anywhere with *her*," Natalie said in a petulant tone, "unless she apologizes for all the cracks about my hair."

"Oh, please," Annie said. "What about *you*? You called me a bleach blonde tramp."

"Like hours ago," Natalie countered. "You've been busting on me all night."

For a moment, Meaghan knew exactly how Owen must have felt when they forced him to drink tea and eat cookies at the historical society.

"Ladies," she said, her voiced dipped in acid, "if it's not too much trouble, I strongly recommend you stow this bullshit immediately or neither of you will have hair to insult. Because I will have pulled it out by the roots while knocking your bitchy little heads together." She put on her most fearsome glare and pinned them under it. "I don't care how addled you are by magic. Get your shit together. Right now. Because you aren't any good to me like this."

"Now, Meg," Sid said, "relax. They're only blowing off steam. Something you should—"

"Don't start with me," Meaghan said in a low tone. "You and I are on the outs at the moment, in case you haven't noticed. I'm tired of being lied to. I'm tired of people hiding things from me. I'm still trying to process the fact that the only one who appears to have been straight with me is a leprechaun, who by all reports should be inherently untrustworthy."

Sid snorted. "Yeah, because he is. Why can't you see that? He hasn't actually told you any of the details of what he did."

"No, but he hasn't hidden them, either."

"Oh, sure, he gets caught and he confesses he lied without actually telling you what it was he doesn't want you to know about and that's being honest? Come on, Meg, are you that naive that you'd—"

"He told me about the prophecy."

Sid's eyes widened in shock. He shook his head. "He wasn't supposed to do that. Matthew didn't want—"

Meaghan had passed through the white-hot anger into icy rage. In a deceptively calm voice, she said, "He also told me about the war."

Sid whimpered.

"How, Sid," Meaghan said, her voice cold, "am I supposed to do the job that's been dumped on me if nobody will tell me the whole story?"

"But," Sid said in a breathless squeak, "Matthew told us not—"

"Matthew is dead, Sid. My father is dead. Which we are all likely to be soon if we don't figure out how to stop these things. Whatever they are. But then I suppose you know that, too." She took a ragged breath. The rage was waning, leaving her shaky and on the verge of tears. "You keep looking at me like I have all the answers, but you don't trust me enough to tell me what I'm fighting. Am I truly that incompetent?"

Sid shook his head. "No, no. You aren't incompetent at all. But you're not invincible either. The prophecy . . . it says . . ." He shook his head more emphatically. "I promised Matthew I wouldn't tell you."

"What does it say?"

"It says . . ." Sid looked up at her, his eyes shiny with

tears. "It says you're going to die. The Order is going to kill you."

Meaghan stared at him for a moment, mouth open, before replying. "That's what everybody's been hiding?" She rolled her eyes. "Let me guess. They want to burn Natalie because this stupid prophecy says they can take me out only if they kill her first." She looked around at her companions. Silently, they stared at her, wide-eyed. "Quit looking at me like that."

"Like what?" Jamie said in a soft voice.

"Like I'm about to explode. You guys . . . Owen was right. Humans will believe anything. *Prophecy*." Meaghan snorted with disgust.

"But they're going to kill you," Natalie said, her earlier peevishness gone. "And me."

"No. They're going to *try* to kill us," Meaghan said. "That doesn't mean they'll succeed. I don't believe in prophecy. Point out one clear, unequivocal prediction that Alastair Eldrich got right."

They continued to stare at her, eyes wide.

"Like I said. I don't believe in prophecy." Meaghan began walking toward Main Street. She didn't care if they followed her.

Natalie scurried to catch up. "Alastair predicted *us*. He predicted that Matthew and Vivian would hook up and have me."

Meaghan shook her head. "No. He didn't. Think about it. He predicted that an impervious man and a witch would have two daughters. Why does that have to mean us?" She stopped walking and whirled around to face Natalie. "Alastair said they'd have two daughters, not a daughter together and a daughter from a previous marriage. I'm not Vivian's daughter. Shouldn't that disqualify us?"

Now Annie caught up with her. "Well, that's kind of splitting hairs, don't you think?"

"Yes, and that's the whole point. A prophecy you can interpret to mean different things doesn't tell you anything about the future. Because you can twist words around to mean anything. Trust me on this. I do it professionally every day." Meaghan stopped and looked around. "Is Sid still with us? Or is he sulking?"

"Both," Sid stage whispered. "I'll follow you, but I can sulk if I want while I do it." In a very small voice, he said, "Are you still mad at me?"

Meaghan was surprised to realize she wasn't. "Not really. That was a big secret. I get why you didn't want to tell me that one."

"You really need to take it seriously."

"No, Sid, I really don't." She began walking again. They were almost to Main. The square appeared deserted. "I'm not living my life based on the incoherent ravings of a madman."

"But," Jamie said right behind her. "It says they'll kill you. Haven't you been listening?"

Meaghan snorted again. "You of all people should know better. You can twist the law to fit any set of facts you get handed. I know. I've read your case files. You're an even more talented bullshit artist than I am. How am I supposed to die? Does it even say that?"

"Yeah," Sid answered. "It says they'll quench your vital spark."

"Which means what exactly?"

"Your heart," Sid said.

She gave him a skeptical look.

"All right, fine. Quit it with the lawyer face. That's the way I've always heard it. Vital spark is the electrical charge that runs your heart."

"But," Meaghan said. "It also says quench, which suggests drowning. And vital spark could also be interpreted to mean brain-wave activity. That's the true measure of death."

"Yeah," Sid said. "I suppose."

"Assuming for argument that I am the one Alastair wrote about, does it definitely say I'm going to die?" Meaghan asked.

"Well, not as such . . ."

Meaghan rolled her eyes. "That phrase could mean so many different things that trying to predict the future from it is useless. Worse than useless, because when people believe shit like that, they'll force events to make it come true. At some point, it stops being a prophecy and becomes a to-do list."

"Your father believed in it," Sid said.

"You sure about that?"

"Well . . . he believed other people believed it."

Meaghan smiled. "Now that I can believe. He sent me a message about it from wherever he is now. Through Finn. He told me to use my head and find the loopholes."

Jamie chuckled. "Yeah, that sounds more like Matthew."

"*Guys,*" Natalie squeaked behind them. "Trouble!"

Jamie whirled to look at her. "What?"

The mob boiled out of the shadows.

CHAPTER FORTY-FOUR

MEAGHAN WAS KNOCKED aside by the mob in their rush to grab Natalie. When Jamie tried to protect Natalie, the mob grabbed him, too.

Annie and Sid were nowhere to be seen.

Rough hands seized Meaghan from behind and pulled her to her feet. A balding, middle-aged man in a gray robe, about her height but paunchy, stepped into her line of vision.

"I've been wanting to do this all night." With a leer, he pulled back his fist and punched Meaghan in the face.

She squealed in pain, feeling the blood pour from her nose and lip.

The wizard pulled back his fist for another blow, then a voice said, "Enough. Cooper wants her awake. He wants her to watch."

The first wizard scowled at her. "This won't knock her out."

He dropped his fist and punched her in the lower abdomen.

Meaghan crumpled to the ground. Searing pain was followed by a wave of nausea as she gasped for air. In her mind, she was screaming obscenities at him, but the only sound she could make was a high-pitched whimper.

The wizard rolled her onto her back and straddled her, pinning her arms beneath her body. He reached under her baggy T-shirt and fumbled for the zipper to her jeans. "The bitch needs to learn her place."

Panicked, Meaghan tried to pull her arms free so she could push him away, but they remained crushed beneath her. She tried to kick him, and he kneed her in the groin. Gasping for breath from pain and from his weight on top of her, her nose clogged with blood, she felt her head grow light. Yellow lights sparked and flared in her darkening field of vision.

The second wizard again intervened, knocking his companion off her. "Not yet. We're taking her to Cooper. He gets her first. After we light up the other two."

The first wizard grunted in disgust and dragged Meaghan to her feet. He pulled a plastic zip tie out of his robe and cinched her hands behind her back. He shoved her hard in the middle of the back. "Move."

Meaghan stumbled, but managed to stay on her feet as he prodded her toward the square. She waited for the powerful rush of anger that normally drowned out her fear, but it wouldn't come.

She had always convinced herself that she could talk or fight her way out of any situation. But she'd been easily bested by a paunchy middle-aged man. If the second wizard hadn't intervened, hadn't wanted to save her for something even worse, the bastard would have raped her right there on the sidewalk. In front of friends and enemies alike.

Meaghan knew she had to keep fighting, but she felt small and terrified and more powerless than she'd ever felt before.

Until she saw Jamie and Natalie. Jamie still wore the scrub pants, but his shirt was gone. Natalie had been stripped down to her underwear. She clung to Jamie, weeping and shaking with fear, while the crowd dragged and shoved them toward the unlit bonfire in front of city hall.

Distracted from her own fear, Meaghan felt the rage finally rise up. She turned to the wizard pushing her. "I'm gonna watch you die, asshole. I promise you."

The man merely laughed and shoved her harder. "You're scaring me to death. I'm gonna love watching Cooper strip the skin from your bones. After you watch us burn your witch friends."

The anger blew through her like a biting wind, clearing the panic and pain away. Even if the prophecy was right and she was doomed to die today at the Order's hands, she was taking as many of them with her as possible.

Dawn was upon them. The sun wouldn't rise over the horizon for an hour or so, but the gray light had turned pink. Meaghan looked around the square, searching desperately for allies.

Still no sign of Annie. Or Sid. Maybe they hadn't been grabbed. Maybe they got into city hall and—

Meaghan felt the momentary flare of hope sputter out. Even if Annie and Sid could get into city hall, then what? What could they do, alone, even with any information Annie might be able to glean from the ghosts?

The sea of people around her seemed unrecognizable. She knew many of them, but their faces were twisted and contorted with malice. Like something else was in control.

She'd seen this before. In Fahraya.

Could the thing that had infected Jamie's uncle infect an entire crowd of people? It thrived on fear and pain and hate. She and John had suspected it wanted a way into the human world, but they had assumed that it could only occupy one host at a time, like it had occupied V'hren.

A man in the crowd called to her as the wizards dragged her past. "I'm stronger now. You won't stop me this time."

A woman on her other side shouted, "Did you really think I was done with you?"

Sally, Nate's wife, stepped in front of her. Good-natured Sally, with her tattoos and freckles and optimism, sneered at her in a way that Meaghan knew Sally was not capable of, and said, "You'll get to watch them all die before I gut you."

With a roar, Meaghan kicked her in the knee and Sally went down with a shriek. Something in her eyes changed and, for a moment, the real Sally looked back at Meaghan in shock.

One of the wizards grabbed the back of Meaghan's neck and shoved her forward. She had no time to see what happened to Sally.

What Meaghan didn't see in the crowd were any witches. They'd been leading the mob earlier, but now there was no sign of them. Only when she was shoved closer to the bonfire, did Meaghan finally see them. About twenty-five women, some she considered close friends, were huddled together near the bonfire, surrounded by a circle of wizards. The most powerful were restrained. She saw Susan, Gretchen, and Lynette chained together, duct tape over their mouths and fury in their eyes.

But the rest merely stood, staring blankly into space. Some were crying, others smiling, but all appeared to be lost within themselves. A younger one shook her head hard, as if clearing it, and threw herself toward the wizards. Before she reached them, a flash of vivid green light enveloped her. She screamed, convulsed, and dropped to the ground.

With a start, Meaghan realized it was the girl who had been at her house the other day. The trainee witch, Cassandra—real name Dana—the 9-1-1 dispatcher who had done such a good job making sure the right people responded to the explosion at Jamie's house.

The balding wizard, the one who had tried to rape her, saw her staring at Dana's crumpled body and shoved her so hard she almost fell again. "Don't worry about her. Worry about yourself. You're gonna die screaming, bitch."

Meaghan turned and gave him the fiercest glare she had. "Don't gloat yet, asshole. I'm taking you with me. Or at least some of your favorite body parts." She sneered at him. "As little as they may be."

The wizard raised his hand and muttered, a look of fury on his face.

Nothing happened.

He took a step backward, eyes wide with fear, before regaining his composure.

"Still impervious," Meaghan said with a sweet smile. "How's it feel to be impotent, shithead?"

He punched her in the gut again so hard that she doubled over in pain, but it was worth it for the look on his face.

They still get surprised when magic doesn't work on me. Could she use that somehow?

"Your witch friends are still gonna burn. Along with the Fahrayan." He twined a hand in her hair and yanked her upright. "I can't wait to get my chance with you. I'm gonna make it hurt. Like it hurt that spell-casting slut we caught in the woods. Only this time her big blond boyfriend will get to watch. We got something special planned for him."

"Yeah, I know," Meaghan snarled. "We're all gonna die. And so are you when those things you're trying to free finally get here."

His eyes widened.

Gotcha. I'm not supposed to know about that am I? She smiled at him again. "You're expendable, shithead. You're gonna be monster chow. If this was Star Trek, you'd be wearing a red shirt."

The other wizard stepped toward them. "Quit flirting with your new girlfriend. Cooper's waiting. He wants to move this along and he's losing patience. You want to piss him off? I don't."

Baldy's eyes grew wider and he shook his head.

The other wizards were afraid of Cooper, Meaghan realized. Could she somehow work that to her advantage, too?

She stared at the witches. Why didn't they do something? They stood there, like cattle, patiently waiting to be slaughtered.

Like bewitched cattle. This mob had consisted of the people, women mostly, who'd been attracted to Jhoro. Judging by the dreamy looks on many of the witches' faces, they were off in romantic head movies where Jhoro was the star.

Meaghan took as deep a breath as she could with her bruised stomach muscles, and shouted, "They're going to kill Jhoro! They took him so they can kill him!"

The wizards kept prodding her along.

She scanned the huddled witches. If she could wake them up, pull them out of their love-spell-induced dreams, they might have a chance. A few women shook their heads as if mildly distracted, but the only reaction came from the trio of chained witches. They stared at Meaghan and began frantically gesturing with their heads toward something.

Jamie. They were directing her to Jamie.

He and Natalie had been chained back to back to the light pole jutting from the middle of the bonfire. Natalie was sobbing, a wad of cloth shoved into her mouth. She struggled against the chains but couldn't move.

Jamie hung limp, the chains the only thing keeping him from collapsing to the ground. His head hung down as if he'd passed out.

Then with a shriek, he threw back his head, and began to struggle. The sigils on his chest glowed red, as if on fire. Natalie screamed in pain as the sigils on his back burnt into her.

With an ominous creaking, the light post swayed, but didn't fall. Smaller chunks of wood from the pile rose into the air and flew at the wizards surrounding them, but without enough force to harm them.

The lorazepam was wearing off.

Jamie wailed with rage, then fear, shrieking, "No! No!"

A wizard walked up and backhanded him hard across the face. Jamie slumped against the light pole, weeping.

Meaghan's heart sank. Jamie had been her last hope. She couldn't see any way out of this. There was nobody left, nobody powerful enough to stand up to the wizards.

Then she heard a car engine, revving high and growing closer. Somebody was coming.

CHAPTER FORTY-FIVE

T HE SOUND OF the approaching vehicle grew louder. Whatever it was, it was big. After a moment, Meaghan heard the whine of a second engine.

She glanced at the wizards. Both stared in the direction of the sounds.

Baldy muttered, "What the hell?"

Meaghan heard a crack, like fireworks going off, and Baldy flinched as if punched and fell face first to the ground. A red stain blossomed on the back of his gray robe.

A second crack rent the air. The other wizard screamed and fell. He held his leg, shrieking in pain, as blood bubbled through his fingers.

The sound of the engines forgotten, Meaghan wheeled wildly around trying to find the source of the shot.

City hall. Somebody was shooting from the roof.

A few more cracks and more wizards fell. The shooter was taking his or her time and targeting only robed wizards.

Whoever was shooting was on their side. Brian, she thought. It's got to be Brian.

The mob broke in panic, running from the square. The witches appeared to be waking up, looking around confused.

The remaining wizards began frantically gesticulating and shouting. They were trying to put up a barrier to block the sniper.

Meaghan sprinted toward the bonfire, clumsy with her hands tied behind her back. She had to rally the witches and get Jamie and Natalie free before the panicked wizards ignited the pile.

A wizard tackled her. He kneeled over her, fist raised to strike. Another crack and he fell sideways, screaming.

Meaghan crawled out from under him and scrambled awkwardly to her feet. She heard yet another crack, this time followed by a sizzle and burst of light.

The barrier was up and the sniper couldn't help her anymore.

She surveyed the scene. The wizards had circled the witches, chanting, and Meaghan watched some, but not all, of the witches' faces go slack again.

Those witches still in control of their faculties conjured their own barriers. The witches began waking up again, but they were trapped. If they lowered their barriers to attack, they'd be easy targets for the encircling wizards.

The mob began to calm and started to methodically line South Street along the square. Another circle was forming behind the bonfire. Between the barricades on either end of the block and the human wall connecting them, the vehicles she'd heard would only be able to approach by mowing over the hexed and possessed townspeople.

She heard the witches screaming and whirled toward them. They were staring in horror at the bonfire. Natalie struggled to free herself, but Jamie still slumped in his chains, weeping. Two wizards were emptying gas cans onto the wooden pile.

When they were finished, they tossed the empty cans away, and moved back. A few more wizards, some limping and bloodstained from the sniper's shots, approached them. They formed a circle and began to mutter and sway. Sparks crackled in the air above their heads.

As Meaghan screamed and ran toward them, time seemed to slow. What felt like minutes was probably only seconds.

A lot happened all at once.

The wizards stepped back and Meaghan could see a ball of flame hanging in the air.

Natalie let out a muffled wail of terror as the witches screamed.

The ball of flame began to spin rapidly, then shot toward the pile. The ball flew in a smooth arc toward Natalie and Jamie, but at the last second swerved, as if it had been swatted aside. It still landed on the pile, but on a far corner.

The wood smoldered a moment and then caught fire, but with a gentle whoosh. By some miracle, the wizards' ball of flame must have landed on a portion of the pile that had not been splashed with gasoline.

Meaghan heard screams behind her and saw the mob lining the street fleeing from something. The whine of vehicles at high speed was joined by a blaring car horn.

The driver didn't swerve to avoid townspeople or the barricade. Instead the first vehicle came *over* the barricade.

It was a pink Hummer—bubble-gum pink—with huge

tires and a snowplow blade on the front. What it couldn't shove aside, it drove over.

An advertising wrap, designed to look like a leopard print scarf, twined around the doors and hood, and featured a photograph of a smiling middle-aged woman with black hair and big gold earrings, next to bold letters stating, "Gigi Nackos, Your Happy Valley Real Estate Expert!"

It screeched to a halt in front of her. The passenger door swung open.

Patrice sat behind the wheel, tiny inside the massive space. She barked, "Get in."

As soon as Meaghan neared the door, hands reached and pulled her into the vehicle. Before she registered whose hands they were, she gasped, "The fire. They're burning Jamie and Natalie. We have to put it out."

"Done," Patrice said. A moment later, the fire hydrant on the east end of South Street exploded. Water gushed into the sky and then seemed to bend in a graceful fountain toward the pile.

The flames went out with a hiss of steam. After thoroughly soaking the pile, the water seemed to bend again, and shot at the wizards like a high-powered fire hose. Screaming, they were knocked off their feet.

Meaghan finally noticed the other occupant of the vehicle. John.

She gaped at him as he pulled her over the console and into the backseat. He produced a knife and cut the zip tie binding her hands.

"What . . . what are you doing here?" she finally managed to stammer.

"Saving you," he said with a grin. He pulled her into a crushing hug. "I'm not so helpless as you think."

"But the forge, the lock, only Terry can open it. Who let you out?"

John nodded in the direction of Patrice. He gave Meaghan a warning look and Meaghan realized he was afraid. "She is strong now. I . . ." He shook his head. "She is more than she appears."

Patrice gunned the Hummer in the direction of the bonfire, not swerving. Wizards dove out of the way. She screeched to a halt in front of the now steaming pile and shouted, "John, you're up."

He reached behind the seat and pulled out a huge set of bolt cutters. "Come. Help me. I'll get him, you get her."

They climbed out of the truck and onto the pile. Grunting, his neck muscles straining, John cut through the heavy chains. Jamie slumped into his arms, and John threw him over his shoulders in a fireman's carry. Meaghan pulled the now loose chains from Natalie and ripped the gag from her mouth.

Natalie clung to her, crying and shaking so hard she could barely stand. Meaghan half-dragged, half-carried her to the Hummer.

John placed Jamie in the front seat and climbed in the backseat with Meaghan and Natalie.

Patrice glanced over at Jamie and caressed his cheek with her fingers. He barely stirred. "Come on, big guy," she said with a gentle smile. She leaned over him and fastened his seat belt. "Let's get those nasty things out of your head."

"Buckle up and hang on," Patrice called over her shoulder to the backseat occupants. She jammed the Hummer into reverse, and screeched backward in an arc until she was facing city hall. She stepped on the gas and accelerated toward the front door.

The sun barely peeked over the horizon. The first rays of daylight highlighted the battered wreck of city hall. The turret where Meaghan's office had been looked like an exploded firework. The roof was gone and twisted girders splayed out like the petals of an iron flower. Meaghan could see her desk, teetering on the edge of what remained of her office floor.

Next to it, where Jamie's office had been, yawned a gaping hole. It might have been a trick of the morning sun, but the hole seemed to be glowing, pulsating with yellow light.

Two wizards stood on the walkway, not moving as the Hummer sped toward them. They looked smaller and thinner than the wizards on the square, like Caleb, the possessed kid who'd attacked Meaghan in June.

"Patrice, don't hit—"

Before Meaghan could finish, Patrice nodded and the wizards were swept aside, gently, like autumn leaves in a light breeze.

Two larger wizards stood behind them, on the short flight of steps leading to the door, carrying semi-automatic rifles. With a savage laugh, Patrice drove up the stairs straight toward them. Before they could flee, she was on them. They both disappeared under the vehicle.

Meaghan and John exchanged a glance. He had gotten to know his daughter-in-law fairly well over the last couple of months and Meaghan could tell by the look on his face that he was as shocked as Meaghan by Patrice's bloodthirsty demeanor.

She looked over at Natalie who sat huddled next to her,

shaking with cold and fear. Natalie met her gaze, wide-eyed, and shook her head.

The Hummer crashed through the front entrance, the snowplow blade splintering the heavy oak doors and shattering the plate glass, then screeched to a halt in the lobby right in front of the security desk.

Patrice looked in the rearview mirror with a smile. "How we doing back there? Everybody okay?"

The three occupants of the backseat nodded, eyes wide, unable to speak.

"Great," Patrice said. "John, would you grab that cardboard box in the back and see if you can find some clothes and shoes for Natalie? And there should be an old pair of Jamie's running shoes in there, too. There's a lot of broken glass on the floor."

While John rummaged for the clothes, Meaghan remembered the second vehicle. "Where's Russ? Was somebody following you?"

Patrice nodded. "That was Russ. In his food truck. It's a little dinged up in the back from the police car, but once we moved that out of the way, it was fine."

Meaghan glanced at John. The police car had been a lump of mangled steel. It would require some serious muscle and possibly a blow torch to untangle it from the truck and break it into small enough pieces to shove out of the way.

John raised his eyebrows and tilted his chin slightly toward Patrice.

"But it's steel," Meaghan whispered to John. "It's impervious."

Patrice sighed. "I know you have a lot of questions. Trust me, I do too. I don't know how I'm doing this stuff. I just am, and until we get this mess cleaned up and get everybody home safe, I'm not going to worry about it. We can figure out what I am tomorrow."

Natalie squeaked with fear.

Patrice turned in her seat. "Please don't be scared. Whatever this is, whatever I *am*, I'm still me."

With a slight tremor in his hands, John handed her a large pair of battered running shoes.

Her face lit up with a smile. "There they are. Good thing I grabbed them out of the minivan. I had a feeling we might need them." She took the shoes and turned back toward Jamie. "Honey, give me a foot."

He didn't move.

Patrice snapped her fingers in front of his face. "Hey, Sleepy, wake up. We're gonna go fight bad guys now." She sighed, then slapped his face a few times. "James, wake up. Now."

He groaned and opened his eyes. He blinked up at her a few times. "I'm sorry," he said, "They made me. I'm . . . if you never forgive me, I understand."

Patrice grimaced. "Don't be a dope. I'm not that fragile." She smiled and caressed his cheek again. "Baby, you're a mess." She leaned over and kissed him on the forehead. "Don't you worry about me. If you ever hit me again, I'll kick your ass to the moon."

He smiled back at her. "That seems fair." He shut his eyes. "I'm so tired." He opened his eyes. "Are the kids okay?"

"Fine. They're at the Nackos family reunion down in Altoona. Gigi took the kids and the minivan and I took her truck."

Jamie chuckled weakly. "Yeah, this looks something Gigi would drive."

Natalie stared out the window, blankly. John handed

Meaghan a wad of clothing from the box. She passed it to Natalie, who grasped it close, but didn't try to get dressed.

"Where's Russ?" Meagan asked again.

"Mopping up and freeing the witches," Patrice said. She raised her eyebrows. "With *Emily* of all people. Didn't see that one coming." She looked around the truck. "Everybody ready to go? If you need to use the bathroom, now's the time. The lavs on two and three probably aren't working too well thanks to Bob the Un-Builder, here." She patted Jamie's shoulder. "C'mon, honey. Let's go save the world."

CHAPTER FORTY-SIX

PATRICE HELPED JAMIE get his shoes on, kneeling to tie them the way she did with the kids.

Natalie seemed to snap out of her stupor, at least enough to wrestle on the mismatched T-shirt, shorts, and sneakers John had found for her.

Patrice pulled a tub of baby wipes out of the console and rubbed some of the grime off Jamie, carefully avoiding the bright red sigils. If they caused him any pain, Jamie gave no sign of it. Patrice's reappearance and casual forgiveness seemed to steady him. Despite the blood and dirt, and the huge circles under his still overly dilated eyes, Jamie looked calmer and more like himself than he had in a long time.

While Patrice was cleaning up Jamie, John used a couple of baby wipes to gently dab the crusted blood off Meaghan's nose, lips, and chin.

"I was afraid you'd be mad at me," Meaghan said.

"Oh, I was. Very angry." John smiled. "Then she opens

the door and Russ and I are too busy to be angry anymore. There. All clean and beautiful."

With her fingers, Meaghan carefully felt her cut lip and swollen nose. "Liar. I bet I look awful."

"No worse than last time," John said. "For either of us. You were all scraped up and had a big bandage on your arm and your head full of Jhoro's special drink. And I was a wingless Fahrayan. How about when this is done, we have a wash, you put on a dress, I put on a clean shirt, and I take you somewhere for a nice meal?"

Despite everything she'd been through, despite her pain and fear, Meaghan laughed out loud. "Are you asking me out on a date?"

John looked puzzled.

"Courting ritual," Jamie called over. He buzzed a Fahrayan word at John.

John, nodded, now understanding. "Yes, I am asking you out for the date."

Patrice giggled. "About damn time."

Jamie glared at her.

She smiled back and handed him a faded blue polo shirt. "Oh, don't be Mr. Grumpy-pants. This is a good thing."

"It's my father, going out with my boss. Tell me how that's a good thing."

Natalie punched him lightly in the arm. The simple task of getting dressed seemed to have calmed her quite a bit. "Don't be a whiney puke. Old people get to have romance, too."

"*Old people*?" Meaghan shook her head. She looked at John. "Did you hear that?"

"Yes," he said, grinning. "So, you say yes? To the date?"

"Yeah," Meaghan said, smiling back. "Absolutely. If the world doesn't end and we aren't dead, it's a date."

John beamed.

"But, I thought you going on a date meant the world *was* ending."

Meaghan whirled around. Russ was standing in the shattered doorway. He waved his fingers at her. "Hey, sis." He stepped closer. "You look like shit."

She grinned at him. "You should see the other guy."

"Shot or squished?"

"Shot. Nice work getting Brian up on the roof top."

Russ looked puzzled. "Brian's in Williamsport." He looked around at everyone. "Isn't he?"

"So, you aren't responsible for the sniper?"

Russ shook his head. "Not us. We were trying to figure out who did it." He looked around again. "Where's Annie?"

Meaghan shook her head, her good mood abruptly gone. "I don't know. I haven't seen her or Sid since the mob grabbed us."

"She got away?" Russ chewed on his lip, looking worried. "You think she's okay?"

Meaghan nodded. She had no idea what happened to Annie, but if it made Russ feel better, she was happy to lie. "And Brian came back from Williamsport. Emily didn't tell you?"

"We didn't really have time to talk," Russ said. "The door opened, Patrice . . ."—Russ waggled his fingers—"did something to the handcuffs. She told us Emily was on our side now and that John was riding in the Hummer and Emily and I were following in the food truck. We picked up Nate on the way."

"Nate?" Meaghan asked.

"Yo!" Nate sauntered in and waved. "Hey, Patrice. I hear you turned into Wonder Woman. I like the pink Hummer. Is that like your Batmobile?"

Patrice merely smiled.

Nate looked at Meaghan. "So, what's the plan?"

Meaghan stared at him. "Why are you asking me? Go ask Wonder Woman."

Patrice laughed. "I'm not the leader." She turned to Natalie. "Would you grab the cooler bag out of truck?" She turned back to the crowd. "Juice boxes, water, and snacks. Everybody make sure to grab something. I'm sure you're all hungry and dehydrated." Now she looked at Meaghan. "You're the leader. I'm the secret weapon."

"And the mommy," Jamie said, grinning. "Black magic can't withstand the power of a chilled juice box and a bag of Chex-Mix. You got trophies in there, too? Participation certificates?" He put his arms around her and gave her a quick kiss. "I love you so much. Those shithead wizards don't stand a chance against you. How did I ever forget that?" Then he doubled over, his hand on his chest, groaning. "Oh, shit, that's how."

Patrice supported him so he wouldn't fall. Her face grim, she said, "That's it. I want these things off you. I'm done with this." She looked upward. "We need to get upstairs. Send these things back to whatever hell they're trying to break out of."

After some arguing, Russ relented and took Nate back out to the truck where Emily waited. Their job was to round up the witches and make sure no other wizards could get into the building. Or out. They were also sorting out the possessed kids in gray robes from the surviving wizards.

The mob had melted away once it was no longer controlled by the Power. Whether the Power was gone or merely lurking, looking for a new vessel, no one knew. Meaghan's bet was on the latter. Hopefully, without the raging emotional energy of the mob fueling it, the Power would again be limited to one person at a time. If not . . . Meaghan shook her head. She wasn't going to think about that right now. She had to keep moving.

Meaghan led them up the stairs to the second floor. The plan was to do a sweep, looking for wizards before climbing to the third floor. They found several wizards in Emily's office. The biggest one tried to hex them.

Patrice dropped him with a look.

"Um, honey," Jamie said gently. "You're kind of . . . glowing. And you're hair, your ponytail, is all . . . floaty. Is that normal?"

Patrice's dark hair floated outward like it was charged with static electricity, perhaps from the pulsing golden aura now visibly surrounding her. "I have no idea what's normal right now. Not a clue." She looked at the two smaller wizards, who huddled together. She smiled. "You boys can go. Take off the robes before you go outside, okay? So you don't get blasted on your way out the door."

"We're . . . we . . ." The taller one swallowed, his face turning red. "We're naked underneath."

Patrice nodded. "Hang on a sec. Let me fix it. Hold still." Shaking, he obeyed.

With a glowing finger, Patrice traced the shoulders and collar of his robe. The sleeves and hood fell away, leaving the boy standing in a gray sleeveless shift. She then waved her finger and the letters "OK" appeared on the fabric over his chest, as if scorched into the cloth. She did the same thing to the other boy.

The boys stared at her, wide-eyed.

"There," she said, standing back to admire her handiwork with a smile. "Off you go. There's a cooler on the hood of the big pink truck parked in the lobby. Make sure to grab a juice box and something to eat before you leave. You're both too skinny."

They nodded and ran.

"Don't forget," Patrice called after them. "I'll know if you don't take anything."

"Baby, you're kind of scary right now," Jamie said. "Sweet, but scary. Like some kind of vengeful mommy goddess."

"Yes," Patrice said, "but I've always been like that, only without the superpowers." She looked at everyone else. "Okay, let's do one more quick sweep to make sure nobody sneaked down the stairs and then we'll head upstairs."

Meaghan looked at John. She didn't need to be psychic to know he was thinking the same thing she was. Patrice was more than "kind of scary" at the moment.

Natalie was thinking the same thing. She grabbed Meaghan's arm, holding her back a moment as Patrice led Jamie and John out into the hallway. Before Natalie could say anything, Meaghan whispered, "What is she? Have you seen anything like this before?"

Eyes wide, Natalie shook her head. "Never."

"Is it witchcraft? Magic?"

"No freaking idea."

"Has she ever given any signs of abilities, magical or psychic, before this?"

"Not that I've seen and Jamie's never said anything. I spend an awful lot of time with them. Patrice has never . . . nothing. We used to joke about how she was the normal one."

"Does she know anything about her family?"

Patrice poked her head in the door. "No, not a thing." She sighed. "I can hear you. In here." She tapped her forehead. "I know you're scared. I can feel it radiating off everybody, even Jamie. But I'm still me. I think I'm more me than I've ever been. I can't explain it any better than that. Whoever . . . *whatever* I am, I'm supposed to be here doing this. Stopping this. And so are you." She smiled. "C'mon. We have to get upstairs. They're almost here."

"Who's almost here?" Meaghan asked.

"*Them*." Patrice's brow furrowed. "I'll explain later. If there is a later. C'mon." She turned and walked out of Emily's office.

Meaghan grabbed Natalie's hand and dragged her forward. "You heard the scary mommy lady. Let's go save the world."

"And then we can have a juice box," Natalie said. "At least this day can't get any weirder. Can it?"

CHAPTER FORTY-SEVEN

"AND YOU DIDN'T think it could any weirder," Meaghan whispered to Natalie as they trudged up the stairs to the third floor.

Patrice had already dispatched several more scared boys—wardrobe change and juice boxes—and a few wizards, which involved significantly more screaming and no snacks.

The climb seemed much longer than it should have. It was like the space had been stretched and the air thickened. Every step took more effort than the last one.

As they climbed, Patrice glowed even brighter. Her hair, now escaped from its ponytail, floated in a mahogany nimbus around her head. The light emanating from her was so bright it hurt to focus on her for too long.

With every step, Jamie grew visibly weaker, his face slick with sweat and contorted with pain. The sigils glowed red, so hot that they'd burned holes in his shirt. He finally tore it over his head, gasping for breath. "Hurts. It hurts."

John threw Jamie's arm over his shoulder to support him. He tried to pick up Jamie and carry him, but Jamie resisted.

"No, you'll . . . they'll burn you." Gingerly, he rested his forehead on his father's shoulder. "Stop, give me a minute."

John gently squeezed the back of Jamie's neck, careful not to brush against the sigils. "I've got you."

"I'm scared."

"I know."

"Don't go away again."

"Never."

At which point, Meaghan's eyes filled with tears. "Goddammit," she muttered. "Damn crybaby."

Natalie handed her a roll of toilet paper.

"Where you'd get this?" Meaghan tore off some tissue and handed the roll back to Natalie.

"Second floor men's room. Figured you'd need to blow your snotty nose at some point."

"Bitch," Meaghan sniffled.

Natalie gave her a grin. "I know you are, but what am I?" She gripped Meaghan's arm. "Fucking scared. That's what I am. We're not going to get through this, are we?"

Meaghan tossed the soggy wad of paper aside and squeezed Natalie's hand. "Yeah, we are. It felt hopeless in Fahraya, too."

"And then you saved the day."

"Yeah, something like that." Meaghan sniffled again, feeling the tears still close by. "But not by myself. I had help. Like I have this time." She pulled Natalie into a quick hug. "We have something they don't have. Family. Each other. All they have is fear and hate."

It sounded good, Meaghan thought, reaching for the roll of toilet paper to blow her nose again. Bullshit often did.

But it seemed to help Natalie rally. She smiled. "Okay." She glanced up the stairs. "Jamie's not gonna make it without help." She dragged herself up a couple of steps until she stood next to John and Jamie. "Let me try something."

Natalie closed her eyes, concentrated, and then moved her hand to Jamie's chest. She held her palm about two inches above the glowing sigil. Teeth gritted, she held her hand there for a few seconds, then pulled it away. She shook it violently for a moment as if trying to flick off something nasty.

Jamie looked up. "What did you do?"

"I pulled off some of the heat. Is it better?" Natalie asked.

"Yeah. Can you do the other ones?"

Natalie did the same thing to the other three sigils. By the time she was done, Meaghan noticed, there were tears in her eyes.

"Let me see your hand," Meaghan said.

Natalie gave her a warning look and a microscopic tilt of her head towards Jamie. "It's fine. Let's keep moving."

When Jamie, with John's help, began climbing again, Meaghan grabbed Natalie's hand. The palm was red and blistered.

"Not a word," Natalie hissed. "He doesn't need to know. I'll be fine."

Patrice had gotten about ten steps above them. She turned and stared at Jamie, concern in her eyes. "You can do it, baby. Not much further now." She looked at John. "I can't help you with him. There's too much power in me right now. I'll burn him up."

"Go," John said. "I have him. You go and finish this."

She nodded. "Natalie, get up here. I need you by my side."

"What about Meaghan?" Natalie asked.

Patrice's eyes narrowed. "She needs to stay in back. She can't help with this. Not yet."

Natalie looked at Meaghan for a long moment. She took a tentative step up.

"Wait," Meaghan said. "The toilet paper." She held up her hands. "For my snotty nose."

Natalie grinned, tossed the roll, and climbed the stairs to where Patrice waited.

Patrice grabbed Natalie's burnt hand to help pull her up the stairs, and Natalie cried out. Patrice frowned. "Let me see that." She examined Natalie's blistered palm, then blew on it gently. "There. All better."

Natalie stared in wonder at her now unburnt hand. "Shit, yeah." She smiled at Patrice. "Let's go kick some monster ass."

Patrice smiled back. "Everybody try to get upstairs as fast as you can." She looked down at Meaghan. "You have a role to play, I feel it. But not yet. Hold back and wait. You'll know what to do when the time comes."

Unless, I don't. Meaghan forced herself to smile and wave.

They continued climbing. Meaghan slipped her arm around Jamie's other side and, together, she and John pulled him up the stairs. Natalie's intervention soon wore off and the sigils burned red again. Jamie's eyes had rolled back in his head and he whimpered like a wounded animal with every step.

John tried to carry him, and Jamie shook him off. "No. I have to do this. I have to be the one."

"Why?" Meaghan asked. "Let us help you."

"You are helping," Jamie rasped. "But you can't do it for me. Don't ask why. You can't. It has to be me."

Patrice and Natalie reached the landing. With a final backward glance and a wave, they stepped out of view, leaving only a golden glow behind them.

Meaghan and John dragged Jamie up the final half dozen stairs. By the time they got there, Patrice and her glow were gone and the landing was enveloped in murky darkness.

The high windows that normally flooded the stairwell with light showed only blackness. Meaghan hadn't noticed the absence of daylight before because of the glow emanating from Patrice. It was not the darkness of nighttime, but the flat blackness of the void. Meaghan had seen it before, in the moments before Fahraya had been destroyed.

A faint brightness came from the shattered remains of the solicitor's office. "This way," Meaghan said, pointing with her free hand. "Almost there." She smiled, trying to hide her fear. "I almost never get to work this early. And during Labor Day weekend, no less."

Jamie merely grunted.

The oak door and its surrounding frame were charred and shattered. Meaghan couldn't see much in the dim light, but the squelching under her feet told her the fire sprinklers had gone off at some point.

"Hang on a sec," Meaghan said. She pulled her phone out of her back pocket. The screen was cracked but the flashlight app still worked. She shone it around until she found what she was looking for—the small fire extinguisher sitting under what remained of Kady's desk.

John looked puzzled.

Meaghan shrugged. "In case the wizards are still fire happy. And it's a metal doohickey we can hit somebody with."

"Made of steel?" John asked. "Like the saucepan?"

Meaghan grimaced. "No idea. Let's hope we don't need to find out." She peered into the murk. The flashlight app was a pinprick in the darkness and as good as useless. She put the phone back in her pocket. "This way."

Yesterday the hallway had been only about twelve feet long, with Meaghan's office door near the middle. But the hallway they entered stretched far into the gloom. All the usual landmarks were gone. In the distance, they saw a pulsating ball of light.

"I don't think we're in city hall anymore," Meaghan said.

"Did we go through a gateway?" John asked.

"Maybe," she said. "The Fahrayan gateway was like stepping through a doorway. No tunnels, no light shows."

John nodded. "Troon is like that too."

Jamie roused a bit from his stupor. "That way." He gestured weakly at the light. "Patrice is down there. They're down there."

Meaghan grinned at him. "So first you trash the office, then these jerks turn it into some kind of mystical portal to hell?"

"I guess," Jamie said, smiling for a moment before crying out in pain and doubling over. He would have crumpled to the ground if John hadn't caught him.

"Enough, boy. I carry you now." He cradled Jamie like a baby and lifted him from the ground. Jamie was a big guy, yet John held him like he would a sleeping child.

They trudged down the hallway toward the pulsing light.

Go toward the light, Meaghan thought. *Isn't that what*

they say happens in a near-death experience? "Are you sure we should we be doing this?"

John grunted and shifted Jamie's weight. "No. But Patrice says we must. And I think I am more scared of her than them."

"Put me down," Jamie grumbled. "I'm not a kid any-more. I can walk."

John sighed, but acquiesced.

Jamie groaned and buckled again.

John caught his arm and tried to lift him, but before he could, Jamie said, "I can do this. If you help me."

Meaghan and John pulled him to his feet and pulled his arms over their shoulders. Jamie swayed a bit, but stayed on his feet. "Lions and tigers and bears," he rasped. "Oh, my."

"What?" Meaghan tucked the fire extinguisher tightly under her armpit and tried to get a better grip on him.

"The Wizard of Oz. When they're going down that big hallway to meet the wizard. Or maybe in the woods before they met the lion—I can't remember."

"Who is this wizard?" John asked. "Is he with the Order?"

Jamie chuckled. "Dad, you need to get out more."

"It's from an old movie," Meaghan said. "They show it on TV all the time."

"I don't have a TV," John said.

"Of course you don't," Jamie said. "You guys promise me something."

Like it had on the stairs, the air felt thicker. Every step was a struggle.

"Anything," John said.

"What are we promising?" Meaghan asked.

Jamie chuckled. He was still on his feet, but John and

Meaghan were doing most of the work. "You're such a law-yer. He says yes, you say not so fast. Promise me you'll look after Patrice when I'm gone."

Meaghan snorted. "You aren't going anywhere. At least not without the rest of us."

He laughed, almost giddy now. "You know that's not true. Even if the wizards or the mystery bad guys don't kill me, my heart's about to explode from all the drugs. I'm not getting out of this one alive. We all know it."

"No," John growled. "We do not know it. Patrice, she does not know it."

"You guys need to make sure she's okay. Make sure she gets on with her life. Gets married again." Jamie gave John a hard look. "No years of drinking and grieving and being all alone. Promise me."

John stopped, his head bowed. His shoulders shook and Meaghan realized he was weeping. "I promise."

Jamie nodded. "Good." He turned to Meaghan. "I'd ask you again, but I know how stubborn you are."

"Good call." She squeezed his hand. "Wherever we end up, we're all going together. You're not ditching me that easy, kid."

"I'm still not gonna call you Mom."

"Fine," Meaghan grunted. "Whatever. Let's get our asses down the hall and get this shit over with. Everybody's wait-ing for us."

CHAPTER FORTY-EIGHT

THE LIGHT GLOWING at the end of the long corridor was not the bright liquid gold that had surrounded Patrice, but something darker and murkier—less like summer sunlight and more like the pits of hell. With a hint of avocado green.

It was malevolent light.

They stepped into it.

They were in what looked like city hall's attic—the part with the unreinforced floor that would drop anyone standing on it into the offices below. But there were almost a dozen people standing around and the floor remained intact, which meant this couldn't be the actual attic and they were no longer in city hall.

Meaghan didn't plan on jumping up and down to find out.

Patrice and Natalie stood at one end of the space, bathed in golden light. At the other end, illuminated in the murky, hellish light stood a gray-robed wizard. And a woman. Dressed like a witch of the Circe wannabe variety—flowing blonde hair, too much silver jewelry, and lots of black leather.

Halfway between them, Jhoro kneeled, head down, arms bound behind his back.

The woman stepped forward. There was some black lace in her ensemble, too.

"Give me a break," Meaghan said, rolling her eyes. She'd meant to mutter it, but it chimed clear, as if she had a microphone.

The wizard threw back his hood and Meaghan recognized him.

Cooper. The ostensible leader of the Order, the man who'd torn off Jamie's amulet and shoved him through the gateway into Fahraya. A tall strong man, bigger than John, he had close-cropped, dark hair, speckled with gray, and a face that would have been handsome but for the cruelty stamped into every line.

"Finally," Cooper said. He turned toward the woman. "Orinda, my love, meet Keele's daughter and—" he gave a cold chuckle, "the former king, if you can call it that, of Fahraya."

The woman smiled, her face equally twisted with cruelty. "You didn't tell me she was so . . . *old*."

Meaghan's fear evaporated. No way was she letting this caricature of a witch talk shit and get away with it. "Who are *you* calling old, Bellatrix? Nice bleach job, but you really should get those roots looked after. And black leather? Not a good look for you. Gives kind of an overstuffed luggage vibe."

Jamie snorted with laughter.

The woman glared at him, waved her hand, and Jamie cried out in agony. He crumpled to the ground, nearly taking Meaghan and John with him.

The woman waved her hand again, and this time John fell to the ground writhing in pain. She looked at Meaghan, smiling, and lifted her hand a third time.

Meaghan stood there, fire extinguisher tucked under one arm, her free hand on her hip, an eyebrow raised. She wanted desperately to help John and Jamie, but stood her ground. She would not give Cooper and his girlfriend the satisfaction of seeing her panic.

The witch flicked her hand at Meaghan.

Nothing happened.

The witch stepped back, startled.

"Tacky *and* stupid," Meaghan said, her voice dripping acid. "Which part of impervious don't you idiots understand?"

The witch bristled. "Stupid? I'm not the one who thought she could protect the town by keeping the wizards out. I walked right in and set all this chaos in motion. Who do you think cast the first love spell?"

Meaghan grimaced. Magically blocking any wizards from getting near Eldrich hadn't been Meaghan's idea, but she'd approved it. *They used a witch to get to us last time. How could I think they wouldn't do it again?*

Because the Order's stated belief was that women shouldn't be permitted to do magic. Except, apparently, the boss's girlfriend. Which was exactly the sort of hypocrisy she'd encountered throughout her government law career. *Some leader I am. Where was your bullshit detector on that one, Meg?*

Orinda gave Meaghan a saccharine smile, then flicked another spell. Jamie and John cried out together in pain.

"Enough," Patrice shouted. "They're under my protection."

Cooper merely smiled. This time he waved his hand and Jhoro cried out along with John and Jamie.

Now Meaghan wanted to run to Jhoro, but knew she had to confront Cooper. "Get out of my town."

Cooper laughed. "*My* town. *My* protection. Maybe for now, but soon it's going to be *my world*." He pointed at Patrice. "Where are your sisters, little one? So much power, but you don't know how to wield it, and," he pointed at the circle of light contracting around her, "it's fading fast."

He turned back to Meaghan. "And you." He laughed again. "No power at all. Being impervious means nothing. Less than nothing. Yet they all look to you. We both know what a bad idea that is, don't we?"

Meaghan's face flamed. The bastard *knew*. Maybe it was only a lucky guess, but she'd been telling herself the same thing since that day in June when she learned the truth about Eldrich and herself.

But, who, Meg, are you going to believe? This evil cackling bastard and his bitch girlfriend? Or the people who know and trust you?

Meaghan thought of Eliot. And Annie. And Russ. All telling her how strong she was, how she could see the world clearly when others couldn't. All calling her boss.

She looked around. John and Jamie slumped on the floor, moaning in pain. Patrice stood like a goddess in her golden circle, but it was now visibly shrinking, the golden light fading. Natalie stood by her side, eyes screwed shut in concentration, chanting, as if fighting against an invisible foe.

Meaghan looked over at Jhoro, hunched on the floor, seemingly in agony. Curled on his side, his golden hair matted with blood, Jhoro had his back to Cooper and the witch. He stared up at Meaghan with his vivid blue eyes, and winked at her, a big Cheshire cat grin on his battered face.

It took all Meaghan's effort not to do a visible double take. Jhoro was faking.

Her heart lurched in her chest and hope flared inside her.

Cooper hit him with another spell. Jhoro cried out, while giving Meaghan a massive eye roll, and shaking his head slightly as if saying "can you believe this guy?"

Her confidence streamed back. Whatever the source of Jhoro's power, it was stronger than Cooper's magic.

Let's see if he falls for this one again. Meaghan buried her face in her hands and began to sob noisily. She was so exhausted by now it wasn't hard to summon up real tears. The hardest part was not bursting into manic laughter at the same time.

"You're right," she wailed. "It's a terrible idea." She rushed to John and Jamie's side and knelt beside them. "Please don't hurt them anymore." She turned away from Cooper and crouched next to John. Now it was her turn to wink.

His eyes widened slightly, slanted towards Jhoro, and then back to Meaghan.

She nodded slightly in return.

John pulled her towards him into a rough hug and whispered, "He is faking?"

"Yes."

"You have a plan?"

"Working on it," she breathed. "Follow our lead. If you see a chance to get out of here, take it."

A pair of rough hands pulled her away from John. One of Cooper's minions. The fire extinguisher fell from her grasp, but John caught it before it hit the ground and tucked it under his legs.

The minion dragged her over to Jhoro and dropped her next to him.

She tried to stand and the hands shoved her down. "Knees, bitch."

Meaghan sighed. Always the knees with these jerks. She gritted her teeth. She might bristle when called old, but she wasn't young and kneeling hurt like hell.

Jhoro looked up at her from where he lay on the floor and winked again.

Back to business. Meaghan slumped onto her side next to Jhoro and commenced with the show. "Please," she sobbed, her face hidden in her elbow. "Let them go."

Already her knees felt better.

The tacky witch laughed.

Meaghan ignored her. Time to see if she could get Cooper talking. He'd fallen for it in June. She let loose a fresh wave of sobs. "Why are you doing this?"

"Because I can," he said and then laughed.

She gave him a moment, but he didn't elaborate.

Come on, already. Start blabbing. "What's going to happen to us?"

He chuckled. "Why you're going to die, of course. But by then, you'll be only too glad to go. After *they* finish with you."

And more silence. He was going to make her drag it out of him.

"Who are they?" she sobbed.

"*What* is more accurate," the leather-clad witch chimed in. "And when they get here, they'll burn the human world to ashes. Except for us."

Of course they will, Meaghan thought. *Will one of you start monologuing already?*

Cooper complied. "They exist outside time and space, and even the most powerful magical beings fear them. They are magic itself. Once they were free to roam the worlds, magical and otherwise, and they fed freely on the fear and flesh of those who defied them."

Ka-ching. Scary bad monsters who, regardless of how bad and scary they were, apparently weren't roaming anymore. Meaghan sobbed louder. "Aren't they free now?"

"Soon, old woman," the witch said. "Soon."

"Yes," Cooper said. "They've been trapped a long time, but soon, finally, they'll be free."

"But won't they . . ." Meaghan sobbed louder. "Won't they kill us all?"

"Not us," the witch said. "They'll reward us."

Cooper, with a faint tone of annoyance, Meaghan noted, said, "We know how to control them."

You sure about that? Meaghan shifted on the ground. Now her hip hurt. And she didn't think she could do anymore faux crying and be believable.

With even more annoyance in his voice, Cooper said, "And that's all you need to know." He turned to a minion. "Bring her. Time for the first sacrifice."

"You aren't using Keele?" the witch asked. "I want to see her burn."

Cooper said nothing for a moment. Long enough to betray his growing impatience with his girlfriend. "In time, love, in time. But the first must be properly . . . prepared. You know this."

The witch sighed in exasperation. "Fine. Let's get on with it then."

The minion dragged a limp figure from the shadows.
Marnie.

Meaghan almost started to cry again, for real this time.

Marnie was naked and filthy and battered. The ring had been torn from her nose and her hair had been shaved, roughly, with a knife, judging by her torn and bloody scalp. Dried blood crusted her thighs and buttocks.

But the look on her face was even worse. She wasn't dead, but she might as well have been. Not even fear registered on her face. The interior light in her eyes was extinguished, replaced with a flat, vacant stare, devoid of hope or feeling.

Seeing the look on Meaghan's face, the witch cooed. "She wanted love. So we gave it to her. Over and over and over."

Meaghan had thought there couldn't be anyone in the Order she hated more than Cooper, but she was wrong.

"How," Meaghan said, her voice shaking with fury, her pretended fear gone, "could you do this to another woman? How?"

The witch laughed. "She wanted it."

"Thank you," Meaghan said, through gritted teeth. "You've made it very easy for me to kill you when the time comes. Cooper's *girlfriend*. Pathetic. You can't even be evil in your own right."

"She's stupid in her own right, though," Natalie said behind her. "So is he."

Meaghan turned to look.

Patrice stood in her circle of golden light, smiling at Natalie. "Nice trick, Nat. I can't believe they fell for it."

"Fell for what?" Cooper sneered.

"My light-dimming trick," Natalie said, as a blinding flash of golden light filled the space.

CHAPTER FORTY-NINE

T HE WORLD LURCHED, like somebody had jammed on the brakes.

When the blinding light faded, the space in which they stood had changed.

It was smaller and grimier. Dust motes danced in the rays of morning sunshine beaming through the huge arched window—now empty of glass—that sat high in the stone wall. Cardboard file boxes lined the wall adjoining the solicitor's office. Debris and office supplies lay scattered across the floor.

They were in the unfinished attic of city hall. For real this time.

Cooper shouted at the minions and two of them stepped toward Natalie and Patrice.

And disappeared, leaving only their screams and a cloud of plaster dust.

Patrice laughed. "Wow, you weren't kidding. These floors are like Styrofoam."

"Unreinforced," Natalie said. "Except for a few key spots."

"Here?" Patrice said.

"No, this is magic," Natalie said. "And it's getting heavy. Would you—"

"Oh, right." Patrice closed her eyes and after a moment said, "Better?"

"Thanks. Would you grab Marnie and Jhoro, too?"

The ropes binding Jhoro's arms dissolved like cotton candy. He crawled over to Marnie and put his arms around her. Marnie stared blankly over his shoulder. Wherever she had gone inside herself, she wasn't ready to come out.

Meaghan felt the floor vibrate underneath her.

Patrice looked at Natalie. "I reinforced the floor."

"All of it?"

Patrice shook her head. "No, I had to pull . . . I don't know . . . stuff from other parts of the floor. So they're even thinner."

"You can do that?"

Patrice nodded. "Apparently."

"Thin it out over there." Natalie waved toward Cooper and the witch. "That's one of the reinforced spots."

Patrice squinted in concentration, then shook her head. "I can't. Jamie's too close to them and he's throwing off too much power."

"Good to know," Cooper snarled.

Meaghan looked a question at Natalie. She grimaced in response. Meaghan could tell by the look on Natalie's face and the way she moved her hands that she was trying to set up a barrier around John and Jamie.

With a loud cry and flourish of his hands, Cooper gestured toward Jamie.

"Patrice," Meaghan shouted. "Stop him."

Patrice shook her head, her face twisted in anguish. "I can't. There's too much magic in the sigils."

John threw himself on top of Jamie, but it was no use. Cooper flicked a hand and John cried out in pain and rolled off his son. He jerked a few times as if struck, then lay still. Jamie's body rose, with a jerk, into the air and flew, as if thrown, landing in a heap at the feet of the leather-clad witch.

"For me?" she said, in mock surprise. She leered at Jamie. "How thoughtful."

"Now that we have the original," Cooper said, "we don't need the other."

"But you promised I could play with the new one," the witch said, pouting. "Before you killed him."

"With the other one back, we won't have to kill the new one. You can keep him as a pet. But now we have work to do, and we still need the whore," Cooper hissed. He stepped forward, past Jamie, and lifted his hands again.

This time Patrice was ready. Cooper's hands were thrust back. This time, it was Cooper who cried out in pain. He stepped back, doubled over, but stayed on his feet. He jammed his left wrist under his right armpit.

"My turn," Patrice said. "Remember? You broke my wrist, back in June." Her look grew dark. "When you forced your way into my home, terrified my children, and kidnapped my husband." She scowled and when she spoke it was in a different voice. "When you hurt my family."

Meaghan shivered. Whatever impelled Patrice now, it wasn't human. Her eyes were a solid, shiny black, like polished obsidian, with no white or iris visible.

"Justice will be done," Patrice said. Her voice echoed with tones Meaghan had never heard in a human voice.

She was no longer Patrice. Up until now, even at her scariest, Patrice's essential nature, her humor, her compassion, had shone through. But a stranger now stood in her place.

Meaghan looked at Natalie, but Natalie had her eyes closed in concentration, muttering.

"You are alone," Cooper hissed. "In an untried vessel."

Patrice smiled. "This child is strong. This vessel will serve. I will have justice for the wrongs you have done her." But, despite her strong words, she staggered and fell to one knee.

Cooper smiled. "Told you so."

The blonde witch turned to Cooper. "Who the hell is this? I thought you had the only one. And where the hell did *it* go? The mob broke up half an hour ago."

"Shut up, Orinda," Cooper said, still cradling his broken wrist. "Heal this. We need to get back on schedule."

"Heal it yourself," Orinda said, annoyance in her voice. She gestured at Patrice. "Who is this bitch and how do you know her?"

"We have no time for your ridiculous jealousy," Cooper said through gritted teeth. "I'll explain later. They're waiting and the window will close soon. Would you like to explain to them how your petty female complaining caused us to miss this opportunity?"

Orinda grew visibly pale. She shook her head, chastened. "No. I'll fix it now." She held his broken wrist between her palms and murmured a spell.

With a grunt, Cooper pulled his hand away from her. "Better." He smiled at her. "Isn't it better when you obey me?"

Orinda nodded and stepped away, her head bowed.

Meaghan could almost imagine feeling a tiny spark of compassion for the woman. If Orinda wasn't such a bitch.

"Cheer up, my love," Cooper cooed. "You've given me an idea."

"I have?" Orinda flipped her hair with a silver-ringed hand, her moment of unease forgotten. "I love it when I do that."

Meaghan rolled her eyes and said, "Pathetic."

Cooper ignored her. "Yes, you have." Cooper closed his eyes, concentrating. "We have the perfect vessel right here. It can bring the whore right to us."

Marnie shoved Jhoro away. "Get off me, you faggot. I should have killed you when I was in your father."

Cooper smiled. "About time you showed up. The mob tired you?"

Marnie stood up and looked down on herself. "Too many good things to eat. I needed a little time to digest. A post-meal nap." She ran her hands up and down her body. "The shame is tasty, but I assume this is merely a snack, and you have a task for me."

The Power was back.

Cooper nodded. He held out his hand. "Bring her to me. She's more than a snack. She's a sacrifice to our masters."

Marnie's breath quickened and she smiled. "Thank you for this honor. I will serve you well."

Jhoro grabbed her from behind. She swept her arms up, breaking his grasp, drove an elbow back into his nose, then turned and jammed her knee into his groin. He fell to his knees with a grunt and curled into a ball.

Marnie straddled him, grabbed a handful of his golden hair, and pulled his head back. She jammed her knee into his neck, pinning him and partially choking him with the weight of her body, then wrapped her hands around his throat and squeezed. "Don't try your shamanic crap on me, boy. It didn't work on me in Fahraya and it won't work now."

"No," Patrice shouted. "Stop!"

"Your crap won't work on me either, bitch," Marnie said. "Not without your sisters."

Patrice grunted and collapsed. Natalie, still trying to cast a spell, ignored her.

"Marnie," Meaghan called to her. "I know you're still in there." Compassion had worked to undermine the Power in the past. "Don't let this thing take you. Don't let them win."

Marnie rolled her eyes. "You again? Going to drown me in another wave of maternal instinct? All I smell now is big fear. Ooh, and the doubt. That was there before, but it's had time to marinate." She licked her lips. "Magic makes it much easier to consume someone, but for you, I'll make the extra effort." Jhoro's pawed ineffectually at Marnie's hands as she throttled him. "Let me finish up here."

Meaghan scrambled to her feet and threw herself at them.

Marnie lost her balance and fell, giving Jhoro the opportunity he needed to escape. He rolled onto his side, coughing spasmodically, his face brick red. He tried to pull himself onto his knees.

Marnie, now on the floor with Meaghan, kicked out hard with her heel and hit Jhoro square on his temple. He collapsed, unconscious.

Meaghan was a good fighter when she had to be, but the Power, with the strength of Marnie's youth, was better.

Now she straddled Meaghan, wrapping her hands around Meaghan's throat, and choking her. With a big grin, Marnie said, "I've wanted to do this since the first moment I met you."

Meaghan's hands scrabbled in the detritus on the floor, searching for something, anything, she could use to defend herself. Blackness surrounded her field of vision and everything else was covered in a yellow haze.

She felt something cold and metallic under her hand and lifted it. A stapler. The new, sleek, lightweight, ergonomic stapler Jamie kept on his desk. The stapler Meaghan had seen levitate.

With her remaining strength Meaghan slammed the stapler into the side of Marnie's head.

Marnie snarled, but hung onto Meaghan's throat with both hands. The stapler was ripped from Meaghan's hand and flew out of her reach.

Not steel, Meaghan thought, as the darkness took her.

CHAPTER FIFTY

WITH HER LAST shred of conscious awareness, Meaghan heard a sizzling sound and felt Marnie roll off her. Small hands touched her face, then shook her.

"Meg, Meaghan. Come on, come back."

Meaghan's head felt like it was about to explode. Swallowing was even worse. Reluctantly, she opened her eyes.

Owen was leaning over here. "There you are. C'mon. On your feet. Natalie can't keep the misdirection spell going much longer. They'll figure it out in a second."

With his help, Meaghan sat up and then made it to her feet. She almost fell, but Owen propped her up. She leaned her elbow on his head.

"This one time you get to use me as an armrest, Meg. Move." He tugged at her.

"Where were you?" she rasped.

"Hiding in plain sight." He smiled. "Where did you think I'd be?"

"Did you hex her?"

Owen shook his head. "Nope. Used a Taser. *Move*."

Meaghan heard Cooper shouting. "Uh oh," she said. "He sees you."

"He sees *you*, messing up the magic again."

Hands reached out of the doorway and pulled her forward.

Annie and Brian wrapped their arms around her and carried her through the file room into the copy room, then out into the hall.

Meaghan looked at Brian. "You were on the roof," she said, her voice small and squeaky. "Nice shootin', Tex."

Brian grinned. "Saved your ass."

"You sure did. Thanks." Meaghan took a few deep breaths. "Oh God, my head hurts." She thought about it a moment as she took another deep breath. "More than everything else." She looked down at Owen. "I'm too old for this shit."

"So you keep saying. Come on. We have to get you out of here."

Meaghan's head cleared more with each breath. "No. I can't leave them back there. Natalie's the only one still fighting. We can't leave her on her own."

Annie grabbed Meaghan's hand. "She's not alone. There are about twenty witches right under her feet in Tony's office backing her up. The bad guys are outnumbered. Your job is to pull back and set up a second front out here."

"But those things . . ."

"Break it into smaller problems," Annie said, smiling. "Right? Sweet memory, by the way. I tried not to peek, but you took me along for the ride."

The doorway from the attic to the file room exploded.

"Oh, shit," Brian said. "Time to move."

Meaghan looked around. Where Jamie's office used to be, the hallway opened to empty sky. A similar view greeted her from her office, but part of the circular room was still there, like a pie with big slice cut from it.

"Front office," she said.

They clambered over the wreckage and debris that filled the hallway to the front area. With the return of the natural light, Meaghan could see the full extent of the damage. The plaster ceiling was gone, leaving a grid of pipes, wires, and exposed iron girders. Puddles of water on the floor confirmed what her feet had told her earlier. The fire sprinklers had gone off.

"Nobody move," Meaghan said. Now that she could see the standing water on the floor, she realized the risk. "There aren't enough outlets out here so we use a lot of extension cords, which might be live."

Brian shook his head. "Power's off."

"How do you know?"

"I shut it off, then monkey-wrenched the backup generator and the transformer box outside so nobody can turn it back on." He smiled. "That's where I ran into Annie. And how she ended up on the roof telling me which wizards were bad and which were possessed kids."

"Sid," Meaghan said. "Annie, is Sid with you?"

Annie shook her head. "No. He's not with you?"

Meaghan shook her head. "He slipped away the same time you did. Did he come in with the witches?"

"I didn't see him." Annie took a close look at Meaghan. "Don't worry. Sid's tough."

Meaghan nodded. She'd spent much of the last twenty-four hours angry with him, but right now she'd give anything to see his little blue face. "Where are Russ and Emily?"

"None of the witches trust Emily," Annie said. "She's outside with Russ handing out juice boxes and Chex-Mix from the stash he found in that ghastly pink truck parked in the lobby. All those Order kids were adamant that they had to have a juice box and a snack or the golden lady would get mad."

In spite of everything, Meaghan managed a small laugh. "Patrice. Long story." She looked down at Owen. "You're the only magical operator here. What's the plan?"

"Get you out of the attic," he said. "We didn't really think much past that. We figured you'd tell us."

"Of course you did. Because I was doing such a good job." She sighed. Every inch of her body hurt. Marnie had really kicked her ass.

Marnie. They still had to get Marnie and Jamie away from Cooper. "Marnie's in bad shape, the Power has her, and they're going to kill her first and then activate the sigils on Jamie to let whatever those things are into our world. They scare Cooper's pet witch, and she's pretty powerful in her own right, so I think it's safe to say we don't want them getting loose."

"Natalie and the coven will hang onto Marnie for now," Annie said. "The Taser broke that thing's concentration enough for Natalie to get a foot in the door. Plus, whatever they did to Marnie broke the love spell. I can't feel it anymore." She shrugged. "At least not that love spell."

"There's more than one?" Brian asked.

"Yes," Meaghan, Annie, and Owen said at the same moment.

"What is it with him?" Brian shook his head. "They do know he's gay right?"

"No time to worry about it now," Owen said. "Meg, what do we do?"

Meaghan stood silent. This felt wrong. Standing in the front office was not where she belonged. Patrice had told Meaghan she had a role to play before the end, and she'd know what to do when the time came.

She had to get back in there.

"I'm not leaving them," Meaghan said. "If those things get through, we won't need a second front."

"But," Annie said, "the witches—"

"Are better equipped than I am to fight these things if they get through," Meaghan answered.

"What the hell are you gonna do in there?" Owen glared up at her. "Besides get killed?"

"If we don't keep Cooper from getting this door of his open, we're all dead anyway. Let me think a second."

She'd been hearing it all day. How being able to see things the way they really were gave her power. How she had the gift of plain sight. How she could see these things' true faces.

Meaghan began to laugh. She looked down at Owen. "You were the first to say it."

"What?"

"When you told me about the fair folk and why they hated Matthew so much—he could see their true faces. Eliot said the same thing. He said I'm the only one whose head they can't screw with. Cooper said they were magic itself and that's why everyone was afraid of them."

Owen stared at her a moment. "And magic doesn't work on you."

"Bingo. Why do the fair folk hate showing their true faces? Because they aren't very imposing. If people could see them as they really are, if they could see through the trick, then the trick wouldn't work anymore, right?"

Owen nodded. "Go on."

"So, what if these things are like that, too? They use magic to make themselves appear terrifying. What if they aren't? How would we know unless we could see them as they really are?"

"And you're the only one who can do that."

"Exactly. If we don't stop them here, it won't matter whether I know what they really look like because we'll all be dead anyway. But even if we do stop them this time, they're going to keep trying. Think of the advantage we'd have if I knew what we were really dealing with."

"But they'll kill you," Annie said, her eyes shiny with tears.

"Maybe. But they can't do it with magic. And if they're like the rest of these jerks, they won't believe it at first. Which gives me an advantage. Every magical bad actor I've encountered has tried to take a shot at me because they're all egotistical enough to believe the rules don't apply to them."

Owen was nodding.

"But they can still kill you," Annie said, looking panicked. "Marnie was doing a pretty good job before Owen saved you."

Meaghan nodded. "Yeah, she was. But she wasn't doing it with magic. And Owen got her off me with a Taser. A human-engineered, completely non-magical weapon."

Annie glared at Owen. "You can't possibly believe this is a good idea."

Owen shrugged.

"Maybe I can hurt them," Meaghan said. "Maybe without magic, they're as fragile as any of us."

"Aren't you scared?" Annie was crying now.

"Terrified," Meaghan said. "It doesn't matter. I have to do this."

Owen gave her a hard, appraising look. "And you know about the prophecy."

Meaghan nodded. "Yeah. I do. And I still don't believe in it."

Owen grinned. "Of course you don't. Where do you want us to be?"

"You won't be smiling in a minute. I want you in there with me."

"I kind of figured. To do what?"

"Sneak people out, interfere, whatever you can do to keep Cooper and the witch off balance."

Owen nodded. "I can do that."

"And us?" Brian put a comforting arm around Annie's shoulder.

"Downstairs with the witches."

Brian sighed. "Yeah, I kind of figured, too. They won't be happy."

"Too bad," Meaghan said. "I'm in charge. And you can tell them I said that."

Annie sobbed.

Meaghan hugged her. "Don't wuss out on me, lady. We've been kicking ass together since this thing started. We need to finish strong."

Annie nodded, wiping her eyes with a grubby hand. "That's what Welland says. He says Cooper is evil to the core, but vain and petty."

"You found him. What else does he say?"

"He says the witch is Cooper's weak spot." Annie pulled away. "And if you don't make it, he and the other ghosts will be honored to have you join them."

Meaghan shook her head. "Tell them thanks, but not today."

CHAPTER FIFTY-ONE

MEAGHAN SMILED AND waved as Annie and Brian headed downstairs. When they were out of sight, she sagged against the remains of Natalie's desk.

"The whole second front thing is a load of crap, isn't it?" she asked Owen.

He nodded. "Yeah. If we don't stop these things here, we're done."

"I'm tired," Meaghan said. "And out of ideas."

"Then make up some shit," a voice said from behind her. "Like you did last time."

Meaghan, her heart pounding, spun around.

Sid stood in the remains of the doorway. He smiled at them. "What? You think I'd miss the big finale? I'm way too much of a diva for that." He gave Owen an appraising look. "You know, you are awfully cute despite your many sins. Which, if we survive, you will be disclosing to Meaghan." Now he looked at her. "I'm sorry I didn't trust you enough to tell you everything. It doesn't matter what I promised Matthew. He's gone and you're the one who has to do the job."

"Where the hell did you come from?" Meaghan finally managed to squeak.

"Emergency stairs."

Owen shook his head. "No, you didn't. I was the last one up those stairs. They were collapsing as I climbed."

Sid rolled his eyes. "No." He pointed across the landing. "The emergency stairs."

Meaghan shook her head blankly.

"On the other side of the building? Don't you people ever do fire drills? There's a big red exit sign—" He craned his head to look. "Well, there would be one if the lights were on."

"I don't care how you got in," Meaghan said. "I'm just happy you're here. Come on. We have to go back into the lion's den."

Sid nodded. "Yeah. I thought as much. Any ideas on what we're going to do?"

Meaghan smiled. "Get our people back. Kick everybody's ass."

Sid smiled back. "It worked last time. Maybe lightning will strike twice." He smirked at Owen. "And if we fail, I won't have to be the shortest one to die."

Owen rolled his eyes. "*Troon.*"

"Do I have to separate the two of you?" Meaghan asked. "Come on. Bad guys, ultimate evil, end of the world." She pointed over her shoulder with her thumb. "This way."

They climbed back over the wreckage in the hallway to the file room.

"You got any weapons?" Sid asked, his voice an octave higher than it had been in the front office.

Owen held his Taser out to Meaghan. "Take it."

She shook her head. "You can do more damage with it. They won't see you coming. Or Sid. Hide him with you."

"But—"

She held up her index finger. "Not one word, Sid. I'm in charge. Do what I say. That Taser's not impervious, and I don't want them to know we have it until they're flopping around like electrocuted fish."

Meaghan looked around the remains of the file room. "I need something made out of steel. Something heavy, but small enough to handle."

"Like your saucepan," Sid said morosely.

Meaghan shifted a pile of sodden paper aside and smiled. "Or this."

On the floor sat the large stapler Kady referred to as the Mangler. It was the one they used for court filings, the budget, and other huge documents. Anything less than about forty pages and the thing jammed, leaving no choice but to pry the offending pages loose with a screw driver. The Mangler had inspired some truly creative swearing from both Kady and Natalie in the short time Meaghan had worked with them.

Meaghan examined it. The Mangler had a lever handle that she could easily grip. It was heavy, but not so heavy that she couldn't swing it or throw it if she had to. But was it made out of steel?

She grabbed the handle and pulled it from the debris. She flipped it over. There was some printing on the bottom, but too tiny for Meaghan to see clearly. "Can either of you read this? Does it say anything about steel construction?"

Owen and Sid leaned in from either side.

"No," Sid said.

"Let me try something." Owen took the stapler from Meaghan, closed his eyes, and stood there. Nothing happened.

Sid gasped. "How did you do that?"

"Do what?" Meaghan asked. "He's just standing there."

"No, he isn't. I see a stapler, floating in the air."

Meaghan grinned. "Sweet. That means it's steel right? It's impervious?"

Owen opened his eyes. "Yeah, like you. You really could see me?"

"Plain as day."

"Damn." He thought about it a moment. "Because the spell doesn't actually change me. It changes your perception of me." He nodded. "Which is why it doesn't work on you."

Meaghan took the stapler from him. "See? Even you don't quite believe your magic won't affect me, and you know better."

"What are you going to do with that thing?" Sid asked.

"Probably not stapling, but you never know. I'll probably chuck it at somebody. And miss. It's been that kind of day. But at least I don't feel so helpless."

She smiled down at her companions. "Gentlemen, shall we?"

They stepped into the attic.

Meaghan surveyed the room.

Natalie still stood, her eyes shut, concentrating. Meaghan could see her lips moving as she muttered incantations.

Patrice, next to her, was on all fours, head down. The golden light had shrunk again to a small circle, but Meaghan feared it wasn't a trick this time. Patrice was fighting against the power being thrown at her and losing.

Marnie now kneeled in front of Cooper, eyes shut, an ecstatic look on her face, as he waved his hands in an intricate pattern over her. Jamie lay in a heap nearby, convulsing.

Jhoro, no longer faking, curled in a ball in the center of the floor. He gasped in pain as Orinda flicked spells at him. With each moan, she laughed. Her face was flushed, her eyes bright with malice.

A hand grasped Meaghan's ankle. Her heart lurched as she looked down.

John, his face bloody, looked up at her. He reached for her wrist and pulled her down on the floor before Cooper or Orinda noticed her. "What are you doing here?"

"Saving you," Meaghan said, pulling him into a rough hug.

He winced.

She let go. "What did they do?"

"Threw me around a little," he rasped. "Broke a rib, I think. What do we do now?"

Meaghan looked for Sid and Owen. They were creeping toward Jhoro. Patrice had said something about thinning out parts of the floor to reinforce others. If they weren't careful, they'd go right through.

She glanced over at Patrice and Natalie. "What's happening to Patrice?"

I'm working on the floor. Patrice's voice sounded clear in Meaghan's mind. *Let's get Jhoro out of here first. He can help from downstairs. I'm not as helpless as I look.*

Meaghan nodded, relieved to find out she'd been wrong.

"I don't know," John said. "She's been kneeling like that since you left."

Orinda threw another spell at Jhoro. He cried out and tried to crawl away.

"Oh, no you don't, pet," Orinda said, a leer on her face. "You'll never get away from me."

Jhoro looked up at her and gave her a bloody grin. He rolled to his left. Something cracked and Jhoro fell through the floor, leaving a cloud of plaster dust behind him.

Orinda shrieked with rage. "Bring him back!"

"No, you snotty bitch," shouted Natalie. "You want him? Go get him."

Orinda's eyes widened, and she stepped next to Cooper. "Did you hear that? Are you going to let her call me that?"

"I'm busy," Cooper hissed through gritted teeth. "In case you haven't noticed."

She pouted. "What am I supposed to do now?"

He grunted, "Light the witch. I'll get the other one."

Orinda smirked. "That's even more fun." She waved her hands and fashioned a ball of flame similar to what the wizards had conjured earlier. "Has she been—" she giggled, "anointed?"

"Not yet," Marnie said. She picked up a dusty jar filled with clear liquid.

It was a Mason jar. More of the Miller's moonshine.

She opened the jar and took a swallow, then poured the rest over her head.

Orinda looked positively gleeful. "Now?"

"Now," Cooper said, smiling too.

"Fire extinguisher," Meaghan shouted, panicked. "Where is it?"

John pulled it from a dark corner.

Orinda flicked the ball of fire at Marnie.

Meaghan grabbed the fire extinguisher and ran, John right behind her, hoping like hell that the floor wouldn't collapse beneath them.

There was a flash and a scream.

Meaghan pulled the pin on the extinguisher and sprayed Marnie.

Patrice shrieked, there was a flash of golden light, and a dark cloud erupted from Marnie and flew toward Orinda.

John tackled Marnie, wrapped his arms around her and rolled away from Cooper. The suddenly unreinforced floor gave way and he and Marnie were gone.

Orinda dropped to her knees screaming, and then abruptly stopped. She looked up at Meaghan, her eyes glowing orange. In a deep hoarse voice, she cried, "Last time, bitch. Last time you fuck with me."

Meaghan hurled the spent fire extinguisher at Orinda. The witch snarled, waved a hand, and the canister crumpled.

The Power had found a new host.

CHAPTER FIFTY-TWO

COOPER RUSHED TO Orinda's side, his face contorted with fury. "Not her," he roared. "Not her. Ever.
Get out!"

"Where would you like me to go?" Orinda hissed. "Not
a lot of choices at the moment. Your whore was the only one
available. If you'd listened to me and we'd used the other
witch, the prophesied one, they'd be here by now. You don't
want to test them. Trust me on this."

Cooper paled. "Can you enter the other one?"

"Give me a minute," Orinda grunted. "She's well shielded at
the moment. A little help? If you're not too busy?" She stood up
and ran her hands over her body. She smiled. "This one is strong.
Now we've both been inside her. Something we can share."

Meaghan's fear evaporated, replaced with disgust. "You are
the most disgusting pair . . . *trio* . . . of . . . Gah." She lifted
her lip in disgust and shook her head. "How vile can you get?
You've both been inside her? Ewww. You deserve each other.

Ménage-a-*ewww*. The end of the world is worth it if means getting away from you creepy assholes."

Cooper and Orinda stared at her, mouths open.

"When did evil get so tacky? So low rent?" Meaghan asked, her mouth now way out ahead of her brain. "Look at yourselves. You're ridiculous."

Orinda recovered quickly. "I'm going to kill you."

"Great," Meaghan ranted. "If that's what it takes so I don't have to endure another nanosecond with you repulsive freaks, have at it. I'd rather be dead than have to listen to any more of this. You've both been inside her? It's not even original."

Out of the corner of her eye, she saw Sid and Owen creeping towards her. She took a deep breath and tried to calm down. They were up to something. Cooper and the Power were still focused on her. She needed to keep distracting them.

"So now what are you going to do? Now who are you coming after? It's me, the well-protected witch, or the . . . whatever the hell Patrice is. All that estrogen, Cooper. Sure you can handle it?"

"She's not that well-protected," Cooper snarled as he conjured a ball of fire larger than Orinda's, even larger than the flames the wizards had conjured when they'd ignited the bonfire outside. He threw it at Natalie.

It exploded about a foot away from her, but instead of dissipating, the sparks formed a flaming lattice. A burning cage now surrounded her. She screamed. The flames weren't touching her physically, but terror was unhinging her.

"Satisfied?" Cooper said to Orinda. "Takes a little longer, but it gets the job done. Now, get the hell out of there. Take the Fahrayan. We have work to do."

"Fine," Orinda said with a pout. The dark cloud oozed from her and rolled across the floor toward Jamie.

Meaghan felt a small hand grasp her wrist and pull her hand behind her back. Something cold and metallic slid into her grip.

The Mangler.

Meaghan felt a wave of hopelessness wash over her as she listened to Natalie's screams. Her sister was dying. The man she loved like a son was about to die. Something unthinkable was about to be unleashed into the world.

And she was holding a stapler. That was her big plan. Throw a stapler at somebody.

Jamie stood up and stretched. "Wow, this feels kind of nostalgic. Been a while since I ate Fahrayan."

"He's human now," Orinda said, a sour look on her pale face. She looked at Cooper, hurt in her eyes. "You promised you'd never let that thing have me. You promised me."

Jamie strolled over to her and grinned. "Now, I can be inside you the other way, too. I know you want it."

Orinda screeched in rage and swung her hand towards his face. He grabbed her wrist and snapped it. She squealed with pain.

"Will you please get your woman under control?" Jamie said, eyebrow raised.

Cooper's face was white with rage. "You go too far."

Jamie smirked. "File a complaint with the new management. When they get here." He ran a hand over the sigils on his chest. "Very soon now."

Cooper said nothing, his jaw clenched.

Meaghan could see the anger on his face. The ghost of Welland Eldrich had been right. Orinda was Cooper's weak spot.

"Get the rest of the spell set up," Jamie said, walking toward Patrice and Natalie. "I'll check on the witch." He glared at Patrice, who crouched on the floor, eyes shut tight in concentration, sweat dripping down her face. "Try anything tricky with the floor molecules, love, and I'll keep him ambulatory long enough so I can beat you to death with his fists. And maybe do a few other things. Would you like that? Some special moments with your husband's rotting corpse?"

Patrice ignored him, then opened her eyes for a moment and stared at Meaghan. *Now.*

Meaghan nodded. "Hey, Cooper," she shouted. "Catch."

She flung the Mangler at the wizard with all her strength.

Cooper waved a hand, but the stapler kept coming. It hit a glancing blow on his left shoulder and the side of his head, enough to make him stumble and fall backwards.

Meaghan turned toward Jamie.

"Too late," he said, smiling. "They're here."

Meaghan turned back toward Cooper. The shadows behind him were growing. He scrambled away on all fours toward Orinda, breathing in a high thready whine, but wearing a triumphant look on his face.

Dark red light began to throb within the shadows, growing brighter.

Behind her, Jamie threw his arms wide, an exultant look on his face, the sigils glowing red on his chest. He began chanting in a guttural language, with Natalie's anguished high-pitched shrieks serving as a horrible counterpoint.

Meaghan wanted to run like hell, but she stood her ground. This was her job. To see. To see with clear eyes what no one else could truly see.

The red glow coalesced into a circle, like a tunnel.

The first thing that hit Meaghan was the smell.

She'd gotten sprayed by a skunk once, years before, when she had found her dog cornering what he thought was a cat. She had thought she knew what skunks smelled like. But up close—it had been like rotten eggs and bulbs of old garlic being sautéed on a burning tire by a chef who'd never bathed once in his life. It was more than an odor—it was like a living presence infecting her nose and mouth.

The odor wafting from the red tunnel, foul and pungent, had a similar effect on her, but smelled like nothing she had ever encountered.

Eyes watering, stomach turning, Meaghan pulled the collar of her T-shirt over her nose and mouth. Breathing through her mouth made the smell marginally less sickening.

The red light grew stronger.

Jamie still chanted, while Natalie screamed.

Then Meaghan heard a shushing sound.

Jamie roared with rage. Cooper joined him.

Meaghan looked back.

Sid and Owen, each holding a fire extinguisher, were spraying the flaming cage surrounding Natalie. The flames may have been ignited magically, but were smothered easily by chemical foam.

Within moments, Natalie was free. She snarled something and shot a spell at Jamie.

Jamie grunted, as if punched hard in the gut, and fell to the ground. The black shadow erupted from his prone body. Natalie snarled and made a throwing motion at the shadow. A flash of golden light blinded Meaghan for a moment and when she could see again, the shadow was gone.

Meaghan turned back to Cooper, who huddled in a corner

near the glowing tunnel, eyes wide, gripping Orinda tightly. Both were staring at the tunnel, Natalie and Jamie forgotten.

A tentacle slithered out of the red light as the smell grew stronger.

Meaghan stepped backward. She wanted to run, but she had to watch. A second tentacle erupted from the red tunnel.

Orinda screamed, eyes wild, and tried to scramble away. Cooper gripped her, unmoving, his look of triumph replaced with fear.

Meaghan forced herself to look at what was coming.

The tentacles were gray. Sort of scaly. But no suckers or spikes or anything. The worst thing about them was the smell.

Meaghan felt her fear begin to lessen. She glanced over at Cooper and Orinda. They were clinging to each other, terror etched on their faces. She turned to look at Owen and Sid and Natalie behind her. Again she saw the wide-eyed looks of horror.

All this for a couple of stinky tentacles? The others clearly saw something different from what was actually there.

"Huh," she said out loud. She called over her shoulder. "It's not as bad as it looks."

Meaghan turned back toward the tunnel. A third tentacle emerged.

Owen and Sid tackled Natalie and the three of them fell through the suddenly paper thin floor.

Orinda began to wail, a high-pitched moaning shriek that was much scarier than the three limp tentacles flopping around in the red light.

What the hell did everybody else see? *This is it?* Meaghan thought. *Three tentacles?* She'd seen scarier stuff on TV.

Patrice shouted, "Meaghan!"

Meaghan turned.

Patrice straddled Jamie, one hand on the sigil over his heart. "Duck!"

Meaghan hit the floor.

Patrice bent to kiss Jamie, then sat up, her eyes again obsidian and inhuman. She gave Cooper a triumphant smile and stretched her other hand toward the tunnel.

Jamie cried out in pain and then was still.

Meaghan felt a rushing, like a strong wind, above her. A golden flash of light illuminated the attic, followed by high-pitched screaming, as inhuman as Patrice's glittering stony eyes.

She turned to look at the tunnel. The flimsy tentacles, blistering in the golden light, squirmed convulsively, but did not withdraw. The red light wavered for a moment and grew strong again.

The building shook.

The pulsing red light flashed off something metallic.

The Mangler lay at the mouth of the tunnel.

At that moment, Meaghan understood what she had to do. Patrice had been right. Meaghan did have a role to play and now she knew what it was.

These things are magic itself? Let's see them choke on something impervious.

Meaghan dove toward the Mangler. A tentacle slithered forward and tried to grab her, but she smashed it with the bulky stapler. With a piercing shriek, it pulled away from her.

Sitting on the floor, Meaghan grabbed the Mangler with both hands and chucked it over her head into the tunnel.

The tentacles retreated. The inhuman shrieking increased

for a moment, and then abruptly stopped. There was a loud popping noise and the tunnel disappeared.

Even the smell was gone.

Meaghan sat up and looked over at Cooper and Orinda, still clinging to each other in fear. She followed their gaze and saw Patrice helping Jamie to his feet. The golden aura was gone and her dark hair hung down her back, tangled, no longer floating.

Jamie patted his chest and smiled. He spun around to show Patrice his back, then pulled her into passionate kiss.

The sigils were gone. Not healed or faded. Gone. As if they had never been carved into his skin.

Patrice came up for air and saw Meaghan staring. With a grin, she gave Meaghan a thumbs-up.

Meaghan, now grinning too, turned back to Cooper and Orinda. "Well," she said, as she pulled herself to her feet. "That didn't go quite according to plan, did it?"

"This isn't over," Cooper said in a shaky voice. "All you've done is buy yourself some time. I'll see you dead for this. As was prophesied."

"Blah blah blah," Meaghan said. "I don't believe in prophecy." Her grin segued into her most fearsome glare. "Now get out of my town."

Cooper, still clutching the now weeping Orinda to his side, muttered something, waved his free hand, and the pair of them vanished.

CHAPTER FIFTY-THREE

WITH THE LAST shreds of her power, Patrice cleared a safe path across the floor and out of the attic.

Clinging to each other like drunks after a wild party, giggling, Meaghan, Jamie, and Patrice stumbled through the remains of the solicitor's office and down the stairs to the second floor.

The crowd in Tony's office erupted in pandemonium when they entered. Like an actor acknowledging an encore, Jamie grabbed Patrice and Meaghan's hands, and the three of them took a bow to raucous cheers and applause.

Then John was on her and Meaghan didn't come up for air for a very long moment. When the kiss broke, they still held each other. He murmured in her ear, "You still want to have the date with me?"

She pulled back, laughing and crying at the same time, and gazed into his deep blue eyes. "Yes, I still want to have the date with you."

Russ grabbed both of them into a bear hug. "Meg! You saved the world. Again."

"No," Meaghan said, gently extricating herself. "Patrice did. All I did was throw a stapler at the bad guys. She did all the heavy lifting."

Russ's giddy good cheer evaporated. "What the hell is she? Everyone down here is kind of freaked out at the moment."

Meaghan glanced around and found Patrice and Jamie talking to a small group of witches. They had their arms around each other and big smiles on their faces. Patrice looked completely normal. The glow was gone. And apparently her powers, whatever their source, had gone with it.

But figuring that out would have to wait. Right now they had more immediate casualties to deal with.

"Where's Marnie?" Meaghan asked, scanning the room.

Russ shook his head and his eyes filled. "Brian got her out of here."

"When we fell through the floor, the witches they catch us and bring us down so we don't crash," John explained. "And then she wakes up. Screaming and crying and trying to hurt herself. I held her the best I could, and Jhoro and Brian came to help."

Meaghan's eyes widened. "Jhoro? How'd that go?"

John scowled. "It was very strange. He got to her first. He held her face in his hands, and stared at her."

"And she stopped screaming," Russ said. "And then she went limp. Jhoro nodded to Brian, who wrapped her up in a blanket he found somewhere, scooped her up, and left."

"He took her outside, away from here," Annie said, suddenly standing at Russ's elbow.

Russ wrapped his arm around Annie, pulled her close, and kissed her on the forehead. "There's my girl."

"What did Jhoro do to her?" Meaghan asked.

Annie shrugged. "No idea. All that empathic stuff I was getting from him has dried up." She pointed behind Meaghan. "He's over there with Sid."

Meaghan looked over her shoulder. Jhoro sat on the floor, his arms wrapped around his knees, his head down. Sid sat next to him, a sad look on his little blue face.

Meaghan turned back to John. "Did you talk to him?"

He shook his head. "No. He has said nothing since Brian took Marnie."

"The grief is back," Meaghan said.

John shook his head. "The grief was always there. Some of it always will be there. Better to feel it so one day he can remember how to live."

Meaghan scanned the crowd and realized who else she didn't see. "What about Natalie? Where is she?"

John didn't know. Neither did Sid or Owen or the witches.

Natalie had been nearly burned alive twice in the same morning and now she was nowhere to be found. Meaghan didn't like that all.

Finally, Meaghan found someone with information. Dana, the young witch and police dispatcher, was sitting on the second floor landing, near the women's restroom, holding a blue ice pack over one cheek.

Meaghan plopped down next to her. "Hey, kiddo." She wrapped an arm around the young witch. "I thought we'd lost you for a minute there."

Dana sighed. "Yeah, me too. Running headlong into a pack of wizards was a really stupid thing to do."

"Brave, though," Meaghan said.

Dana snorted.

Meaghan smiled. "The line between stupid and brave can be a fine one. Trust me. I've spent more than a little time tap dancing on it."

Dana leaned her head on Meaghan's shoulder. "I was so scared."

Meaghan felt the maternal feelings well up. "You and me both, honey." She held Dana for a moment and then said, "Have you seen Natalie?"

The girl pointed behind her at the restroom door. "She wanted to clean up a little. She got me the ice pack and then she wanted to be alone, but I didn't want to go too far." She lifted her head from Meaghan's shoulder. "She's really freaked out."

"Yeah, I thought she might be." Meaghan sighed. "I'll take over if you have somewhere you want to be."

"Like home in bed with the covers over my head for the next fifty years?" Dana smiled. "I'd better go find Heather."

"Heather?"

"Circe. Her real name's Heather."

Meaghan started laughing. She couldn't help herself. "Of course it is. Of course." They stood up and Meaghan gave the girl a hug. "You don't need to be anyone else. Dana's pretty awesome. Be Dana from now on, okay?"

The girl nodded, her eyes shiny with tears. "For sure."

When she had left, Meaghan cautiously pushed open the door. "Natalie? Can I come in?"

Meaghan heard a muffled grunt. She stepped into the tiled room. There was some water on the floor, the mirror was broken, and one stall door hung askew, but the facilities were relatively intact for having survived a near apocalypse.

Like many older buildings, city hall contained odd little spaces left over during renovations and updates. This particular restroom had a quiet little alcove off the main area, containing a battered Naugahyde sofa.

She found Natalie curled up, eyes shut, shaking. Meaghan sat down on the far end of the sofa and waited.

Finally Natalie spoke. "I'm sorry I'm being such an idiot. Hiding on the cramp couch."

Meaghan sighed. "You were almost burned alive. Twice. You aren't being an idiot. I'd be worried if you weren't hiding somewhere freaking out."

"You aren't freaking out," Natalie said in a small voice.

"Only because I'm too damn tired. And much better than you at shutting down and refusing to feel things, which, in case you haven't noticed, isn't such a great way to deal with shit." Meaghan settled back into the sofa. "Ooh. Ouch. I need a shower, a good night's sleep, a pot of coffee, and about a zillion milligrams of ibuprofen. Only then will I have the energy to freak out."

They sat in silence for a long time until Natalie stopped shaking and said, "Do you think they'll come back?"

Meaghan nodded. "Yeah. I'm sure they'll try."

Natalie shuddered again. "Do you . . . what did you see? What did those horrible things *really* look like?"

"What did they look like to you?'

Natalie sat up and shook her head violently. "I can't . . . it was . . . I can't even describe it."

"Well, I can. I saw three tentacles. Three gray, scaly, not-very-big tentacles. They didn't have suckers or spikes or anything. Kinda squirmy, but that's it. The worst part was the smell."

Natalie frowned. "That's it? Three not-very-big tentacles? Really?"

Meaghan nodded. "Really. Whatever the rest of you saw, it wasn't real. Those things were screwing with your heads like Eliot said they would. They were even screwing with Voldemort and Cruella."

Natalie smiled, just for a moment, but it was enough to make Meaghan feel much better. "Really? They were talking like those things were on their payroll."

"Yeah, I'm thinking not so much. I'm thinking old Coop realized too late that he'd bitten off a little more than he could chew."

"So these things aren't dangerous?"

Meaghan sighed. "No. I'm sure they're dangerous, but I'm also sure they don't look as big and scary as they would like us to believe."

Natalie stood up. "Well, now I'm pissed. A bunch of freaking extra-dimensional stinky space squid think they can bamboozle *me* with magic? Huh. We'll see about that." She tilted her head, thinking. "Maybe an amulet . . ."

Meaghan held out her hand. "Help me up."

Natalie pulled and, with some groaning and creaking, Meaghan got to her feet.

As soon as they were both standing, Natalie threw her arms around Meaghan and held her tight. "Thank you."

"For what?"

"For saving me so many times. You were right. About why we'd win."

Meaghan looked confused. "Which was?"

Natalie pulled back and stared at her. "You know. On the stairs. About how we were family and had each other and all they had was hate and fear."

Meaghan rolled her eyes. "That was total bullshit. You do know that, right? Me saying something inspiring to prod you up the stairs?"

Natalie punched her gently in the arm. "You're such a bitch. It worked though, so nyah nyah."

Meaghan pulled her back into a hug. "Let's get out of this dump. We still have to figure out a cover story for this mess."

"Aye-aye, Captain Bullshit," Natalie said in her ear.

CHAPTER FIFTY-FOUR

THE OFFICIAL STORY was a natural gas explosion precipitated by a freak earthquake. Although rare, earthquakes were not unheard of in Pennsylvania, and—to use Natalie's name for them—the extra-dimensional stinky space squid had provided the necessary seismic shaking to make the story plausible.

Magical intervention and standard Eldrich denial were sufficient to smooth over the rough spots in the story—like how almost all the windows in city hall had been blown out eighteen hours before the supposed earthquake.

Not everyone returned to a state of blissful denial. Within a week, for-sale signs began sprouting on lawns throughout Eldrich. For many, the reality of life in Eldrich could no longer be denied. They wanted out.

But some people could deny anything. The mayor, for instance. Brian had returned the Escalade to Tony's driveway with an empty gas tank, blood stains on the backseat, and a note of apology.

Tony never responded. A few days later, he traded in the Escalade for a Range Rover. He appeared to accept the earthquake story without reservation, and pledged loudly to seek state and federal money to rebuild. But the weak cover story would unravel rapidly if subjected to the scrutiny that would accompany a request for disaster funding for such a localized catastrophe.

Owen came through for them again. His employer, a reclusive venture capitalist, generously agreed to donate the necessary funding to restore city hall and to finance Ruth and Eliot's efforts on behalf of the refugee Fahrayans.

Owen was all over town negotiating sweetheart cash deals with desperate homeowners. At the rate he was scooping up houses, they'd have everybody indoors by Halloween.

Meaghan wasn't clear on whether Owen still expected her to try to negotiate access to Matthew's redacted files. Owen told her they could worry about it after they took care of the Fahrayans and processed the events of Labor Day weekend.

"Those things will be back," he said. "You know that."

"One crisis at a time," she told him. "The stinky space squid will simply have to wait their turn."

Without the influence of the love spell—or more accurately, *spells*— general sanity returned. There were even some happily-ever-after stories—the best one belonging to Tim Lyons, the police officer purloined by the Order in front of Jeff's garage.

Despite Meaghan's fears for his fate, the wizards had merely abandoned the magic bus—Lyons unconscious in the back—in the employee parking lot across the street from city hall. Injured, he made his way to the nearby home of a woman he'd known since childhood. Recently divorced, back in Eldrich, and love hexed, she had spent the day mulling over old photos of her childhood friend, Tim Lyons.

Each had nursed an unrequited crush on the other for more than twenty years. When he knocked on her door, dazed and bleeding, it was mutual love at first sight.

"The son of a bitch is getting married. It's been like two weeks." Brian shook his head. He was sitting on his front porch with Meaghan. "Tim's the last guy you'd think would do something that impulsive."

Meaghan smiled. "He's known her since childhood?"

"Yeah, but—"

"I guess, once you know, you know."

Brian gave her a skeptical look. "I guess."

"How's Marnie?" Meaghan asked.

Brian had taken Marnie directly to his house from city hall. She was still there, much to Natalie's chagrin. Natalie had finally fallen for Brian, but he remained unmoved and claimed he was done with her.

He was silent for a long moment, then shrugged. "Considering what they did to her, she's coping."

"Are you and she . . . involved?"

He shook his head. "God, no. It's not like that at all. She's . . . I don't know if she'll ever be able to feel that way about a man again." His face grew pink. "And I don't know if I'll—I wasted a lot of years loving someone who didn't love me back. I'm not doing that again. She needs me to take care of her and I guess I need somebody to take care of." He shrugged again. "It works for now."

Meaghan found Marnie inside, curled in an armchair in

Brian's small guest room, staring out the window. Her hair had begun to grow back, but the gashes healing on her scalp were still visible.

Clad in an oversized Eldrich PD T-shirt and baggy sweatpants, a coffee mug cradled in her hands, she looked small and frail, nothing like the confident, beautiful woman she had been before her ordeal.

Meaghan knocked gently on the door frame. "Hi, got a minute?"

Marnie nodded. "You want to see how I am."

"Um . . . yeah. Can I come in?"

Marnie gave her a weak smile, but didn't make eye contact, and gestured at the bed. "Have a seat. There's some coffee in the kitchen if you want it."

Meaghan shook her head. "I can't stay long. But I wanted to drop in and see you."

Marnie nodded, but said nothing. The awkward silence stretched for a few moments until Meaghan broke it.

"Marnie, if there's anything you need—"

"I'm better than I thought I'd be," she said. "Jhoro, he . . . I'm not sure what he did. But it helped."

"That thing he did in the mayor's office?"

Marnie nodded. "Yeah. It's not that he made me forget what happened, but somehow it doesn't feel so . . . immediate, I guess. It's something that happened to me, but I know it's over, and now I can put it in the past."

"You need to process what happened or—"

"That's what he did, I think. Brian got me a book on surviving trauma and I think that whatever it is that makes someone keep reliving awful things, Jhoro took it away."

"Do you still have feelings for him?"

Marnie shook her head. "Not like that. Those feelings weren't real. I think we both got hexed. I knew he was gay, that he was grieving for Finn. I wasn't trying to get romantic with him. I only combed out his dreads for the challenge. For a hairdresser, that rat's nest on his head was like Mt. Everest."

Meaghan sighed. "I've received several confessions from witches in town about casting their own love spells." She decided not to mention Orinda's spell for now. "I think you both got caught up in that."

Marnie bit her lip. "Maybe. I should have known better, but when a god invites you into his bed, it's hard to say no."

"Jhoro initiated it?"

Marnie nodded. "Like I said, I wasn't even thinking about him that way. Not seriously, at least."

"So why did you cast a love spell?"

"I didn't." Marnie finally looked Meaghan in the eye. "I wanted to ease his grief."

"Make him forget Finn?"

"Not forget. But make it less . . . close." She gave a small humorless laugh. "I was trying to do for him what he did for me. Make it hurt a little less. Give him some distance."

Meaghan sighed. "I wish it had worked. He's a wreck. He's spending most of his time out in the woods at Finn's grave."

Marnie shrugged. "Maybe that's for the best. You can't get over something you won't let yourself feel."

They sat in silence for a long moment.

"Brian's a good man," Marnie said.

"He is. A very good man. One of the best."

Marnie nodded. "He deserves somebody who will love him back. Not somebody broken."

Meaghan felt her eyes prickle with tears. "You're not broken."

"Yeah, I am. For now at least. Maybe not forever." She stretched and stood up. "Thanks for checking on me, but now you need to go home and get ready for your date."

Meaghan was glad she hadn't accepted a cup of coffee because she would have choked on it. "How," she spluttered, "do you know about that?"

Marnie smiled, really smiled, for the first time. "I may be broken and traumatized and hiding from the world in Brian's guest room, but I still hear stuff. Also I gave John a haircut yesterday. He looks good."

Meaghan headed home. Until permanent office space was found, the solicitor's office had relocated to her seldom-used formal dining room.

While most of city hall would be habitable once the electrical system and bathrooms were repaired and the windows replaced, Meaghan and her staff would be located off site until January at least. But part of the design and rebuild of the space would involve locating and minimizing mystical hotspots, so it would be worth the wait.

The details of her and John's date were a secret that apparently everyone but the two of them shared. There had been many whispered, giggling conversations between Natalie, Kady, and Russ, who had become an unofficial member of the staff because "it's my house, too, and I'll go anywhere in it I please, and you're not the boss of me, thank you very much."

At home, Kady waited for her. "Hey boss. Ready for your date?"

"Not really," Meaghan said. "I'm freaked out by the whole thing to be perfectly honest."

"So's John. At least that's what Jamie says, but he's freaked out by the idea of you dating his dad, so he's probably projecting."

"Where is everybody?"

"Jhoro's been gone all day. Jamie and Patrice hit the road after lunch to take the Hummer back and pick up the kids from that Gigi lady."

Patrice's former foster mother had been keeping the kids. Liddy had been due to start kindergarten the Tuesday after Labor Day, but she was so fiendishly bright that her parents decided missing the first few weeks wouldn't be a problem. Jamie seemed to be doing a lot better and Patrice's new powers appeared to be in remission, but they needed some time together as a couple to get their marriage back on track.

"And the terror twins?" Russ and Natalie, no longer forced to hide their connection to each other from Meaghan or from Kady, who had been let in on the secret, were in a giddy competition to see who could plan the most extravagant evening for Meaghan and John.

"Plotting. Go get ready. Natalie says wear a dress."

"Any idea what they're up to? How bad is it?"

Kady smiled. "Not bad at all. Don't worry. It's actually quite nice. Natalie swore me to secrecy in a witchy way so I can't say anything else. I have sealed instructions to give to John when he arrives." Her expression changed abruptly. "Not again."

"Morning sickness?"

"All-stupid-damn-day sickness." Kady ran for the powder room.

Meaghan chose a simple black dress that she knew looked great on her, put on some jewelry and makeup, and even dug out a pair of heels from the back of the closet.

After a moment's reflection, she stuffed a pair of socks in her hiking boots and carried them with her. It was Eldrich. Anything might happen. Best to be prepared.

John arrived. Kady met him at the door and handed him an envelope on her way out.

Meaghan came down the stairs, her stomach fluttering.

John's mouth dropped open, and then he smiled. "You . . . *Wow*."

"I clean up pretty good, don't I?" She giggled like a teenager, her face flushing. "So do you. Damn. You really wear that suit well."

Meaghan suspected Owen and Eliot—still on crutches but healing well—had a hand in dressing John. If it had been up to John, he'd have put on jeans and a clean T-shirt. He wore a black suit, perfectly cut, with a simple gray shirt and no tie. Marnie had shaped his shaggy dark blond hair into a sleek mane that framed his face, accentuating his cheekbones and setting off his vivid blue eyes.

"Thanks. I even borrowed a nice car, so we don't have to ride in my crappy truck."

John escorted her outside where Edna's Crown Victoria, freshly washed, sat gleaming in the fading September sunlight.

Meaghan glanced over at Edna's house. Edna peered back through binoculars and gave Meaghan an exaggerated thumbs-up.

John tore open the envelope and started laughing.

"What? Where are we going?"

He handed her a sheet of thick, high-quality paper, covered in ornate calligraphy:

Welcome to La Petite Maison (aka Natalie's house)

Your chef, Russell Keele, has prepared a delicious gourmet meal, which you'll find waiting in the kitchen with simple reheating instructions.

The guest room has been prepared for your comfort.

Have fun, you crazy kids!

We won't be waiting up.

(Hint, hint.)

"Oh, God," Meaghan rolled her eyes. "They really want us to . . . you know."

"Only when you're ready," John said, smiling at her.

She smiled back. "I'm starving. Let's go."

ACKNOWLEDGEMENTS

BIG THANKS GO out to my beta readers: JoAnn Bradley, Susan Emans, Nooce Miller (noocemiller.com), Sarah Miranda, Brenda Moyer, and George Nackos. Your comments and insights helped make this a better book. Thanks again to my editor, Susan Lindsey, Savvy Communication LLC (savvy-comm.com). And thank you to James T. Egan, Bookfly Design (bookflydesign.com) for the cover design.

A NOTE TO READERS

CRUSHED IS THE second of seven books in the City of Eldrich series. More information about the series is available at laurakirwan.com.

www.ingramcontent.com/pod-product-compliance
Lightning Source LLC
Chambersburg PA
CBHW030650120726
47905CB00001B/142